DREAMER

Other books by Elisabeth Zguta

In The Woods
Murder In The North East Kingdom

Seeking Redemption
Curses & Secrets book 3

Exposing Secret Sins
Curses & Secrets book 2

Breaking Cursed Bonds
Curses & Secrets book 1

"In The Woods *tells the story of Samantha Tremblay, a self-reliant but lonely young woman of Abenaki descent ... suspenseful investigation of what becomes a horrible series of murders proves to be a painful journey of self-discovery for Sam... Vivid descriptions of the Vermont landscape, an in-depth portrayal of the main character, and a rural town full of buried secrets make* In The Woods *a great read for mystery and suspense fans. I couldn't put it down."*
—Caroline Davis, Author of Night Vision

"This book was a great read, full of suspense and intrigue that kept me up late at night. A dangerous killer is hiding among the beauty of the wilderness awaiting his next victim...Samantha's determination to find the killer puts her in more than one dangerous situation. I would definitely recommend this book to anyone who likes a good mystery."
—The International Review of Books

"This is a well written complex tale of romance, family drama, paranormal intrigue, and mystery with touches of emotional horror, historical investigation, and threatening twists."
—Kerrry L. Reis, Author of Legacy Discovered

"In *Seeking Redemption*, Zguta wrote Robert's story, another spellbinding suspense novel... Robert wants redemption for his past indiscretions ... decision resulted in murder, attempted murder, and kidnapping ..."
—Cygnet Brown, Author of The Locket Saga Books

DREAMER

*This is the story of a Ukrainian boy named Ivan Rudenko
and his family from Galicia, of how they survive
World War II without raising a weapon...
They discover new unlikely friends along their journey,
each with their own story to tell.*

A novel written by
Elisabeth Zguta
Edited with Jerry Zguta

Library of Congress   1-8856071181

ISBN13   978-1-7351263-1-9

 Tryzub Press

Tryzub Press is an imprint of:
EZ Indie Publishing
2960 Green Line Way
Minerva Park, Ohio 43231

EZIndiePublishing.com
Book and cover design by EZ Indie Design

DEDICATION

For all the brave people who survived WWII from all sides of the atrocity. I pray they've found peace and joy in the remaining years of their lives.

For the rest of the world, the watchers, may we all learn from the past instead of rewriting it. I have written this *fictional story* in the hope that truth will be revealed for all to explore.

"Fiction is the lie through which we tell the truth."
— *Albert Camus*

God bless my family and friends who have helped me during the pursuit of this work and have enriched my life.
Mnohialita!

Please note: When you come across an unfamiliar term, check the Word Index in the back

FROM THE AUTHOR

Inspiration for this Book

Before I married my dear husband, Jerry, I didn't know much about Ukraine or Ukrainian culture. Like many Americans, I only heard about Ukraine as a reference to a section in Russia, like in the Beatles song, *'Back In The USSR'*. I didn't know the truth about an entire culture that was being denied. International current affairs were rarely taught during my education. More time was spent on learning ancient history than the real world we lived in. Years before the internet were in some ways, a dark time, when it was easy for governments to lie to the citizens and covert policies were the norm.

Then I was introduced to a new culture which opened my eyes to many new ideas about the world we live in, and myself. How easy it is to take for granted the freedom we have always experienced, to have the ability to call out injustices once you catch an influencer's ear. But in Ukraine and places like it, such things could lead to imprisonment or your death. Of course, things have changed since the 1990s when the internet opened accessibility to knowledge. The world was afire with people declaring their freedom. There were other such renaissances, but to live through one was an amazing experience.

Dear family members and friends who have roots from Ukraine inspired this story. The concept brewed after a particular conversation with Uncle Ron. He had a short but clear recollection of a train explosion and his red sweater.

Motivated, I wanted to tell a side of World War II that had rarely been heard.

Some incidents are too grisly to re-tell and I felt I could not do them justice, preferring not to poke at the deep wounds of those who have chosen to forget. Liberties were taken to fill in the gaps, so this is truly a story of fiction. Yet, one truth remains—Ukrainians cherish freedom. The following quote attributed to the great author, Emerson, about the job of fiction, inspired me while writing this story:

'Fiction reveals truth that reality obscures.'
— Ralph Waldo Emerson

Most Ukrainians during the war were peaceful people willing to help other persecuted groups. Ukrainians perished more than the public acknowledged. There is no denying a few Ukrainians had participated in horrible atrocities, but they were the minority. Yet, their history was flaunted to shame other worthy Ukrainians. The majority, who remained quietly getting on with life, suffered an evil reputation undeserved. Ukrainians are people who look ahead and don't spend time obsessing in past despair. Optimistic people, loyal people, and God-fearing.

Ukrainians have suffered centuries of annexation, incarceration, and being regarded as inferiors. Still, many Ukrainians remain inspired by the great Ukrainian writer, Taras Shevchenko. Over the years, he has been one of the most revered throughout the world.

Taras Shevchenko, the celebrated poet was exiled in Russia when his words below were written. I have included an excerpt from his poem, *A Dream*, which illustrates his glimpse of the future, his dream come true, the only way he considered possible while enduring his captivity in a foreign land. How wise his words... He never lost his dream for a free Ukraine.

An excerpt portion from:

"A Dream"

From Orsk Fortress, written end of June – December 1847 by Taras Shevchenko

"...The tears he wiped were hardly cool,
And weren't the ones of youth...
He recalled his blessed bygone years...
What occurred? When, where and how?

Some was lived, and some was dreamed.
The seas that he traversed
And the shady verdant grove,
And the dark-browed youthful beauty,
And the shining moon amid the stars,
And the nightingale on the guelder rose,
That in turns would hush and chirp,
Singing praises to the scared Lord;
And all, all of it was in Ukraine! ..."

"A Dream" continued

"... Such was the dream I dreamt
In a foreign land!
As if born again to freedom
In this world of ours.
Permit me, God, whenever,
Even in old age, to stand
Upon those looted hills
Inside the little house.
Let me bring a heart
That's ground by grief
And tortured,
So it may rest
Upon the Dnipro hills."

Excerpts used in this novel from Zapovit (title translated as Testament), and A Dream from Orsk Fortress, written end of June – December 1847, were written by Taras Shevchenko and translations were taken from the following book: **The Complete KOBZAR The Poetry of Taras Shevchenko / Translated from the Ukrainian by Peter Fedynsky,** Glagoslav Publications Ltd, United Kingdom ©2013 ISBN 978-1-909156-55-5 The text was used with permission granted by Ksenia Papazova, Managing Editor for Glagoslav Publications

PROLOGUE

Summer 1939

People rushed around me in a panic. Blows to the back of my head pushed me forward as the mob drove me into its wake of hysteria. Something was wrong, I felt a twisted knot in my stomach. I couldn't see what was happening, the adults around me wore their wool winter coats, and the thick of them blocked my view as they pushed onward.

Driven by the throng, one tightly knit swarm, we were crammed and moving as one.

"Watch out, kid."

An unshaven man shoved me. My face rubbed against the scratchy coat in front of me; it burned my cheek. I searched for my mother, father, sister, or brother. I couldn't see faces, only legs, women's legs donned in stockings with thin lines running down their calves. All of the shoes pounding against the walkway, black or brown, low heeled shoes, everyone wore the same.

The men's shoes were of old worn leather, most needed a re-sole. Pan Shevchuk would have liked a few of these men as customers; just the other day he said to my father how no one cared about repairing their shoes anymore. No one had money, and no one dared to spend it if they did. Instead, the people hoarded as much as possible.

Store owners in the city had been closing their shops, some mysteriously disappeared overnight. It seemed to me that anyone remaining in the city stood here in this mob, waiting for the train, trying to get out of Lviv no matter the cost.

"Ivan."

I heard my mama calling out my name.

"Ivan Rudenko, come here."

I ran into her outstretched arms, relieved that she had found me.

GALICIA 1939

Occupied Ukraine

CHAPTER 1

Four Months Earlier

"Hurry up, Ivan. We'll be late again." My brother, Petro, always nagged me to rush. He was always in a hurry to do something, but I couldn't imagine why it was so important. I picked up my hand-me-down satchel with worn corners and followed my brother out the door.

Mama stood on the stoop and grabbed my shoulders as I passed her. She stopped me, pulled off my cap, and kissed the top of my head.

"You be a good boy today, Ivan. Listen to the teacher and work hard."

"I promise to do my best."

My tato walked out behind me, placed his hand on my shoulder and said, "that's all anyone can do, their best."

Petro yanked my arm and dragged me away. I turned to make sure my parents noticed me waving to them. They did, and I smiled.

"Hurry, we're late."

Petro sprinted ahead and I followed. We hustled down two streets lined with weathered houses, some had stucco falling off the sides, others needed paint just like ours. I jumped between puddles, balancing myself not to slip on the wet stones and concrete. We reached our teacher's house. It was older than ours, one of the original buildings in the center of town, but since Pan Vasyklo fancied himself a historian, it seemed only right that he should live in this old building. Petro looked around, then we slinked behind the house into the barren back yard, and entered through a back door.

The glass panels rattled as Petro pulled the storm door open from the swollen jamb. We followed a hall to the door that led down to the cellar. Hastening down the steps, our feet clomped, but the echo sounded muffled in the damp open space. We entered the classroom through another door-way, latching it behind us.

"Good, we are all here now," Pan Vasyklo said. "Now, we can begin. Gentlemen, please take your seats."

He waved his hand to the only seats remaining. The cellar walls were white-washed in this space, lamps were sitting on various desks lined up against the wall. A multi-colored map was hung on the front wall, it showed all the historical borders of Ukraine from years ago, mountain ranges, rivers, and railways.

Near to where Pan Vasyklo stood was a desk, piled high with books. There was also a framed photograph of him, taken years ago when he taught at the university, posed with other men dressed in black robes. They all stood so straight, shoulder to shoulder mustached men, but our teacher was the tallest and thinnest of the group. The proud men weren't allowed to teach there any longer, the Ukrainian universities had been shut down first by the Russians, and then by the Polish occupiers.

Pan Vasyklo had volunteered to teach the children in town, at least for the few whose parents dared to chance them learning Ukrainian lessons in secret. The study of our culture and language was against the law, banned by the oppressor's governing rules.

"Now children, since there are only twelve of you today, I think we can break up into two groups. Petro, you can lead the older students, and I will concentrate on the lessons with the younger students. You, older students, turn your chairs to face Petro."

The other five started moving their chairs and formed a semi-circle facing Petro's desk.

Among the commotion, I noticed my sister sitting with the others. She had the habit of arriving before us, meeting her friends early. They walked to school together while I was still eating my breakfast. She and another girl giggled, and I thought how happy she looked when she was with her friends, and how when she grinned, Olena was beautiful just like Mama. I liked making my sister happy, often joked with her just for a smile. Lately, she was sad most of the time, and I wondered why.

"Fine, Sir. Our desks are set."

My brother sat with his back straight against his chair.

"Which lesson should we begin to study?"

"Please, take turns reading aloud the poems "*My Friendly Epistle*" then "*Testament*" written by Taras Shevchenko. Use the book on the top of the pile on my desk, pass it along to the next person in the circle after having read a stanza. After each poem, stop and talk about it. Answer the questions: what does it mean to you, how did you feel while reading it, and explain the literary style he used."

Petro had written the questions down in his notebook, the one he carried with him all the time. Someday he might be a reporter, if not a famous explorer.

I wished I could be in the circle with the older students. I liked reading poems, especially *Zapovit*. It's a beloved poem written by our hero, Taras Shevchenko, a poet who was imprisoned in Russia in the 1800s but he dreamed of coming home to his beloved Ukraine before he died. He expressed himself eloquently when he wrote in 1845 about man's determination to fight for freedom. He had an unquenchable faith in Ukraine's ultimate victory. His words inspired many.

My tato often read the poem to me at night before bed, and it sounded so dreamy, my father's voice so dramatic and yet romantic as he read.

> *"When I am dead, bury me*
> *In my beloved Ukraine,*
> *My tomb upon a grave mound high*
> *Amid the spreading plain,"*

I cried while listening to the sorrowful verses, envisioning the Halychyna Grave nearby, even though the poem referred to another grave. I didn't have to hide my tears from Tato, he understood my sentimentality. Other stanzas of the poem were more hopeful.

> *"And in a great new family,*
> *A family of the free,*
> *Forget not to remember me*
> *With a kind and gentle word."*

I liked to dream about freedom and wondered if we would ever have the chance to know what liberty meant, or how it felt to be free. I enjoyed listening to Ukrainian folklore about all the spirits in the woods and the things lurking beyond the visible world. My favorite fairytale, *Forest Song*, was written by a girl named Lesia Ukrainka. It's about a nymph who falls in love with a mortal and instigates all kinds of trouble. Drama is better when it's imaginary.

"Children, please turn your attention to me." Pan Vasyklo tapped his cane on the floor.

I turned my head toward the teacher, and he peered back directly at me. His dark eyes held mine in place. Then his expression mellowed, almost smiling, as he blurted our instructions.

"Today I will tell you more history about our town." He nodded his head, as if affirming a decision to himself, then began his flow of information.

"Years ago, Halych was an important trading place, many more people lived here, and it was the capital of the area."

A plump boy named Yyri, who was about twice the size of any of the other students, raised his hand.

"Yes, Yyri."

"Sir, isn't our town still important?"

The teacher smiled and twisted his mustache, pinching the ends into a fine line.

"Yes, of course, our town is important. However, things change. Not as many people live here any longer. Lviv has become a bigger, more important city. They have a big railway station that was built during the time of the Austro-Hungarian Empire occupation. The government established many great railways to further trade with other parts of the empire, so of course, the railways in Lviv attracted more people."

He scanned our faces and nodded.

"That's something we all need to remember, children. As time passes, things change. Our borders change, our leaders change, but if we embrace and learn our culture, that is one thing that won't ever change."

We all nodded, with mouths opened. This wasn't the first time the teacher told us this, and if the other children's parents were like mine, they heard all about saving our culture every day when at home.

"Children, always remember the songs that come from our Ukrainian hearts, the dances that come from our spirit, and the land we call home which gives us wheat of yellow and skies of blue. Those colors of nature, blue and yellow, are displayed on the flag that we've honored since 1848, after the *Spring of Nations* when all of Europe was in a wave of revolution for freedom."

Pan Vasyklo stared into space, his eyes saw something from his past. His voice grew dramatic as he continued.

"We raised the flag again in 1917 after the *Russian Revolution* and kept it flying until the Western Ukrainian People's Republic was forced to disband after the First World War when the League of Nations gave Poland the freehand to govern over us by use of martial law. Now our return journey to independence is even harder, but never impossible..."

His voice faded; the last sentence was almost indiscernible.

I raised my hand, eager to add something.

The teacher jerked back to wakefulness.

"Yes, Ivan, what do you want to say?"

"Someday when I grow up, I'm going to be the king. I will give everyone money so they can buy things and I'll share all the food."

The other children laughed.

"That's stupid, Ivan. You can't be a king," Yyri said. "You always pretend things that are impossible."

The teacher tsk-ed.

"Yyri, that's not nice."

"But Pan Vasyklo, he makes things up all the time. He's a liar."

"I am not."

"Are, too."

"Children, be quiet." The teacher held a ruler in his hand.

We both shut our mouths; the bickering was hardly worth a beating on our knuckles.

"Dreaming big things can be good," the teacher said. "If people didn't dream great things then we would have no engineers to build bridges, we would have no artists to paint the likes of the Sistine Chapel, and we would have no leaders brave enough to dare create a free Ukraine. This is exactly what we need—dreamers. Perhaps Ivan will not be a king, but he might be a leader like his father, Pan Rudenko."

We all settled down and listened to the history lesson, then went on to a language lesson, then mathematics. Later in the afternoon, we left class to go home. I was thankful we still had some daylight remaining to play outside, though I enjoyed classes, sitting still for too long made me anxious. I was about to take off, to run down the street and meet the other boys who didn't go to class, but I halted in my tracks when my brother called out to me.

CHAPTER 2

"Ivan, follow me." Petro turned in the opposite direction and sprinted down the street.

I followed him and we zipped past the Orthodox Church, past the butcher's shop, then stopped in front of the space between two buildings. There was a footpath that we often took, back in the alley. It led up a hill and through the woods, heading for the old castle ruins.

"You want to go?" he asked.

"Of course, I do."

My brother, Petro, always took me places around our town. It was 1939 and the Russian digs were still going on at the old castle ruins even though the Poles had martial law over us. Sometimes my brother and I spied on the workers while they excavated the old Halychyna Grave, and he whispered to me things like, *'watch and learn, Ivan. You may need to do this someday.'* Though I never dreamed of being an excavator, in my dreams I was always a leader.

We scurried down the narrow passageway between the stone buildings and then climbed the steep hill, grabbing hold of boulders and small trees to pull us along. We marched through the woods for two kilometers or so, the sun was warm, I sweated, my face felt hot and flush. Despite the rigorous climb and temperature, Petro never slowed his step.

Finally, we arrived close to the top, near the ruins. The castle remnant was Halych's most valued architectural monument. I hoped that this sacred place would last forever but knew that many significant landmarks were destroyed by war and revolution, and the thought of anything other than time wearing on the castle saddened me. Two years ago, back in 1937, an excavator named Yaroslav Pasternak unearthed the sepulcher and found the remains of a notable man, presumably the mortal remains of Yaroslav Osmomysl, our great ancient leader, who united much of Ukraine.

The thumping sound of someone pounding the ground pulled me from my thoughts. Two men excavating the area lingered near the ruins, now packing up the tools, ready to go home for the day. We hid a reasonable distance away.

"Petro, I can't see." I tugged my brother's sleeve.

He shushed me, and then crept closer, I followed until we were about four or five meters away. We could hear the men talking. The older of the two spoke first.

"The city goes on squabbling. What do they think will come of it? They should embrace the authorities and then perhaps we could get more supplies and do the work properly."

"You're right, they're using up valuable resources with their troublesome uprisings, but in the end, they will submit to the Motherland. Why bother fighting? Such a waste of time, they will lose anyway."

"I heard the Soviet Army will be making an appearance soon, then they'll kick the Polish out of power. Then we'll get more funding for our project, the Soviets are good about funding the excavations."

"One can hope, brother."

They slapped each other on the backs as if they were heroes. I didn't like their poking around the castle ruins, taking things away. These were our ruins, our Halychan castle, not theirs. I noticed there were lumps in the cart covered with a heavy cloth. I urgently shook my brother's arm, my heart pounding in my chest.

"Look, Petro, they're taking something. In the back of their cart. Stop them."

"I can't stop them," he shushed. "We could get shot. Be quiet before they hear you."

It was too late, I looked up and saw one of the men standing over us. My stomach dropped, and I thought I'd be sick when his gruff voice reached my ears.

"What are you two doing here! Go away before I report you."

"Sorry, Sir." Petro jumped to his feet and grabbed my arm, yanking me away.

We fled as fast we could, running through the woods, navigating our way, and trying not to trip over dead branches and roots. I stopped to catch my breath when we reached the top of the hill.

Petro pushed me.

Sliding down, the dirt plumed around me and I gagged. The flinging rocks nicked my legs and scraped my fingers, as I frantically plummeted to the bottom. By the time we landed on our feet, I was crying. I couldn't help myself, the terror and senselessness of it all overwhelmed me.

Petro grabbed me by the shoulders and screamed for me to stop. Shaking me, he said, "Ivan, stop being a baby. Come, hurry, let's go home before those men come through town."

I wiped dirt from my eyes with the back of my hand and followed my brother, limping and berating myself for crying. I didn't want to be a baby. *How could I ever be a leader if I cried?* Seven years older than me, Petro kept me in line, thought it his duty. He often punched me in the shoulder and said things like, '*grow up, Ivan.*' Then he flashed me a broad smile and his blue eyes shined with mischief.

Petro looked like our father, blond hair, fair-skinned, and blue-eyed. They were both strong social beings, kindhearted, and in return were liked by other people. I wanted to be like them, wished my hair was golden instead of brown like the neighbor's dog.

We arrived at our house and Petro made a quick attempt at patting the dirt from my clothes, brushing off as much as possible. He hurried, looking up the street, then shoved me up the steps. We stormed through the doorway.

Mama turned from the stove and looked us up and down.

"What have you two been up to?" She held up her hand. "No, I don't want to know. Go get yourselves cleaned up for dinner."

We didn't dare do anything but follow orders. We washed with soap, then seated ourselves at the table, each in our favorite chair. I sat across from Olena. Her eyes were red and puffy, and I wondered what had happened.

"You two boys arrived home late," Tato said. He unfolded his napkin and placed it on his lap. He gave me the stare, and so I grabbed my napkin and did the same. Manners were important to my father, and I felt it best to remain in his good light.

"We were checking out the castle," Petro admitted.

"Tato, they are taking things away. I couldn't see what it was, but they had something covered up in that cart of theirs."

"I told you, boys, not to go there," Mama said.

She placed the bread on the table and sat down. Now it would be polite to eat, I thought. As I reached for a slice, my mama slapped my hand.

Tato cleared his throat and crossed himself. We all said grace, then filled our plates.

While eating dinner, Tato subtly questioned Petro and me about our day. My sister, Olena, remained quiet, looking at me, then at Petro, then toward me again. Her eyes were wide-opened and looked at me as if she expected something to jump out at her as if I hid some jack in the box under the table or held some secret to be shared.

"Olena, don't be so afraid. It was all in good fun. Please don't cry anymore. Those men won't report us."

My father stopped eating, his fork hung mid-air.

"Do you mean they saw you there, snooping?"

My brother cleared his throat and kicked me under the table at the same time.

"Don't worry, they aren't planning to report us for trespassing or anything. Besides, they don't even know our names."

My father put down his fork and took a deep breath, he waited a few seconds.

"Petro," he said, his voice soft. "There aren't many children in town any longer, ever since Holodomor. It would be easy enough for them to find out your names and where you lived. Promise me not to go there again."

Tato's expression meant business, his eyes were stern and unbending. Petro's face reddened but he didn't argue. We both promised never to go back there. That day was the last time I saw my Halychan castle. The only place it existed for me now was in my daydreams.

CHAPTER 3

My father was named Pan Taras Rudenko, he served as a public official for Halych and religious counselor for our small city. Other men in town respected him and sought out his advice whenever there were troubles, they trusted my father with their secrets. Tato wasn't a big man in size, but no one was held higher than him in the public's heart. He liked music, dance, and poetry, and he loved to be with other people, anyone who needed help only needed to ask my father.

For years our town had struggled with poverty, but things were getting better—there were jobs, food, and the supplies needed for the farmers to plant the fields. Halych supported itself once again after suffering for years. We had been extorted and deprived of the things necessary to sustain ourselves, but with my tato's leadership, we were back to a halfway decent place.

Tato occasionally went to Lviv to meet with city storekeepers to barter for supplies our town needed and sell the goods produced by the people from our area. I would tag along sometimes.

My mother, her name Leysa, made delicious cakes with many layers, flavor after buttery flavor. Everyone in the city loved her cakes, and the restaurants often ordered them ahead of time for fancy parties. The best sellers were her Koroliwsky or Royal Torte, and her Napoleon Torte, which was many layers of crispy pastry filled with scrumptious custard cream. My favorite tort was the fruit layered cake.

My sister, Olena, liked to paint, needlepoint, and sometimes was paid when she helped at the weaver's shop. She had beautiful warm brown hair and wore it braided and pulled up on her head, her blue eyes sparkled when she smiled, and her voice was like a Thrush Nightingale when she was happy or chattered with her friends like a songbird.

Our closest neighbor wove baskets and needle-pointed fancy blouses and tablecloths to sell in the department store, another woman made cheese from her goat's milk to be sold at the city grocer. My best friend, Michael, lived close by, his father was a butcher.

The people in my town were good tradesmen. Halych had once been a great trade center, centuries ago, our teacher had told us all about the local history. I loved to dream of those days of the Princely Halych, of living in the castle by the Dniester River. Most days there was no time to dream, we worked to get by, and prayed no one else would ever starve to death like during the Holodomor.

The last trip to Lviv had taken us over two hours to drive. We were on official business, so my tato drove the old brown milk truck that belonged to the town. We packed it full of items to sell to the stores in the city and traveled on the only decent road to Lviv. Many depended on this income and Tato took his duty seriously.

The road was bumpy in spots, a few times we bottomed out, and I felt the thumps on my bottom. When Tato navigated the sharp turns, I heard the crates slide and bump into the metal sides of the truck and I prayed that nothing broke, or that produce didn't get smashed. When we arrived and opened the vehicle's back door, everything inside seemed right.

We worked together, heaving up crates filled with produce or boxes filled with hand-made goods, emptying the back and carrying things into each shop until the truck was empty.

After all the transactions were completed, we stopped at a stand so Tato could buy a newspaper. A small group of men milled about, reading the news, and discussing politics among themselves. A few of them left, only two men remained. They soon drew my tato into their conversation.

"Please, Pan Rudenko, you must understand the severity of the situation."

The man speaking looked wise and trustworthy, with his high cheekbones that dramatized his kind dark eyes. His angled nose, so defined, revealed him as a personable character like an opened book. He was someone to be admired, and my father soaked in his rhetoric as he whispered his chosen words, spoken softly but in a passionate tone nevertheless.

"We know you, know that you care about what's happening. You're a God-fearing man and friend of the Church so you must empathize. Every day, the Polski government's policies harass us and try to destroy our culture, our heritage. We are being persecuted, like in the past when the Russians threw us into that stinking cell, that NKVD prison Lontskogo. You remember the indignity."

My tato glanced at me, his eyes two slits. I lowered my head and pretended I wasn't listening. The man never noticed, he kept talking inflow.

"They've banned our books, our university, and we can't teach freely any longer. Our religion is forbidden, too.

We can only attend sanctioned churches. Now they tell people what they can eat. The Jews were ordered not to make kosher meat. Do you believe that, and that's just the beginning, my friend? We're next on the chopping block, mark my words."

Every other second the man peeped toward the door, like a twitching bird, as if he expected someone to enter the store at any minute.

Another man stood with them, his face more angular, with a high hairline. He was dressed in black clothes from his pants to his hat, which he held tight in his long boney fingers. His expression was angry more than impassioned as he stepped closer to my tato and added to the discussion. His baritone voice made his words almost musical despite the sense of urgency in the delivery. Listening to him speak was like listening to one of those operas transmitted over the radio. I had heard part of a show once when we were in a city store doing business months ago. The impassioned voices had called out from the radio speakers; an emotional cry so loud and at times shrill, that it made me want to jump out of my skin. I shivered at the memory, then tried my best to make sense of the current conversation.

"Andriy is right," the man said. "Ukrainians are a minority in the center of Lviv, but we are the majority in all the surrounding areas, towns, and villages like your Halych. Our voices should be heard, we need to unite, and become an active force. We must take a stand and claim our independence again, now while we can."

"Yes, Stepan, that's right," the first man went on. "We were somewhat better off before the Polish took over Galicia and it's time to stand our ground, to declare our Ukrainian independence. We need to kick those Polski out of control and take back our nation, but we must take care not to hurt ourselves as we do so, Stepan. We need the Churches to be behind our efforts. We can't whack a bee's nest with a stick and take the chance of being stung. We need all the people's support, or else it won't work. If you do things too radically, then not everyone will follow, and that, my friend, will lead to disaster."

The men seemed to be at odds on some points. I watched my father listening to the men, his face patient, like when he listens to my mother when she talks. He nodded, squeezed his eyes now and then, but as the minutes ticked, I noticed his cheeks turning red. I knew he wanted to get away from the conversation, even my tato had his limits.

"Yes, yes, I understand," Tato said. "Andriy and Stepan, you both have our best interests at heart. I know you've had a hard time Stepan, but you are no longer in prison. Perhaps you should try to keep it that way for a while. Tensions with the police have existed since the last treaty," my tato said. "The riots in the streets between all the various forces, the Polish, Ukrainians, Jews, and Russians, they all fight for control. It's dangerous. But in the small towns and villages, it's different, we have lives to live, work to do, and families to care for. I can't afford to be part of a group promoting violence."

He folded his paper and looked ready to leave the store.

I jumped off the stack of newspapers near the door that I had been sitting on, gathered up our packages, and prepared to go home. The intense man named Stepan grabbed hold of my father's arm. I think I stopped breathing for a moment. Startled, I wondered if he intended to hurt my father. I was ready to help my tato, I'd kick and scream, or do whatever I could to stop this dangerous man.

"Remember," the serious man whispered, "that Ukrainians are being persecuted every day, we've been pushed away from our chance as a republic ever since the Ukrainian National Rada had to be incorporated into the Ukrainian Galicia Army and it grows worse with time, more than you know, Pan Rudenko. The clashes with the Polski police happen too often in Lviv. They arrest us just for teaching at the university. How can we do our work? The tension grows among our professors and leaders, too. There are so many small local groups cropping up now, that we don't know who is who any longer. So, we decided to finally form a group of activists from among ourselves, those of us who will do the work that needs to be done. Consider joining us, brother."

My father looked curious; his eyebrow raised.

"A militant underground?"

His face lit up. The resemblance between tato and my brother, Petro, crystallized in my mind at that moment. They both have golden hair that lights their faces, golden boys. I wanted to look like my tato, too. I have my father's blue eyes, but my hair is dark like my mama's. The other children sometimes called me mama's boy. I wanted to grow up and be a man like Tato, brave, and loved.

"Yes, a movement, and we need you, Taras. We call ourselves the Organization of Ukrainian Nationalists, but we're not like the old OUN group. We're more energized than in the past. We have to be more radical, to survive, and keep Ukraine our own."

The conversation continued for half an hour longer, the entire time my stomach was in knots. We finally made our way home. I hadn't understood everything they talked about, but I knew my father agreed with much of what the men had said. Somehow, that knowledge left me feeling unsettled. Still, he hadn't agreed with it all, my father was a peaceful man. I wondered if my tato would get into trouble with these men. We drove in silence. I was happy when we arrived back home to our quaint sleepy town of Halych.

CHAPTER 4

It was dusk, the sun setting, the air cooling as a breeze from the west blew across the river. I smelled the grass and flowers that bloomed during the heat of the day, their fragrance wafted through the air and welcomed us.

The streets were quiet, everyone already inside eating their dinner, the aroma of cooked cabbage and onions lingered as we passed some of the houses.

We approached our stone house, the front was simple and painted white. The shutters were worn, the wood that used to be painted blue had faded to a grayish hue. Flowers were planted along the front wall making our house look bright. I remembered what Mama had told me about the flowers. The pale mauve of the mallow flowers represented our love of homeland, the reddish-orange poppies signified fertility, and the blue cornflowers meant youth and were supposed to be worn by young men in love. The blue-purple periwinkle flowers promised eternity and love everlasting.

Each year the blooms were picked, dried, and laced together to make headpieces for the young girl dancers. Mama also grew herbs like spindly dill and savory chives among the flowers and used them to flavor her canned goods. Her small hands worked miracles with any kind of craft and cooking.

My stomach growled.

"Hungry, Ivan?" Tato looked down at me as we walked toward the house, assessing, measuring me against some ideal son in his mind's eye. I hoped that he was happy with who I was because I didn't know how to be anyone different.

I was young, only seven and barely old enough to go to school, but I understood much. Sometimes, too much.

"You know, Ivan, I love you with all my heart."

He tousled my hair. His touch filled me with happiness.

"Tato, I love you, too."

I grabbed my father's leg; his pants were baggy, but I held on tight as he pretended to shake me off. We played around and danced in the yard, laughing until Mama came out and called us in for dinner. I looked up and saw her standing there, hands on her hips but smiling. The light from inside the house glowed around her saintly body as if she were the Virgin Mary. At that moment, I felt joy.

The kitchen was warm and smelled of freshly baked babka. I hurried to my seat and waited patiently for us to say our meal prayers. After crossing ourselves, I ate the bread first, ravished after the long day in the city. We sat around the table eating and conversing as usual, and I listened to their prattle and enjoyed the gossip much more than the men's banter at the newsstand. Olena talked about her girl-friends and the silly things they did after school, pulling out worms from the mud for the boys to use as bait, and braiding the new flowers to make crowns for their heads for the next dance.

"Let's hope there will be a dance," Mama said as she looked across the table at Tato. "Nice visit? I hope you sold everything."

Tato sipped his borscht and nodded.

"Yes, we sold everything. The people in town will be happy with the money earned. We also met up with some old friends, one from Plast and one from the university."

"Oh?" My mother's voice sounded wary, and her face blanched against the paisley print on her khustka. The scarf was tightly wrapped around her head, and its colors seemed too bright, almost harsh, against her pale skin.

I dropped my eyes, stared at my folded hands, thinking she disapproved of my father's meeting up and talking with old friends. Her voice sounded disappointed, and since I had been with him, I felt somehow complicit. Besides, I had promised Mama that I'd take care of Tato while we were away.

"Should you be talking with them, Taras, considering the situation?" she said.

I peeked up; her eyebrow was raised.

"Yes, it's all right, Leysa. You know Stepan Bandera and Andriy Melnyk, right? But don't worry, no one noticed us speaking together. I'm not sure if Stepan was released with a pardon or if he escaped." Tato smiled. "They are talking about reorganizing the OUN."

"Hmm, and what did they say? Do they want you to join the cause?" My mama seemed like herself again, and I wondered why she had been so worried.

Tato nodded.

"Of course, they want us, Leysa. I told them that we supported them, but only as long as they use peaceful means toward our declaration of Ukraine as a nation. But I'm afraid, after listening to them speak, that peace may be impossible. Some of their views have become too radical for me. Especially Stepan. He still fears the Bolsheviks and he's willing to go too far against them, willing to accept help from the devil himself."

My tato grinned and winked at Mama. Her face lit up, her cheeks blushed. No longer pale, she looked more beautiful than the angel painted in my religion book that I kept under my mattress, the one I dared to take out only on Sundays. Mama's sandy brown hair feathered out from her scarf, surrounding her soft face. Her smile shined, showing all her teeth.

"Well, let's not openly cause trouble," she said with a wink back.

"No violence, I promise. I'll never hurt anyone. I pray for peace and freedom from the tyranny around us. The question is, can I find a way to do this without becoming a tyrant myself."

"All we can do, Taras, is live our lives as best we can. Raise our children to love God and to remember our heritage." My mama had the last word of that discussion.

CHAPTER 5

My father had been arrested by the Polski police before, and when he returned home, he explained to us that they hadn't liked some of the things he had said. Ideas about how Ukraine should reclaim their independence, and how Lviv and all of Galicia should be part of Ukraine, and not ruled by the Polish. The Versailles Treaty had stepped in and stripped us of our right as a nation, a wrong that needs correcting. My father had strong beliefs, and even though I was young, I knew his ideas were important and yet very dangerous.

The first time my father was arrested, I had been so young that I hadn't understood the ramifications, but for the first time, I felt terror in the pit of my stomach. I learned the taste of fear.

It was three years ago, in 1936, I was only four years old. I had just begun my school lessons, my education started early. They said that I'm a smart boy, special, and should go to classes with the older children. I was eager to learn. The most important lesson of all was to keep *the secret*. We couldn't tell anyone about our classes or that we were being taught about our heritage, nor brag about the things we learned of our culture. Pan Vasyklo told us all kinds of truths about our history. If the wrong people heard about the lessons, he would be arrested, so it remained our secret.

Pan Vasyklo feared being arrested as my father had been. During the history lesson on that same day of my tato's arrest, the teacher told the class about the aftermath of the First World War, and why we were no longer a nation.

"Listen carefully, children. In June 1915 the Ukrainian Sich Riflemen pushed the Russian army out of Halych. That had been a miraculous day for Ukrainian freedom fighters," the teacher said.

My grandfather had fought with them, I heard the story from my parents. While the teacher continued the history lesson, I imagined the Ukrainian men sitting high upon their horses, dressed in glorious coats embroidered with red and gold, swords drawn high in victory. I tried to recall the things that my dido had told me, but they were only vague images, so I took liberties and filled in the details with my imagination until the teacher's voice snapped me back to attention.

"Four years later, in the summer of 1919, the city of Lviv witnessed several battles between the Third Corps of the Ukrainian Galician Army and the Poles, it was referred to as the *November Uprising*. We won," Pan Vasyklo said.

"The Ukrainian National Rada ruled the area from 1919 until 1923. But when the Conference of Ambassadors made decisions on behalf of the Allied powers after the First World War, things changed drastically."

He rubbed his eyes with his hand.

"On March 15th, 1923 the conference approved Poland's annexation of Galicia, with many of the details concerning our autonomy put off," the teacher continued, "to be determined at a later date. The conference held in Vienna recognized the Polish-Soviet border that had been outlined in the '*Peace Treaty of Riga*.' Although the Ukrainians of Galicia protested the decision to let Poland rule the west and Russia the east, the decision remained irreversible, and the Western Ukrainian National Republic was forced to dissolve itself in

Vienna, and the Ukrainian government went into exile. Ukrainian land was split, half ruled by Poland, the other half by Russia."

I clearly remember the words spoken by my teacher that day, they had impressed me, stamped my mind about the evil deceptions that man was capable of when they only sought self-interests.

Our teacher stood in front of us, twisting his dark mustache between his fingers, his eyes set deep in thought. Pan Vasyklo's voice had boomed.

"Other countries try to grab our land, whenever possible. They want to turn our land into part of their empire. This concept is called colonialism. Galicia remains in turbulence. Every country wants a piece of our land. But we..." he softened his voice, "we only want to be free...with no one ordering us what to do, or stealing our food. We, the citizens, want to live free and in peace. Let's hope that day will come sooner rather than later."

Pan Vasyklo sounded a lot like my father.

CHAPTER 6

The city of Lviv had problems but most days our village, Halych, was peaceful. The surrounding countryside had scattered farms, most had been in families for generations. Farms that lay to the east of our oblast in the Russian portion were swallowed up and turned into cooperatives.

The Polish weren't much better in Western Ukraine. They renamed our area the Stanislav Oblast, and they took large shares of the crops to feed people in other towns and cities far away. Between the Russians and the Polish political regimes confiscating large portions of the harvests, most farmers didn't have much remaining to feed their own family. So many Ukrainians were left hungry and deprived.

The Russians confiscated all the food supplies from the lands they occupied, and by 1933, thousands of people had fled until the borders were closed, and then the millions who remained were trapped and starved to death. It was called the *Holodomor*, which means *death by hunger*. The atrocity happened within the Russian occupied borders of Ukraine, where they had taken control from Kyiv and east, and from north to south.

It began the year I was born, a year later millions were dead. I first learned about it one day while my mama hung the laundry.

A few years ago, before I started school, I was playing quietly, sitting on the summer grass while Mama hung the laundry nearby. The clothes blew with the wind, snapping the sheets, and the smell of laundry soap filled the air. The sun was bright, and the clean wash flapped in the breeze, the white undergarments and aprons blended with the white clouds when I looked up to watch them fly.

I listened to my mother's conversation with another woman, they talked about the town gossip and enjoyed each other's company. The women were laughing and joking as friends do, then abruptly, the other woman stopped mid-sentence.

"You're lucky to have your children, Leysa."

The woman said this as she stared at me.

"Good that you weren't in Kyiv."

I looked across the lawn noticing the other woman's eyes, they flooded with tears that rolled down her face, the sun made the wet lines twinkle on her cheek. She wiped them to the side, but they kept spilling.

Mama dropped the wet sheet into the basket and went to her, rubbed the woman gently on the back, and cooed as she did for me when I was hurt.

"I'm so sorry you lost them," Mama said. Her voice was soft, almost as if she were singing a lullaby.

Lost them? What could a person lose that would make them cry?

The woman sniffled, wiped her nose with her handkerchief, then stuffed it into her apron pocket. She bent over, grabbed up a wooden clothespin, and started hanging the clothes again.

I looked away and started to play with my toy train, then heard her tortured voice call out.

"Those damned Soviets. They came to our town and took everything from us."

My head jerked up to see what was happening. The woman stood frozen. A desperate expression shrouded her face as she gazed off at nothing in midair. I waited for her to cry again, but this time her cry was a mournful wail, a deep wrenching agony. An outburst of pain erupted as if she were an injured animal caught in a hunter's trap.

"Come, please, we'll sit." My mother gently guided the woman to the bench near to where I sat on the grass. Mama sat next to her friend in silence, holding her, and waited for the woman to compose herself. The woman lamented some more, rested her head on mama's shoulder. Then with a shaky voice, my mother's friend wailed aloud her troubles.

I listened and wanted to cry, but I had no tears, only sadness in the pit of me.

"Just like that, they took over and told us that we worked for them from now on. Remember?"

My mother nodded but remained quiet as she soothed the woman.

"They took all the food, everything we worked for, all the yield from the fields, and left us nothing. How many people suffered and starved to death? Did anyone bother to count? My poor babies . . . "

Red-faced and bloodshot eyes, she sobbed again, then wiped her nose with her apron. "My poor babies . . . " she whimpered. "They didn't have a chance. Why? And I had to watch them wither and die. No one cared that they were dying. My parents, too."

My mama shushed her and patted her softly.

The woman shrouded her face with her apron. She bent over, her head in her hands. Her body rocked back and forth as she wept into her lap.

Mama tenderly rubbed the woman's back but said nothing. Instead, Mama looked up to the sky. I followed her gaze then realized she was praying.

"We tried to hide food, you know, under the floorboards. But then they came with their damned sticks, poking the ground around our house. Then they stormed inside and tore up the floorboards. They found our reserve—mere morsels, hidden under the floor. Then Bohdan was arrested and taken away—sent to Siberia. When he returned, he came home to an empty house, no children left. And then he died, too, he made sure of that—A mortal sin, oh God, forgive him. Why didn't I die? I'm all alone. It's been four years, Leysa, and I'm still hurting so bad inside. When will this pain go away?"

The woman looked into my mama's eyes, then a crazed glare appeared as she nodded.

"It will never leave me, I know."

My mother continued to console her friend, wrapped her arm around her, and said words like, "thank God you're alive, things will get better, I'm here for you."

But how would they get better for that woman who lost her family? She lost everything. I couldn't imagine losing my family and being left alone with no one to love.

Later that same night, my tato had come into my bedroom near the kitchen.

"Time to tuck you in, Ivan. Have you knelt to say your prayers?"

"Yes, Tato."

I giggled because he knew I had; he watched with Mama from the kitchen table as I said them. Tato pulled the quilt up to my chin and tugged at my dark curls.

"Ivan, you are a blessing from heaven. You have so much life in you."

"Tato, do you mean more alive than the dead children of Holodomor?"

His face squished up like a raisin, his blue eyes mere slits.

"How do you know about that?"

"I heard mama's friend crying about it, plus Petro told me about it, in secret."

"Oh, yes, of course. Well, I don't want you to worry. I promise that nothing horrible will ever happen to you. Your mother and I will take care of you, Petro, and Olena. You will all grow up to be strong. You are our future, full of life and vigor."

I smiled, closed my eyes, and felt better. The horror I had heard earlier in the day was forgotten for now. I believed in his words, and when my father hugged me one last time before I slept, I felt safe.

"I love you, Tato."

"Sweet dreams, Ivan."

CHAPTER 7

Every morning when I woke up, I knelt to pray. It's cold getting out from under the warm featherbed, and the wood floor felt like solid ice blocks and hurt my knees. But it didn't matter. I thanked God for my life, for my family, and I honestly felt special. I couldn't wait for my adventure to unfold. The future seemed like a magical place, and one day I would fly into the middle of it and become a king, like the one that lived in Old Halych.

The other children in the town said I'm crazy for thinking that I will be important and famous. They said that no one will leave Halych unless it's our turn to be persecuted by the Soviets or the Polish, and sent to prison.

I should believe them, after all, my father was arrested more than once already. The Russians came and took him away one night, and sent him to Siberia where he was forced to work. But they finally let him come back home when they were convinced that he posed no threat to their government. Then he was arrested again in the city of Lviv by the Polski police when they didn't like something that he had said.

Once soldiers came and arrested Tato in the middle of the night. I remembered it as my worst nightmare. They banged on the front door, trooped through our home, clomping on the hardwood floor with their thick leather boots.

I heard the commotion and stayed hidden in my bed, under the covers. I was a coward. My room was downstairs near the kitchen. My parents had me sleep there because it was the warmest bedroom in the house. It was winter, and they didn't want me to get sick like some of the other children. The bedroom door was opened a crack like always to let the warmth from the stove into my room. I spied from under the blankets, holding my breath and praying that they would leave us alone, terrified they would see me and steal me away to prison.

One of the men yelled out orders in Polish and spoke so fast that I couldn't make sense of what he said. His face reddened as he pointed at the stairs, barking orders to the other men.

It happened so fast.

The soldiers searched the house, knocking over our things and one of them broke my tato's bandura on purpose, yanked out one of the strings. The wooden neck splintered and cracked, an awful sound emitted from the instrument and made my legs hurt as if my limbs had been broken like the bandura. The strings droned a twangy noise, a dying vibration that faded into dull nothingness.

My heart was broken, I covered my eyes for a moment and tried to think of the soft blanket instead of what was happening. Then a heavy, strong man, stomped down the stairs. I looked and saw his black boots; they were shiny and reflected the light. The man dragged my tato behind him. I heard the thump of father's legs as they slammed against the wooden treads. I cringed with fear, clutching onto the blanket for dear life.

The man in charge of the group yanked my father back and forth, even though my tato pleaded.

"I'll come peacefully. Please, let me walk on my own accord."

The Polish soldiers dragged him away, leaving my tato to fight the night's cold air wearing only his nightclothes. The red-faced man turned toward Mama.

A lump stuck in my throat, I couldn't breathe, and a bolt of fear shook my entire body. I stared at my mother, her face seemed so pale and vulnerable.

"Your husband is arrested for treasonous acts and accused of secretly working with the Organization of Ukrainian Nationalists. Pan Rudenko is labeled an instigator, and he will be sent to the Janowska detention camp and stand trial there."

"No, please, I beg of you. This is a mistake."

My mama knelt on the floor, her hands raised.

The officer turned around, grumbled words I couldn't comprehend, and left, slamming the door behind him.

My mother remained slumped on the floor for a long time, she cried for hours that night. My sister Olena appeared from the dark shadows and drew close to Mama's side. Olena hugged Mama, and cried along with her, their weeping brought tears to my eyes, too. I wanted my father back. I was afraid, a coward, and not brave like Tato. How could I dream of being a leader, ever, if all I did was shrivel away from danger?

Tato often spoke openly in the public market area in Halych and Lviv about his beliefs and how our country needed to keep the Ukrainian language alive, to nurture our culture, and religion. He spoke of how the people shouldn't allow other countries to take away our rights within our boundaries. After the First World War, we were patrolled by the Polish police, and they treated us just as badly as the Russians. Our lives were persecuted by unfair laws and penalties. Tato and Mama both wanted something better for us, but how would it be better with my father arrested?

The next morning when the sun streamed through the kitchen window, Mama stood and began cooking breakfast, as if everything was the same. Her eyes were red and swollen, but her entire demeanor had changed to one of resolve. Mama softly hummed hymns about Jesus rising from the dead and mumbled prayers as she worked. By the time our food was ready, she was able to smile, though I realized it took much strength for her to do this. Still, she had smiled for her children. She wanted more than anything to keep us alive, protected, and happy.

Though only a young boy, at that moment, I realized that my mama was strong and brave. She was as much a hero to me as my tato.

Petro had joined us in the kitchen.

"Don't worry, Mama, they'll let Tato go just like last time. They only want to scare people, to keep them quiet. He's being used as an example. They know he's harmless. Someday I'll help Tato, and together we will force the soldiers to leave our country."

My brother's words didn't comfort Mama, instead, she seemed more horrified.

It was a haunting memory that I carried with me at all times. I couldn't breathe as I recalled that night in detail. I resigned to God's help, and in my prayers, asked for it to never happen again. So now, I know it won't happen again because God listens to my prayers. I truly believed this, and my mind accepted nothing else.

CHAPTER 8

My father's face flared, his eyes grew wide. I watched from the window and sensed he had learned important news from a neighbor, Kosko, who worked in a city factory. Standing beside my father on the stoop, Kosko flew his arms in the air and pointed. Tato waved the man off and hurried into the house.

"Leysa," my father rambled, "the Germans have invaded Poland, and they're heading in this direction next. Everyone wants to own Lviv, and the Nazis are no different. Leysa, they're whispering about it in the streets. The Germans will come."

"Is it true?" Mama said. "Perhaps it's only nonsense. That Kosko isn't so bright. Even his mother says so."

Tato drew in a deep breath and released it slowly.

"If it is true, then I fear a great war is heading our way. Leysa, get a few things together, only what we can carry. Maybe we'll have time to catch a train before it's too late. I'll be back soon. I have to warn the others in town, give them a chance to leave, too."

Tato slammed the door as he left, hurrying to spread the word. I couldn't understand what this meant, the idea of leaving confused me. *Would we be gone a day? A year?* I watched my mother fold things into a few bags she had placed on the table, her hands worked fast, she was efficient. When my father returned, Mama had things ready and waiting. Two brown suitcases and three stuffed satchels placed by the door.

"We will leave in the morning, before dawn. That's the plan. Anyone who wants to join us will meet us by the truck." My tato said nothing more, except his usual "say your prayers and go to bed."

"We all need our sleep tonight," Mama added.

I thought sleep would never come, I was so excited and scared about the things changing around me, but sleep finally found me.

In the morning Mama woke me, and I hurriedly dressed. When I stepped outside, the cool morning air greeted me, and I took deep gulps of it to wake me, then I followed my parents without a word of protest. My family rushed to the town center, our footfall echoed in the dimly lit street. We met up with others who lingered near the truck, we all hoped to catch one of the last trains leaving Lviv before the Germans arrived. Perhaps we could head toward Vienna, Tato didn't care where the train went as long as it was away.

We filled the truck, sitting on each other's laps in the front cab, and the others heaved up into the back; we managed to find room for everyone. Traveling in tight quarters for hours wasn't pleasant, the smell of cabbage, garlic, and perspiration filled the cab. I wished I had been old enough to sit in the back with Petro and Olena. I wanted to complain but knew it would have been counter-productive. The adult whose lap I sat upon might slap my head if I whined. So, I sat quietly and turned my mind to other things, like the castle I was leaving behind. I daydreamed about grand armies that battled years ago, and won, waving their flags of victory.

Lviv, 1939

The city lived in fear. It was apparent, even the lion heads that adorned the buildings were forlorn. We passed the tall buildings in a blur, then Tato slowed and parked the truck on a vacant side lane. We unloaded ourselves from the truck in silence. We scurried through the back streets toward the Lviv-Holovnyi Railway Station. I had heard many people talk about the station. It was supposed to be a beautiful building for trains, one of the best examples of Art Nouveau architecture designed in Galicia. I wondered what it would look like and daydreamed as we walked until a slam of a door brought me back.

A frightened citizen locked their bolts as we passed their apartment house. Squeaky hinges and heavy wood shutter panels banged with a thud as more people along the street hid away. The inhabitants in the old brick buildings pretended they weren't home as we raced by their stoops. They were afraid, like us.

We turned a corner and the street became more crowded, heavier traffic as we drew closer to the station. It seemed that many from the city had the same idea as us. We ran toward the train platform. I looked around trying to get a glimpse of the famous building but realized we were arriving from the back, not the main entrance.

I sighed, disappointed. I so much wanted to see the Tuscan columns with gigantic mythological sculptures on the facade. I fancied the magnificence I had read about and bobbed about in the crowd trying to get a glimpse. But sadly, the grandeur was nowhere to be seen. I resigned to give up my search then realized my family was nowhere in sight. I jumped up and down, trying to spot them.

I lost my family in the crowd and panicked. All I saw were coats, a mob of people wearing winter coats on a warm day. We had taken our warm clothes, too, dressed in layers so that we'd have them later on when the weather changed.

Panting, I loosened my collar, I couldn't breathe, and my heart pounded so hard I thought my head would pop off. Then I heard my mother calling my name.

"Ivan Rudenko." She spotted me, pushed through the throng, and then pulled me into her arms with a hug. "Ivan, you can't wander off."

"Sorry, Mama. I wanted to look at the building."

"That can wait." She straightened up. "Quick, let's get back to your tato."

She held my hand. Instantly I felt better. Mama hustled us back to the edge of the platform, squeezing through the crowd with me in tow and holding my hand so hard I thought it might get pulled off. We made our way to Tato and stood crushed together in a line, my family waiting for the train to arrive, ready for the adventure.

I heard a whistle in the distance, the sound grew louder until it was so close, the noise pierced my ears. I flung up my hands to muffle the noise. I loved the sound of the whistle. I couldn't help smiling despite the tension all around us. I anticipated the train would come and take us away to some strange but wonderful world, maybe Vienna.

Tato grabbed my other hand and gripped it like a clamp. My family stood together at the edge of the pavement, waiting for the engine to stop so we could be the first to get a seat.

The train drew closer. I heard the chugging and the squeaking wheels against the tracks. My stomach knotted up, and for a moment, I had to remind myself to breathe. I let out the air I had been holding in, and the knots lessened, then my stomach felt as if I had swallowed butterflies. I wanted to laugh with glee, but I knew that would have been wrong.

Last night my brother had said the most delightful things, his confidence about the places we might see excited me. He spoke of our possible freedom and the thought made me giddy.

Petro recently turned fourteen, just finished a growth spurt, and his pants were too short for his long legs. I teased him and he punched me in the arm.

"Stop that, boys. And Petro, if you don't slow down, you'll be wearing father's pants soon," Mama said.

We all had laughed at that, and while Petro stood there in his shrunken pants, he still looked like a giant to me. My brother's voice was filled with contagious excitement.

"We'll be able to go to school and read books without worrying whether they're banned. Tato, I hear in America people can read anything they want," Petro said.

He continued with optimism, his eyes glinting like diamonds in the sun, and I hung on every word.

"Imagine being able to study anything. The possibilities. They have large universities there, filled with architectural journals and engineering books."

"Petro, we have books here in the universities, too," our father replied.

"Tato, they arrest people at the universities here. I hear the gossip. I know what's going on. Not hard to believe when we know firsthand that they arrest innocent people like you."

Mama stood up.

"That is why we are leaving on the next train. We'll go west, find a new home, maybe Vienna, a safe place where my children can get an education in peace."

She smiled and took my sister by the hands, then pulled her to her feet. They pranced around the room as if dancing around a maypole.

My tato retrieved his bandura from the pegs on the lathed wall and played a tune, strumming the remaining strings of the repaired instrument. My brother picked up his instrument, and together they performed a duet. The music sounded pitch-perfect to me despite the glued neck.

"Olena, you are so beautiful when you smile," Mama said.

"Oh Mama, I'm so happy we are here together, dreaming of a better day when we will finally be free. No more worries about Tato being arrested."

We sang a song about our love for God, Ukraine, and the famous Kozak freedom fighters. The lyrics were the words from the great poet, Taras Shevchenko, and the poem was *Hamaliya* put to music. We knew the lyrics and sang aloud, together our voices blended well. We often sang in our house about freedom and God. I had never felt so much happiness as those moments when we harmonized, our voices raised, full of life, together, living in the same dream.

There were good reasons for leaving, but we had to be careful. I knew about the Polish-Ukrainian wars from listening to my father while he spoke with friends visiting in the late night. The war had split Galicia apart, and people were bitter. We were under Polish rule, and the other areas of Ukraine were under Soviet control. For Catholics, this was the most terrible fate. Though the Russians were to the east, they had their sight on Lviv again too, like the Germans. We lived in fear, hid our faith, practiced in dark rooms, and buried our religious items in the backyard with hopes of unearthing them in the future. I haven't seen some of our sacred holy relics in years, can't remember what they looked like. Tato said it wasn't safe for anyone to say Mass in public.

The opportunity to leave for the west, to a better place where we could be free, seemed heaven-sent.

My attention returned to the train as it chugged closer. The cars passed in front of us, swishing as they sped by, a warm breeze of air fanned my face. I could smell scorched oil from the friction of the metal wheels, and anticipated they'd be stopping any moment now. Then the green caboose flew by and vanished into the distance until I couldn't see it any longer. The train never stopped, it passed us by and slinked into the horizon like a phantom snake.

Tears smarted my eyes. Sinking thoughts of darkness welled up inside of me. Heartbroken, I knew Tato would be so disappointed. I looked up and watched father's throat as he swallowed his anger, his Adam's apple moved up and down. His eyes were slits, and his brow crunched with many worry lines popping out on his forehead. I prayed he'd find resolution quietly and quickly without calling out some remark that could get him arrested. I had noticed policemen lingering about, too close for comfort.

I looked to the side and saw that there was a squadron of police patrolling the nearby square, waving their hands, and herding the people to leave the area. They were sweeping us out like the trash.

"Do you think there will be another train?" Mama asked.

Her face paled, blending with the cement wall behind her. Tato shook his head. My sister cried and wiped her hand across her face, trying to hide the waterfall rolling down her cheeks. Mama hugged Olena, close to her side, and patted her braided hair. Tato wrapped his arm around them both.

Petro and I stood there, stunned into silence. I didn't know what to do, but our father would give us direction at any moment.

Tato simply said, "let's go home."

We picked up our bags and headed back toward the truck. The streets were crowded near the train station, some people wailing, others screaming out in frustration and anger.

"Hurry, we need to move away from here quickly before there's trouble," my tato said.

I heard the clip-clops of horse hooves in the distance and looked over my shoulder, down toward the main street to see what was happening. Men, dressed in regal guard uniforms and wearing helmets, sat tall with hubris upon their battalion of horses lined in ranks. They marched in sync like a re-hearsed dance. I wanted to witness the pageant, something momentous was happening.

"Quick, down this street." My father's urgent voice jolted me; we were in danger.

We followed tato's lead and weaved through the crowd. Within minutes the soldiers on parade were out of sight. We walked back toward the truck and piled in, then when all the others were accounted for, Tato drove down the back streets until we reached a highway.

"Did you see the soldiers? Russians. Taras, the damned Bolsheviks have returned." The man tightened his mouth as if afraid to say more.

Soft whimpers came from all directions.

"What do we do now, Taras?" a woman asked as she tightened her grip around her daughter.

"We go home. We pray and stay vigilant." My tato uttered the last discernable words.

The return trip home seemed to last for days. We all agonized over why the train left us standing there, flying by us as if we were nothing but forgotten cargo. No one said another word, we didn't have to because we knew what was on each other's minds. We remained in our thoughts because we were afraid to state the truth, the city of Lviv had been taken over by the Bolsheviks, again. My father's worst dream had come true.

CHAPTER 9

When we arrived home, Mama and Olena started a fire in the kitchen stove.

"I'm going to warm up some kompot for everyone," Olena said. "We could use a boost."

Mama grabbed the kettle. "Let's make syta instead. It's quicker, and we could use a sweet drink. I have a jar of honey in the cupboard."

She crossed the room to find the jar.

"But Mama, it's not Christmas." Olena pouted.

"That's a great idea," Tato said. "We need a special drink today. We can't let our spirits die. Even though there was no train today, it doesn't mean there won't be one in our future."

The matter was settled, but Petro was too thirsty to wait, so he poured himself a glass of water and offered the same to me. I didn't refuse. It quenched my thirst after walking home in the hot sun from the center of town where Tato had parked the community truck.

Why didn't the train stop? It bothered me that our father didn't explain, and I couldn't fully understand what it all meant for us, but I knew something terrible had happened.

A knock on the door broke the silence. Everyone froze.

"Taras, it's Gabriel. Can we talk?"

The room breathed again. The local butcher, Pan Fleishman, stopped by to talk with my tato like he often did. My father pulled his pipe from his pipe rack then he stepped outside to join his friend.

I sat by the window, opened it, and watched as tato struck a match. The glow reflected the sorrow in his eyes, now ice-cold blue eyes. He puffed the pipe until the bowl smoldered. He and his Jewish friend spoke about the small stuff, the warm weather, and then finally, the subject of what had happened in the city rolled out.

"They took the entire street," the butcher said. He turned and his belly wiggled.

My Father nodded.

"We left right away," my father offered in reply. "That's one parade my children needed to miss. You should have seen them, those pompous—The Red Army marched into the street, in full form, high and mighty upon their horses, looking down at the people edging the streets. The people at the train station were angry, and some vowed to fight the soldiers if they had to, and I don't blame them, of course."

"I heard there was some bloodshed," Pan Fleishman said. He scratched his full beard and nodded as Tato spoke.

"I only pray the soldiers will stay in the city limits and don't come here to the countryside. We don't need them to bother our little city. I'll do my best to keep us safe from those Bolsheviks."

"No worries, they're miles away now." Pan Fleishman waved his hand and chuckled a nervous laugh. "No, I suppose we don't want them here. You've had enough of them already, my brother." The butcher tapped my father's back.

"That's the truth."

Tato drew in another puff. My father was remembering the torment from the last time he was arrested, I could tell by the way his face scrunched tight, and his eyes looked ahead with a blank stare. He had seen horrible things that he never spoke of, not even with Mama. There were times he seemed distant, like a stranger, and I didn't recognize him. That's when I knew he was reliving the prison.

"We've all lost so much because of those Soviets, what more can they take? They took our food, our people, killed thousands, and left us crumbs to survive. Then they dare call us comrade! Now, just when we're getting back on our feet, by the hard work of our own two hands. Now they storm through the city to declare we are their subjects!" Pan Fleishman's eyes gave him away, brimming with fury and fear.

Tato waited a moment before replying, contemplating his thoughts. "I wonder if other trains will be allowed to come into the city, and if it will be possible to get another ticket if one does, or even safe to get on board? I wonder who's in charge of running the trains. The Germans took Poland to the west, but the Russians took over the city... We're stuck in the middle without answers, aren't we?"

Pan Fleishman looked down at the ground, his massive head swung.

"Expensive, too," he said. "And didn't you use all your extra money for the tickets you bought for today? Tsk, tsk."

Tato nodded, and looked at the ground, too. They stared at the same spot.

"Gabriel, I don't know what I will do next."

The Jewish man's face paled, he shuffled his feet, leaning his weight on one foot and then another, until he found the words he sought.

"My friend, what will I do? Some have already packed it up and are moving east, into the Soviet's hands. I say to them, are you crazy? Do you think the Russians care about you? But the Polish police have been so harsh on the Jews, as you well know. And there's talk about Germany. They say that they deport Jews by the thousands, confiscate their belongings, no one knows what this means, but they are frightened. What hope do we have? It's not safe to go east or to the west, and our homeland is so far away... and it's dangerous there as well. Oy vey."

I noticed tears rolling down his chubby face, and sadness filled my heart. I knew Pan Fleishman was right, some of the children in the village were already gone. They must have fled toward the east, into deep Russia. I won't go there, not to the place where they had imprisoned my father. Those same Soviets who had starved the villages. *Why would anyone go there?*

My father nodded to Pan Fleishman.

"Yes, well, this is my homeland, Gabriel. Halych is my town. Yours, too. Unfortunately, here there is no future for us. I'm afraid for you, my friend."

"Taras, you must lead the town as you've always done. People need your guidance now more than ever."

When I overheard those words, I straightened my posture like a good soldier, proud of my father. He was the leader of this town, and everyone looked up to him for advice. I glanced out of the window again and watched my father. I swear I saw the heavy burden of us all, resting upon his shoulders. He bore it all and yet remained standing tall.

We had tried to leave, he warned them to catch a train as soon as possible, but it had been too late, the last train had left before we even arrived at the station. Now my tato would have to find another way to take care of the people. I knew he would, I had absolute faith in his leadership.

"Gabriel, the villagers need us both right now. When we were in Lviv, I heard men talking about the terrible situation. Constant scrimmages, fighting back and forth, not enough food to go around. Worse than you or I had imagined. In the city, it is Poles against Jews, and Poles against Ukrainians, and Russians against Poles, Russians against Ukrainians. You and I—we are the minority.

"And now the Soviets have arrived, taking over with a mighty force. The OUN is speaking out against the Polish police and also against the Soviets. It's a volatile place, and I fear it's the beginning of an explosion. Forces pitted against each other, will against will, man against man. I'm afraid the OUN will be so desperate that they will try to align themselves with the devil from the west. We'll be fighting for our lives very soon. People with common sense need to stick together to get out of this alive."

Pan Fleishman nodded.

"I've got to find a way to get people safely away from here," Tato said. "Word about the European war's status is quiet, no one is receiving any messages. We have no idea what any of us would face if we fled to the west, but I do know the Nazis are no good. I also know that going deeper east, into the Soviet side, is a definite no for me. I fear the Bolsheviks the most."

My father's words made my heart pound so hard in my chest that I thought it was in danger of cracking my ribs. Confusing thoughts raced in my head, and I had a hard time making sense of any of them. *Fighting for our lives, who will we be fighting against?* The Polish people who claim Lviv as their own, the Russians who decided to retake control, or the OUN a dangerous rebellion group? Aren't they supposed to be for Ukrainians, and if so, why is my father worried about them, too?

Sometimes I wished I hadn't eavesdropped and instead minded my own business, then I wouldn't know of these things and of the dangers my family and the town faced.

I heard my sister calling out my name. I turned, my head still spinning, lost in a state of confusion.

"Time for dinner, Ivan. Don't just sit there with that silly look on your face."

I came back to my senses and walked away from the window. Depressed, I wished the train had stopped because then things would be better. I had been so ready for an adventure, had dreamed of living in a place safer than here, someplace where the police wouldn't drag anyone away to prison, even if it meant we had to work for practically nothing. As the recruiting posters said, they have work.

CHAPTER 10

Rumors of the problems in Lviv weaved into the local gossip. News drifted into conversations by those who witnessed things in the city. The Battle of Lviv had lasted ten days, but the aftermath of fighting in the city streets still lingered. A struggle ensued in Lviv; the Polish police were losing against the Russians. Our village of Halych remained quiet on most days, we did our daily business, stole away to school, worked, and kept a vigilant eye out for trouble.

Each afternoon I sat near the open window watching people walk by, eager to learn news, and curious about what was going on. I hoped to hear the whispered stories between the adults. One particular sunny afternoon, my father was working in the garden when a man ran toward him, waving his arms. It was Kosko, again. He lived in our neighborhood and traveled to the city to work in a factory, staying in Lviv all week. Then he came home on the weekend to take care of his mother.

"Pan Rudenko, Pan Rudenko," Kosko cried aloud.

He slumped for a moment, panting to catch his breath. His skinny body seemed to need more than air.

"I've heard some news. Poland has been completely captured by the Germans—the Nazis overtook the entire territory, and now they will march into Lviv as we feared. The Russians don't stand a chance. It looks like the agreement between them is over."

My tato lifted himself from the ground, dusted off his pants, and then encouraged the young man to sit on the step to tell all.

"Are you sure of this news? They are headed for Lviv?"

"Yes, I saw a bulletin at a newsstand. But that's not all, Pan Rudenko. Remember the rumor that there was a secret agreement between the Soviets and Germany?"

"Yes, of course. What did you hear, Kosko?"

"I didn't hear, Pan Rudenko, I saw. With my own eyes. The Russians are fleeing. They were gathering up all the city leaders and the shop owners with money. All the leading businessmen and their families were being led to the train station. They are making them evacuate to Russia. Do you know what this means?"

My father sat down on the front steps and dropped his head. At that moment, I wanted to run to him and hug him, push my love into his heart because he seemed so deflated.

"This means the Russians are afraid of the Germans, as they should be," my father said. "The secret agreement seems to be off, Kosko. The *Molotov-Ribbentrop Pact* between the two countries was a farce, to begin with. The Russians are behaving as if they don't trust the Germans to adhere to the pact, retreating from the Nazi advancements like this. We should all be afraid of the Germans."

Tato stood up. "We need to let everyone know. Go tell anyone you see to meet at the old church tonight. We need an emergency plan in case the Germans come to our town, too."

The wafer-thin young man shook in disagreement.

"No, this isn't bad news," Kosko said. "It's good news. Those Soviets are running, and the Germans are going to help us return to normal. The old days seemed glorious compared to how we live now. Certainly, better than how the Soviets ever treated us."

My father's face turned a shade of beet red.

"No, Kosko, don't allow yourself to be fooled. I have no love for the Soviets either, and for reasons better than most, but the Nazis aren't like the old Prussian state. The soldiers coming here aren't going to save anyone. They will be here to use us, then kill us. Don't you understand? We need to leave here right away! We need to warn people."

"More warnings." The young man's expression turned sour, he waved his hand at my father and strutted away. Tato turned and ran into the house, calling out in alarm.

"Leysa, Leysa, please come quick. I need you to pack our things."

I ran to the kitchen, crying.

"Mama, are they coming to kill us?"

She wrapped me into the fold of her skirt and burned a look at my father. I wished I had been braver, instead of whimpering and causing her to give my father that stare.

"We will be fine, Ivan."

She patted my head.

My father bent down, pulled me away from Mama, and hugged me. I smiled then, feeling much better.

"I love you, Tato. Please don't let them kill us."

He rubbed my head and said, "*dobryj chlopec*, good boy. No one will be killing anyone around here."

Tato recruited Petro and me to spread the word. We knocked on doors and told those interested to meet later that night, at the old church. The building hadn't been used for Masses in ages, just a relic in the former town center that lay close to the Dniester River. It sat high on a hill, so anyone standing at the top had the advantage of seeing if someone was coming. My brother often took me there to play king of the mountain if the diggers weren't there of course. He always won.

The old timber frame had been spared once, during the first World War. I hoped that it would be spared again if the Nazis or Russians tried anything underhanded like burning our town. One never knew what to expect from the oppressors. The old stories I heard of the great battles with swords that spilled blood and guts, might not be true. Still, the grisly horrors from the past haunted my dreams. Those nightmares might happen again. I had a vague recollection of my grandfather's stories.

Dido spoke as if it were an honor to fight for freedom. My grandfather glorified his battles like old people often do. Bragging while they stare off into the ghostly past, clinging so memories stay alive. My mama told me that though my dido was brave, God blessed his soul, it was even braver to match wits with strategic words rather than swords. I missed my dido and his warm bear hugs.

But the mere thought of a battle sent chills down my back. What did I know of the war, I was only a boy? Perhaps the war stories Petro shared with me weren't genuine like he claimed. Maybe the school teacher had glamorized the historical life of Ukraine before the Soviets took control. Maybe it hadn't been so wonderful after all. *Was war as important as portrayed?*

I refused to believe the babbles of Kosko, of how the Germans might save us. My tato was the smartest man in town, and if he said the Nazis were no good, then they weren't. Besides, Kosko wasn't the brightest person around, even I knew that. *Would they chase us from our homes so Germans could take over our land?* That's what the Russians had done. My mind debated possibilities back and forth until I was so confused, I decided not to think anymore.

I sat on the wooden floor and tossed my rubber ball against the wall, not a care that my mother might chastise me for rough play in the house. Mama was preoccupied, my game never caught her attention.

At dusk, my father left for the meeting, and while he was away, my mama sewed. She was embroidering a shirt for my father, a blue and cranberry-colored design on white cotton. A thick stitched band around the collar and cuffs in an intricate geometric pattern that stood out from across the room. Mama's hands moved expertly, her fingers tugging the threads and pushing the needle with skill. I closed my eyes and thought of how Tato will look handsome in his new shirt when he stands in front of the town, giving speeches.

My sister and brother sat at the table reading. They were so immersed in their stories that they never gave a glance in my direction. I pretended nothing worried me, and tried not to look at the clock while waiting for Tato to return. A yawn came over me, so I stretched then went to bed.

I left the door open and waited for my father's return. After saying my prayers I couldn't fall asleep. I stared up at the ceiling and watched the shadows move as my mother got up, put her sewing away, and tidied the kitchen. Petro and Olena had already gone upstairs to bed. The soft glow of light from the front room beamed through the crack of my ajar door.

Finally, the entry lock turned. I crept out of bed, peeked through the door crack, and caught a glimpse of the bleak night sky behind Tato as he opened the front door wider. A cool breeze flittered across the room and drafted into my bedroom, tickling my feet. The kitchen was dimly lit from the one lamp my mama had left on. I heard my father drape his coat over the back of a kitchen chair, then he sat. The cane of the seat crunched under his weight. Mama leaned on the wooden arm of the chair and lovingly kneaded tato's shoulder.

"That feels wonderful, my dear Leysa."

"You are so tense, Taras."

"Yes, and with reason. I want to take us away from here, but I'm afraid it's too late. It's confirmed, the trains have been commandeered by the Nazis. One of the townspeople saw soldiers arresting the remaining university professors when they were in Lviv— they executed one of them right in the street for show."

My mama covered her mouth, as if she were about to be ill, then looked up at my tato to listen. She wanted to know the truth, like me, no matter the ugliness.

"The OUN is useless now. They've all scattered. I'm afraid that some of the extremists will follow the Germans and become vigilantes, and we know what happens then."

"Who was arrested, who killed? Anyone, we know?"

My mother rested her head on tato's shoulder. I think she was crying.

"No names were mentioned, but soon more German troops will arrive to push out the remaining Russians and then they'll take over the entire city. Everything has to be underground from now on. Everything. The soldiers ordered those who remained in the Polish police to gather up the remaining groups of Jewish businessmen. They took them away to Janowska."

Mama gasped.

"What are we to do, Taras?"

"We will help, however we can."

Tato turned the chair, pulled Mama close. His hands remained around her hips as he looked up into her eyes the way he does. My father cherished my mother. I could tell that he had teared up as well, his voice was soft, his words slow.

"Leysa, there are rumors that the Jews are being sent to the prison camps to be killed. We need to help the Jewish families from our town. They need to hide before the German soldiers come to Halych."

It was silent, except for the clock over the stove. It had a low tick, usually a soothing sound, but at that moment, I thought it would make me burst into tears. I couldn't stand hearing the tick-tock; it sounded like a pendulum, never motionless, never stopping to rest.

"We can't help them," Mama said. "It's too dangerous. If any soldiers discover that we are helping Jews hide, then they will shoot us."

Tato took her hands to his lips and kissed them.

"My dear druzhyna, if we don't help them, then our souls will die. What good is living without a soul?"

Tato raised his head and reached up to kiss her cheek.

"Fear of death takes away the joy of the living, Leysa."

She slid into his lap, and they embraced, kissing like there would be no tomorrow.

Carefully, I closed my bedroom door tight and scampered back into my bed. As I pulled the covers up to my neck, I vowed to help my father as best I could because I didn't want my friend, Michael, to disappear. He was a Jew, whatever that meant, and I didn't want him to be sent to prison, and I didn't want him to be taken away to a death camp, either.

All the dreams of running away to a new land suddenly seemed scary. Staying in Halych seemed dangerous, too. Our future was filled with too many unknowns.

I shut my eyes and prayed that we could stay home, that our village would be spared from all the fighting, and that the Bolsheviks, nor the Nazis, would find us. Tears came to my eyes while I prayed, and finally, sleep found me between my sobs.

GALICIA 1940-1943

Confusion Begins

CHAPTER 11

Galicia 1940

The men from town gathered in the park each day, sitting on the old weathered benches as they shared any newspaper that had managed to get printed in the turbulent city of Lviv. Most news gained was from newsletters circulated by the underground presses.

Men smoked cigarettes pinched between their nicotine-stained fingertips until the very ends almost singed their mustaches. Some older men toked their pipes, pulling in deep puffs, blowing out swirling rings that floated up until they dissipated, all for the other men's amusement. They needed an excuse to laugh. Bottles were passed around, each took swigs of vodka or vyno that they had stolen from the back of their cupboards. Only slim pickings these days, so each toke of smoke and each drink shared, turned into a special communal event among the gathered men.

One particular chilly spring day I followed my tato to the park and watched as the men bantered about what was going on in the other parts of the world. I knew I wasn't supposed to be there, my father didn't like for us children to hear the things that were happening around us, but I spied anyway. I sat on the ground behind a bush, my private lookout. I wrapped my arms around myself and felt comfortable as I eavesdropped once again.

"Thousands were arrested," an old man said. "Packed into cattle cars, and sent to Siberia, and Kazakhstan most probably, sentenced to work as slave labor..." the man's voice faded.

He dropped his eyes and stared at the new spring grass, completing other thoughts quietly to himself.

"The thought of being captured and shipped away frightens me," another man with bushy eyebrows added to the conversation.

"I wonder how long it will take for them to do that here, to us?" a third man asked.

"Can Russia get away with doing that here in Galicia?"

The man with bushy eyebrows pinched them as he spoke.

"I thought the Polish had control? But since Germany took Poland, what does that mean here? Then I heard the Russians took over, but now they are leaving? Who's in control of Lviv? Does anyone have a clue?"

"The Russians marched into the city, I saw it myself," the old man said.

"They arrested people and carted them off, they don't care. The lucky ones already left, headed west to Poland to escape being taken by the Russians. Every day the fighting still goes on. I heard that the Bolsheviks forced the important people back to Russia, they want to keep them—you know, the rich people and smart people, owners of factories with money and the industrialists. No matter, soon it will all be run by the Nazis, mark my words, they will march in and take over everything," the old man said. "May God help us all." He hung his head and returned to looking at the ground.

Information was flung about in discourse, engraining the details into their minds. Worldly things that were happening in Europe, news of the war, Church news, no matter the topic, they added their opinions. One hope remained consistent among them all—that one day Ukraine would be a free independent country. That was the dream, to be free from the tyranny of any kind. When my father quoted our favored writer, they all looked up toward the sky, many teared up by the sentiment.

I listened to them all, curious about the outside world, knowing that one day, my father might take us away from here to a place out there. It didn't seem much better anywhere else by the remarks of the men. I was frightened but pretended that their talk didn't bother me. I wanted to know what was happening, and if I showed fear, my tato would sense it. If he discovered I came to the park to hear the conversations...well, I wanted no excuse for him to ban me from listening.

A sudden movement grabbed my attention. A tall man wearing an old cap and wool jacket stood to talk. Everyone turned to listen.

"Look what I have."

The man held up a small object.

"A postage stamp with the tryzub and a coin with the same Ukrainian symbol on the front. These small symbols will help us to get recognition as a real nation. We need to make others take notice and see that we are more than a territory. We have our own identity. These small tokens are the first steps for acknowledgment that we indeed exist as a nation. Soon other countries will realize that Ukraine has its thumbprint and that we're not part of Russia or Poland. We are Ukraine."

"Sit down. You crazy fool," someone called out.

The man passed the coin and a bottle around, the others nodded their acceptance.

"What countries are going to recognize us, old man? I heard Belgium, and the Netherlands surrendered to the Germans, they had no choice," another man said. "They were bombed, and then the German tanks ripped up the land and all of the crops. Paratroopers landed on people's roofs from the sky, for God's sake. Soldiers forced their way into the homes from under their very own rooftops, and literally pushed the people into the streets. Thousands were forced to leave their homes, just walking in a long line. The people marched away, not knowing where they were going, or what awaited them."

"How would you know?" someone called him out.

"I received a letter from a cousin. Soon it will be Paris."

His panic spread, and whispered conversations grew like wildfire.

Another urgent voice from the crowd spoke out.

"I heard some were rescued at Dunkirk by the Royal Navy."

More replies, men began to speak over each other, a babbling mess. The conversations turned dark, adding more graphic details about smoke streaked skies, and dead bodies mangled by the bombs. Family members had written about the distress of the situation, and told their little horror tales.

I didn't want to listen any longer and wondered if there was a chance of hope remaining for us. I closed my eyes to get away from the assault of bloody visions that popped into my head.

Instead, I envisioned the ancient castle that I held dear in my heart. I daydreamed about the noblemen who fought to protect this land ages ago. I wondered why the men in town just sat around complaining, why didn't they grab whatever weapon was available to stand guard and protect our town.

The Kozaky we often sang about in ballads had fought to keep our people safe by killing our enemies. *Where were they now? Couldn't these men get off their asses and act like Kozaky if it meant saving their families?*

Frustration welled inside of me, and all I could see in my mind was fire—bright orange, reds, and blue, fiercely burning hatred. I needed to punch something, someone, and felt helpless.

Time after time I was told how special I was, and I did feel God residing in my heart and knew that He would give me strength. I vowed that one day, somehow, I would fight for our people, for our freedom. Someday I'd create something to make this world a better place. A brighter future was in store for my family, I had to believe.

All I had to do was ask for His help. I bent my head and mumbled a prayer, asking God to take the anger away and make me brave instead.

CHAPTER 12

Galicia 1941

The hardships and confusion intensified. The Polish reigned political power over us the first month of the year, then the Russians marched in and reined control. Once again all the Catholic Ukrainians lived in daily fear. The Russian takeover proved to be brief.

On June 30th the Nazis invaded the city of Lviv, days later we heard the news that the Nazis had taken Paris as well. The entire world seemed to be overpowered by the German forces.

A few men sat around in the park and yakked about the things they've heard. How the statue of Lenin standing in Lviv had been pulled down by the incoming German troops—A defiant insult to the Russian Bolsheviks. Many people applauded as they saw it coming down; no one remaining in this oblast was a fan of the Communists. We worried about what would become of our town, our Ukrainian culture, our chances for freedom.

One late afternoon, a man came running into the yard calling out for my father. I rushed to the window and saw that it was that crazy Kosko again.

"Pan Rudenko, Pan Rudenko." He kept yelling.

My father appeared from the back room and went out to the yard.

"Kosko, what is it? What's your problem?"

"It's the Ukrainian nationalists, your old friends from the new OUN."

The man panted and spoke between breaths.

"They held a demonstration after the Nazis took over, you know, marching and calling out for a free Ukraine. They gathered at the Lviv Opera House and spoke so fancy. They said the Nazis would help us, that they would support the '*Act of Revival of the Ukrainian State*'. That's what the OUN had told us all along, that the Germans would help us after they occupied our land. So, they made a public announcement, that we were a nation."

"Really," my father said.

A hint of hope slipped into his tone, and for a second, my blood rushed with anticipation that something good might materialize.

"And what happened? The Germans agreed to let us be, after all this time?"

"No." Kosko snapped. "Not at all, Pan Rudenko. Just the opposite, it was horrible. You were right. Everything happened so fast like a fuse was lit and exploded. The demonstration turned into a slaughter. Your friends, Stetsko and some other OUN members, they proclaimed the independence of Ukraine. And then they were surrounded by soldiers, like a swarm of wasps let loose. Armed Nazi guards stormed forward and arrested them all. I heard that Bandera was arrested in Krakow, too."

My tato slumped on the step, rocking his head.

"That's not good. Not good at all. All the hard work they've done will be for nothing. Fools! Why hadn't they taken more care?"

"Our hopes of working with the Germans are dashed. The Einsatzgruppe rounded up the OUN leaders and sent them away. They posted a notice declaring that they were sent to the camps to be executed." Kosko collapsed to the ground, folded his legs, and hung his head. "I ran away as fast as I could, all I could think of was to get home and check on my mama. Now, what are we to do?"

"We move forward, Kosko. We do our jobs, live our lives, and try to help whoever we can in whatever manner possible. We can't depend on the underground, political parties, or occupying forces to save us. We build our life by our work and deeds, no one else's."

Kosko looked up and squinted. The setting sun blinded his eyes, he covered half of his face with his hand as he spoke.

"I'm afraid. Some of the things I intended to do, to help my fellow Ukrainians, would land me in jail."

Tato nodded.

"Follow your heart. Good deeds are often the hardest to act on."

Word of the arrests blazed through the Ukrainian community. Until then, I had never appreciated our efficient rumor chain. The news passed along faster than if we could have used telephones.

My parents were approached by many men and women who were happy to share secrets, and my sleuthing techniques improved each day. I discovered better ways to hide my whereabouts, and believable alibis to keep my parents from checking on me.

They learned that the few OUN followers who weren't arrested remained working for the cause of a free Ukraine using the underground. Everything was a big secret.

A split in the OUN philosophy created a gap. Rumors claimed that some more radical OUN members who followed Stepan Bandera joined the German ranks. A few participated with the Nazis, did unspeakable things, in the hope the Third Reich might change their agenda toward Ukrainians. They disgraced our heritage, and people didn't speak of them often, as if that could erase their bad deeds.

There were whispers about how the Germans were forcibly taking young Ukrainian men for their regiment. They threatened to arrest their families if they didn't comply. After hearing those stories, our tato kept Petro in the house most days, asked him that he not leave without permission.

As a leader, Tato preached to the town about the real German agenda, and how they, like every other captor, wanted our land, our labor, and our lives. He spoke of remaining peaceful and not giving in to our darker side out of fear.

"As we wait for the day when we can proclaim our freedom without fear of arrest, we should remember to help each other. That's how we'll survive any occupier, by remaining human."

My father spoke profoundly to the small crowd in the park and always knew what to say to help people overcome despair. He refused to see the German invaders as any kind of savior and pleaded with the others to keep their faith in God and the dream of a free Ukraine.

A German soldier drove into the town center and jumped from his vehicle to post another bulletin. More rules, already we had too many restrictions. I watched as an old man from town walked by with his head bent toward the ground, trying to look as inconspicuous as possible. Public meetings of any kind have been outlawed for a while now. Soldiers arrested anyone who threatened the peace with an original idea about our lives. So people kept their heads down and worked in silence.

Weeks and months passed, the people in town shared news they heard but waited until the coast was clear of soldiers patrolling the streets.

Going to our secret school became too dangerous, so we read the books we had at home, and helped with chores more often. When Mama hired a cleaning lady to help tidy up the nearby Church, it seemed odd to me. She did the work instead of asking us, now that we had lots of free time.

Mama went out early in the morning to unlock the back door of the Church and then let the woman into the Sacristy. The woman secretly left the same way in the evening after sunset. I didn't understand why the woman behaved like this, hiding her actions as if it was a big secret that she cleaned the old Church. It's not like anything public was happening. I never asked my mother about it, she seemed to want to keep it a secret mission of some sort. I put it out of my mind, knowing my mother would never do anything wrong. She was too afraid to call attention to Petro.

Everyone in town walked around in the shadows. Voices kept low, as unassuming as possible, to remain unobserved by random soldiers who canvased the streets. Even I didn't venture outdoors to play much these days, except on days when I walked down the road leading out of town.

There was a small farm a couple of kilometers away from home where I sometimes worked with my friend, Michael, feeding and mucking the horse stalls. The old man had no money to pay us, so Michael and I went home with cheese or wheat instead.

My father remained extra careful to cover up the secret project he had started. Our town had begun digging sewer lines for our small city, though most of our houses still had outhouses in the back yard. There were some buildings already connected as the work was ongoing. Lots of digging by day. The soldiers often stopped by to inspect the workers.

Things went on during the night, too, dangerous things. Tato led a small group dedicated to helping our Jewish neighbors to get out of town to safety, putting them as far away as possible from the Nazis. The families were smuggled through the newly dug waste tunnels that dumped into the river. From there, they escaped across the river using a hidden towboat. The idea came from a story we heard about a Polish man named Leopold Socha. He helped the Jews in Lviv by hiding them in the city sewers to save them from ghetto deportations. My father borrowed the idea so that our neighbors could be saved, as well. But it was difficult, and we had to be careful.

My brother and I did our part by packing travel sacks for the people. We filled them with bread baked by Mama and other women, scavenged canned goods, matches, and any other survival supplies we could get our hands onto. We stuffed the meager rations into the cloth bags that had been sewn by Olena and her friends. The girls had no idea why they were so busy sewing, but Olena was good at getting

87

them to follow her lead, and they happily did the work without knowing why.

We dared not tell anyone outside of our small circle of close friends about what we were doing. We feared they might be secretly working with Einsatzgruppe, the terror police lead by that brutal German dog, Erich Koch.

I spit on the ground; I did this every time I thought of those soldiers and their evil leader, Koch.

Our neighbor, Pan Fleischman, heard that all the Jews in Lviv were forced into the ghetto. They were systematically being sent away in groups to be killed. Like the Bolsheviks killed all the Ukrainian men in the prison hours before they fled the city, now the Nazis were killing the Jews.

I spit again, this time it landed on my shoe.

"Dammit."

"What's wrong with you," Petro asked.

"Nothing. I hate the Nazis, that's all."

"We all do. Now get working, we need to finish in time."

I picked up another bag that sat on the picnic table and filled the cloth sack. It was a warm summer afternoon, and the birds were singing, and the sky was powder blue. A few bugs buzzed by my ear and I batted them away, thinking about the work we had to finish.

Later that night, we would be handing out bags to more good people who had waited their turn to escape. The family leaving was a young couple who had befriended my parents. They had a son and a daughter. For some ungodly reason, the soldiers had labeled this family as the enemy. I spit on the ground again, three times for good measure. I took any kind of luck.

Tato walked across the lawn and stood by our side, his eyes were mere slits, his wrinkled forehead divulged his deep-seated distress. I knew he hated us doing this work with him, but the extra help was needed, and it was dangerous to trust anyone else.

"Remember boys, some of our Ukrainian neighbors in town are different from us. They're against the Jews and believe the propaganda promoted by the Nazis. Some people believe in their rhetoric and false promises. We must be cautious tonight and every night. It's hard to determine who to trust, so don't stop to talk with anyone, that's the best way to stay safe."

"Don't worry, Tato. Ivan and I know to be careful," Petro said.

Tato rustled our hair, one hand on each of our heads, then he patted me on the back.

"*Dobryj chlopec*, good boy. You're good sons and I trust that you will do a good job again tonight."

It was exciting, everything accomplished covertly, scampering through the streets like quiet mice, no one could know what we were up to. We left no evidence for anyone to use to point us out. Otherwise, we'd be labeled as traitors. If our clandestine alliance got caught, there would be no one remaining to help anyone.

CHAPTER 13

Late Summer 1941

A tragedy happened in our town that touched my soul in such a horrific manner, that I was never the same again. My wildest nightmare could never have contemplated such evil. If only I could close my eyes and open them again, to discover that it had been a dreadful hallucination—that it hadn't been real.

Things changed for the worse since the Nazis took over Halych. The children were kept in their houses, so there was never anyone to play with during the day. Especially not the boy next door, Michael, who used to be my best friend. Kosko stopped by our house every so often and told my father the latest gossip, but it happened less and less. I thought that was probably a relief for father because he never trusted Kosko, I could tell by the way he shook his head when the man talked.

Sad news filled the few papers printed about the city of Lviv, and of how there were killings, beatings, and barricaded ghettos. People were carted off to prisons, these were all daily events. *If everyone went to prison, who would be left?*

Halych still had many Jewish people living in town. It was dangerous being a Jew. They were often picked out of the crowd and humiliated by soldiers or beaten, so they tried to blend in with the others to avoid the Nazis' wrath. Fear veiled our daily lives, but this particular day the Jews were caught in a quagmire. The saddest day of my life, a nightmare that would forever be in my head, the last day for many people.

It was a late afternoon in August, the sun was hot. We went to the Church to clean the pews and place flowers on the altar for the Holy Day of Obligation. Religious ceremonies and gatherings of groups of any kind were banned. We still occasionally met in secret. The patrolling soldiers had a predictable schedule. The adults thought it worth the chance to celebrate the *Feast of the Transfiguration*. It was a remembrance of when Jesus was proclaimed the prophet and son of God, the bridge between heaven and earth. They thought we needed this time to be together as a Church.

Some of us Catholic children gathered summer flowers from the fields: yellow Sonyashnyk—sunflowers, dark blue Voloshka—cornflowers, a few white Shasta daisies, and deep-red Mak better known as—poppies. The flowers had a meaning: the vigor of life, virtue, and purity, and the infinity of the universe. They protected against evil spirits and worked as a good luck charm. Olena and her friends roped them into a long braid. We all helped to drape the flower swag over the altar.

We kept all the windows and doors sealed tight despite the hour of the day to remain safe from the soldier's view, or from anyone from ransacking. Still, the altar looked beautiful, the brilliant colors warmed my heart. The yellow, blue, and red spilled brightness into the darkness of the room. Looking at the altar, I was delighted and thankful for the rainbow of flowers that cheered our day. But that simple moment of joy was quickly taken away.

The Church doors burst open. I spun around to see. German soldiers rushed into the nave and surrounded the group of women who stood upfront by the altar. The men spread out and went in all directions.

I watched in horror as one of the soldiers went to the tabernacle, opened the door, and stole the gold Communion chalice.

My eyes roamed to another soldier as he grabbed the bible that sat on top of the pulpit where the priest said Mass. A third man confiscated the gold candlesticks. Everything happened in a blur.

My stomach twisted into knots, my skin crawled, and my pulse raced. I thought I might faint.

From the edge of my vision, I caught sight of the Nazi leader stepping toward my mother.

I sprang forward. No soldier was going to put a hand on my mother.

Mama held up her hand, inclined her head and gave me that look, that stern stare, freezing me to the spot. The soldier never noticed as he handed my mother some papers. I heard the pages crunch as my mother crumpled them and let them fall to the floor. Mama had high ideals, no doubt furious that the men intruded our Church, but she should have known better than to antagonize these men.

I stepped to her side, frightened that the soldiers would take her away to prison. No one belonged in a dank place like that, especially not my mother.

The soldier made a clicking sound with his teeth then spoke.

"Fraulein, you can no longer meet here. It is banned. No religious ceremonies are allowed. But you know this already. I have no personal issue with your ceremonies as the Bolsheviks had, but you need permission to use this building again. I suggest you straighten out those pages and fill them in. Hand it over to the local command station, and you might be able to have your ceremonies legally."

The leader clicked his heels and saluted with that strange hand movement.

"Heil Hitler."

I breathed in deeply and let it out, relieved that the problem was averted. I looked up and spied another soldier resurfacing from the priest's Sanctuary, pulling the cleaning woman with him.

I had learned that Mama was hiding her in the Church to protect her true identity. *My mother's secret mission.* The woman was waiting for her husband to return so they could flee the area together, but what would become of her if he never returned? My mother no doubt thought that it was a romantic gesture to help her. But I'm certain my father thought it unwise since the Germans wasted no time sending any Jewish person away to the camps or worse.

I watched in horror as the woman struggled at the hands of the Nazi soldiers. They pushed her from one man to another, making lewd comments, taunting the woman with bawdy gestures while she shook with fear. Her clothes torn, the soldiers yanked at them more with each shove, her dress shredding more, until I could see her slip and undergarments. She grabbed at the tattered pieces of cloth and tried to cover herself.

My stomach dropped to the floor, and I wanted to vomit but had no choice but to stand there motionless, watching them mishandle her.

"Let me go, please, I have done nothing wrong." Her desperate pleas faded.

The head soldier turned to my mother and the other women that now stood huddled together in silence, staring at the scene playing out in front of them.

"Do you know this woman?"

No one spoke at first, then my mother stepped forward.

"Yes, she is our cleaning lady, Sonia. I ask, no I demand that you unhand her, she is harmless."

My mother's face remained stoic, and if I hadn't known her, I would have thought she wasn't moved in any fashion at all. She was strong and brave to stand there and show such calm because she was crying inside. I knew my mother, and she was weeping for her friend that was caught in the hunter's snare. I was crying inside, too.

"She is a Jew!"

The Nazi soldier yelled, his face boiled, his cold gray eyes bulged.

"You are hiding Jews here, in the church."

The soldiers stopped tossing the woman.

"No, please, Sir, you are mistaken. This woman is one of us," my mother declared.

The Nazi leader shook his head.

"Perhaps, I should arrest you all for keeping a Jew!"

One of the women started to bawl, and soon, all the women were weeping.

"Take this one," the leader ordered.

He shoved Sonia forward, into the arms of the soldier who had discovered her in the back room.

"Bring her to the riverfront, where she can join the other Jews. This town will see what we do with the likes of them, then perhaps they won't be so moved to help them hide in the future . . . once they realize the seriousness of their situation."

Sonia's voice wailed softly, helplessly.

My mother stepped forward, about to go to Sonia to help her, but the Nazi leader put his arm up to stop her.

"Fraulein, you will do well to remember to fill out the paperwork."

He smiled; the kind of shitty grin bullies like to give after they've punched you in the gut.

The other soldier pushed Sonia along, again and again, until she was obliged to walk forward on her own. I saw her face, desperate, frail, and her eyes wide-opened with fright. I'd never forgotten those eyes, dark, pretty eyes, but so terrorized. Sonia pleaded as the soldier ushered her out of the building.

She never stopped pleading, her voice a fading cry until she was out of earshot.

The other soldiers formed a line and marched out. The Nazi leader turned and swung his arm up in salute, flashed his chagrin, then stomped off, slamming the doors shut. The bang echoed and an eeriness filled the church. I looked at the flowers that had been knocked off the altar, the colors strewn all over the floor, and I thought of how useless they had been against the evil.

One of the women ran to the window and opened the shutter.

"Look," she cried out.

The others went to the window and watched as the remaining items from the Church that had been confiscated were piled into a truck parked outside. The women prayed aloud together for this to end, crossing themselves over and over again.

When the soldiers finally drove away, my mother turned to me.

"Go home, Ivan. Take your sister. Tell your tato what happened here. Tell him to go to the riverfront right away, and say that I'm afraid something very bad is about to happen there. And then, after your father leaves to meet me, I want you to stay home with your brother and sister, and lock the door."

Her blue eyes were intense, stern, resolute. I knew not to argue with her or ask questions.

"Go, hurry. And don't get stopped."

Nodding, I did as promised. I ran home, pulling my older sister along.

I sweated and panted under the heat of the afternoon sun. The bricks of the road pounded against my shoes. I felt every bump and crevice of the street, and when our house was in sight, I gave one last burst of energy and flighted through the doorway.

"Tato, tato, where are you?" I called out from room to room.

My father came running and grabbed my arms.

"What is it, Ivan? Are you hurt?"

Tato looked at my sister and wrapped his arm around her. Olena was crying but without releasing a sound.

"No Tato, I'm fine. The Nazis . . . "

I shook my head while catching my breath.

"They came to the Church and took everything. They took Sonia, too, and dragged her down to the river. Mama said something horrible is going to happen there and to tell you, and that I should hide with Petro and Olena."

At the mention of his name, Petro popped his head into the room, his face washed with panic.

"Watch your brother," Tato ordered. His eyes were on Petro, now. "Stay here, inside. I'm going to find your Mama."

In a flash, Tato was gone, and the three of us stood there in silence. After a moment, Petro moved, bolted the latch, and stood there a moment longer, staring at the door. His hands remained on the wood frame as if he had turned to stone.

"Petro, let's go help. Let's follow Tato."

"No, Ivan. If there's trouble and we're there, it will only make things harder for Mama and Tato. We'll get in the way, or at least take away their concentration. Let's do as we're told, stay here, and wait for them to return."

The front window was open, and the curtain flung up with the breeze. I could smell the sickled grass; the heat of the sun had warmed the clippings and dried them into fresh hay. That pure pleasure, the scent of warm grass and the bright light beaming across the room, the sunny day—it warmed my heart for a moment. I embraced it, rejoiced in the simplicity of it, and never wanted that second to end.

A loud noise reverberated. The sounds of violence filled the room, *bang, bang, bang, ratatattat.*

Guns went off, over and over again, it seemed to last forever. The acrid smell of gun powder drifted through the open window.

Petro darted to the window and slammed it shut, but still the muffled sounds of continuous gunfire went on.

Bullet after bullet blazed, the sounds rung in my ears. I closed my eyes and saw Sonia's eyes—big dark eyes—pleading for me to help. I felt so guilty to be home, alive, while other people were being killed.

Olena kneeled and started praying ferociously. Petro joined her and pulled me down beside him, so it was the three of us kneeling together. I folded my hands, closed my eyes, and prayed before ugly visions could enter my mind. The first words that popped into my head, *Our Father, Who art in heaven, please help us. . .*

Hours later, our parents returned home. Mama's face was red and swollen, her eyes tiny slits. Tato's forehead was forged into layers of sorrow, stress written all over his expression.

We didn't dare to ask what happened—we already knew the worst. All those people perished and we survived.

The soldiers had said they took Sonia to the riverfront to join the others. *Who were the others, Jews? Is that what happened? All Jews were shot dead?* The thought of her and the many others shot down, dead, scared me senseless. I knew it was true, didn't need to see it, we all heard it happen. Some things are too horrific, too monstrous to even imagine, so our mind blocks them out in vain.

My poor parents witnessed the gruesome killings. I knew that much. Death was all around us, smothering us with its black veil.

I can't remember what happened after that, how we managed to get through the remaining day. We had the routine of praying at every meal and every night before sleep, as a family. Kneeling on the hard, wooden floor that night, I faced the wall with the only small crucifix that tato allowed to remain in the house. I asked God, please help those poor Jews, and to please save us all. Nothing was safe any longer.

CHAPTER 14

After the mass shooting at the riverfront, everyone in town remained hypervigilant. No one spoke about what happened, and no one went into the Church again. Instead, we stayed inside our homes and prayed in private. Tato said that was fine, that the Lord heard our prayers no matter where we recited them, and God would answer our calls to Him.

The very next night I heard my father whispering with his friend, Gabriel Fleishman, my best friend Michael's father. They were Jewish and feared for their lives. The alarm had gone off loud and clear when a thousand Jews were shot dead the previous day. Somehow, through sheer luck or divine intervention, the Fleishman family escaped the dragnet that had executed the others at the riverbank. Pan Fleishman was a butcher and had been able to put some money aside, and though he knew it was dangerous, he planned to leave.

"Yes," my tato said. "We must get you out right away before it's too late. But not to Lviv. I can help you escape away from here."

"Taras, no. It could be very dangerous for you. Don't think the Nazis will be happy killing only Jews. You heard of all the turmoil in the city. All the Ukrainian leaders, even those that had gone along with the Nazis, were arrested and sent to the prison camp to be executed. Those Gestapo understand no limits."

My father nodded.

"Yes, Gabriel, exactly. But the Germans forced all the Jewish shopkeepers and businessmen into the ghetto in the northwest city limits."

My father empathized with his words.

"Jews in our town were attacked yesterday in the worst way, and soon they will come for you. You can't go to Lviv, there is no chance for you there. You must find someplace else to ride out the storm, and I can help you get across the river."

My father's stern voice sounded like a soldier's voice, harsh, commanding and forceful. It scared me, that I didn't recognize my tato. I hated the changes the carnage of yesterday had brought on him.

"Thank you, Taras. Please, get my family out first, the wife and son. I put my trust in you to keep them safe, and I will hold down the fort, try to keep things seeming normal. Surely, a butcher would be missed right away, those Germans need their rump roasts." He snickered. "If I disappeared there would be an investigation. Let's hide what we're doing as long as possible because if they catch us, we're all dead."

My stomach tensed, and I felt ill. I rolled over. I didn't want to listen to my father's conversation any longer. To take my mind off things, I daydreamed about the days of kings. It seemed a much happier time. They fought with swords, and there had been much bloodshed, still, the escape through fantasy allowed me to keep the trauma under control.

Plans were arranged. The next day, Petro and I stuffed food and supplies into bags for our neighbors who were desperate to escape through the underground tunnels. I would miss Michael, we had fun together while working on the farm and playing around. Those days were gone forever.

The summer months rolled into autumn, then before I realized it, a new year arrived.

CHAPTER 15

Halych 1942

Every day, I tried my best to understand what was happening, to cope with the uncertainty around me, knowing that even my brave father was afraid. Still, I wondered why the men weren't fighting back for our homeland. No one raised their arms, no one spoke aloud, no one challenged the Nazis.

My birthday arrived and I turned ten years old, but no one celebrated much. Only my family sang the traditional tune, *Mnohialita*, wishing me many more years of good health. My family sang so softly that it hardly felt special. I was disappointed even though I knew it was too dangerous to draw attention to ourselves. Now, even when inside the house, we remained as quiet as possible. Home felt like a prison.

Halych 1943

1943 arrived with extra turmoil, though Tato said he couldn't believe things could get any worse. The past few months I have behaved badly, hated being cooped up inside, and didn't give my family a moment's peace. I knew I was wrong to be so malicious, teasing and whining. Instead, I should have been thankful to be alive. But, it didn't feel like much of a life. I needed to roam outside, breathe fresh air, and play with my friends...but they weren't around either. It was a ghost town.

The people remained divided. Some were thankful that Nazis helped the Ukrainians by overthrowing the Russians, but the majority of us knew they weren't to be trusted.

People like us might as well have been fighting the entire world, there was never a more lost cause. In my short lifetime the Russians controlled us, then the Polish, then the Russians again and now the Germans . . . It was just like those old stories in the history books, except there was no happy ending in sight.

We lived in the breadbasket of Europe and every country wanted a piece of us, our land, our rivers, and now with another world war striking—our oil. No matter who governed the area, our people were second class citizens to them or worse slave workers. We were treated poorly and lived in fear of a foreign government's strong hand. Still, we did the best we could with what we had, always with hope in our hearts that one day we would have lasting freedom.

The patrolling soldiers increased each day, and I began to see why Tato and the other men in town had remained passive—there were too many of them. The men in uniforms haunted my dreams, I'd wake up covered in sweat and on the verge of tears.

The cloak and dagger secrets that we kept had changed my view of things, I didn't trust anyone except my family. Hiding the remaining Jewish families became more complicated, they were afraid to be found out while waiting for their turn to escape. Brave friends hid them in back rooms, attics, and toolsheds.

Hearsay placed the OUN-B complicit in some underhanded schemes and of horrors that had been done. Some worked along with the Germans led by Koch, the man I hated, Hitler's man.

I spit on the ground again. I did this every time I thought of his name and prayed that good would win over evil. I wanted more than anything for my dreams of being free to come true.

One day a woman stopped by my parent's house.

I was in my bedroom, sitting on the bed reading when she arrived. The woman was crying as she entered the house, I heard the sniffles between her introductory words. She asked for help to locate her son's body.

"Pan Rudenko, I don't know what to do. My son, Olec, was taken against his will. I begged for them to leave him with me, but they said he was needed."

I dropped my book and went to the kitchen to hear her story. She looked frail, dull, wearing an old faded house dress. I immediately felt sad for her and listened with care.

"After a couple of weeks, I received a letter. He wrote about the horrible treatment he received. Olec said that he and the other Ukrainian boys didn't have much food, and were hungry all the time, but the German soldiers ate well. He hated marching with them, as did the other boys who were stolen away. They ordered my son to do things that he knew was wrong, and when he refused, they beat him. He said he was going to escape from the regiment, but he never made it home. Someone heard word that he was shot in the back, along with the other boys trying to escape the Ukrainian regiment under the Nazis."

My mama's hands flew to her mouth. Then she reached over to the woman.

"You poor soul."

Mama pulled the woman into an embrace, and the woman cried into mama's shoulder.

"The boys dragged away by the Germans didn't have a chance," Tato said. "Better to die a hero trying to come home than to live with death on his hands. Olec was a brave young man, who stood up for his beliefs."

Tato said the words, but I knew in his heart, he didn't believe them. He would do anything for his sons to stay away from being a hero.

"We will all pray for his soul at dawn. I'm sorry that's all we can do."

A plan quickly sprung into form, with whispered instructions from one Catholic family to the next.

The following day at dawn, we all slipped into the old Church, the first time we were gathered there for some time. With resolve, we bowed our heads to each other and stood close. After making the sign of the cross, we mumbled *Our Fathers* and *Hail Mary's* for Olec and the other boys who were taken away. Standing side by side in quiet prayer, we prayed for the souls of the departed, those taken before their time because of war.

We took a big chance and could have been arrested because Mama never filled out the paperwork for permission to use the church. I was afraid of getting caught. *Dangerous deeds for a good cause.* The mothers of the lost boys felt some closure, I saw it in their eyes as they recited the Rosary, though nothing would ever take away the pain they felt.

The haunting memory of the day they took Sonia, suddenly filled my head. Her dark pleading eyes stared back at me when I closed mine. I wondered if this situation would ever change... *is it possible to win? Could the Allies build enough strength to obliterate the Germans?* I never prayed as hard.

CHAPTER 16

My family never spoke about politics in public any longer. Instead, my parents talked about those things at home after dinner, using low voices, trying to keep the horrible things from our ears. Since we couldn't go to Pan Vasyklo's classroom in the cellar any longer, our parents insisted that we read every night at home.

One night I didn't want to read. Instead, I sat at the table near my sister and pretended to read. I stared at the pages and kept my face turned away, flipping the pages as I eavesdropped on my parents' conversation.

"How was your day, Taras? You're so tense."

I could hear the sound of Mama's hands massaging my father's neck. He sighed the occasional—ah.

"Some of the men in town were talking about another group that sprouted up," he said. "The UPA—It stands for the Ukrainian Insurgent Army—and it has already changed its name," Tato chuckled. "They renamed it the Ukrainian People's Revolutionary Army."

I turned my head and saw my tato's smile. He looked up at me, his eyes met mine. He had a look so mischievous that it troubled me. It was a private look. I snapped my head down again and pretended to read the lines using my fingers to run across the page.

Mama giggled. "Sounds like they're the new topic among the men in the park."

"Yes. Leysa, this group might turn out to be a new hope needed. It started as a paramilitary group and they did bad things. But then they reorganized into this partisan army. It sounds like its building up steam, more each day. They engage in guerrilla-type conflicts against the Nazis and Soviets, taking them by surprise. And let's not forget the Czechoslovakians. It seems they've gained some ground against us as well."

"My goodness, the list of those against us grows longer every day."

"This new group, the UPA, is stealing the hearts of Western Ukrainians throughout the oblast. At least those who want freedom without an all-out massacre."

My tato spoke some more, but his words were mumbled, I thought on purpose. He attempted to keep the horrors of the war away from us. No matter how old I get, I will always be treated as a child. I huffed, gripping the book tighter. I was dying to know more.

I listened more carefully, making sense of what I could, as my parents discussed this new group. My father poured out his hope.

I discovered that I had acquired a new feeling—skepticism. I didn't believe this group was any better than the others. *Keeping our spirits up, only to be disappointed again.*

"Nations filled with people who are starving do impulsive acts," Tato said.

The memory of that poor woman who lost her family flickered in my thoughts. How her husband was arrested for hiding food, yet the children starved anyway. I understood the dire need that drove many to act out without rational thought or becoming so afraid that they were paralyzed.

But the Nazis were the opposite—well-fed people and healthy, they wanted for nothing. They even planned to make people like us their workforce, discard us when unwanted, to save themselves for better things. My fists balled up with anger. I wasn't going to be anyone's serf, I was special. I wanted more in life than to exist, I have dreams.

Tato was still speaking.

"I heard that the new leader of UPA called out for all Ukrainians to refrain from anti-Semitic activities. His name is Roman Shukhevych. He asked that those who had been against the Jews and had accused them of being Bolsheviks, to stop it, and to be sympathetic to their dire situation."

"Roman sounds like a good man," my mama said.

"Yes, he is. Roman was once part of the Schutzmannschaft Battalion 201, one of the units trained by the Germans. But when they assigned him to a new post along with the other Ukrainian soldiers in that battalion, he didn't re-enlist. Instead, he did the opposite–the entire battalion fled. Many were caught and arrested, some shot like that poor woman's son we prayed for, but Shukhevych managed to escape."

Tato blew out some air, sounding like a relief valve on a steam engine.

"Then Roman joined the OUN and became part of the leadership, and in August at the Third Special Congress, he was elected Supreme Commander of the new UPA. I had no idea until now. The underground news has been slow coming. Word is he assumed the new position of commander and immediately issued the order banning participation in anti-Jewish activities. They say he and his wife are hiding a Jewish girl and that he provided fake documents to keep the girl safe."

"That's a wonderful and brave thing to do," Leysa said.

"Rumors about his wife spread like wildfire. Stories of how she saved the Jewish girl from being killed by standing up to a soldier. I'm told the girl's family had owned one of the big factories in the city. I think it was the one where Kosko used to work. Early on, when the trouble began in Lviv, the factory was taken over by the government. The family was forced to split up. The father was killed, her mother and sister were sent to prison. Shukhevych's wife had taken a shine to the youngest daughter. They say that they had been neighbors with the family."

I managed a peek and saw my mama nodding. I bowed my head, back toward the book pretending to read, but the story I heard fascinated me. I wanted to hear more.

"So," my tato continued, "the wife saved the youngest girl and hid her from the police when they were moving the Jewish people into the ghettos. Her husband came up with false documents using his influence while in the army at that time. Of course, this was before he walked away from the battalion. The papers were created with a new non-Jewish name to protect the girl. It seems they are educating the girl, sending her to schools, fooling them all."

"What a lovely story—to show such kindness. This is a great example of things that can be done to help save others. In our situation, this kind of action is better than fighting a wall of ignorance." Mama clapped her hands. "What a kind act."

"Yes, a brave woman. Her husband's away most of the time, so the girl, no doubt, makes for a good companion for

Pani Shukhevych, when she's not in school, that is. Her husband and his men spend most of their time fighting in the forests. They roam from village to village, never staying in one place long enough to be caught. UPA members are trying to gather up the small national forces that have cropped up along the countryside to form one united, larger and stronger underground army. Maybe then the fight for Ukrainian independence has a chance. Shukhevych would be shot on the spot if the Germans caught them and discovered who he was."

"His story reminds me of a folktale I heard once when I was little girl, about the hero Oleksa Dovbush from the Carpathian Mountains." My mama laughed. "He lived in the woods with his men, back in the 1700s, they called themselves *the opryshky*. He stole from the rich landowners to help the poor serfs. Like a Robin Hood."

My mother had just raised her head and looked at me, I could feel her eyes staring on my back. She wanted me to hear her folk tale. I smiled but kept my head turned as if I hadn't been listening.

"Well, Shukhevych is no folk tale, not yet anyway," Tato said.

"He organizes meetings between the various political parties, hoping to bring unity. He wants to form an underground parliament governing body for the revolutionary movement. Maybe I should help in that regard, I am a diplomat after all. But I cannot condone the fighting."

The fire in the hearth popped.

I raised my head and noticed my tato, he was gazing at my brother, watching him intensely. It was as if my father was taking an inventory of every feature of Petro's face, each freckle, each golden strand of hair.

Lately, Tato kept a close eye on Petro and often spoke to him privately. My brother told me that father said things like, *stay close—always within earshot.* Teenagers like my brother were quick to follow the dreams of Shukhevych and heroes of the like. Even more dangerous was the chance of being picked up as an army recruit against one's will for the wrong team.

Tato moved his head away and paid attention to Mama again. He kissed her hands. "Followers are asked to uphold basic tenants—to oppose all forms of totalitarian government, to construct a democratic state system in Ukraine that guarantees the right for self-determination against imperialism, and they work to free Ukraine. They believe in the free press, unions, and the like, but not in the same way as the Bolsheviks."

"Taras, it sounds like the code you believe and live."

"Yes, I'll never give up the dream of a free Ukraine. Those of us who aren't fighters can still help by keeping as many people as safe as possible."

CHAPTER 17

In the Park, Spring 1943

My parents tried harder each passing day to keep the news away from my ears, they dreaded that our world was falling apart. I heard them say once that they wanted us to be normal children, without worries of war. But I needed to know what was happening. My parents had no idea that my brother and I knew as much as we did… still, there were so many gaps in the details.

Adults often spoke with hushed voices about what was going on, trying to keep secret the horrors that happened to people. Some incidents were too ugly for the person speaking to repeat without gagging between their words or crying into a handkerchief making a big ordeal of the telling.

One spring afternoon I spied a big man dressed all in black, walking fast down the main street. The man wore a large gold cross dangling on a thick chain hung around his neck. His bushy beard was long and white like St Nicholas's. His hair stuck out in parts like he'd slept funny, and was also snowy white. An outer cloak he wore flared out as he stepped with determination, leaving a wake behind him like he was some superhero on a mission.

He stopped a man along the street and politely introduced himself as Andrey Sheptytsky. He asked where he could find Pan Rudenko. Seeking out my father, he entered the park with his hand outstretched toward my father.

My father's eyes widened with recognition. He immediately bowed and kissed the man's hand. Curious, I hurried to the nearest tree which thankfully was large, and I leaned against it, my body hidden. Tato offered the man a seat on the bench and told him he was honored and humbled to have his holiness visit.

I gulped, impressed, and worried at the same time that a prominent member of the Church was here to see my father.

"Archbishop, what can I do for you?" My father's voice was soft, almost as if he was reciting a prayer.

"Pan Rudenko, Taras, it's been a long time since I last saw you at Oselya. I've heard of all the good you've done here, in Halych."

"Please Holy Father, you give me too much credit, I'm a mere servant."

"As you know, Taras, I've been working on uniting the churches and trying to gain some political advantages. My mission has been to help the unfortunate Jews, and I continue to petition those in power to intervene. However, things move slowly, in Rome especially."

He blew out, his lips vibrated.

"I have done my best to help those I can, but my time is ending soon. I can feel it in my bones. I wanted to thank you personally for your aid to others, it's appreciated. You're a great leader, a good example for others to follow, and your benevolence to the Church has been noted, my friend. Unfortunately, I feel the need to reveal some ugly truths to you today. I pray that someday, no matter where you land at the end of this war, that you can make the world aware of what's happened here. History cannot repeat itself."

I popped my head to the side of the tree and caught sight of my tato, kneeling in front of this man. My father kissed the man's hand again. Things were stranger by the minute.

I wanted to know the truths this man mentioned. I slid myself down along the tree trunk, the bark rubbed hard against my skin until I was sitting on the grass. I leaned and waited for the details.

"Did you hear about the incident at the prison, back in June of '41? Yes, well, it proved beyond question that the Russian secret police are monsters. What the NKVD did will never be forgotten by those who lost friends and loved ones."

The man stopped talking for a moment, but I heard mumbling. He was praying. Then Tato replied to the man.

"Holy Father, we knew that the Russians fled when the Germans took over Lviv, the news was everywhere. We know about the executions of all the prisoners held in the Zamarstyniv, and even though it was a political prison, it was an outrageous act. Some people here in Halych had family executed there," Tato said.

The man nodded. "Fr. Zynoviy Kovalyk was among those who perished by the NKVD, but at Brygidki prison."

"My condolences."

"Thank you, Taras. Father Kovalyk had been arrested by the NKVD the previous December sited for his sermon on the *Feast of the Immaculate Conception*. According to them, it wasn't allowed. Well, we knew the Soviets were atheists, and yes, they outlawed our services, but we never anticipated the extent of their cruelty. He thought merely the arrest for a few months, then he'd be let go." The man paused for a moment.

A rush of sadness overwhelmed me, making me feel as if I was about to experience some kind of awful cruelty. My instinct knew I would regret this news, but I remained rooted to the spot.

The Archbishop exhaled and began talking again, his voice low and secretive. "All the prisoners were shot dead before the Russians fled, except for the priest. They decided to use his death as a terror weapon against the Church. They stayed back and took enough time to crucify Fr. Kovalyk and then they displayed his body in the courtyard for the people to see."

"Oh God in heaven, have mercy," my tato exclaimed.

"I am sorry to bear this burden of knowledge on you, Taras, but I didn't want this tragedy to be forgotten. Some in the Church would rather pretend it never happened. A web of treachery even darker and deeper grows."

The Archbishop paused as if he needed to find strength before continuing. His face paled. He breathed deeply, closed his eyes, and then he continued.

"After the German troops conquered Lviv, the families rushed to the prison in hopes of finding their relatives alive and waiting for liberation. Instead, they found them all killed. They were greeted with the horrific sight of Fr. Kovalyk..." The Archbishop huffed. "He was nailed to a cross that leaned against the prison wall in the courtyard, near the chapel. His belly was slit open. A dead human fetus had been placed inside of the wound."

Feeling sick, I lowered my head between my knees. Deep red blood covered the ground. I blinked to erase the vision. I wanted any other image than a crucified priest flashing in my brain. I wanted to scream. The suggestion of guts ripped out of the man, made my stomach ache. I held my mid-section and leaned sideways. I dry heaved.

My father's outraged voice trumped my discomfort.

"An unforgivable sin, may those who participated in the sin rot in hell."

I didn't need to see my father's face to know it burned with anger. His voice sounded tortured and outraged at the same time. The urge to come out of my hiding place and hug my father filled me. I turned to see them, my tato looked older in years.

The Holy Father's eyebrows were drawn tight together, his eyes looked straight at me, without seeing me, his glare unbroken and yet without malice. The man was in deep thought, he looked weary. The bags under his eyes told the story of many sleepless nights, his mouth was pinched tight as if holding back his words.

"Well," the man continued as if in surrender, "after that tragedy and many other incidents the NKVD performed, one can understand how frightened the people became and why they sought relief from the brutality. Why they placed hope in the Germans. Even I thought they'd treat people better than the Bolsheviks."

The man shifted his weight on the bench.

"Some Ukrainians still believe that the Germans will allow us to begin practicing our religion again, but clearly to me, that ship has sailed."

"Yes, I understand," Tato said. "They listen to the German rhetoric about how it was the Jewish people who shot all the prisoners of war in the Janowska camp."

"Yes," the Archbishop said. "That was a horrific act, too. And so many listened to the lies and propaganda. They hated the Jews, beat them, killed them. Horrific. But of course, it wasn't the Jews—the Russians had killed them all—the scorch earth policy. Still, some won't listen."

"We remain cautious," Tato said. "Some of our neighbors believe the nonsense. They might be compelled to hand us over for helping Jews, with the hope of staying in the oppressor's good graces. What good are we if arrested... or worse. People depend on us. Holy Father, please bless me. I don't know what to do next."

The man raised his arms and blessed my father. I watched, then jerked to looked around, checked for any witnesses. I feared that if others in town learned of our secrets, they would leak the information to Erich Koch's men. That would be deadly—we feared Einsatzgruppe and the dreaded Gestapo. If we were found out we'd be sent away to prison or killed. The German secret police were brutes without a conscience, vile executioners who sent people away to death camps, perhaps they were worse than the evil men who crucified the priest.

I had heard many wild stories told among the men in the park about the brutal ways of the SS, how they pulled people out of their homes in the middle of the night, shoved them into the streets, and took all their possessions down to their last piece of clothing, and dehumanized them in public. Those imprisoned had to live fifteen people to a cell meant for three. Horror stories told of what happened to the people deported from the Jewish ghetto section in Lviv and then transported to the death camps.

One Ukrainian man was arrested and taken away to a prison camp, then wrote home about the things he witnessed while on a train. His brother read the letter aloud in the park one day when no soldiers were patrolling. He said that the people in the train car were packed like cattle, some had letters written on them for identification. P stood for Polish, U for Ukrainian, but the poor Jews had been stripped naked.

Hearing about their mortification made me sick.

The man had gone on to write about one cruel German guard. How he had grabbed a Jewish baby from its mother's arms for his enjoyment. Then the guard threw the baby overboard while the train was moving. The baby smashed against a building's wall as they flew past, and the sick bastard laughed. He was a monster. *Were all German soldiers fiends like him?* I couldn't imagine the mother's pain. Soldiers could easily do the same to us in Halych, a few Jewish families remained hiding. We did all we could to help the remaining people getaway, but we had to be careful. These Nazis were very good at detecting lies. If only my family could leave, if only that train had stopped three years ago. I was more afraid now than ever.

Later that night, I lay awake thinking of the people we helped. Did those who fled go undetected? I wondered what they were leaving behind and if they had already lost loved ones. *What happened to all their things?*

I had just turned eleven on my last birthday, and my brother was almost eighteen. We were allowed to help our father get the people to safety on many occasions, especially when he needed a diversion.

Petro ran very fast and made a great decoy. On our last mission, he knocked over trash cans, making such a loud ruckus. The patrol soldiers ran to investigate the clatter. My brother was already a few houses ahead of them, then he ducked into a friend's home, and enjoyed a cup of cocoa with his friend's mother. No one the wiser, but the commotion gave Tato enough time to get the people away.

No matter when or who we were saving, when my father opened the trap door to the new sewage tunnel, a strong odor floated up from below and reeked. I held my nose tight and still could smell the gaseous fumes from human waste. The people were warned about this smelly part, but no one can truly appreciate the assault to your senses until it's experienced firsthand. There weren't many houses hooked up to the refuse system yet, and I wondered how it would smell later when all the homes dumped their waste into this system.

A hollow echo clanged as the people stepped down the metal ladder into the darkness, their feet navigated each rung with care. The sound gave me shivers. Eeriness, a dark abyss, awaited these people, but they all showed such bravery.

Once a child cried, but the mother immediately looked at him with that special stare mother's do so well, shaking her head, and he quickly remembered the rules . . . Absolute silence.

I handed the lantern down to the husband, Petro handed him envelopes with pieces of paper, and the sacks that he and I had packaged. Then Tato closed the heavy lid in place again. They would be gone, swiftly into the quiet night. The new sewer tunnel stunk, but if it meant an escape and leaving for a better place, maybe we should try.

I asked my father one night, "Tato, why don't we leave?"

"If we left, Ivan, who would be here to keep the Jewish people safe?"

I nodded, and we walked together, happily, never running into a soldier on the way home.

CHAPTER 18

Summer 1943

German soldiers had infiltrated our quiet Halych. They drove through our streets and stopped to recruit new soldiers whenever a stray young man dared to walk in public. The Nazis would grab the boys as if they owned them, forcing them into a truck, then into their rank and file.

The heat sweltered. I watched the translucent fumes rise from the tarred pavement. Every living thing outside had withered, choking from lack of water, even the deepest roots found no underground oasis. The night before we had prayed for rain, but the pleas went answered.

Tato appeared from nowhere, he ran into the house, panting. His shirt was spotted with his sweat, his voice sounded foreign as if the grip of fear had its chokehold on him.

"Petro, quick hide now."

My brother had been upstairs in his bedroom, working on his stamp collection. I heard him clomping down the stairs, saw his face pale to a milky-white as if all life was rushing away.

"Are they here?" His voice sounded scared.

I panicked for my brother, he had never looked so vulnerable, and I wondered if I should hide with him. I watched as he headed for the assigned spot.

"Yes, yes. This isn't a drill. They're here. Go below the floorboards as we practiced."

Mama had already pulled up the rug, and Petro pulled up two planks and shimmied down into the small space below the floor.

"Help me, Olena."

Mama and my sister covered the floor with the carpet then moved a table to sit on top of the space. Mama fled to the sink as if her life depended on it, wiping her hand across her forehead.

Olena quickly sat at the table, picked up her sewing, and tried to behave casually. She stitched. I watched Olena's pale blue eyes tear up, then she wiped them with a quick hand, just as the knock on the door sounded.

I jumped.

My sister swallowed hard and pushed her needle through the cloth. She was embroidering a pillowcase with a red and black design. Olena moved her hands without concentration, her eyes kept glancing at the floor, then corrected herself and looked away.

"Ouch."

She pricked herself and sucked the blood from her fingertip, at the exact time a soldier entered our home. He looked at her, then at my mother.

"Fraulein, don't you have a young boy?"

Moving backward, I pushed myself against the wall, fearful the soldier was here to take me away from my family. I swore to myself when I saw his face. I'd never seen such a scary soldier before, his bumpy skin looked like cheese that had gone bad, and his nose stuck out big and red. He turned and ogled me, his eyes popped out, the blood vessels were pumping and ready to explode.

A warm sensation went down my leg. I longed to melt away through the floorboards like my piss. The odor of my urine turned my stomach, but I couldn't move, didn't care if I needed to wipe myself clean. I was a frozen ice-statue and afraid I'd shatter with any false move.

"My son is very young."

I heard Mama say the words, her voice appalled, and she waved her hand at me. My face burned, I thought I'd burst. They were all looking at me, that's when I realized I had been holding my breath.

"Ivan, my poor baby, don't worry. Breathe, son, this nice soldier doesn't want to be your nanny."

Mama smiled, though it was faked. She was trying to show him that we were with them, on their side, so they would leave us in peace.

"No, not the child, Fraulein. I have noted on the list that you have another, older son. He's sixteen or more. I've noticed him myself, entering this house on occasion."

The soldier's eyebrow rose, his jaw set firm, his scowl held in a tight line.

"I'm so sorry to disappoint you. We have no teenagers. Just these two youngsters. Perhaps it was a neighbor you noticed or a delivery boy from the market?"

"I thought surely he belonged here."

Mama shook her head and then averted her eyes to her shoes.

"My apologies, Fraulein."

He didn't look apologetic, but Mama curtsied anyway. I watched her slowly bow her head, performing that small quaint gesture, the way aristocratic people did when meeting royalty, but of course, no one thought the German soldiers were royalty, especially not my mama.

Her display offended me, caused my head to pound in anger. I wanted to scream out, but couldn't muster the strength to overcome my fear. Scared and confused, I wanted to be somewhere else…

I pretended that Mama was dressed in fine gold clothing, a queen's satin dress. In my mind, she was dancing in a ball-room as they did decades ago when we were part of the vast empire. No, not royalty. My mother was a brave and talented actress, pretending not to be frightened by the soldier. She was like *Maria Zankovetska* on the stage, an actress who never forgot her roots, but instead, worked to lift the common folk of Ukraine. She gave us dignity, her very presence on stage demanded respect. My mama was a heroine, too.

Finding that safe place to hide, my imagination swam with visions inspired by the stories that Pan Vasyklo had told us about the rulers from long ago. Lessons that seemed more like fairy tales about Scythian kings before the years of our Lord, back when the Greeks ruled. Tales of the expansion and defeat of the many great empires at the hands of the Visi-goths, Ostrogoths, and the Crimean Goths who had roamed and conquered. Battles of man against man flurried in my mind's eye. In the final battles, they were overtaken by the fierce Roman soldiers. I imagined the Romans' metal helmets and shiny chest plates, adorned with jewelry made of gold embedded with precious gemstones, and of how they slew each other in war with broad swords that glinted in the sun. They fought the other men who wore animal furs and rustic garments, brutally attacking each other, for the golden crown. Brave warriors, all.

I retreated to my favorite story about the leader Vladimir the Great, the first baptized Orthodox Christian who converted the Kievan Rus' people to Christianity. We learned about the first Christians of Ukraine at home and in our studies. Vladimir was an important man, but his son, Yaroslav the Wise, was the leader who the people called the Grand Prince of Kyiv, but his story was sad.

Yaroslav had to fight against his brothers for his right to rule since he had been a bastard child. When I heard that story, I had felt sorry for him, I wouldn't want to fight my brother for a crown. In the end, it was Yaroslav who the people respected, and in return for their loyalty, the Grand Prince of Kyiv created the first Ukrainian library. How wonderful it must have been for the people, I fancied them cheering in the streets as Yaroslav rode past them.

Yaroslav built Saint Sophia's Cathedral in the Byzantine architectural style and added a library, nestled within the bowel of the church. When Yaroslav died, his body was buried in that church, resting in a white marble tomb on top of a fancy tiled floor. I saw pictures of it in a research book that Petro had found among our teacher's things on his desk. Carved with the Christian symbols of palms and crosses, the box panels were also etched with new moons and stars. The walls surrounding his coffin were decorated with painted icons of angels with wings outspread, welcoming him to heaven with the holy ghost. The Church and grave were works of art and an anchor of our culture.

According to the book, Yaroslav remained buried there even though the Soviets had ordered the Church to be destroyed. They hated the Church and anything that reminded them of our Ukrainian roots. Pan Vasyklo, prays for the safety of all churches, but especially that one because it represents a big part of our heritage, a piece of our culture that the Soviets wanted to erase forever. I'll never forget that history lesson. Since then, I've prayed for the survival of the churches.

Petro had also been fascinated with that lesson about the special church, how it survived the centuries, and how it remained of paramount interest. We planned to go there someday, together, and visit the tomb to see it for ourselves. My brother read articles about it, of how seven years ago, a team had dared to open the sarcophagus and to their surprise, two skeletal remains were laid in the grave, a male and female. *Who was the other body?* I still wondered. Curious about such odd things, when my brother and I read of this great mystery, Petro searched for articles about Saint Sophia's Cathedral and what had been discovered.

He read that the male skeleton had been identified as Yaroslav, the great leader, but the female body remained a mystery. Later, in 1939, a newspaper article said the sarcophagus was opened again, and the remains were removed for research purposes. When my brother read this, he tried to buy more newspaper articles, magazines, or any public journal that talked about the project. We both wondered what the research proved and if the bones were ever returned to the tomb, *or had the Bolsheviks destroyed the bones?*

There were other things we learned about our Ukraine in the newspapers that we had managed to confiscate. Like how the Dnieper Rapids in the center of the country were dredged by the Soviets to allow ships to sail to the Black Sea. Amazing things were accomplished by scientists and architects every day, the new heroes of today.

Instead of modern champions, our teacher taught us about our history and the old warriors, like the Kozaky who were nationalists and freedom fighters. He taught of our local Princely Halych and the castle up on the hill near the river. My parents said that when we were occupied by the Russians, they had forbidden anyone to teach the truth about our country. We had to learn these things in secret, just like we met for secret Masses, and buried most of our religious treasures in the back yard in fear they would be confiscated. All things about our Ukrainian heritage were challenged, and today our customs had to be spoken of secretly.

The Russians didn't want us to know or remember anything. They wanted workers for Stalin. They tried to Russify us into thinking like them, to speak like them, and be Communists like them. But freedom was all we wanted.

The Nazis printed leaflets and wrote that the Jews sympathized with the Soviets and wanted us to all be Russian, but it was another lie. Our Jewish friends didn't think like that, they were forced to choose between two evils as well. Propaganda surrounded us, and the only truth we knew was that one day we would be free. We had to keep the dream alive.

We must survive this hard time because too many have already died. The Soviets killed millions of Ukrainians with the Holodomor. They blockaded the borders so those who hadn't fled yet would die, then people from Russia moved in and took over the farms.

The few Ukrainians who remained had to preserve our culture; it was a big responsibility. Every day in school, I was taught these ideas, of holding on, and how it was my generation's responsibility to keep it alive. I thanked God for my teacher, my parents, and my life. I prayed and hoped of being free someday from all the occupiers. One day we will have our own country, as God is willing.

Recalling these thoughts and letting them spin in my head, I managed to escape the moment, forgetting what was happening… that my brother was hidden under the floor.

Frozen, up against the wall, I wore my saturated pants and feared the soldier with the ugly face, he was just one more oppressor. I prayed for my brother Petro to remain safe, hoped he would stay hidden under the floorboards. He had to survive because one day, my brother would be the great explorer like he dreamed of being.

CHAPTER 19

Word quickly spread when the Americans had finally entered the World War on European ground. *Could this be the miracle I had prayed for?* For the past two years, the United States was busy in the Pacific. I had seen pictures of their bombed ships, wrecked by Japan. The photos were splashed on the front page of the newspapers that were stacked neatly in the rack. The store owner did this on purpose so everyone could come in and browse the headlines without buying a paper. He only had the one copy.

The Germans were getting nervous, marching, yelling orders, and pushing people about on the street as if we were dogs. At least that's what an old man said to my father this afternoon in the park. From the stories I overheard, it reasoned that anxious soldiers were a bad thing, and would only lead to more people being hurt.

Later at night, I listened through the crack of my bedroom door. When I realized what my parents were talking about, I got the butterflies. My pulse raced in my veins, a quickening of excitement took hold of me. They were planning another attempt to leave and travel west.

"I met with some of the men from town, secretly. We thought up the best plan to escape Halych for good. But none of us know what we'll be running into. Whether Poland or Austria is best... well, it's nothing more than guesswork."

Tato whispered the directions, as he pointed on a map. My mother whimpered, no doubt she was conflicted, not wanting to leave our home, but knew it would be for the best.

We had been ready to flee once before, but now it seemed scarier, the situation was more dangerous with mounting risks. Soldiers lurked about in the streets everywhere. We were trapped in a web without options.

I tried to make out what my father said. Smiling to myself, I realized that I wanted to see another part of the world, to experience faraway cities, and hear people speaking in other languages. A chance to observe beautiful women, who wore fashion dresses that sparkled when the spotlights of the stage shone them . . . Germany was the top of the fine arts. I heard that they even produced movie films and they had modern movie houses with cushy seats. They darkened the room to make it a memorable experience. I used to scan the glamour magazines sitting on the store shelves when Tato and I went to Lviv. My daydreams were shot down when I heard my father's words.

"What we're attempting to do is dangerous. Leaving has its risks."

The words pulled me down like quicksand. *Could it be more dangerous than staying here in Halych waiting for more Nazis to come and kill us?*

The next morning when Tato told us about the new plans, I pretended that I wasn't scared. I had no intention of embarrassing myself again by pissing my pants, not ever. I pledged to my father that no matter what happened, I would be strong like him.

After I pledged this my Tato smiled and rubbed my head.

He said with a soft, comforting voice, "*dobryj chlopec,* good boy."

We completed making arrangements to sneak off into the dark of night a day too late.

A decree came from Germany. They desperately needed men and women to work in German factories. A few years ago, Germany had begun recruiting workers. At first, some young men from the town desperate to getaway had signed up and volunteered to be an Ostarbeiter. Later, they sent letters home and warned others not to come. All the promises were lies, propaganda, and the conditions in which they lived were harsh. The Ukrainian workers were treated no better than slaves, some women had even been raped by their overseers. The word spread fast, and people didn't want the German jobs, and they stopped volunteering.

Our plans to get away were ruined when the German patrols were given orders that were promptly executed. The soldiers canvased the streets with lists, went door to door, and escorted people away. Our neighbors were herded to buses that would take them to the trains, they were destined to become the dreaded Ostarbeiter.

The first session of recruiting passed us over. The bus had been filled and left. I watched from the window as the vehicle drove away, relieved that we weren't snagged. They would be back. I hurried and packed my things, I was ready to leave.

I heard a thud. I ran to the window and looked out. A military man pounded on the door so hard that I thought the wood would crack in two, split down the middle. I heard him call out.

"Taras and Leysa Rudenko, open the door."

I ran to the front room and saw my mother opening the door. My father stepped forward and blocked the entrance, giving the man a slight bow of his head. The man was younger and stood taller than my father, but he was just as pale. His right cheek was maimed with a scar at least three inches long and he looked like a man no one would trifle with if there was a choice.

"You are hereby ordered to go to the Lviv railway station tomorrow, where you will be sent to Germany, to a factory that needs workers. Pack one bag each and be ready to leave on the morning bus."

My father cleared his throat.

"Yes, of course, we understand. Please, officer, can we take our children with us? We have no family here to watch over them, and they will make excellent workers, as well."

"No, that would be highly irregular. Leave your brats with the neighbors."

My father stepped closer to the soldier. I swallowed the spit in my mouth, waiting for him to be knocked down within seconds. He spoke again with deliberate words.

"I would leave them if I could, but you see, our neighbors were Jews. They are all gone now."

The soldier's face reddened and looked as if he was about to scream back, that's when tato opened the door wider and nodded for the man to come in. The soldier's expression mellowed as he entered. Tato then pulled some gold coins from his pocket.

"Please, Sir, this is all I have in the world, but it should easily cover the cost of their fare. If you would be so kind, and let us take our children, I would be grateful to you. Indebted to you."

My father jingled the coins.

"Is this real?"

My father nodded and handed one of the pieces for the man to inspect.

"Yes, of course," Tato said. "It's authentic gold."

The soldier looked at the coins, turning his head, inspecting the way the light hit the face and edges, then he looked down at the papers in his hands.

"Pan Rudenko, do you have a pen?"

Mama hurried to the desk, grabbed our only fountain pen, and handed the man the instrument.

"What are their names?"

"Petro, Olena, and Ivan," my father said.

He snatched the pen, scratched in some lines, and scribbled our names on the sides of the pages. The soldier finished correcting the forms, handed my father his copy of the orders, and greedily accepted the coins offered. They were imprinted with a Tryzub, but the man never took notice, all he cared about was that they were solid gold.

"You must all be in the center of town for the early bus tomorrow. You'll arrive in Lviv in time to board the ten o'clock train. If you don't report to the Lviv railway station, you will be hunted and killed. Understood, Pan Rudenko? Go to the overall roof next to the third-class section of the station building. You can't miss it, it's the platform that's not destroyed—yet."

"Yes, I understand, perfectly."

The soldier nodded, snapped his heels together, and saluted with his arm up in that funny way, then he said, "Heil Hitler."

My parents nodded and closed the door behind him.

"Mama, he took our pen."

"That's all right, Olena. We have no use for it now," she said.

"Oh, Mama, how will I write my lessons?"

Olena sat down with a huff, let her head fall onto the tabletop, and she wept.

"You know how much I like to write poems," her words muffled by her soggy sleeve.

"It doesn't matter right now, sweetheart," Mama's voice crooned.

"We were recruited and must report to the train station, we must do as ordered. No need for pens and paper there, but at least we'll be together. That's the most important thing."

Petro leaned in.

"Tato, you offered the man a bribe for our papers, so we could travel together. Does this mean that we are all going to Germany?"

Petro sounded confused.

"Yes, whether we want to or not," Mama said.

"But at least we'll be together," Tato added. "And when we arrive in Germany, we'll buy a new fountain pen."

"Now, to bed with you, children. Everyone will need to get their rest because tomorrow will be a long day."

"Mama, it's still daylight," I protested, thoroughly confused.

"Then go to your room and pack," my tato said.

I had packed already, but I wasn't going to push the issue. We all left the room so our father could be alone with Mama.

I went to my room, closed the door, and hurled myself onto the bed. I had no idea what to think about our new situation, nor how I felt. Part of me was happy to leave. *Could working in Germany be worse?* They might separate us and send us to different locations. I got up and tossed my bag onto the bed and went through my things again. Tired of packing, I jumped onto my bed, rolled and pulled a magazine out from my nightstand drawer. The cover was a photo of the train station. I flipped through and found the article and began to read about the great train station... my imagination wandered to better possibilities for our future. This might work out for the best, after all.

Petro knocked on the door and entered, landing on the bed beside me.

"I thought you might like to talk," he said.

"About what?"

"Well, maybe you're afraid about this journey. You know, going to Germany."

I shook my head.

"Good, because it might be our ticket to freedom. If we go there to work, it might not last long. The way I see it, the Allies will win the war sooner or later. When they do, we will be liberated."

I listened with an open heart. Petro knew exactly what I needed to hear.

LEAVING GALICIA

CHAPTER 20

We woke early before sunrise and took one bag each.

"We need to wear as many clothes as we can fit," Mama said. "Children put on one layer after another, like last time."

I struggled to put on a second pair of trousers over two sets of underwear and my first pair of pants, cursing under my breath. I tumbled to the floor and squirmed until they were on and belted. I blew out and swore to myself, then gazed up to make sure no one noticed me using foul language. They didn't—everyone was concentrating on their wardrobe issues.

I layered my socks, my shirts, and last I put on my favorite red sweater that Mama had knitted for me. We didn't need to wear any of these clothes today, it was warm outside, but there was no way I would leave my sweater. It was special to me—a present from my last birthday, and I planned on wearing it for Christmas. I was exhausted by the time I finished, sweating as if I had sprinted a million yards on a track field like Jesse Owens.

"Come on, Ivan," Petro said.

He pushed me toward the door.

"Let's get going."

We made our way to the town center to catch a bus to Lviv. The bus was packed. We sat cramped together, no one talking, all still dazed and half asleep. I looked at Olena and wondered why she was sitting by me, and not her friends. Then I realized few children had joined us, the bus was occupied by adults, most of them younger than our parents but much older than me.

The time on the bus didn't seem too long. I entertained myself watching the others, making up stories about what would happen to them once we made our way to Germany. I had never been on a train before, and part of me was excited. *Would we get a window seat?* Perhaps a train car of our own since we were a family and my tato had paid the soldier extra money.

The bus crawled through the city and down a long avenue then stopped in front of the building. It was huge, but sadly a long barricade blocked the front façade. I scanned the immense framework that rose above. Three sections, each topped with a dome that showed some damage from recent bombardments. The center had the largest dome, the main entrance.

I had never seen the front of the building before, the last time we had gone directly to the back of the building, never glimpsed this magnificent façade. Though it was beaten, I was still amazed by the doorways adorned with intricate carvings. We walked through a space in the barrier and stepped into the main entryway. It was magical. The walls were covered with deep, dark, rich paneling. The high ceilings decorated with an elaborate design.

A soldier approached and in a huffy tone, told Tato we needed to leave this area and go to the third class. We hurried through the vast space, our footfall echoing into the lofty height above. Looking up, my heart sang at the wonder of it all. We entered another area, not as grand, but still beautiful. The wooden benches had slats that curved as if it could cradle the weariest of bodies.

We walked out the back doors to the train-shed. In this platform area, the walls arched and became the ceiling. Steel bent and formed a grid, windows above were built into the grid-like forms. The railings and balustrades were designed in the Art Nouveau style of Paris, the new trend everyone wrote about in the newspapers. I was astonished to see such graceful architecture here. It made my head spin to think the world had such beauty in a place that held so many ugly, sorrowful stories. I may never become a king or even a leader, but at that moment I decided. I would become an engineer and design beautiful things. I would fill buildings with light and brilliant colors everywhere to brighten people's days.

"Hurry, Ivan, we have no time to lose."

My father and mother rushed ahead, walking away from this magnificent sight and into the open air again. The cobbled walkway soon turned to a dusty path, but they kept walking.

"Where are we going?"

Petro shrugged his shoulders and kept following our parents. Soon, everyone was ahead of me, even Olena. I kept looking back over my shoulder at the beautiful building that faded more with each step. I looked in front of me and saw a crowd of people standing around. Looking left and right, I noticed the web of train tracks, all snaked together, some landing in front of the people waiting. This must be where we get aboard our train. My idea of a window seat and possible train car vanished. The third class didn't entertain such things, I realized that now.

A creepy sensation came over me. I looked around, tried to find my family. I didn't see them, none of them. I was alone and had no idea what I was supposed to do next.

Someone pushed me hard in the middle of my back. I jolted and turned to see the culprit, but it was impossible to tell one person from another. The shoving back and forth and the smell of dried sausages and cheese that filled people's pockets made me queasy.

Then I heard a familiar voice. Pan Tereshchenko, the man who always smelled like vodka, yelled out directions with his cracked voice. I jumped up and down a few times. I caught glimpses of him waving his arm wildly in the air, pointing toward a train coming into the station. I listened for the sounds of the whistle, but it was too faint to hear over the maze of people. The crowd pushed against me. To cope, I pretended that we were one massive wave going toward the sea and then back again, battering against the sand of the shoreline.

Someone grabbed my arm. I turned and sucked in air. It was my mother. I released my breath as her face appeared in front of mine; she looked weary. Her sober, angry mood, had aged her in years, and the sparkle that used to glow in her eyes had vanished. Mama grabbed onto the material of my coat's collar and held it firmly in her fist and nudged me forward alongside her. I moved quickly so I wouldn't get choked, the tightness around my neck somehow made me feel a little safer. My mother had me and wasn't about to lose me in this mass exodus.

I bumped into a woman standing in front of me, the wool of her coat was rough and scratched my cheek. Trapped between the woman and my mother, a smothering sensation made me ill.

Suddenly, I was lifted from the ground. Mama pulled me close to her chest, shrouding me with her coat as if it were a comfy blanket, but I was already too hot. It was a warm morning. Still, my parents had insisted that I wear every piece of clothing I could fit under my coat. I was sweltering worse than any fever I've ever had.

The smothering sensation exacerbated, and all I wanted to do was to tear my clothes off and run far away from this congested platform. I felt I couldn't breathe right, and started gasping for air.

My mother cooed in my ear and patted my head. I closed my eyes and tried to think of something else, someplace else, where the air was crisp, and the wind blew through my hair. Someplace where I could be a boy playing instead of a scaredy-cat cowering in my mother's arms. I was eleven years old, but still, my mother's embrace comforted me more than I cared to admit.

My thoughts were interrupted by the train drawing closer. I heard the chugging, the squealing wheels against the tracks, metal against metal, and the sounds shrilled against my nerves. A whistle blew, and the mob around us started shouting at the same time. My mother let go, my Tato was now standing next to her. My parents each took one of my hands and kept me in the middle, as we followed the horde to board the train.

We moved forward, together as one large mass, then managed ourselves into an orderly line. I worried that if we let go of each other's hand that we might get lost or worse, trampled. The idea frightened me, so I tightened my grip and looked up at my father. He patted my head, fluffed my hair, and smiled for a brief second. Then his face became intent, looking ahead at whatever fate we faced. I held onto my father's hand so tight and willed mine to meld with his.

We were steered to our left and passed open doors to some of the train cars. They smelled foul, like animal stench, as if there was a stable nearby that needed mucking. It was the same stench that we sniffed the previous summer when my friend Michael and I worked for a local farmer cleaning out his plow horse's stall. I had enjoyed talking to the horse and the money we were paid but hated the smell. I wrinkled my face, then pulled my hand free, so I could pinch my nose closed as we walked closer.

The smell got worse, exuding a rancid earthy smell other than manure, it was more vile and rotten. The feral stench assaulted me, burned my nose and eyes. I rubbed my hand across my face, vigorously. *Cows or pigs must have been transported in this car.* I prayed we wouldn't have to ride in that fetid car. Scrutinizing the car's floor from eye-level, I noticed a layer of dung underneath the strewn straw that covered the wood, a weak attempt to hide the filth.

A group of people lined up and began to fill that filthy train car. I felt terrible for them. Every person in that train car wore a star patch, they were Jews, not from our neighborhood, but I recognized some from the city stores. They had sold the best meat and jewelry, according to my mother. She had always wanted Tato to stop into their shops. The people pulled themselves up and then lifted others into the train, filling in space until it looked cramped. Still more were forced to climb aboard. That's when I noticed my friend, Michael, mixed in the crowd. He was with his grandmother and mother. I lifted my arm and started to wave. Tato pushed it down.

"Not now, Ivan. Please pay attention to where we're going."

"But Tato, it's Michael."

He gave me that 'listen to me' glare, and I quieted down and followed my mother. I looked again over my shoulder, but Michael was out of sight.

A man in a uniform inspected the papers Tato handed to him, he nodded and pointed to the next train car. We managed our way to the edge of a cement platform. My mother was lifted into the ratty car by another uniformed man. The steps were missing, and I wondered if they were gone on purpose. Mama reached down and helped me up as my father hoisted me from the ground, pushing me up by my rear end. I turned and panicked a moment, worried my father wasn't going to follow us into the train. Relieved, I watched Tato pull himself up, that's when I noticed it.

A patch had been pinned onto my father's lapel. It was square-shaped, and the color of a summer sky, with white letters, stitched onto the blue patch. OST. I looked, and Mama had one on her coat lapel as well, stayed with a large safety pin.

My parents eyed each other with their distinctive look. A language that only the two of them shared. Then each took one of my hands, and we went further into the train car. My big brother was waving us over. He wore a patch, too. Petro stood with my older sister, Olena. They had climbed into the train ahead of us and claimed a spot. We made our way toward them, huddled together as more people piled in. We squeezed into the bench seats, they were hard and uncomfortable.

Petro stood near me, leaning against the wall with his arms folded on his chest. I watched him as he looked around, assessing the situation and trying to be like a mighty Kozak, like in the stories we used to read at school. Petro liked to envision himself an exceptional freedom fighter, thought that he was in charge all the time. The older he grew, the bossier he became. He often pushed me about when he thought he could get away with it at home. Anytime I whined or complained about it, Petro told me to stop being a baby. *"No one wants to hear about your troubles, Ivan. Grow up,"* he would say to me, then he'd shove my shoulder harder. He did this on purpose to toughen me up for the real world.

Of course, when he did this, I cried even more, and Mama came to my rescue, administering Petro with a slap to the head. None of this mattered now. I would gladly take my brother's rough play if it meant going back home. I missed our kitchen filled with the pleasant smells of mother's cooking, the savory soups, and her sweet cakes. On most days, a fresh breeze blew through the window. The warm earthy fragrance drifted in from the wheat fields down the road, filling the kitchen with a wholesomeness that touched my heart.

More and more people piled into the car. My sister, Olena, stood so close to my face that I thought I might disappear behind her skirts. Maybe that would be a better place, I could hide there until this was all over. She looked down at me and smiled, but I saw the hollowness behind her eyes. For months she had been crying over the things that happened. If soldiers came and took someone away, she cried. If Mama scolded her, Olena cried. If she spilled her cup of soup, she cried then too.

But today Olena wasn't shedding a tear. Tato had asked us all to be brave, and she wore her resolve. Her stare looked past the people, out toward some unfathomed horizon that only she could see, then she looked down at me.

"Don't worry, Ivan. This will be a short ride. We're going to a better place, a place where Tato doesn't have to worry about being arrested again, and Mama won't cry herself to sleep anymore."

And you won't cry anymore. My sister's words comforted me. I didn't want them to take my father away again, either. Any place else seemed safer than staying in Halych or Lviv.

CHAPTER 21

While waiting for the train to move, I busied myself with diversions. I tried blocking the unpleasant scenes playing out among the people around me. I heard babies crying outside. Young mothers entered the train car, leaving their wailing children behind. Some men were being handcuffed and dragged away—maybe they were fathers—who knew? They were arrested to rot somewhere in prison. Memories of my tato being dragged away flashed before me.

My pulse raced and I sweated more if that were even possible. I closed my eyes and mumbled prayers that the officers would leave my family alone, hoping I could suppress the bad memories. Too late, a vivid recall of the last time the Polish police came to our home in the middle of the night, flooded my thoughts. They had broken down the front door, locks and all, and ransacked our house.

My pulse raced, a rush of sweat dewed my skin. That happened years ago, but the memory was still so real. Our entire way of life was under siege, and we had no place else to flee. We lived the best we could, helped as many as we could, until they forced us here, and we boarded the train.

My sister said we were going to a better place, but what could be better? They gave my parents that blue OST patch to wear. I knew what it meant. A guard handed them out, he said it meant worker, *Ostarbeiter*. *A worker for who? Would Tato and Mama be paid, or would they be slaves?* I'm young, but I listened well when the teacher taught about old rulers, and how they used people to do all the work—they ended up dying.

When the Soviets turned the farms into cooperatives, the people worked the fields but had to turn over all the food, and our people starved.

I wanted to believe we were traveling to a better place. I just wasn't convinced yet. Our future didn't look like life in the glamour magazines, of that I was certain.

A loud noise sounded from above. For a moment, I thought it might be angels coming to save us from this horrid place. I squeezed my eyes shut and said a prayer to the Lord.

The train was packed tightly, the air dense, and it was difficult to breathe. A whistle blew again, this time louder and a moment later, the train tugged and started to roll. Squeaky wheels and huffing sounds from the engine grew fainter as the train gained speed. The tracks leaving the station had connections and joints which we felt. All passengers tossed back and forth bumping against each other as the car jerked into the correct lane connections. No one fell, our tight quarters kept us upright, but I felt the weight of my brother bear down on me, as his body leaned against me, squishing me like liver pâté.

Once the train connected to the straight tracks, it picked up speed and the ride became smoother. I pushed my sister's coat to the side and stared at the people around us. I saw that everyone was wearing their coats just like us and sweating.

"Mama, can I take my coat off now?"

My mother helped and pulled off my sleeves. I felt instant relief. She folded my coat and laid it on the dirty floor at my feet. Feeling a little more comfortable, I scrutinized the faces attached to the other winter coats. I recognized some of the neighbors from our section of town, others were from Lviv. The fishmonger from the corner of Main Street in the city, the lawyer Tato liked to talk with, and the priest from another Church.

Most of the women had scarfs wrapped around their heads. Some were off-white, others were beautiful paisley rainbows of bright reds and deep blues. I concentrated on the designs and colors, it made me feel better. The vibrant reds were my favorite, red like my sweater, the color came alive and excited me. Perhaps Olena was right, and this trip would be the best thing that ever happened to us. I dared to smile.

Someone pulled on my trousers. I looked down and saw another young boy smiling up at me.

"Want to play with me?" I recognized the narrow face and dark brown eyes that shined with a spark of mischief. It was our neighbor's young boy, he was only four or so.

"Later," I said.

For some reason, the boy made me think of my friend Michael. The last time I had spoken with my friend was minutes before they left that night to escape through the waste tunnel. He had been with his mother, but Pan Fleishman was nowhere in sight—I knew that he was taken away just minutes before Michael left with his mother.

I heard my mother talking with the young boy's mother who was now holding tight onto his collar as if his life depended on it. I tugged on mama's coat to get her attention.

"What is it?" she said.

"I saw Michael before we got on the train."

"Are you sure?"

Mama turned to Tato and said, "Ivan saw Michael."

My father reached around my mother.

"Where did you see him? Are you certain it was him?"

"Yes, I'm certain. I know who Michael is, he is my best friend, after all. It was before we got on board. He was with his mother and grandmother near that smelly train car. What does that mean? They left—"

I raised my hand to cover my mouth when I remembered that I should be careful about what I said aloud in public. I finished my thoughts in whispers.

"You know, they left the other day, and now they're here."

My tato nodded. "I don't understand what could have happened. Perhaps they went to Lviv to look for Gabriel after he was arrested, though I told them it was too dangerous."

My mama whispered. "I wonder how many others didn't make it, Taras?"

"Want to play a game, Ivan? Something to pass the time?" Olena interrupted. She must be bored if she wanted to play with me.

"Yes," I replied. "Stick out your finger."

She did, and I caught it easily.

"Awe, you're not trying. Do it again. This time try not to let me catch it."

Olena nodded and seemed to enjoy this challenge. She stuck out her finger and managed to evade my grasp for longer than I had thought. She smiled, enjoying that I was losing. Finally, I caught her, and the tables turned. She grabbed hold of my finger much quicker. I felt a little demoralized that I lost to a girl. This game didn't involve much

153

movement, and soon I imagined jumping off the train and running across the grassy fields that blurred by as we passed. How I wanted to run . . .

"Ivan, why did you stop? Wake up, you're daydreaming again."

Olena grabbed my finger and pulled hard, demanding my attention.

"Are you all right?" she said.

"Ouch," I said then smiled.

"Yes, I'm fine. Let's think of a new game."

We decided on a different game and looked out of the window even though the glass was smudged with dirt. We pushed our faces against the streaked pane and watched the scenery fly by, counting cows, buildings, and even tried to count the clouds in the sky, but that proved near impossible.

As new places streamed by, we took turns guessing where we were with the clues of our observations. We saw fields, houses, farms, barns, then stores and churches. In and out of towns, after a while, they seemed the same and the game got boring.

Once or twice my sister giggled, but quietly. Somehow it seemed wrong to enjoy ourselves in this horrid train car. Though we were entertaining ourselves, the time dragged, and I wondered if we would ever arrive at this better place that Olena spoke of. A place filled with opportunity and peace.

Earlier, my tato said to another man that the train was scheduled to stop in Bratislava, in occupied Czechoslovakia, and then go on to Germany.

The man responded, "you mean the Slovak Republic."

Tato waved his hand and turned away.

I wondered what those places looked like and day-dreamed about the possibilities.

Hours later, staring out of the window from our seat in silence, we spent the time in quiet contemplation about a future that we dare not dream aloud. Someday I would be someone important. I could dig up buried treasures, or write lovely poems. Or work as a farmer who feeds thousands of people. Maybe I could be that engineer who created the best of the best, beautiful buildings that reached for the sky.

I decided to always dream big. It seemed right for me to do so, after all, people often told me that I was exceptional, *special*. I conceded that all people were unique. Everyone has a special place in this world, a certain destiny.

I felt sorry for myself cramped on this wooden seat squished between my mama and sister, but I knew this was a much better place compared to that stinky train car that Michael boarded. My mind wandered, and I thought of my friend Michael.

A tear rolled down my cheek, envisioning my friend's dismal face the last time we had spoken. His dark eyes were wide-opened, but he looked straight ahead as if he had seen a ghost. I wondered if he had seen his future—his destiny.

Michael was eleven like me, but he had to be a man already. His last spoken words to me had been ominous, yet he said them bravely. *'Your father told us that my papa was taken away by the soldiers. I must be brave and take care of my mother, now.'* Speechless, clueless, I had wrapped my arm around his shoulder and comforted my friend like I'd seen my mother do so many times before.

In the back of my mind, I worried his father was dead, like so many other Jews taken away. *Why did they wear yellow stars, and now my parents wore blue square patches?* That last time I was with Michael, I had said, *'It will be alright, Michael,'* but I had known it was a lie. Pan Fleishman was Jewish. Bad things happened to Jews, like what had happened to them in Halych. I thought he and his family had been lucky when they escaped the river massacre, but their luck ran out.

My father wanted to save the Fleishman family, but it had been too late, they had arrested and sent Michael's father to Auschwitz in Poland because the Janowska camp near Lviv was too full. We had managed to help Michael and his mother to get away, but now they were on this train, too.

I wondered if bad things would happen to all on this train. I hoped we would find a work camp at the end of our ride instead of a death camp.

CHAPTER 22

A roaring sound grew louder until it completely drowned out the squeals of the train. *Was there another train on a track close by?* For a fleeting moment, I envisioned us crushed — a major collision. If another train collided with ours, surely, we would be killed.

In a high alert, I listened anxiously. *Wait, it wasn't another train.* This engine roared above us. A familiar sound, and yet different than the grinding groans of a train engine. I had heard this noise before, I was sure, and tried to recall where and when.

Tilting my head up, I followed the noise as it drew closer until the roar was directly above us. Of course, it was a plane. The sound began to fade as the plane flew away.

I pushed my face against the window's glass. No not a plane, a fleet of them, flying above us like birds of prey circling their victim. *Definitely, there was more than one.* I heard the whining engines grow louder as another plane appeared on the horizon, growing bigger by the second.

I swallowed my saliva, the reflex action felt grueling, my throat was swelled-up. I turned and poked my brother until I got his attention.

"What is it?" Petro snapped.

My attention went back to the window, my porthole to the outside world. Spying right then left, I caught sight of a plane and pointed, pushing my finger so hard against the dirty glass that I bruised it.

Petro's face sparked with acknowledgment.

Watching through the filthy pane, we waited to see it again. We heard one of the planes swooping closer, and then it zoomed overhead. The outline of one of its wings was over us for a brief moment, then it was gone. I thought I glimpsed a white star in a blue circle.

"Holy shit!" my brother said.

Now two more planes joined, it was a team of three, a mini-fleet. They flew away from the train, so far off that we couldn't see them anymore. Then the small squad returned and crossed each other's path in a fancy flying pattern.

"Look, they're having fun, Petro. They are playing in the sky and doing tricks."

The planes turned and proceeded together in formation, back toward the train, flying closer for another pass.

"They're spying on us, Ivan. See it's only three of them, probably scout planes. They'll decide if they should shoot this train or if we're peaceful. Wow, did you see them? They look like Thunderbolts—like the P-47s—remember seeing them in the magazine?"

I nodded. The planes flew above us again, the engines roared like an angry lion. Petro turned and spoke fast with Tato and pointed up, then my father spied out of the window with us. His body stiffened, he held his hand to his head.

Straightaway, Tato turned and yelled orders to everyone in the train car. His voice sounded fierce, and for a moment, I couldn't believe it was my gentle father speaking.

"Listen, everyone."

Planes soared overhead. One of them swooped down for a closer inspection. In its dive, the plane's engine sounded like a buzzing bee. After it had its once-over the plane thundered away, the turbulence reverberated the metal walls of our small train car. Every person inside stopped yakking. We all heard the roar of the distancing plane moving away from the tracks, a ghostly trail that frightened and excited me at the same time.

"Did you hear that?" Tato hollered. "Fighter planes are surrounding this train. You heard me, fighter planes. There's no time to debate. We need to get out of here now. I saw the wing of one, it's an American fighter plane."

The folks on the train started mumbling to each other all at once. One woman yelled for her husband to open the door as she hit him on his back in a panic. Babies began crying, all at once, as if they had been wound up with the same key.

An older man called out, "we're safer to stay inside while the train's moving."

It was madness. I covered my ears.

"Listen to me," my tato shouted. "They have no idea if we're peaceful people in here. This is a German train; the Americans will bomb it to paralyze the Nazis. For all they know, we are carrying ammunition. They don't know we are innocents in here, how could they know? We cannot stay here, we will all be killed if we do. Quick, let's help each other get out. We have to jump while we can."

The brakes squealed with a piercing noise, blocking out every other sound. My ears hurt. I flung my hands to cover them but clumsily missed, after being jostled about. The others inside the train car also jerked back and forth, crashing into each other.

The train stopped with one last jerk. Sobs filled the air, and people called out about the safety of their loved ones. From the far corner of the cramped space, my brother and others raced toward the door.

I looked out the window and saw the train conductors, they were running away. I cried out in my loudest voice.

"Wait, come back and let us out!"

My words were drowned out by a plane making a pass, plummeting down close to the ground, as it discharged a barrage of bullets. *Rat-a-tat-tat* sounded as their guns fired at the men fleeing away from the train and into the nearby field. Their Nazi uniforms dropped out of sight. The green and golden meadow folded over, then the grass rippled with the wind without a glimpse of soldiers.

The people in the train car panicked, men began bellowing orders, and women began to scream back at them. My mother and father took hold of my hand, my sister grabbed my coat from the floor, and we followed my brother pushing toward the only exit.

The door was locked from the outside. A small group of healthy young men helped Petro. Their faces puffed, red, and sweaty as they struggled to pull the door free with all their strength. Finally, they managed to heave it open.

A rush of fresh air breezed in and it was easier to breathe as if the embers in the furnace had been doused. Petro wiped his forehead with his sleeve and said, "Come on, let's get moving."

For a moment, I felt happy about getting out of this trap. Everyone must have felt the same, they pushed ahead and exited with speed, stopping only to help the old and young to take the jump down to the ground.

Two people in line before me fell when they leaped down, after catching their foot on protruding metal. A twisted rod stuck out and was left hanging from the old missing stairs.

When it was my turn, I heaved myself out, jumping as far as I could, evading the scrapped tread. I landed and rolled on my shoulder, then got up and brushed myself off as I watched all the others escaping.

Stones crunched under my feet, I was out of the train car and walking. A moment of joy, a twinge of happiness, I was grateful to be alive. The air smelled fresh, clean, and I drank in as much oxygen as I could afford until I was grabbed by the hand and led away.

Looking back at the length of the train, I saw Petro and the other men working together. They slid the train car gates open, making their way down to each car, to free the people. So many bodies flowed out of the cars. A gust brought an awful fetid smell toward me, then with a shift of wind, it was gone again.

A buzzing swarm rung in my ears—the planes were back. They roared above us and made a sweeping arc. I had almost forgotten about them and the danger they represented. The Americans were the good guys, our liberators, yet they didn't know who we were.

Looking up at the pale blue sky, I could barely see them and wondered if they had an American flag painted on their tails, the famous red, white, and blue flag. The planes' silver bodies reflected the glint of the sun, the painted colors brightened for an instant, then washed away with the light.

Those hotshot Americans must be flying, I could tell by the graceful maneuvers they circled in the sky. I admired the show, thankful that they were the good guys. Now that the Americans were in this war against Germany and fighting in the European theatre, there was hope that the war might end soon.

Hope is a funny thing, like a fairy it flies right in front of you and for a moment, happiness seems within your reach. But then it hides, concealed in an invisible spell, and it all happens in a split second.

My brief hope abandoned me when I realized one important fact, which my father had recognized right off. This was a German train. *Would the pilots think we were German, too? Would they shoot us down?* The thought of being mistaken for a Nazi nauseated me.

There had been no other choice for us, we were forced to take the train, and all departing trains from Lviv traveled toward Germany. Our only option for evacuating the Eastern Front had quickly become our deathbed. We still had no choices. We had to run into the field and pray we didn't get shot, killed like what happened to the Nazis who had been on board.

Fear rose from inside of me. Revolted, I realized that we might all die here beside this German train. I was afraid to die. Horror filled my gut, I felt sick. I bent over and vomited. I wiped my mouth with the back of my hand and then crossed myself out of habit. I thanked God for my life.

My parents had taught me to always be thankful for my life, it was a gift. Then I remembered the words my father had said to my mother, *"fear of death takes away the joy of living."* Tato was right, and I took solace in the fact that at least our family wasn't separated. If we were to die, then we would die together.

"Ivan, quick." Petro was with us, and he waved me forward.

Whoever had led me away from the train was no longer by my side. Most of the people were running into the fields.

"No, they'll shoot at us like they did the men from the train, thinking we're Germans, too. They will kill us " Turning around, I looked for my father. "They will shoot us in the fields, Tato."

My father didn't speak. He grabbed my arm, and we followed my brother, mother, and sister into the field. The only thought in my head was that I was wearing my red sweater. It had been my favorite of all my clothes, Mama had made it for me to wear to church, but it was so bright. Now with my coat off, my sweater was the outside layer. My favorite red sweater would make us a target, a red bull's eye.

I had to take it off, so I stopped and started to tug at it. My father almost tumbled to the ground. He turned and picked me up, then he carried me across the field. He ran with me over his shoulder. I raised my head and saw the fleet of air raiders, they were making a design in the air, like a flock of geese traveling together to go south. The victorious V formation.

This was it, the end of the line. The planes would fly toward us, zero in and shoot us down with bullets from the fancy guns attached to the wings.

I prayed to God for a miracle. Prayed that they would recognize us as refugees. Prayed they would know in their hearts that we weren't Nazi's but instead we were Ukrainians fleeing for our lives. I folded my hands together, bouncing on my father's shoulder, I mumbled prayers with my eyes squeezed tight. "Lord, please save us."

CHAPTER 23

Suddenly, I was on the ground, my head hit hard. I stayed down and didn't cry because I had promised my father to be brave when we left our house, and I intended on keeping my vow.

Looking around, I saw that we were all crouched down in the grass, trying to hide.

"Mama," I cried out. "Help me to take off my sweater. They'll see the bright red."

I grabbed at the sweater and pulled to yank it off. There was so much noise around me that I became distracted, and the sweater got stuck on my head. I breathed and exhaled so deeply that steam filled the air around me and heated my face. Commotion confused my efforts, making hard work of the simple task. I stopped dead when I heard the screams.

Someone nearby cried out wails which carried across the field. The eerie voice originated from close by. I managed to wriggle the sweater off and pushed myself up, onto my knees, to have a look at what was happening.

A tall thin woman wearing a star armband cried out to someone still by the train. The woman waved a white scarf as she screamed, "hurry, come here. No. No. Don't go underneath the train."

My head spun around, my attention focused on the train, I wanted to see who was stupid enough to stay there, never mind going under it. My eyes nearly popped from my sockets when I saw my friend Michael standing by the train with his mother and grandmother. He seemed to be yelling at the women. Michael grabbed his mother's arm and tugged, pulling her away. But now the women won the scuffle. They were crawling under the train, trying to hide, totally ignoring Michael's plea.

"Come here. Hurry, run into the field."

The woman screamed, but Michael's mother shook her head, and the two old women crawled even deeper beneath the train.

"Michael."

I screamed louder than the Jewish woman.

"Run to me, Michael. Run now."

I saw Michael look up—he was searching the field trying to find me. I jumped up and down, waving my red sweater in the air so that he'd see where we were hiding. But Michael was gone, I couldn't see him. He must have crawled under the train with his mother and grandmother.

I felt a tug and was pulled down. Petro had pulled on my arm so hard that I hit the dirt with force.

"Stay down close to the ground and stop waving that red sweater."

My face hurt, and an involuntary tear dripped down my cheek.

"Don't be stupid," my brother said. "If you wave something, make it a white flag."

Still, with tears in my eyes, I lay next to my brother, and I cried out as loud as I could to my friend.

"Michael. Run into the field."

I rolled toward my brother.

"Petro, Michael is under the train. I need to get him. They're going to bomb the train, you know it. I need to help my friend."

I turned onto my other side.

"Tato, please. He's my friend." I sounded like a baby again, but I didn't care.

"Shush, Ivan, and stay down." My tato spoke as he pulled off his shirt. "There's nothing we can do for Michael now. Don't you think I would if I could? I promised his papa to keep him safe, and I have failed."

My father made a flag with his white undershirt tied to a stick, and he was waving it up in the air, his outer shirt back on unbuttoned, rippling freely in the breeze. I sat up to look and saw that many others were waving white flags of scarfs, shirts, any old rag that still looked somewhat white. My father unfailingly waved his shirt.

My brother weighed his arm over my body, holding me in place.

"We can't get closer or else we'll die, too," Petro said. "Now, be smart. Do you want our tato to die trying to save your friend? Hasn't father done enough for people?"

Petro pushed my head down. The dry weeds scratched against my face, and the fresh scent of new hay filled my nostrils. I sneezed. *Was there enough time to go back and pull my friend away from the train?* I rolled over onto my back, and a slight breeze ran across my body and cooled me. The open-air felt so much better compared to the crowded train car. A brief smile crossed my lips, then I frowned thinking of my friend, stuck under the train near the hot greasy undercarriage. I wanted so bad to run to get him, grab him away from there, but Petro was right. I couldn't, I was too afraid there wasn't enough time.

A loud sound roared, the noise filled the air. Then a swooshing breeze wafted across my body. Quickly, I checked that my bright red sweater was underneath me, then I looked up at the bright blue sky, hoping to see the planes. They flew in formation and came straight toward us.

So powerful yet beautiful, they glided toward us, a box formation, a sound like giant bees, Bzzzzz Bzzzzz. I knew I should be frightened because they might blow us away to oblivion. Still, excitement surged in my veins, as I witnessed the hotshot Americans fly, taking rounds and loops with their planes.

Swallowing hard, I turned around again and stared at the train. *Michael.* For a split second, I thought that I saw my friend, and swore he was waving to me. I waved back, then it happened.

In a flash-of-a-second, a millisecond, my eyes filled with bright colors, yellow, orange, and red. Then a loud kaboom sounded, and the ground shook. My teeth rattled. The explosion echoed in my head, my ears were ringing from the high pitch and it blocked out every other sound. I couldn't hear a thing. I ducked and shifted closer to my mother. She wrapped her arm around me. If we were to die, we would be together, a comforting thought in the middle of the madness.

I don't know how much time passed before we dared to look up. Tato touched each of us with his hand, his touch made me feel safe for a moment. We nodded to each other, Tato, Mama, Olena, Petro, and I. We were all alive. My eyes wandered across the field.

Rolling over onto my stomach, I watched my father get up. He inspected the area, his expression grave, his hand flew up to cover his mouth. He soaked in the gruesome scene. Sadly, I understood the horror reflected in his eyes.

I got onto my knees and followed his stare. The train was gone. All that remained were flames licking through black twisted metal and dark billowing smoke funnels. The drone from the fleet faded away until we couldn't hear them any longer.

The Americans left us alone in the field, free to live. Happiness overcame me, a feeling I'd never forget for the rest of my life. Euphoria. Despite the smoke filling my lungs, I took a deep breath. I felt free and laughed aloud.

Then I remembered Michael. He had to have been killed by the bombs. I was afraid to look for his body, most likely, it was under that dark beast of metal. My mind had a difficult time processing reality, I didn't want to face the loss. Darker thoughts filled my mind, and fear took over. *What would happen to us, my family? Where would we go now?*

Bliss left me faster than it had surfaced, replaced with horror. Doom filled my thoughts, sorting out the facts, I searched for something to hang onto, anything that might be a sign of hope.

First reality, we were stuck in a field, in the middle of nowhere, with no food and danger all around us. This fact wasn't helping, and I cursed all the soldiers, the Germans, the Russians, and the Polish who pushed us to this point. I cursed everyone who had been cruel to us when all we wanted was to be safe in our home.

The second fact, the bad men were still out there some-where, and we had no place to go, no place to hide or call home anymore. *Why had this happened? Why?* Faith in my fa-ther was lost at the moment, I knew that he had no answers either.

Panic set in, and I started breathing heavy, gasping for air, choking on the smoke. The bubble had popped, this wasn't a planned excursion to freedom like I had day-dreamed, we were fleeing for our lives. People were out to kill us because they didn't think we were good enough to ex-ist. We spoke differently, dressed, and danced differently. We sang religious songs and weren't skilled fighters. We were peaceful people, and that's why everyone else trampled over our homes, farms, cities and took whatever they wanted.

Why couldn't we be barbarians like in the old stories, or like the Kozaks? Then we would teach them all a huge lesson.

My face burned, either from the anger within me, or the heat of the flames raging red-hot as the fuel was swallowed-up in small explosive eruptions.

This was wrong. I hung my head in shame for those vio-lent thoughts and prayed to God to please make the ugly im-ages in my head go away.

Time passed. I don't know how long we stayed motion-less, but finally, the people around us began to rise and leave the field.

My father stood, hands on his hips, and he looked around taking inventory. The ground near us was marked with singed grass, we were lucky to have our lives. Gray smoke still swirled from the bent iron and torn up tracks.

I drew in a deep breath, then coughed out the smoke that filled my lungs. The burnt smell singed my nostrils. Gagging, I thought I'd be sick. No, I refused to regurgitate the last meal I had devoured, who knew when we would eat again. Swallowing back, the burning reflux went down my throat. Every piece of nourishment was needed, and I refused to vomit again, ever.

I stood and went to be near my brother and father, and we three men watched as the fire finished destroying what remained of the train. This had begun as a good day and then evolved to not a good day, not at all.

People gathered their meager belongings and ambled toward the nearest road, or toward wherever they thought the closest sign of civilization. Some were crying, others moaning, as they moved along.

Numb, I couldn't move forward and barely noticed when Mama and Tato took my hands and led me out from the fields. My sister's voice, my brother's reply, they spoke, but I had no idea what they said because my mind couldn't process one more thing.

The only voice that registered belonged to my father.

"Our best hope is the United States, Leysa. There or Canada. We will find our way to America. There we will finally be free of this nightmare. A man from town had heard rumors that refugees will be accepted there. We will go to America, somehow, I promise."

His words penetrated my fog, sounding like a horn blaring in the grim, and an ember of hope returned to me. Sparks are a funny thing, they feed on air and smolder until it's a flame, then they burn and can keep you warm.

I looked up and saw an opening within the billows of smoke, a window filled with a bright blue patch of color. A miracle unfolded before our eyes—a small rainbow painted the sky in that small space above. For me, our future was visible in that tiny patch of sky.

The sun beamed through that open window, and I sensed some kind of power was given to us at that moment. It was a sign, and my confidence returned. Somehow, we would find America. My faith in my tato's words renewed.

INTO THE WOODS

CHAPTER 24

I followed the others, keeping a few paces behind my brother. It was a group of us from the train, trailing each other along a back road. Those who knew my father decided to follow him, uncertain of where to go. The adults discussed the situation among themselves, but I was in no mood to eavesdrop.

As we met a junction, some turned left, others right, but I followed my father and brother straight ahead. After a few hours, most of the other families had wandered off in different directions, deciding to find their way.

The Zeminski family had Polish relatives to seek out, they went north by a different route. They didn't think it wise for us to tag along. Most of the Polish blamed us for the *Huta Pieniacka* massacre, understandably so. Our Ukrainian underground army had been there with the Nazi troops when it happened, according to the newspapers. We were unfairly branded by the deeds of others, but the stain was there even so.

Another woman and her beautiful teenaged daughter Zelda decided to head west toward the nearest city, Bratislava, to see if they could find some type of sewing job that paid room and board. My mother had thought of that idea for them, but she had no intention of doing the same and leaving us men without her and Olena.

Now that our family was traveling alone, there was less work for Mama, and she no longer worried about the others. She became inventive when we took a break, re-bundling our things into rucksacks, making them easier for us to carry.

We walked and walked. My feet got hot and sweaty. It felt as if the bottom of my shoes were melting to the road. I looked up and noticed a small house in the middle of nothing. My tato signaled us to stop. I collapsed onto the grass and watched as my father walked closer to the front door, then cautiously he knocked.

A man opened the door, shook his head as he said something to Tato, then the man slammed the door in my father's face. I watched as the heavy door swung closed, registered my tato's face, eyes opened wide in surprise, then falling to the ground, disappointment written all over his body. At that moment, my father seemed so vulnerable, not at all like the tato I knew and respected. His charm and negotiation skills meant nothing here. I pitied him. His humiliation was also mine.

We walked on and stopped at more doors, and each time we looked on with the hope that the locals would be understanding, perhaps compassionate to our plight. So far, they were not, and every door we approached turned us away without a kind word.

The first time we stopped in a town for a meal, Tato learned from the newsstand papers that the train we had been on was bombed northeast of the city Bratislava, the stop before Vienna. It was a blessing in disguise that we never arrived at Bratislava. The Nazis had a strong-hold of troops there and took people away to concentration camps. The newspaper said the train had been destroyed, but we already knew that first hand.

After reading the newspaper that was on the stand, we moved along the street and looked for a cheap place to buy food. As we passed stores, I felt the people stare at us, sensed their antagonist attitude. They made faces as if they smelled something foul, then turned their eyes to the ground. We were in occupied territory, and the people here didn't seem to care for us Ukrainians much. As soon as they heard my parents speaking, they dropped their eyes, with disgust written all over their faces.

My parents planned to travel northwest toward Brno, located in an area known as South Moravia. Then we'd turn in the westerly direction toward the area known as Bohemia, which was also under German occupation.

It seemed as if there was no avoiding the Germans. They had occupied every country possible. In the back of my mind was the cold truth, that we needed to keep Petro safe from being snatched and recruited as a soldier by the Germans. I hoped that the OST badge made him invisible to any soldiers we might come across during our travels. I was glad he had it on his lapel.

Each day we walked and walked, I didn't feel anything. The hours dragged into days, but time meant nothing to me any longer. I was so tired, scared, afraid to speak, and hungry. We stayed away from town centers as best we could, except for when we needed a meal.

My feet had never been so sore. I tried to stay out of any puddles after it rained on those summer days, so my feet would remain dry. There was nothing worse than walking in soaked socks.

At night we took refuge away from the roads. Once we huddled and slept in a dark stairwell, not the most comfortable night. Another night we spent in a drainage ditch, resting our heads on our sacks while trying to ignore the dirt and pebbles underneath our sore bodies. Olena complained every night, whining like a sick crane. Finally, I screamed aloud for her to stop, which only made her cry. That night we slept in a park, using a grove of trees for cover. That was much better, more comfortable sleeping on the grass. In the morning an officer approached Tato and explained we couldn't sleep there again, there had been complaints. It seemed no one noticed us until they decided they didn't like the site of us.

Whenever we walked through a town center, Tato bought us food, usually bread, and we always drank water in the public fountains if we could. We had bottles and filled them up, careful never to be without water.

The people in the houses refused us when we knocked on doors looking for work. One man ran after us and chased us away. We speculated there were bounties on Ukrainians, perhaps some might try to claim that we were Russian spies. Each town we wandered into seemed larger and more unfriendly, no doubt many came before us looking for the same. My father always offered to work in exchange for whatever help they could lend, but the days of loving thy neighbor had disappeared.

Food was scarce in the stores, the display windows were bare showing off shiny metal shelves. Our money was even thinner than the inventory. When we reached the foothills of the Záhorie, between the Little Carpathians to the east and the Morava River to the west, Tato announced that we would continue our journey in the forest.

Camping life suited me, it was better than walking through these unfriendly places. The idea brightened my outlook, and for the first time, I started paying attention to details like time and weather. As we began to climb into the forest, Olena complained and complained. No one noticed, we just climbed until we found a spot for our first campsite.

"Here, this is the spot. Let's stop for the day, catch our breath and rest tonight under the stars."

Tato stood tall as he grabbed mama's waist and pulled her close for a kiss. Dropping his pack, he searched for his knife.

"Let's hunt some rabbit," Tato said. "We must first study the area for animal droppings to find their paths, then we'll set up our snare to catch them. No worries, Leysa. We won't starve to death with nature's bounty at our feet."

"I will join you," Petro said.

"Can I come too?"

I wondered if my father would allow me to tag along. I had never gone hunting with him before. Excitement made my stomach flutter as I waited for the invitation.

"Yes, Ivan, you come, too. Promise you will follow us and stay quiet."

I nodded and we were off, leaving Mama and Olena to set up our small campsite.

The woods were quiet at first until you listened. Suddenly, the sounds of scurrying feet, branches swaying, and the nibbling of animals came to life. Petro found the tracks and traps were set.

We circled back and discovered the first catch in a snare. It didn't take long for one to work. Tato used a cloth sack that he had found in a garbage can the previous day to bundle the catch. We walked to the nearest stream to clean the kill.

"Come, follow me, boys."

Tato paced himself so we could follow.

"Do you think these are private woods? Could we get arrested for poaching?" Petro asked.

"Let's not worry about that right now. We need to get this creature cleaned up and cooked."

I followed, wanting to see how it was done. When we arrived at the river bank I noticed the sack twitching. I guess I didn't expect the rabbit to be alive, but of course, it would be.

My father pulled him out by the ears. He was so cute, I wanted to pet him, so I reached out my hand. Just then, I heard the snap. Tato had twisted its neck and killed it.

My eyes flew wide-opened and tears stung. I wiped them with the back of my hand and pretended it never happened. Then I smelled the iron scent of blood and looked down at my father's hands, they were covered in blood. He used his knife, the one with multiple tools and sizes that pulled out, and he cut the animal open with its sharpest blade. I heard the tearing of its skin, saw its guts being pulled out, and had to close my eyes. My gut ached and I felt faint, I was about to pass out.

"You slice the animal down the middle like this, then you cut the ends off and pull the innards out." Tato was making fast work of it, I heard the blade go in for another cut.

Petro came close to me and held my arm.

"This is what we do to survive," he said. "So, don't think of him as a nice bunny. It's food for us to eat."

I nodded, then looked up.

"Petro, I think I like fish better."

I turned away and ran as fast as I could. When I arrived at the campsite, I rummaged through my bag.

"Did you catch anything?" Olena asked.

"Ah yes, a rabbit."

"Oh, that's wonderful," Mama said.

"I better make a spit. What are you doing, Ivan?"

"I found it. I'm looking for this string. I'm going to devise a fishing pole with this string from my pocket. Do you have a spare safety pin or paper clip I can use to design a hook?"

"You are in luck, young man."

Mama handed me an actual hook. I looked down at the shiny miracle in her palm.

"I had this tucked on my coat from last year when I went fishing with your father. I almost forgot it was there. Lucky break."

I smiled and thanked her.

From that day on, whenever there was a stream or pond around, I'd dig up some worms from the darkest dirt I could find, hook them, then throw in the line.

The catch of the day, whether rabbit or fish, was roasted over a fire and shared by all. We ate right off the stick and passed the dinner around and picked out small bites. It was fun to eat with my fingers and not get scolded. When I was hungry, I didn't mind eating the food, but I blocked the image of a live rabbit being killed, from my mind.

CHAPTER 25

First Week In The Woods

We kept moving by day, never staying in any one place too long. We walked through the woods, heading northwest with the guidance of our compass, always on the lookout for streams. When found, we'd drink from the fresh spring to our heart's content, then filled our bottles with the precious life-giving water. To survive a person could go without food for days, but the water was vital.

After the first week of sleeping in the woods, we looked like we had the measles. The skin on our legs was speckled with pocks, covered with bug bites. Tato said they would get infected if I itched them, so I tried hard not to scratch. They felt better when I waded in the cold river waters.

Mama was the best camper of all. She used our winter coats to make a cover for us at night. She draped them over the lean-to she erected with sturdy branches, and whenever we moved camp, she took those sticks with us.

She had always been a good cook. But Mama excelled at roasting our hunt on a spit rotisserie. It was held up by two spicate posts she fashioned from an old petrified branch that she had found in the woods near an ancient hickory tree. She cooked the rabbits over the fire, turning the meal while looking out and dreaming about something no one else could fathom. She worked the spit until the meat was juicy and ready to eat.

Olena wasn't handy at all, she remained quiet most of the time, always terrified there might be snakes near our bed. She hated the mosquitoes and was afraid that hornet nests might be in the ground. My sister was a mess of worry. I tried to cheer her up, talked about the things she liked, as we traipsed through the woods. We sang the songs she loved best. For a few seconds, she'd smile. But it never lasted long, the poor girl agonized over every minute spent in the woods.

On the seventh night of camping, we woke to the sound of barking dogs.

Arf-arf-arf

My eyes opened wide, and I jerked.

Olena screeched. Tato covered his hand over her mouth in a snap movement. Listening with such intensity, his eyes grew big and round until he didn't look like himself at all.

My lungs filled with air, and I held my breath.

Tato gazed down at Olena, she nodded, and he moved his hand away. Then he put his finger to his lips, shushing us all.

Mama took the blanket and draped it over our heads, then she lowered the stilts holding up our makeshift tent. I felt the weight of the coats on my body.

We lay silent, scrunched together trying to remain invisible in the night's darkness. I pretended that we were a sizeable gray boulder near a tree, instead of a group of frightened people. My head began to pound, it hurt so bad, and throbbed so hard, that I thought it might knock me out.

Olena whimpered, and my father covered her mouth again. I felt her head moving, and, he removed his hand, ready to cover her mouth again if needed.

If Olena gives us away, I'll be so angry. This was a matter of life and death—I could feel it. Strangers lingered in the woods, perhaps hunting for deer or worse, hunting for spies. No matter who they were and what they were doing, they no doubt meant danger for us if they discovered us hiding here under the trees.

More snarls and howling echoed in the woods, I couldn't tell how many dogs there were, but it was a pack of them. The dogs yelped out fiercely, they had found something or someone they hunted.

I read once about how the English used dogs for hunting fox and made a great big show of the hunt. This was different—these dogs weren't hounds searching for fox—these animals were brutes. They growled more like a wolf, perhaps they were the big shepherds used by German guards.

Terrified, I wondered if they were after us. Maybe a local had spotted us in the woods? Perhaps the landowner was after us for poaching his rabbits?

I heard men's feet trampling the forest floor, sticks and leaves crumpled, then a man shouted orders in German, and another man called back. A chase ensued, whoever was running went away from us, thank God. Shots blared through the night air in sequence. *Rat-a-tat* again *rat-a-tat*. *Rat-a-tat* again *rat-a-tat*. Then a deadly silence seemed to cover us with a shawl of ignorance.

I felt pressure against my skin from the coat covering me. The pounding of my heart thumped so hard it moved my clothes; I could see the cloth of my jacket move up and down. Panicked, I wondered if this was how Michael felt before the bomb had exploded and killed him. *Did he even know it was coming?*

Frozen, with no sense of time, I waited on my back, scared to death with my eyes squeezed shut. I stopped thinking except for the thought of my blood rushing through my veins. I was alive. Then I reflected on the innocent blood of all those who had already been killed. I considered whether it was our turn to die this time, then decided it was not.

Whoever had come into the woods had finished with their secret business, the intruders were leaving, and taking their dogs with them. The barking sounds of the beasts faded until all that remained was an eerie silence.

Someone or something was shot close by, meters away from where we hid. Knowing that horrified me, wondering what we might find when we decided to look. No one was in a hurry, we remained huddled together in stillness, not speaking, barely breathing for the remaining night. When the sun inched its rays over the hills and through the trees brightening the woods, we uncovered and looked around. No one was within our immediate vision.

Tato picked up a large thick stick from the ground and held it firmly in his hands, a weapon to use, ready to strike.

"That's the good stick to hold up our tent," Mama said.

She was grumpy. "Make sure you bring it back."

"Of course," Tato said. "But first, I need to check what's out there."

"I wish you had a pistol, Taras."

He shook his head and turned to leave, edging toward the area where the sounds had originated from the night before. I started to follow.

"No, I'll do this alone."

He motioned for me and Petro to stay back, and he continued alone to investigate. Less than five minutes later he returned, his face pale as the milk I hungered, his expression that of a beaten man.

"Taras, what's wrong? Who was it?" Mama said.

He looked down at her face and then began to cry. She embraced him, rubbing her arms up and down his back.

"Taras, it will be okay," she cooed.

I couldn't believe my father was acting so emotional, *what did this mean?* He talked into her shoulder letting out his pangs of frustration.

"It was a woman with two children—they killed a helpless family. They were shot dead."

No one spoke for hours. Tato went back and dug the strangers a shallow grave and prayed for them. Petro and I wanted to help, but he refused. He didn't want any of us to see their bodies. I could only imagine how horrific that sight must have been for him. I felt sorry for those people, and for my tato, who bore witness to their deaths.

We gathered our things while waiting for our father to return, and prayed with hushed voices for the woman and her children. I'm not sure how we managed to move at all, but we did, and we finished our tasks. Since our departure from home, I've learned that when something needs to get done, you do it somehow.

No matter how terrified, we had to keep going.

When Tato returned, we drank our water, ate the last of the wild raspberries we had picked the day before, and then started walking. We left that area of woods where the dogs had come, we couldn't get away fast enough.

CHAPTER 26

After the incident in the woods, it took us six days of walking from one town to the next, traveling westward, until we stopped in a small village. It was called Hardegg, a border town of Austria, close to the Slovakian border.

Hardegg was nestled along the *Thaya River* basin.
A castle that had seen better days, overlooked the old village. The river wrapped itself around the hill where the relic stood, meandering like a snake curling itself around its prey, waiting to squeeze the life from within its victim.

There were worn out signs which suggested that in previous days, this dingy town was a splendid vacation spot, but no longer. Things looked shabby. The ramshackle houses were dilapidated. Sagging remnants of a decaying mill from a previous manufacturing heyday matched the eroding condition of the crumbling castle walls. This town was dying.

We strolled into the village center at the exact time when a small church opened its doors for Sunday service. We entered with the other good people. Ignoring their stares, we sat on one of the back pews. No one asked us to leave, but they didn't look friendly, either. Still, it felt good to be in a church with a chance to pray appropriately.

There was no Holy Communion given out, this must have been a Protestant church. I heard my tato's words play in my head, *Ivan, God hears our prayers wherever you say them.* That memory gave me great comfort, and I didn't feel so guilty for being in this non-Catholic church.

After the religious service, Mama browsed the window of the small general store and bought some supplies:

matches, sugar cubes, and bandages. The woman at the counter stared at us, no doubt wondering why we purchased such strange items.

Few people had to stay outdoors at night or worry about lighting a fire to cook, so of course, they didn't understand. They didn't rely on sugar cubes for a burst of energy to keep walking, they probably only used them for morning tea. These few supplies helped us stay mobile while maintaining some degree of normalcy. I laughed to myself, there was nothing normal about our situation, nor for the others who lost their homes. But that was a small price to pay compared to losing one's life.

In the center of town, we used the community well and filled our bottles. Most people had returned home for their mid-afternoon meal, the few who remained in the village never looked our way, as if we were invisible. We gathered our few packs and returned to the woods.

We hiked northwest on a trail for hours, it led us high into the hills overlooking the *Thaya River*, and a thick forest revealed itself. The earth smelled rich, and the deeper we walked, the more abundant the soft moss underfoot. Dark shades of evergreen painted the view, their fragrance filled my nostrils, and I was contented.

Stumps, damp and rotting, displayed huge mushroom blooms on its leftover bark.

"Look, Mama, hen of the woods."

I pointed to the bottom of an old oak tree. There protruding on its bark was a glorious mound, a cluster of Grifola frondosa mushrooms.

"Good eye, Ivan. Let's cut them and save them for dinner."

My mama pulled out her knife and carefully sliced pieces and handed them to me.

"Petro, Olena, look around for more," Tato called out.

We spent a good part of the afternoon hunting mushrooms that day, one of my favorite days spent in the woods.

The forest became our home for weeks. Each day we walked further up the mountains and westward, discovering new delights for our senses to experience. Parts of our climb were rocky, so we grabbed the stone wall and forged ahead. A trickling stream was always found nearby.

The forest provided us with plentiful water supplies wherever we traveled, and that helped us survive. The beauty of the greenery gave us even more, a boost to our spirit. We felt human, like good scouts who were camping to enjoy life rather than running away from it. For myself, it was like being in a grand dream, perfect surroundings, and family love.

The remaining days of summer were spent hiking and camping in the rolling forest hills, where everything was big. I appreciated the cooler temperatures, the lower humidity, and we slept more comfortably at night.

I looked forward to every minute of my day. Solid ground supported me with each step. Surrounded by nature, my soul felt alive. Surely this was freedom.

At nightfall, we slept covered by a canopy of fir trees and a starlit universe peeking between the boughs. Looking up at the night sky, we stargazed, and watched as comets fizzled-out along their journey across the sky and dropped to their death.

We passed a huge reservoir dam that backed up the water for miles. The lake that it formed mesmerized us. Its glassy surface reflected the sky and surrounding trees in dark tones upon its surface as if it were filled with ink. Nothing rippled across that smooth sheet, no breeze or fish, only the water's skin so splay, so perfectly stable, that we were tempted to make waves.

We flung off our clothes and dove in; Petro and I swam in our underwear and splashed about, causing all kinds of movement to the lake's expanse. Even Olena swam, but she kept her clothes on and said it was the easiest way to wash them. We all laughed and spent the afternoon swimming and sunning ourselves along the nearby banks in leisure.

On the rougher day treks, especially in the highest elevations, the rock scaling was rigorous. We were challenged by steep rises of gray cliffs, but the views from on top were worth every step. Even Olena was happier here and didn't seem to mind being away from civilization. *Civilization*, the thought of that seemed odd to me, we hadn't seen any sort of human compassion by civilized people in a long time.

I had a lot of time to think as we journeyed, pondering the devastation we experienced. I didn't like the way others stared at us with distrust, and the slaughter of innocents splayed across the newspapers when any were available. I wondered what civilization would look like after this war if there would be anything recognizable.

People were hollowed out, always cautious, unwilling to trust. War was an ugly beast that changed us all.

Determined to remain positive as Tato preached, I returned to my daydreaming. But now my imaginings were about America instead of castles. I wanted to be great someday, I didn't know how, but I was determined to figure it out. *Hope has to survive.* Like a dormant plant waiting for the right moment to seize the day, and then when spring finally comes. The sun warms the ground, the roots dig deep into the fertile soil, and the plant grows and thrives.

One day we came across the ruins of an old Gothic pilgrimage church. The crumbling remains made me think of our old castle in Old Halych, and for the first time since we had left, I was homesick. I said this to my father and brother.

"Ivan, forget about Halych and the old castle. It might be gone because of this war. We have much better things to see," Petro said.

"Yes, that's right. Listen to your brother. Never look back. We will have better days, I promise. One day you will be looking at the Statue of Liberty in the greatest city in the world—New York."

My father smiled and closed his eyes. He was dreaming.

Immediately, my mind began imagining the mysterious city of New York. In America, I will be special and will do something truly fantastic, and then I can say, *I am the king of my world.*

LIFE ON A
BAVARIAN FARM

CHAPTER 27

After camping and walking throughout the summer months, autumn was near. The nights were getting colder. Tato decided that we needed to find a better place to sleep.

"Leysa, we need to know what's going on in the world. It's best to continue in the direction we're heading, but we need to go down the mountain, out of the woods, back to civilization."

"Is it the right thing to do, to go west? Head straight into Germany and say, 'here we are,' go ahead and use us as you see fit. And then what about Petro? You want them to recruit him into an army? The German army on the Russian front?"

"I'm betting on the war being almost over," my father said.

His head was down, watching the grass under his feet as he walked.

"What if it's not over? If we hear gunshots, are you willing to climb back up into the woods? By then there will be snow. I think not."

I had never heard my mama speak against Tato before and it unsettled me. I understood her fear, it was real. I only hoped that what my father said was correct and the war was over. How would we know unless we went somewhere with people? At the end of a lengthy discussion, the decision reached was to continue heading west.

We were in the area known as Bohemia, now part of Czechoslovakia, and its control was taken over by the Germans. There was no escaping the Nazi hold. We had the German paperwork to travel as workers. And my parents still had the OST patches they were given by the guards at the train station. They hoped no one would arrest us for being vagrants in this foreign land. We had been given a destination to work in a manufacturing plant. *Maybe they still needed our help? Did we want to help the Germans?* The place might be gone now that the Allies had been bombing over Germany.

Perhaps the war was over, and we were unaware. That was another reason my father argued for us to go back down from the forest—we needed to know what was going on with the world war.

Traveling downhill proved a faster undertaking than going up. At times on sunny days, the colors of the trees seemed so vibrant that I had to shield my eyes. The golden and bronzed foliage fell so fast that it felt as if we were in a race, to see who could reach the bottom first. It took a couple of days to reach the western side of the forest. I had taken for granted the fresh air and the beauty of the mountains, but when we met up with a road, things suddenly felt crowded.

We walked for a couple more days, taking occasional sojourn hours away from the road to rest. We sat nestled in the golden foliage and fir trees, before continuing our expedition. The closer we got to a village, the more nervous we all became. We passed others on the road, most were too weary to do anything more than a nod. They were thin and dirty as if they had no water to bathe. I felt lucky, *special even*. My family had managed to stay healthy, clean, and fed.

Our conversations were slight, nearly non-existent. I spent the quiet days walking and dreaming to myself, entertaining myself with old stories to pass the time.

One afternoon we stumbled across a small farm nestled into a hillside. No one seemed to be around, the yard was empty except for a few golden-colored hens hopping freely and pecking for grain in the brown dirt.

We traipsed across the yard toward the barn. The door slid wide open. We froze in our tracks, our instincts fully alerted.

A tall, thin young man came out and greeted us. He was smiling, a rarity.

"Guten Tag," the man said. "Good day. How can I help you, Sir?"

The man smiled a lot and seemed happier than anyone else that we've met along our journey. He was in his twenties, older than Petro but much younger than Tato. His eyes were blue like a summer sky, his complexion once pale, now sun-kissed from working outside.

"Hello, Sir. My name is Pan Rudenko. We have traveled from Halych," Tato said in German. He walked toward the man, his arm bent behind his back, waving for us to hold off.

The man whistled through his teeth.

"That's a long way to wander, my friend."

"Yes, indeed, our excursion has taken us months to get this far."

The man's head bobbed up and down as he listened to my tato explain our situation. He seemed to empathize with our predicament.

"Please, Sir, this is my family. My wife Leysa, sons Petro and Ivan, and our daughter Olena."

We all bowed our heads as Tato continued our introduction.

"We are good workers, we could help you around the farm in exchange for a roof over our heads, perhaps you could let us sleep in the barn? We are not asking for a hand-out—we will work for what you can spare."

The farmer said something in German that I couldn't understand and soon my tato waved his arm for us to come closer and join him. We stood by Tato, and the man walked up to each of us and shook our hand. The man spoke again in German.

Mama said to us, "he says we can sleep in his barn."

I clapped my hands, and everyone laughed. The man led us into the barn, we shadowed him, like children following the Pied Piper. It was a massive space inside. Warmth filled the air, and I smelled fresh hay.

We passed four cows, then another pen holding one pig but the side door was opened, and I spied more pigs outside in a penned-in area. There were also laying hens nearby, I could hear their clucking. It smelled of dry straw and animal, the way barns do, but it was tidy compared to others I had seen.

We marched to the back where there was another door that led to a tackle room, then another door to a back room. Six bunks flanked the wall, a small table with old wooden chairs around it, and a potbelly stove in the room's center. The ceiling slanted, the walls were clean and painted an off-white. This might have been a space reserved for their workers, so I guessed that we were now his hired help.

The man left us and returned twenty minutes later with his pregnant wife. She was blonde and small-framed, but her

belly was big. She smiled like her husband, but more discretely. Her hair was short and curled, a more modern style
than worn in our hometown.

They brought us food. Clearly, the woman liked to bake.
It smelled heavenly. Inside the basket were goodies, some
kind of fruit cobbler. The man asked my father to help him,
and they returned with buckets of water for us to wash.
Within hours we felt glorious. We were fed and clean. For the
first time in days, Olena was smiling again.

Tato explained to us that the farmer's name was Herr
Baumann and his wife was Frau Baumann. They were new-
lyweds and were expecting their first child. They desperately
needed help around the farm with chores and had told Tato
that we were a God-send.

"They own this farm?" my mama asked.

"Yes, they do. Things are different here, Leysa. Common
folks aren't treated like we were, they can own land and make
a decent living. It's more prosperous here. They bought the
farm cheap because it needed so much work."

"So, Taras, you arranged with Herr Baumann, that we
help them, and they help us? They will let us stay here?"

My father smiled; months of worry melted away.

"Exactly, my dear. We have found a haven in the middle
of the madness. The couple said the soldiers pretty much
leave them alone. There is no front here, at least not yet."

My father's eyes saw something none of us could see.

"So, the war is still going on," Mama said.

He nodded.

"Sometimes they hear bombs, but kilometers away. This
is a small farming area, no city to blow up."

Tato smiled then planted a kiss on Mama's face. He stood up and addressed Petro and me.

"Ready for some honest hard work, boys?"

We both agreed eagerly and followed our father out of the barn to start the job.

My first project was to build up a bed for planting garlic. It was the first time I used a hoe, and blisters soon formed on my fingers. They hurt but I kept going. When I finished I showed my hands to Tato.

"They'll turn into callouses, eventually."

No pity from him. I must be getting older.

Tato and Mama tried hard to understand the intricacies of the German language. They translated what Herr Baumann said as best as possible so that we children understood and learned the language as well. Each day we were taught more words. Since we lived here now, we needed to know how people spoke.

Each morning after breakfast we were given instructions to follow. Mama reminded us to always smile while we worked, that was the best way for us to show the strangers how much we appreciated their kindness.

CHAPTER 28

The Baumann couple didn't remain strangers for long. Tato, Petro and I worked all day beside the man, cutting the last of the dry hay in his fields and gathering the remaining harvest, preparing the vegetable beds for the next crop season, feeding the chickens and livestock, even milking the cows.

Mama and Olena spent all day working with his wife. They scrubbed the floors, patched walls, and painted. Olena designed a beautiful mural of butterflies for the soon to be baby's room.

The women baked stollen, a bread made with dried fruit, cooked up fruit jams, and canned the last of the vegetables for the long winter storage. Work never ended, there were so many things to do to resurrect the old homestead. But after a few weeks of intense labor, the farm looked like a polished stone.

Colorful produce from the fields, fresh paint around the house, it all completed the scene and showed the full potential of the place. The Baumanns were grateful for our added labor, and in truth, we all enjoyed the work. It felt good to be part of something bigger than ourselves, a common goal, even if it wasn't our farm. The couple made us feel welcomed, part of their extended family, and for the first time in a long time, it felt like we were in a real home.

One afternoon the women needed my help—I shredded the cabbage for a batch of sauerkraut. In Ukrainian, we call it *kapusta*, but it's all the same, a staple cuisine of country life.

For hours I pushed heads of cabbage across a grate that was affixed across a basket with a sheet draped to catch the shredded strands. We stuffed the strings into a large ceramic crock. Frau Baumann added lots of salt and vinegar so the cabbage would ferment. Though jobs in the kitchen were considered a woman's work, I enjoyed the tasks.

Every day I learned something new while on the farm. There were varied chores that proved to be more fun than the monotonous work for the farmer back home, cleaning out the horse stalls with Michael. I thought of my friend often while I worked, and I prayed for him, hoped that he had gone to the Jewish heaven.

Olena smiled most days now, after living on the farm these past few weeks, things seemed natural. Over time we were invited into the main house and began eating supper with the Baumann couple. After dinner, we shared stories about our town, and they told us about their families and friends. They spoke freely about what had happened in Germany.

Herr Baumann's family had lost their home during a bombing. Tato was too polite to ask for details, though I was curious. In my heart, I knew that we supported the Allies, dreamed of going to America and to be Americans. We couldn't tell the Baumanns this, the people who took us in after their family had lost their home in a raid by Allies. The airstrikes were a big part of this war, stories of British air raids had been splayed across the newspapers all year according to Herr Baumann.

We hoped the Allies would win the war, but we didn't have to wave that flag in front of our hosts.

As the days went on, it became clear that the Baumanns weren't happy with the politics of the war and felt threatened by the German soldiers. That was one reason why when the government posted the property for sale, they had bought this run-down farm in Bohemia, away from the German cities. They never mentioned in conversations what exactly had happened to the previous owners and we never asked.

"They are pacifists," Tato said to us one night before we said our nightly prayers. "They want nothing to do with the war, like us. We are the same, stuck in the middle of this ugly business. They are very sympathetic to our situation and promise to help us as long as they are able. We agreed that peace is the best goal, and we choose to live our lives in that example."

My father enjoyed most people, but his feelings for Herr Baumann ran deeper. I could see it the way he laughed with the man, I heard it in his voice when he said praises of him. My father respected the way Herr Baumann lived his life, helping others, and working hard.

That was fine with me, but I wondered how long we could stay here...

My brother spoke aloud, waking me from my thoughts.

"That's wonderful, but what about going to America? Are we still going?"

My brother looked worried. My father smiled and wrapped his arm around Petro's shoulder.

"Don't worry son, we are still going there. We can't stay here indefinitely. We aren't German, after all. We aren't native Bohemians, either. All we are to the Third Reich are Ostarbeiter, and they may not even want our labor any longer. We'll never get ahead here in this society, so that's why we have to wait, see what happens in this war, and pray the good guys will win."

"You mean the Americans, Tato?" I knew what my father meant, but I needed him to say it, to verify for us all that they were the good guys, like us.

"Yes, Ivan. The Americans are the good guys."

After the fall harvest, we moved into the back bedrooms of the main house. Frost covered the ground most mornings and Frau Baumann said the barn was too primitive to keep us warm during cold nights. But I knew it was better than what many people had these days. The barn was warm and cozy. Still, Frau insisted. My mother thought that perhaps she felt safer with us nearby. The woman was getting closer to her due date and had begun to depend on my mother's help around the house.

I was thankful to God that we had a roof over our heads at night instead of sleeping under a tree or in a stairwell. I had enjoyed the camping during the late summer and early autumn months, but soon the snow would come along with the cold north winds.

One afternoon Herr Baumann returned from the supply store with news.

"I heard from a few different folks that they've seen transient people walking along the roads. People in town talk about new security troubles around their places, strangers stealing,"

Herr Baumann took off his cap and rubbed his head.

"Sometimes things are found broken for no apparent reason. Almost like it was a deliberate act."

My father drew in a deep breath. He sympathized with the homeless strangers who roamed the countryside, they were hungry, like we had been. But he felt a stronger allegiance to Herr Baumann. We owed him our protection for his kindness.

"No worries, Herr Baumann," Tato said. "We'll help safeguard your farm."

The men nodded to each other. The agreement understood.

"Petro, Ivan. Keep a close eye on things. If you see anything strange, let me know about it right away."

"Yes, Tato. We rarely see anyone, so of course, we'll notice them right off." Petro picked up his tools and headed for the barn.

I followed. No matter how old I get, it seems I'm always following my big brother.

For weeks whenever Herr Baumann went to the market, there was another story upon his return. He had sympathetic tendencies as he had for us when we first arrived, but things were different now. His concern was for his family first. My father reassured him and promised Herr Baumann that we would remain on guard.

Often at night, when things went quiet as I lay in bed after reciting my prayers, I would hear faint echoes of bomb explosions and bursts of gunfire pops. Even though it sounded far away, I couldn't sleep, terrified that the war was getting closer and would soon ruin everything.

One afternoon while baling up the hay to add to the winter storage in the barn, we spotted smoke in the distance. It was kilometers away, but the black clouds billowed up into the sky and reminded me of the day when the train was bombed. I prayed as we finished the work, that this small farm would be spared the scars of war.

Time passed, we worked hard, and the war got closer. Daily we heard the stutter of machine guns and the thudding of bombshells off in the distance. Tato looked up and gauged the distance, then he nodded at Herr Baumann, and returned to his work without saying a word. A mutual understanding grew. All the more reason to thank God for our blessings, so far, the farm was spared the casualty of war.

CHAPTER 29

We celebrated Christmas Eve with the Baumann family, and it turned out to be one of the most joyous holidays that I had ever experienced.

Frau Baumann was young and inexperienced about many things around the house, so when she asked my mother to handle preparing our traditional Ukrainian Christmas Eve dinner, Mama was delighted. She smiled and hummed for days while cooking the holiday meal. Asking my mother to do this was a great gift from Frau Baumann, and I wondered if the lady of the house had planned it that way, knowing precisely that it would brighten my mother's spirits. Frau Baumann was a gracious lady.

Friday arrived, the eve of Christmas, and the dining table was covered with a fine linen cloth, white like the snow. Evergreens were placed in the middle of the tabletop, and the fragrance of spruce filled the room, giving the house that special scent of Christmas. A sheave of wheat was placed on top of the boughs to decorate the center.

Mama situated her fancy braided *Kolach* on top of the wheat and stuck three candles into the bread's core, which represented the Blessed Trinity.

"Let me add some red ribbons," Olena said.

"Oh, it looks so festive," Frau Baumann said. She clasped her hands together. "Please, let me add my Weihnachtsstollen, too."

She placed her bread next to Mama's kolach.

"There, it looks so colorful. Festive with the red ribbons, thank you, Olena."

My sister beamed after being praised. Olena completed her centerpiece and then set the dishes carefully. Finally, we were invited to gather around the holiday table. Herr Baumann said a brief prayer of thanks.

Tato picked up a plate and passed to each person a small piece of bread with a drop of honey and said, "Merry Christmas." This Ukrainian custom was a gesture representing best wishes for good health and happiness.

Dinner was served, and we ate holiday specialties like my favorite *kutia*, a sweet whole-wheat dish made with poppies, nuts, and honey added to the cereal concoction. There were twelve courses and one by one, my parents explained to the Baumanns the various meaning behind the food. Twelve courses for twelve Apostles, all meatless dishes the night before Christ's birth, this was our tradition.

We enjoyed pickled herring and beet borscht that was served with small *uszka*, which are small *pidpenky* or mushroom dumplings that are shaped like little ears. We all laughed after that explanation. Another dish the Baumanns enjoyed was mother's *holubtsi*, which are cabbage leaves stuffed with rice, mushrooms, and savory spices then rolled up tight and baked in a tomato sauce. My favorite, besides the sweets, was the *varenyky*, which are dough dumplings stuffed with potato and some stuffed with a cabbage filling.

"I helped mother make them yesterday," I told the Baumanns. "It was a challenge to wrap the dough around the filling and seal it so it wouldn't leak when boiled. But I was careful and did it like Mama."

"My mother was from Poland, and she used to cook something similar, but she called them *pierogi*," Frau Baumann said. "Sometimes she filled them with blueberries."

"That sounds delicious," Olena chimed in.

Nodding our agreement, we finished dinner with the final courses of fruit compote and a poppyseed roll sliced in meticulous even pieces.

Frau Baumann had baked ginger cookies, shaped like little people, one designed after each of us. She passed them out, smiling as we took our caricature.

"Thank you, Frau Baumann. I like cookies," I said.

"You are most welcome, Ivan," she said.

She seemed pleased that we all appreciated her sweets, even after such a filling meal. I was happy to boost her baking confidence, especially if it encouraged her to bake more cookies in the future.

We all helped clear the dishes away then Herr Baumann had a surprise.

"Is everyone ready?" he asked.

"Yes, please open the door," Frau Baumann said.

He pushed the door open and, in the salon, stood a five-foot tree alight with small candles in holders attached to the ends of the boughs.

"It's beautiful, just like on the postcards with the old-fashioned trees," I said.

"Ivan, that didn't sound nice," my mama scolded.

"I mean it as a compliment, you know like the old Currier and Ives scenes. They are famous, Mama."

Herr Baumann bowed.

"Well, thank you, young man. It is supposed to look like that, and since you seem to like the tree so much, you have the honor of placing the first ornament."

He handed me a delicate glass ball, painted pink with a fancy design of angels with widespread wings. I hung it on a branch, gingerly moving the hook over the twig.

"There."

Everyone clapped, then took turns placing ornaments on the tree. It sparkled with such beauty that I almost cried. It seemed a miracle to have such happiness in the middle of the war. We sang a carol and watched the tree for a bit, the candle lights reflecting on the colored glass, and the silver tinsel strung about the tree.

"The tree is our special holiday tradition," Herr Baumann said.

"Yes, every year we wait until after dinner, then reveal the lit fir tree," Frau Baumann said.

"Then we exchange presents if we had any to exchange, of course." She giggled.

Everyone laughed as well, knowing money was too tight to buy gifts. No one seemed to mind a presentless Christmas. But then my mother pulled a package from behind her back and handed it to Frau Baumann.

"Please take this, I know we weren't planning on exchanging gifts, but this is something you'll appreciate," Mama said.

Frau Baumann unwrapped the present carefully, opening it without ripping the paper, and flattening it out and folding it in half. She smiled and held up the small blanket my mother had knitted for the baby.

"It's beautiful and so soft. And the baby is due to arrive soon, so this is very much needed. Thank you," Frau Baumann said.

"You're most welcome. I managed to knit a little section each night. I wanted to do something special for your baby because you have been so kind to my children," Mama said.

The rest of us didn't receive presents, but we didn't care. We were happy being in each other's company, at peace, together, more than enough to be thankful for. We all knew that others were in a precarious situation while we were enjoying ourselves with merriment. We were blessed to be safe and warm.

"Please, pass these to the next person beside you," Herr Baumann said as he passed out cups filled with mulled cider.

"Merry Christmas," he toasted. "Many more blessed years. May the birth of the Christ child give you peace in your heart."

My father took a turn at toasting good wishes. "Thank God for our blessings, wonderful family, friends, and bounty. God bless all those who have less and please comfort them with your grace tonight, Lord. Amen."

Tato raised his cup.

We all said, "Amen."

We had a grand time, sang another carol, and joked around with each other. It was beautiful noise to my ears, I heard the laughter, a sound that had been vacant from our lives for so long. When the merriment settled down a bit, Herr Baumann produced a guitar.

"Will you do us the honor? I discovered this instrument in the attic while I searched for more blankets last week. I remembered that you said you played, so I thought I'd save it for this special occasion."

Herr Baumann beamed as he handed it to Tato.

"Thank you, I'd love to play a song for you. I hope I'm not too out of practice."

My father laughed at his quip and accepted the gracious honor. He strummed familiar carols for the young couple, they marveled at his talent, sang along, and shared their lovely voices lifted in chorus. We sang together the Austrian carol Silent Night. Looking at everyone's faces as we sang the tender words, I saw compassion for life in all their eyes, and I felt honored to be with them.

"I'd like to play something special for you next," Tato said.

"This song was composed by Mykola Leontovych, back in 1914. He devised this ostinato, which is based on a four-note melody. The tune is beguiling. A little enchantment."

My father's eyes wandered off dreamily.

"It inspires me with an endearing sentiment when I play it. The inspiration for the music came from an ancient chant that had been sung for ages, even before the days of Christianity in Ukraine. It's the story known as 'Shchedryk'. It's about a little swallow who flies to an open window and wishes the household within much luck and happiness. So, I too wish you much success and happiness, Baumann family."

Tato nodded and strummed a practice note, while Mama added another tidbit to his charming story.

"You may have heard the English version of the song, it's called 'Carol of the Bells'," she said.

"The revised words were added to the music by Peter Wilhousky a few years ago, in 1936, I believe. Well, it doesn't matter. What's important is that in his new verses, the songwriter describes ringing bells, because that's what he envisioned when he first heard the alluring music. Now, it's a famous holiday song for many."

"Oh yes, I have heard the song. Please play it for us," Frau Baumann said.

My father played the music, and we joined in by singing the verses in Capella. My family harmonized the Ukrainian carol for our hosts, and they thoroughly enjoyed it. The second round, when we played an encore performance, they joined in.

The song left me with a haunting retrospect, as we sat contently in the salon, quietly digesting the music and the feast.

Herr Baumann sat on the sofa next to his wife admiring the tree, smiling like a man content with his lot in life. *He'll be a great father when the baby arrives, he's a kind man, hard-working, yet gentle inside.*

My father sat in the large armchair, my mother was on his lap with her head on his chest, contented. Tato was at peace today as well, instead of worrying about our future, he probably was remembering past Christmases that were happy as well.

I indulged in daydreams about my favorite castle left behind in Halych, reminiscing about the stories that I enjoyed dearly.

CHAPTER 30

I don't recall how long we relaxed with our thoughts, but they were interrupted when Herr Baumann stood, walked across the room, and turned on the radio. He sat again, this time in his rocking chair, smiling, of course. He rocked and listened.

The station announcer said, "Jetzt spielt die Musik, *Aus Böhmens Hain und Flur* aus der Aufnahme des Leipziger Gewandhausorchesters."

Tato translated.

"That means he's playing the recorded song, '*From Bohemia's Meadows and Forests.*'

"It's lovely music," Frau Baumann said.

We nodded, and the radio filled the house with the dramatic music, from a recorded concert of The Leipzig Gewandhaus Orchestra. The music was spectacular, and I found myself fantasizing again about the old stories that we learned at school. I imagined Pan Vasyklo standing in front of the class, pointing to places on the map and telling stories. It seemed like ages ago when he explained about the old tomb of Yaroslav, about the Goths, and the Kozaky, but in fact, it hadn't even been a year since the last time we saw him.

So much had happened, so fast. I hoped that we could stay here on the farm a little bit longer, to help the Baumanns get settled in their new lives with the new baby. And we could try to get ourselves settled, as well. I liked living here.

As I relaxed, giving in to the lure of the music, the program was interrupted with a news bulletin. The announcer spoke fast over the music with words I couldn't make out.

Herr Baumann said, "the man says that the people of Germany were amazed when the church bells rang to celebrate *Heiligenacht*. He credits the Royal Air Force, says that it was only because of the reprieve of the British bombing. The RAF had stopped their air attacks over Berlin for the past week. The Germans are thankful and celebrate with the bells."

"Yes, that is good news for this special evening. I'm glad there's no bombing going on for Christmas Eve," Frau Baumann said.

Herr Baumann squeezed his eyes; he was trying to hear more. He leaned his head down towards the radio, as he translated more of the news announcement.

"Canadian soldiers are in trenches in Ortona, facing off against the German stronghold of the Italian city. Paratroopers were sent at Hitler's command to assist and hold the line for the Fatherland, buildings have been bombed to block the streets making it impossible for tanks to pass, turning it into a face to face battle. Reporters said the city is a death trap for the Canadian troops."

My mother and Frau Baumann both gasped.

"That's horrible, especially on this holy day," Mama said. "You would think they would stop at least for the day's sake."

Herr Baumann continued, his voice, deeper than usual, his expression serious.

"Meanwhile, it's reported that the Red Army claimed a Soviet victory yesterday; they won the Battle of the Dnieper, and the second Battle of Kyiv, though there remains some stray fighting in your dear Ukraine, Taras. On Tuesday, a German submarine U-284 suffered damages in the Atlantic."

"Hooray," I called out.

The others looked and smiled at me, and then Herr Baumann continued.

"In light of the holiday, they are repeating a story that happened on Monday, December 20th. They say an ace fighter of the German Luftwaffe, Oberleutnant Franz Stigler refused orders to shoot down a severely damaged American B-17 bomber. Instead, in the spirit of the holiday, he escorted the plane away from the German airspace until he was free and clear to return to his home base. Later, intelligence learned the American flyer was Second Lieutenant Charlie Brown, and that he landed safely at the RAF Seething base. The American flyer announced over the AFN Europe radio station his gratitude to the ace fighter for the escort."

Everyone in the room clapped with excitement.

"Thank God!" Frau Baumann said aloud. "Maybe the German soldiers have seen enough. This Franz Stigler and Charlie Brown can teach them all a lesson."

"How did they think this would all work?" Tato said.

"That they would bomb London, then the world, but the world wouldn't strike back?"

"Unfortunately, my friend, many do think that way. I pray for Stigler's life. Heroic deeds like that aren't encouraged by Gestapo," Herr Baumann said.

"I mentioned to you before, Taras, that my parent's home was in Hamburg. What I didn't say was that last summer I went back home to check on them. I had hoped to convince them to come here, to the farm, because it had been so hot and everything was dry. Very unusual weather—that's why it all burned so fast. It turned into a nightmare that I'd never wish on anyone. The British had their reprisal."

He looked at his wife. She bit her thick lip, then he went on with his story.

"The Royal British Airforce hit hard in Hamburg, they bombed in teams, first the factories and the transportation ports. They were trying to bring Germany down to their knees, after all, we blitzed them, right. An eye for an eye.

"For seven nights the raid lasted, nonstop. Firebombs turned the streets into walls of flame. The force of tornado winds created by the pressure of the heat blocked our way and formed a gigantic wall of fire. There was no leaving, the streets were lit up bright red, and debris blocked the way, strewn all over the road and sidewalks. I had to walk around bodies to get to my parent's apartment, though it was challenging going against that hot wind. People moaned in the street asking for help, but there was no helping them, they were half dead.

"Once I made it to the floor of my parent's apartment, I found them hiding in a closet. We covered ourselves with wet blankets and stayed crouched until the raid moved to another section of the city. I pulled them through the debris, headed for the waterway, and we barely made it out in time. The fire destroyed the entire neighborhood. Afterward, no part of the city was left standing, only stacks of brick with nothing inside. Fire destroyed everything."

"We're so sorry you experienced that," my mother said.

I looked over at my sister. Olena wasn't smiling anymore. She sat staring at the floor, frozen, trying to block every word from entering her head.

"I'm lucky I survived. My parents live with my sister now," Herr Baumann continued.

"You would think that after such a catastrophe that the German Reich would seek out peace for the people's safety, but instead, they follow a crazy man. They waged more retaliation—working along with the fascists in Italy, and Japan. Trying to conquer Africa and the Middle East, war all over the world—it's insane. Will it ever end?"

I was terrified by Herr Baumann's words. I had no idea there was fighting in so many places or that he had been from Hamburg. We all had read in a newspaper what had happened there last July, but no one ever spoke of it, it was too horrible. Even after such trepidation, Herr Baumann remained a gentle soul and smiled most of the time. It made me wonder why some men morphed into Hitler-like evil dictators while other men were virtuous and never wavered. *What part of us controls our humanity?*

"Wait, there's more," Herr Baumann said, holding up his finger. "They are announcing a reminder bulletin. On December 18th Heinrich Himmler announced new rules concerning the arrests and deportation of Jews and those Gentiles married to Jews. There will be no more exemptions, all must be deported to Theresienstadt beginning in January."

The women gasped. Herr Baumann motioned for them to quiet down.

"Also, on Tuesday . . . it was announced that all German boys aged sixteen and older are required to register for military duty, this takes effect in January, too."

"God, save us. Sending boys into the war."

We all heard the disgust in my mother's voice. Our Merry Christmas was overshadowed by the ugliness of the war, tainted by its reality. Though we were blessed to be safe, and together, we realized so many others were in need. How long could we turn a blind eye?

CHAPTER 31

December turned into the new year and farm life remained busy. There were a couple of occasions when strangers stopped by and spoke with Herr Baumann near the gate. I noticed his nodding while listening to the people, and then he allowed them to stay in the barn for a day to rest before they continued on their way. They seemed genuinely thankful for the night's lodging as they shook his hand.

I think Herr Baumann felt good too, his small way to help, and some of the guilt lifted off his back, though I knew he had nothing to feel bad about. Many suffered, yes, but it wasn't his fault. Herr Baumann was a kind man, and we prayed for him because sometimes his kindness was abused or viewed as a weakness when strangers passed through.

I recall one frigid day when another group arrived, two men, looking for a haven. Once again, Herr Baumann offered them a place to rest for a night in the barn, but one of them spoke out enraged. He was tall, muscled, and intimidating when he raised his arm, his hand fisted. He argued with Herr Baumann, demanding permanent lodgings, threatening him.

My tato stepped out from the side of the barn, his stern expression said more than words could have conveyed. Tato walked closer to the gate, despite the cold wind slapping against his face. He remained steady, squinting against the snow, never wavering.

The gypsy man lowered his arm when he took notice of my father, then cursed under his breath. The other man was either embarrassed by his friend's demeanor or intimidated by my father's approach. He tugged at his friend's sleeve, and urged him to walk away. We never saw the men again.

February 1944

It was early morning. I was milking the last of the cows. This milk was destined for the container that Herr Baumann used to make his cheeses, and the last pail was put aside to carry to the house for breakfast.

Olena came running into the barn, her hair flying every which way, waving her hands with excitement. I turned away from Betsy, who still needed more of my attention because she always gave more milk than the others, that's why I saved her for last.

"Calm down, there's no fire in here. I'm almost finished, Olena. I'll bring the milk in shortly."

"No, that's not why I'm here. Where's Herr Baumann. Hurry." She stamped her foot.

Tato and Herr Baumann heard her commotion and came out from the back room where they had been sharpening the tools to get ready for the spring planting. My father had oil on his shirt, and I knew he'd be in trouble as soon as Mama noticed it. Herr Baumann was wiping his hands on a dirty rag. He stood tall and looked as if he'd grown a foot since we had first met him. His beard was thicker now, too, but his eyes were still bonnie blue like the sky. He had bright, honest eyes, like angel eyes.

"I'm here, Olena. What is it?" Herr Baumann said.

"The baby is on his way."

Herr Baumann and my tato shared a look, then dropped their rags and ran to the house. I slapped Betsy gently, and followed them, then turned back to grab the pail of milk.

Maybe they would need it for the baby. We rushed in one after the other, making a lot of noise until we heard the screams of pain that came from the upstairs bedroom.

I heard moans, so loud, I thought someone was dying up there. Blood rushed from my head to my feet. I placed the pail on the table and sat down before I fainted.

My mother rushed down the stairs and took command. Pointing she called out, "I need boiling water, at least two big pots. And string. Don't forget to bring something to cut it with, too."

She pointed at my tato. "You, I need towels, three or four at least, and the softest blanket you can find."

Herr Baumann and my father followed her orders without hesitation. They ran about doing the tasks while Olena, Petro, and I sat at the kitchen's farm table, not daring to say a word or ask questions. We stayed out of the way, while the grown men helped. More cries of pain echoed from upstairs. Mama ran back up to tend to Frau Baumann.

I winced with each sharp yell. Then I heard Mama's soothing voice.

"Look at me," my mother said. "Breath out, like this."

Heavy breathing was heard from the room above, more groans, and it sounded as if the young woman was using up all her strength to push the baby out. She breathed like my friend did when he removed a boulder from his father's garden that had weighed a ton. He lifted and pushed, used all his strength, and when he had finished the job, he was a complete sweaty mess. I imagined that Frau Baumann was upstairs perspiring like that, as well. That explains why Mama needed water and towels.

I cringed every time she moaned or grunted in agony. I felt so helpless.

Then, a baby cried out.

I had never heard such an incredible sound, soft yet loud, sweet yet a selfish cry. A voice that was so pure, so natural, so human. This baby was real, alive, and kicking.

"It's a boy," Herr Baumann called out from upstairs.

We jumped from our seats and danced in a circle, holding hands and swinging them with delight, happy and relieved that the wait was over. My mama descended in slow motion, holding the new baby in her arms. We hurried to meet her.

Mama announced, "meet the new baby boy Baumann. Frau Baumann is resting now, she worked very hard."

"Yes, we heard, Mama. I felt so bad for her," Olena said. "I'm never going to have a child."

"Oh, don't be silly. And don't worry, she's fine." Mama smiled. "I washed this tiny bundle of joy and presented him to his father. Herr Baumann asked that I show off his new son to you while he thanks his wife in private for the beautiful child. Isn't he precious?"

The baby was wrapped up in the tiny soft blanket that Mama made of lambswool and looked so small, pink, and chubby with rosy cheeks. He moved his head back and forth, then opened his eyes for a split second before cooing.

"He's beautiful," Olena said. Her voice was a whisper.

"I think he's hungry. Was I that small when I was born, Mama?" Petro asked.

"Yes, you were all like this, so soft and precious. So sweet. I fell in love with each of you when I saw your innocent faces."

Tato came up behind Mama. He looked over her shoulder and gently traced his finger over the baby's forehead, then drew an invisible cross.

"God bless this baby. Look, this one is already smiling like his father."

We laughed at that because Herr Baumann's smile was glued onto his face.

That early-winter we welcomed the Baumann's new baby boy into the world. A few days later, he was ceremoniously christened Herbert Baumann at his Baptismal ceremony. The men celebrated together with a glass of beer, "to the new heir."

Life continued, things bustled on the farm, and spring entered with the melting snows. The dirt roads were mud. The local ephemerals that poked up in small clumps of brightly colored blooms of purple and yellow, edged the soggy ground in the fields. Life budded all around the farm, the fruit trees and, annuals.

First, we heard the cries of baby Baumann, followed by the neighing calls of a birthed calf, and later a couple of baby goats arrived. Spring gave way to new life and new hope on the farm. Everything smelled fresh and newfound. It was a pleasant time, and I caught myself wondering if this happiness could last, or would the war eventually come to find us.

A BRISK ESCAPE

CHAPTER 32

We were happy living on the farm. At the end of the day, my arms were sore, my back ached, and I looked forward to sleep. We labored hard, but it was enjoyable, we were motivated to help charitable people like the Baumann family.

Now that the baby was born, there was even more work to do around the old place. Watching the way Herr Baumann fussed over the little one every night after dinner, pacing the floor with the small bundle in his big arms, humming to him softly with so much love in his gaze, it inspired us to value the living. Little Herbert was the future, and we all felt the need to nurture the young boy.

One early afternoon Petro, Tato and I walked back toward the barn to put away the tools after digging in the fields all morning. It was warm and sunny, a slight breeze did little to cool us off after tilling the field to prepare it to plant seed. I was exhausted. Tato carried a hoe and rake over his shoulder, his step was slower than a few hours ago. Petro shuffled his feet, the dusty row plumed with puffs of dirt, the sun filtered through small brown clouds.

The callouses on my fingers and palms hurt, I looked down and saw that a blister had broken open, so I wrapped my bandanna around the hand.

No one spoke, no one complained, it was quiet companionship. I heard the spring songs of the citril finch floating in the air. A cool breeze caught my hair, my brown locks flipped back away from my sweaty neck, and for a moment I felt nothing but peace in my soul. I closed my eyes and listened to the sounds of life all around us, then I heard someone running toward us, their feet plodded against the dirt road, ricocheting rocks in their path.

Opening my eyes, I saw Herr Baumann sprinting toward us from the road, waving his hat in the air like a madman. Tato quickened his pace to meet him. Something was wrong.

Tato's head bobbed up and down as he listened while Herr Baumann's mouth moved fast with his arms flailing wildly in the air. Tato dropped his rake, right there on the ground, and ran toward us.

"Run to the house," he ordered. "Grab your things, only what's necessary, we must go. Now!"

I had seen that desperation before. Petro and I followed our father's orders and ran into the house, flew to our room in the back. I heard Tato calling into the kitchen, telling my sister the same thing.

"Why?" Olena said.

She hurried down the hall, her feet softly pattering against the hardwood. Tato followed her without offering an answer. He entered the room behind her and looked down at her, his eyes stern as ever.

"Now. No time for questions," he said.

Mama hustled down the hall to the back room where we slept and took her pack from under the bed, and then she hurried us along. She helped us stuff the last of our things into our bags, then we followed her as she went to the kitchen, and we all exited through the back door of the house.

"Hurry," Tato said. "We have no time left."

My heart was pounding, I was breathing through my opened mouth. All the muscle aches were forgotten, replaced with that dread I remembered having months before—a lifetime ago.

Tato led us toward the woods, which began with a small hedgerow that edged the Baumann's yard about thirty meters from the house. We ran through the thicket, up a slight hill, then through the woods another thirty meters at least. When the foliage hid our immediate proximity, Tato turned around, his attention peered down at the house below. We all did the same.

Tato motioned for us to get down. Crouched close to the ground, we looked through the spaces in the bushes in front of us. We spied a military vehicle approaching, heard it drive up the road and it braked to a stop in front of the Baumann's house. The couple came out from the front door, Frau Baumann was holding baby Herbert. Some of the soldiers exited the vehicle and rushed past the Baumanns and entered inside.

Then we heard barking. *Dogs!* The sound sent shivers up my spine, and my skin prickled with goosebumps.

"Quick, we need to get as far away from here as we can," my tato said.

He was right. Dogs would pick up our scent and follow, so we went deeper into the woods. Tato led, and we followed like ducklings, staying in a straight path, afraid to stray an inch. After ten minutes or so, the sounds of a gunshot blast echoed from somewhere behind us.

We all stopped. Frozen in time. We were all thinking the same thing, then Olena whimpered, and Mama shushed her.

"It could have come from any direction—we often hear sounds of gunfire echoing throughout the area." My father spoke in a soft tone, he sounded as if he was trying to convince himself.

"Yes, someone is practicing their aim," Petro said.

"Or they are a new war casualty." Olena's tone sounded hateful.

No need to think the Baumanns were shot, after all, they never did anyone harm. An image of Herbert's face, so small and defenseless, all by himself . . .

"No, they are fine, shots ring out all the time. Even Nazis wouldn't shoot a baby's parents leaving him orphaned," I said. Then I mumbled to myself, "they're fine."

No one else mentioned the shots again, no one talked at all.

Tato turned, then began walking again and we followed in line. We hiked for a few hours, never looking back, not a single word uttered between us. The trees all looked the same, and I had no idea of where we were heading, none of us knew. We followed our father silently and cautiously.

Ever vigilant, I listened for dogs that might be tracking our steps. I wondered why the soldiers had come to the farm in the first place, maybe Herr Baumann's parents had taken ill. No, Nazis didn't seem to care about things like that, if they had, they wouldn't have sacrificed so many soldiers for the war effort. I couldn't come up with one good idea that didn't lead to the macabre.

We had lived on the farm for months, and there had never been any sign of trouble. If the Nazis had learned about us, so what—we weren't a danger. Maybe one of the strangers that Herr Baumann helped said something to save themselves? *Perhaps they thought Herr and Frau Baumann were*

Jew sympathizers? Could someone have mistakenly thought that we were Jews? The Baumann family would help anyone, yes. Would they give us up to save themselves? No, I didn't think so. Herr Baumann was a principled man—he'd find another way to keep his family safe. Besides we weren't Jews, so he never broke the law by hiring us. *But perhaps another family he helped was Jewish, and they told on him to save themselves?* That thought made me nauseous.

I prayed as we aimlessly marched through the forest. The Baumann's kindness should be rewarded, not punished. Surely God knows that and will protect them. *The shots we heard couldn't be anything that harmed them, just random gunfire,* I convinced myself.

I had to think of something else. Otherwise, my mind would sink to a dark place with no return. So, I looked around us, noticed the trees, the soft needles underfoot, and appreciated the smell of pine in the air. This was proof of life, the abundance of all that was good and worth living for—nature.

We climbed along natural paths grooved in by the animals of this habitat, some dry beds of rocks, once a flowing river but now covered with soft moss. The timberline changed as we moved higher, from mixed trees to mostly thickly nestled evergreens. The ground we stepped on grew softer as the red needle carpet became thicker. I wondered where we were and what kind of magical place this forest was? I had never seen such deep tones of green, such heavy, lush moss, or such dark, moist ground.

By late afternoon we managed to reach the top of one of the mountains of the range. Looking across the vista, we saw the green fields below, separated by stone walls, tree lines, and fences. Everything seemed so small from up high. I tried to find the Baumann farm, but that was long gone, only visible from the other side of this mountain.

We had traveled many meters west. After a quick break and eating a few berries we found for a late meal, we started walking again into the deeper woods.

"You know, Ivan, this is the Bohemian Forest, and in some places, the woods are called The Black Forest," Petro said.

His voice faded low, almost to a whisper.

"How do you know this?" Olena asked. "I've never learned of such a place."

"Yes, you have, too, Olena. Remember the Magyars and then the Hussite Wars? Remember—they eventually became part of the Austrian Empire, like Ukraine."

"Oh, yes, I remember. So what."

"So, this is part of the Bavarian Forest, the part between Bohemia and Germany."

Petro stopped walking and lowered his voice again as if he were telling us a secret.

"They say that there are packs of hungry wolves in the woods. And bear and wild boar. It can be very dangerous. I'm trying to warn you. You must stay alert at all times."

"Tato, is Petro telling the truth?" Olena asked.

Her eyes were agape.

"Yes, Olena, it is true. The forest is beautiful, but it is also wild. It can't hurt to remain vigilant of your surroundings, but you need not worry. We are here together. No wolves will bother us while we're together."

"The best part is that there are no Germans here in the woods," I added.

"Sorry to say, we can't assume that either, Ivan."

Tato watched the ground as he walked. I could tell he was thinking of something that troubled him deeply.

"Do you think they'll bother us here, in the deep forest?" Petro asked.

My father stopped and took a deep breath, and slowly let it out, thinking of what he'll say next as he did. He had his fatherly expression across his face, his wrinkled-up forehead, and squinting blue eyes.

"Unfortunately, I heard a troubling story the other day. Herr Baumann said that some escaped POWs were caught again by Hitler's dragnet. Afterward, the Reich promised the Allies that all the escaped prisoners would be returned to the stalag barracks, but they lied. They were chauffeured to the forest and shot dead."

"That's ominous," Mama said.

She slipped her arm through Tato's and called back to us over his shoulder.

"No worries, children. We are here, and we will protect you. Besides they don't care a damn about us, we have nothing to offer them, no secret plans, no money, nothing."

"The bears and wolves, on the other hand, they may give us a little trouble sleeping tonight." Tato chuckled. He was trying not to think about the Nazis.

We walked for a long time, and I became more aware of my surroundings. I listened to every sound, heard a faraway hoot of a Pygmy Owl, and the throaty knocking call of a Capercaillie bird defending its territory. I recognized the tussling in the brush by Red Deer playing or fighting each other. Deeper in the woods, I heard the sounds of swift flight as rabbits darted away after being chased by a fox.

A nearby stream splashed water against the rocks along its banks, most of the time only a low trickle reverberated. Along the trail every so often, we spotted a pool of water collecting in the river. It would swirl and then the water rushed over walls of rock, glorious waterfalls that fed the thirsty plants and animals of the forest.

The forest glowed in a surreal array of greens in the long afternoon light. *Could I trust my eyes?* The beauty of nature surrounding us seemed impossible, yet here it was before our feet.

It seemed strange that there could be danger in such a mesmerizing place. *Was there anything to fear here?* I rationalized that Petro wanted to scare us with talk about wolves, but I had heard of them hunting together in packs. They were meat-eaters, and we were meat.

A cold shiver ran through me, and I shook myself from head to toe. I decided if we were confronted by a wolf, I'd pretend the creature was my dog, and if it dared to come near me, I'd offer him my supper instead of me. Then we'd be friends, and he'd be loyal and protect us from the rest of the pack. Changing the story to one of friendship helped my stride bounce a little faster, and soon I was in the lead, hiking to the top of the next hill in the forest.

The sun was setting, the sky shone yellowish-orange hues through the trees.

"We'll camp here for the night before it gets too dark," she said. Mama dropped her gear. "This is a perfect spot, we're up high and can see all around us."

"As soldiers do," Petro added.

Tato hugged Petro's shoulders and then, like a snap of the fingers, we were back into camping mode. These woods were dense, the Bavarian Forest seemed to have gotten darker and thicker as we hiked. At least this time we were a little more experienced, more fortified, and knew the dangers we were dealing with, or at least we thought we knew.

CHAPTER 33

We traveled for days, trapping our food as before. We stored water from fresh running streams in bottles. We slept under the stars on beds of soft pine needles with a roof made from Mama's lean-to sticks covered with our coats. It was ideal, and each night the temperature was a little warmer as spring morphed into early summer.

Before we were forced to leave the farm, Tato and Herr Baumann had tuned in to a newscast, listening to the AFN Europe radio station, a new program for the American forces. It broadcasted all over Western Europe in the hopes of cheering up Allied soldiers. They entertained the troops with shows like *The Golden Record Gallery*, playing old favorite songs to help them remember their home.

I had overheard some of the songs myself and loved the upbeats. The station also played other music, comedy skits, and announced sports records. Most importantly, they broadcasted the news about the war advances, and where the significant attacks had taken place. Herr Baumann and my father tried their best to translate the English-speaking broadcasters.

Last year, 1943, there had been many bombings over Germany, lots of destruction by the firebombs like in Hamburg, the usual war destruction to railways and ports like in Regensburg, and damage to factories that manufactured military aircraft like the Focke Wulf that was made in Marienburg. Now, in 1944, there were more air raids waged over

Germany, and the USA took part and aided in the RAF strikes. More fliers roamed the sky, *surely the war would be over soon,* I had thought while listening to my tato's translation of the news.

We had never divulged to Herr Baumann and his wife, that we hoped the Allied forces would win the war effort. They didn't need to know about our dream of going to America, either. If they had known, they might have thrown us out or handed us over as an enemy of Germany. *No, the Baumann couple were kind and wouldn't have done that to us, I know that positively.* I thought that perhaps the Baumanns hoped the Nazis would surrender, as well. They didn't appreciate the war's violence that was written about in the newspapers, and they were afraid of the Gestapo. *Was it the Gestapo who arrived at the farm the day we fled?* I hated not knowing the full truth. I prayed that the war would be over soon, then people could go on and live their lives in peace.

Suddenly, my father's voice jolted me back to the reality of my immediate surroundings. We were in the middle of the forest.

"We have no idea what's in store for us, but somehow our path is destined to lead us to America," he said. "That's a good thing because I like the music that they played on the radio station."

Petro laughed, appreciating the sentiment, then he bent over and gathered some long branches and busted them up for Mama to use to build a fire. When Tato said such things, it helped me to believe in a bright future again. If my father could joke, then all was right with the world.

"All these nights sleeping in the open air is good for our health," Mama said.

Then she started humming a hymn. Olena joined her voice, as we all made busy with the chores of setting up our little campsite.

The forest was beautiful, the fir trees filled the air with the thick scent of pine, reminding me of the enchantment we experienced on Christmas Eve. That was a memory I'd never forget, and I'll always remember the Baumann family with love for them in my heart.

The stars finally filled the night sky. We lay there in silence staring up at the glorious scatter, only the sound of the occasional owl, and Mama's and Tato's murmurs could be heard. They were making plans, deciding together what our next step would be, though I couldn't make out all the words, I understood the gist of the conversation.

As I gazed at the heavens, I imagined all kinds of things we could do and places we could visit in our future. We could live in a big city like New York and have a prestigious life among movie stars and famous people. The old magazine covers that I used to thumb through in Lviv came to mind. Beautiful French and German actresses were displayed across the racks, the covers showing off the clothing by famous designers. Photos of high buildings constructed by modern architects and posters printed in the Nouveau style filled my mind.

Germany had led the way in contemporary films and built many music halls. The culture was at the edge of art, and

I wondered if the famous places I had read about still existed. Would the movie stars all move to New York? Hadn't Hitler realized that the beautiful German cities would come to harm after his careless bullying all over the world?

It seemed like ages ago when I waited for Tato to complete his business in Lviv, allowing me time to scan the magazines. Photos of the famous movie stars posing for the articles captivated me. Spellbound, lost in the fantasy, I had been taken by their flawless faces, infatuated with their skin so smooth that the images glowed on the paper.

Color and glamor had filled the pages with the smiles of actresses like Ingrid Bergman and Rita Hayworth from America. Smoky eyes had looked back at me from the likes of Marlene Dietrich and Pola Negri. *Were those beautiful people, and the swanky clubs, and prestigious restaurants they visited still standing? Or had the war claimed them as well?* I wanted to find out, wanted to visit these places, and most of all, I wished to watch the films they performed in.

Sleep found me under the night sky, dreaming about stars of the human persuasion, and with the hope of someday meeting the beautiful women who had been displayed across the provocative advertisements.

CHAPTER 34

I awoke in the middle of the night, it was pitch dark, the stars were gone, hidden behind cloud cover, and I couldn't see in front of me. Then I heard mumbling.

"Petro, is that you?"

"Shh."

I waited for a second.

"Petro," I whispered. "Psst. Did you hear that?"

"Yes, it sounds like someone is talking nearby. Be quiet."

My brother was right, someone was talking close to us. The throaty, deep voice sent chills up my spine.

I closed my eyes and listened and tried to understand what they were saying. It was a strange language that I never heard before; the sounds didn't make sense. After a minute, the peculiar sound left and faded into the darkest dark.

"Who was that?" I whispered.

"I don't think that was anyone. It wasn't a human voice. Maybe it was a wild boar, they like to eat at night. Do you remember the fairy tales about the Bavarian Forest?"

I nodded, though Petro couldn't see me.

"You mean the Brothers Grimm?"

Petro turned around so that he faced me, still lying on his side but close enough now that I could see him.

"Have you heard of the Morbach Monster," Petro asked.

"No, what's that?"

"Well, it's a legend. It's kind of scary. Do you want to hear it?"

"Yes, tell me."

"No, I shouldn't—you'll never be able to sleep again."

I punched Petro in the arm.

"Ouch. Okay, I will tell you. But don't say I didn't warn you."

"I'm not a baby anymore, Petro."

"Fine. Listen, then. The legend begins with a soldier named Thomas Johannes Schwytzer. He served in Napoleon's Grand Army, back in 1812. Schwytzer failed as an officer, he wasn't able to conquer the Russians because the people of Moscow abandoned the city instead of surrendering. In a fit of anger, he ordered his men to set fire to the abandoned city. Schwytzer was a ruined officer without any spoils of war to show Napoleon after a battle. Worse yet, it had been winter, and his men suffered from disease and starvation, leaving the army defeated and fearing for their lives. Schwytzer did what any hothead coward would do, he deserted his men and left the remaining soldiers to fend for themselves.

"He fell in with a bad group of Russian deserters that were traveling to France. They stopped in a small rural German village called Wittlich, along their way. The men desperately needed supplies, so they raided a nearby farmhouse. Tragically, the family was home, so the bad band of deserters murdered the entire family."

I sucked in my breath.

"That's awful. Did they get caught and punished, Petro?"

"Well, according to the legend, the farmer's wife was the only survivor. She saw the slaughter. Watched from her hiding spot in a wardrobe. Frozen with fear for her life, she was. They killed her husband and sons, so the woman placed a curse on Schwytzer. As the ruffians were leaving, she went crazy, lost all her fear and cried out a curse aimed at Schwytzer, 'At every full moon, you will change into a rabid wolf!'"

"Did the wife live?"

Images of the traumatized woman filled my mind. *What if that had been Mama?* I knew she would be brave enough to stand up for us against an evil monster.

I heard something in the nearby woods. I pulled myself together, tightening up every inch of muscle into the tiniest ball I could muster.

"Sorry to say, no. The wife did not live. Schwytzer was so infuriated with the woman that he crushed her skull. He stomped on it until it caved in then crushed it between his hands."

Petro moved his hands as if crushing something between his palms.

I punched his shoulder so he'd stop.

"But, it was too late," Petro continued, "the soldier had already begun to change because of the curse. He became a monster and continued to do crimes. He embraced the brutality of robbing, raping and murdering and his appetite for debauchery and blood lust grew so much that the other deserters left him, in fear for their lives.

"Then one night, Schwytzer turned into a werewolf and abandoned civilization altogether. He made a separate camp for himself, far away in the woods."

"So there's no more werewolf, no more monster," I said.

"Whispered tales of a wolf that walks tall like a man soon spread among the villagers. Then the killings began. The mysterious wolf was blamed for the brutal slaughter of the local livestock. Of course, they suspected Schwytzer. The whole thing was costing them their livelihood. Herds were being slaughtered. But there was little evidence to connect him to the crimes . . . until one day, Schwytzer made a big mistake."

Petro stopped for a moment.

"I don't know if I should tell you about this part."

"You must tell me, now, I'll die if I don't know how it ends."

"Okay then, you asked for it. One night as he prowled the forest for his next kill, he spied a beautiful farm girl. His lust grew as he stalked her through the woods, following her as she walked down the path. Then he pounced and raped the young woman named Elizabeth Beierle."

"Disgusting. That's horrible."

I closed my eyes and tried to block out images of a were-wolf hurting the farm girl. I pictured her with blonde hair, braided and pinned to the top of her head.

"Later, a group of villagers decided that they wanted justice," Petro said.

"They ambushed Schwytzer as he sat by his campfire, and they demanded that he pay for his crimes. Schwytzer fled, and being a werewolf, he was fast, but the mob relentlessly pursued him. They were fired up with revenge in their hearts. They cornered him in the village called Morbach. The vigilantes killed Schwytzer on the spot and buried his body."

"So, he's dead."

I swallowed, waiting for my brother to confirm the kill.

"Yes, he died."

"Hooray," I said.

My body loosened up, relieved by the knowledge that the werewolf had been caught.

"But—

I turned my head and tried to see my brother's face...was he kidding me?

"The vigilantes took the woman's curse seriously. They believed that Schwytzer was a werewolf, who could come back on the next full moon. So, they made a shrine at the gravesite with a candle that burned, and they kept it lit forever to prevent him from returning in the form of a werewolf. Legend says as long as the candle is burning, the creature will be bound to the grave."

"Good."

"Yes, but what happens if the candle goes out on a windy night? What if there's no one left to check on it?"

Just then a breeze gently touched my face, the skin on my right arm felt the flutter, and my hair stood up on end.

"That place is very close to here," Petro said. "Nestled in the Bavarian Forest. Perhaps that sound we heard earlier was the Morbach Monster, running through the woods, looking for another victim."

The idea of a werewolf hanging around in the forest made my blood rush.

"No, it wasn't a monster," I said. "It sounded like people—someone speaking a different language. Maybe they are trying to escape the Nazis like us."

I said it more to convince myself.

"I'd rather face a werewolf than a Nazi monster," Petro said. "But if I do face someone who wants to kill us, I will rush him, pound him to the ground, and crush his skull in, like Schwytzer did."

I punched him again. Petro's voice sounded committed to the idea, and I wondered when he started to think about killing other people. For so long, our parents have tried to protect Petro from being recruited as a soldier, but he sounded like he wanted some kind of revenge. That thought scared me more than anything.

"We should try to go to sleep, goodnight, Petro."

He reached over and messed up my hair.

"Goodnight, Ivan. I hope I didn't scare you, too much."

TRAIL TO GERMANY

CHAPTER 35

Daybreak came too soon. Tired, I stretched and looked around. The sun was beginning to show its color. I rose, trying not to disturb the others and walked to the edge of the hill and looked down. In the valley below the rolling hills were filled with a dense ghostly fog that lingered throughout the timbers, wrapping itself around the trees and branches as a ribbon weaves through a girl's curl. In the denser areas, only the tops of the fir pines showed themselves like dark spikes popping from within the phantom mist. The wind picked up, moving the fog, mysteriously slithering away, as if it were alive. There could have been a dragon sleeping in its lair below, the scene was magical enough.

I'd never seen a more beautiful sight, it was hypnotic. I closed my eyes, tried to memorize the scene in my mind, opened them again, and closed them once more. I wanted to paint those muted gray and green colors, to record the moment of that slow, laborious movement as the mist roamed across the trees so that I could remember it forever. Birds screeched from all directions, caws and elusive songs, all early risers looking for their meal before the sun began to scorch the grass dry.

"Ivan, come back and get yourself ready."

I heard my name called. Mama was in charge this morning. I trudged back to the campsite and gathered my things, packed them tight in my sack, then followed Petro's lead as we searched for the stream to fill the bottles. We all bent down and washed the sleep from our face, rinsed our mouths, then took our fill of drink. When our morning rituals were completed, we went back to our small campsite for breakfast.

I knew something was up, Tato wore his serious scowl, and Mama kept herself moving around and checking our packs, like a nervous chipmunk storing away nuts. Finally, we were all sitting on the ground munching on a breakfast of wild raspberries and a few chestnuts that remained from those we had roasted the night before. Our parents explained the new agenda.

"We've decided that it's too dangerous to remain in the Bavarian Forest," Mama said. "Here, deep in the woods, there are too many wild animals, and we have nothing to protect ourselves."

"Mama, we can each make a staff and use it to keep animals away, plus we could keep the fire burning longer at night. We could take turns as watchmen."

Petro wanted to remain in the forest like me. I nodded my approval.

"The dangers are more than wildlife, son. We've heard that the German soldiers are executing men along the dirt roads here, a bit closer to the villages. We hoped it wasn't true, but the other night we heard shots fired," Tato said.

He wiped his mouth and squinted his eyes.

"In other words, staying in the forest isn't without troubles. And we know firsthand that they use dogs to hunt out people hiding. People like us. Though we aren't Jewish, how different are we? Even if we give them our vow that we aren't Jewish, who's to say a soldier would believe us anyway, seeing us hiding as they do. Leaving and getting back to civilization will save us from being accosted in the woods by a trigger-happy soldier."

I wasn't happy about this decision, why, summer was only beginning, and I'd much rather stay in the forest. But our parents had made their decision and didn't care what I thought about it.

"The Germans are after Jews, and we aren't Jews," Petro said. "We're Ukrainian."

"Yes, the same Ukrainians they need to work for them," Tato said.

Petro threw down a stick he had been holding and stormed away.

"Get back here, now Petro."

Tato's face turned ten shades of red.

Petro's fists balled into hammers, ready to punch. He raised them, turned and hit a tree. Mama ran to him and grabbed his hands.

"Petro, are you all right?"

Petro shrugged and stepped back, lowering his head. It was quiet for a few seconds but it felt like an eternity. Things were so strained between my brother and father.

My stomach twisted and my veins raced with a fear that this was bad.

"Look, I agree to do as you say," Petro said. "You're my father, after all. I suppose you're right, it would be best to go look for work. We can't hide in the woods forever."

I knew that he was still angry, yet he caved to father's wishes. *Turncoat.*

"I want to stay in the forest," I said.

No one heard me. I repeated myself, resorted to stomping my foot.

"I want to stay here, in the forest, away from the other people."

"Stop behaving like a baby," my brother said.

Then he glanced at me and winked.

"We have work papers with us. It's better to work for the enemy than to be caught by them and killed," Tato said.

"Tato, you're good at talking with people," Olena said. "I'm confident you can keep us safe no matter where we go."

"Of course, he can," Mama said.

"Your tato can persuade most, and your father never had a better reason to sway others. If it means our safety, then he will convince whoever we stumble across that we are no threat. We are good people, and only want to make our way."

"I want to stay in the forest. It's summertime, Tato. It would be fun."

I pleaded and stomped my foot, one last time.

"Fun. No. We will find work someplace where they can use us and then at least we will have a roof over our heads. No more talk about what is fun," Tato said.

"Eventually the Allies will take over, and when that day comes, we should be there, wherever there is, but it most certainly is not in the woods."

My father looked more confident than he had in days, and I hated to be the one who went against him. But it felt wrong to me, going to an unknown country, begging for work. I would miss being here in the dark, rich forest. I had to speak my mind.

"What if we meet up with an unscrupulous Nazi who doesn't care about our papers, or worse, end up somewhere that gets bombed? Isn't that a danger, too, Tato? What if they take Petro and me away to fight at the Eastern Front?"

My brother kicked the side of my leg and glared that *'shut up kid'* stare. I had no idea what his game was, but I still didn't want to go to a city.

"Yes, Ivan, yes. But it is a chance we must take. I need to believe that there are still some German people who have a conscience like the Baumanns, and people like us who believe that doing what they have to do to survive can still be humane. I pray the soldiers will be returning home, soon. No more fronts to fight if they all fall."

CHAPTER 36

We hiked northwest through the forest. My brother walked by my side, waiting for a chance to say something privately to me. Finally, we turned a corner and ran ahead for a short distance. Petro turned and grabbed my shoulders, so I had to stop.

"Why do you keep teasing Tato with your whining? Ivan, if we go to a city I might be able to sign up to fight with the Allies. Don't mess things up for me."

Then Petro nudged me back a bit, turned, and kept walking. I followed and the others soon caught up to us. I wondered why my brother wanted to be a soldier, knowing that our father discouraged that kind of behavior.

It had taken us most of the day to find a small road with sporadic traffic. We walked alongside the curb for the remaining afternoon and into the evening, prepared to explain to anyone who stopped us that we had work papers and were hoping to report for duty at a factory somewhere in Germany. It hadn't been our fault the train was bombed, nor that we survived.

Maybe then a stranger would give us a lift to a place where we could live if we remained cooperative. Tato would do his best to keep us together, as always, a family. Nobody stopped, no-one noticed us. Others were walking ahead of us. People like us, displaced by war. We seemed to have more energy and passed them as we continued on our way.

Late in the night, a loud truck drew near. I heard the grinding gears as the driver shifted down for the approaching incline. His load was getting closer, his breaks squeaked.

I wondered if we should hide at the curb, but Tato kept walking, ignoring the truck, and we followed him like the little ducklings we were. It was pitch dark until the headlights appeared, casting our shadows down upon the pavement. They stretched and made us seem bigger than life. Tato turned around and watched it descend the steep hill, then we all turned around, the headlights blinded us.

The heavy truck stopped; it was lifted high off the ground with large, thick rubber tires. It seemed to be an army vehicle of some sort. German voices called out for us to halt. My heart skipped a lot of beats, and I think I stopped breathing.

Tato raised his arms and explained who we were. They allowed my father to fish the papers from his jacket pocket. One of the men grabbed the papers and stood reading them, nodding. He handed them back to Tato and motioned for us to climb into the rear of the truck.

The other soldier took my sister's hand to help her up, he smiled at her. He was young and handsome.

Mama pushed herself between him and my sister and heaved Olena into the back of the truck. We all piled in and sat on the hard metal benches. The truck immediately took off, nearly knocking me to the floor with the jerk.

The night air was crisp, and we wrapped our arms around one another to keep warm. The engine's roar soon turned into a rhythm that lulled me into a semi-sleep. I leaned my head against my mother's shoulder and imagined the sound was rushing water, flooding into a lake. I envisioned blue skies and the warm yellow sun. My vivid dreams warmed me inside.

The ride lasted a few hours. Finally, the truck jerked, the brakes scraped, we were jolted back and forth. A man opened a flap door and ordered us to file out. We stood on the sidewalk while the driver spoke with Tato. He nodded and seemed satisfied with whatever the man said to him. Tato folded his papers, stuck them in his pocket, and joined us.

"There's an office on this street where we can register for work and find a bed to sleep on," Tato said.

We picked up our bags and walked half a block. It was dark, sometime around midnight, and it was a challenge to make sense of our surroundings. The buildings we passed were constructed of old brick, stone, some stucco, knit tightly together with hardly any side alleys between them. The air was cold from a breeze coming off the river, though I couldn't see it, I recognized the fish smell rising from the turbulence.

We stopped in front of a shabby storefront. There was a light shining onto the sidewalk from the window, making slanted box designs on the concrete. The exterior lights were turned off or broken.

"This is it," Tato said.

Mama frowned.

"Are your certain, Taras?"

He nodded, and we stepped into the old shop. A small bell attached to the top of the door jingled as the door opened. My father walked to the counter and rang the handbell. An angry-looking, little man appeared from behind a doorway and made his way to the front.

Tato handed over the paperwork. The little man sat on a stool that was behind the counter, and he read through the papers slowly, as if reading a novel. He turned each page with thoughtful nods. When he read the parts the soldier had penned in the margin, the old man looked over at the three of us kids standing awkwardly near the closed door. Whatever the soldier had written worked like a charm. The man stamped the pages with a loud thump and then signed the pages with a flourished pen swipe as well.

"Welcome to Regensburg," he said with a gruff tone, and he stood.

The man's height barely extended past the counter's height. He directed us into a back room, and we followed.

"Here's how it will go. The women will be sent every morning to sew. Different places on most days but close by and within walking distance. Mostly you'll be mending uniforms. Stop at the counter in the morning to get the address for the day."

Mama nodded and gave a sideways glance at Tato. He squeezed his eyes once and confirmed everything was all right.

The angry little man twitched his head as he read from a ledger. I couldn't stop staring as the mustache over his mouth moved up and down strangely when he spoke.

"You," he pointed to my tato, "will go to the ball-bearing factory, or the aircraft factory, at least to what's left of it. A bus comes at daybreak to take the workers there. It's clean up labor."

"That sounds fine," Tato said.

"Your eldest son will be fitted for a uniform tomorrow, then he will enter training."

"Training? Training for what?" My mama took hold of the angry man's arm, and he was forced to look up at her.

"Frau, you are aware that since January all boys, sixteen and older, have to report for duty?"

My parents nodded.

"Yes, we heard an announcement a while ago," Tato said.

Mama had tears in her eyes, a few rolled down her cheek like shiny silver tinsel that reflected on her face from the soft light of the lamp.

"There's nothing I can do, it's out of my hands."

The man turned away and ignored her sadness.

"Good, we understand each other. Last the younger boy. He will remain here and work for me doing errands as I need things done. There is a basic apartment upstairs, you will live there. Be ready to board the bus early tomorrow, at day-break."

He didn't allow for any more responses or questions, but pushed ahead, and waved for us to follow him. We climbed an old squeaky staircase nestled in the back of the building. The old man withdrew a ring of jingling keys from his jacket pocket and unlocked an old wooden door. We were led into a one-room apartment. The place smelled strange—a mixture of dankness covered up by sour vinegar.

"Well, here you are, this is the place where you can sleep. Just enough beds."

There was a small stove and sink in the corner, and four beds with pillows and blankets rolled up waiting for the next customer.

"The bathroom is down the hall."

He pointed then exited, leaving the door open.

As soon as the little man left, Mama sat at the edge of a bed and started to cry. She whispered in a desperate tone.

"Taras, we can't let them train Petro to fight. This cannot be. They will send him to the front line."

Her tears morphed into sobs.

Tears smarted the corners of my eyes, too, and I wanted to throw myself to the floor and have a tantrum, screaming out, *I knew we should have stayed in the forest. Now, they will take Petro away from us.*

"Don't worry Mama," Petro said.

He knelt in front of her lap.

"I promise to stay safe, no matter where they send me. Besides, I won't leave right away, not for a long time. It takes months to train a soldier. The war will be over before they need me."

She smiled at that, grabbed my brother, and squeezed him.

"Don't worry, Petro, your father and I will think of a way to get you out of this situation. You will not be sent away from us. We will pray all day and night."

She scowled up at my tato, and he nodded. He lowered his eyes, they shadowed the sadness and anger we shared.

CHAPTER 37

Olena ventured to the sink first and was happy to find running water.

"Eek!" she screamed.

"What is it?" Mama ran to her, then smiled. "No worries, it's only a spider."

"Mama, I don't like this place."

Mama stroked Olena's hair gently then grabbed her shoulders almost in a hug.

"Don't worry. We'll clean this place up in no time, and soon it will feel like home. Finish up now, wash your face, and let your brothers have a turn. It was a long day."

We all washed our faces, Petro even splashed water under his arms.

Mama found a pan near the stove and filled it with water. She struck a match and lit the old gas stove, I smelled the gas fumes that escaped before the flame lit, it made me nauseous. She opened and closed more drawers and doors in the kitchen corner, some were cock-eyed and didn't close tight, so she slammed them into place.

She finally found an old silver tea tin; it was dinged up a bit but still had some Earl Gray leaves remaining. She spotted an old teapot and poured the boiled water and let the tea steep. We had a pot for us to share and a box of Leibniz keks, a German shortbread biscuit. The snack filled our stomachs enough to let us sleep in peace without hunger pangs.

We each took a small bed, Mama and Tato shared the largest and fell sound asleep.

Before I drifted off, I heard my father drawing in deep breaths, my sister whimpered in her sleep, and the floorboards creaked. I sat up in bed and listened intently. Someone was out in the hallway. A door opened and closed, and then it was quiet again.

"Go to sleep, Ivan."

Petro sounded annoyed.

I laid back down and tried to block out the strange noises. I decided to say my prayers and must have fallen asleep right away. The next thing I knew it was morning.

A sound woke me. I opened my eyes. The room was dark. Where was I? I felt achy in my arms and legs and was still tired. The bed my brother slept in squeaked and reminded me that we were someplace in Regensburg. I cursed to myself, the morning had come too quickly. I tried to pretend that I was back in Halych, in my comfy bed with fresh linens, but the memory of it was too far away.

It was no use. I stretched my legs and arms then rolled out from my skinny bed, lifted my body from the squeaky spring mattress as quietly as I could manage, went to the window, and looked out through the dusty grime.

Regensburg wasn't a large city, but it was old and hugged the Danube River, which I hoped would make it an interesting place. I watched as a few small boats went by, they drifted past the larger ships that were moored and sunk at the shore. The sun was still hiding but leaving enough light to see the early birds on their way to work, or wherever it was they were heading to.

Color wasn't discernible yet, everything was a washed shade of grayish tan, perhaps as the day dawned, the sun would brighten things up. Colorful things intrigued me, that's one of the reasons the forest was one of my favorite places. Petro said that they called it the Dark Forest. Still, I had seen for myself the many shades of green, the small bright flower buds popping out from the crevices of the rocks, and the blues and reds of the birds. It had been a rainbow there compared to the city street I spied below.

I sighed thinking about my destiny as a helper for the little angry old man. I wasn't looking forward to the day, but at least my family would return in the evening, and we were safe here. We were together and luckier than many displaced people.

My brother and sister mumbled something to me about taking my turn in the bathroom. I turned around and saw that everyone was awake now.

"Ivan, go wait in line," my father said.

I looked down the hallway and saw that the other people living in the building stood in a line, waiting their turn to use the toilet. I dragged myself to the end of the line, tried hard not to make eye contact with any of them, not to seem too friendly nor too awkward. Tato had said, try to fit in and remain inconspicuous. It felt weird for me because I was the curious type. Harder still because I couldn't make out half the things the people said.

I stood against the wall, moving up the line until I had my turn in the latrine then hurried back to our room to change into a set of cleaner clothes. We all had two sets, one to be cleaned, one clean enough to wear.

Mama held up a sheet to hide Olena as she dressed in her second outfit. It's odd to think of her so modest still, even though we had passed many bodies lying in the streets half-naked. We had seen many bad things along the roads.

Our parents tried to hide the atrocities from us, hurrying us away, but we knew others had been beaten, we saw their bruises. It only took a second to see that some women had been raped. When we slept in the parks in towns, we heard people crying out in pain in the middle of the night. And all too often we saw orphaned children who ran loose in the streets while trying to survive.

Mama tried to help a child once, but the boy took off, afraid that her kindness had a price. War was a sad business.

We never discussed the things we witnessed, we carried on, forged ahead, pretended it wasn't happening, and thanked God for our blessings. *'We have to look forward,'* my tato would say. *'You must remain, gentlemen,'* my mama lectured Petro and me.

What would the holy priest, the Arch Bishop Andrey Sheptytsky, say about what was going on? He had been upset about the prisoners who were killed in Lviv. I wonder if he knew about the farmers and everyday people in Poland, Czechoslovakia, and Bohemia who were tormented daily. We saw their suffering and experienced their pessimism as we marched aimlessly west looking for our future. Did the Arch Bishop know that Christians closed their doors and refused to help anyone, even if it was only a request for a piece of bread? What was happening in my hometown?

Daydreaming a bit, I was roused when Tato handed me an apple. He gave each of us one as he went over what was expected of us for the day.

Olena and Mama would be together, a good thing. Hopefully, whatever household they were assigned to for sewing would provide them with lunch.

"Petro," Tato said, "you will have to be brave, polite, and remain as unmemorable as possible while training. Listen carefully to what they say today. I'm certain they won't have you do anything bad on your first day. Train well and get physically fit, but do not volunteer for anything, you understand."

"I understand more than you know, Tato."

Tato placed kisses on each of our heads. "If we can get through this day, we'll make it," he said.

Tato left first. Mama grabbed his arm on his way out. He turned, and she reached up on her toes then kissed him so passionately that I had to turn my eyes away.

"Be careful, Taras."

Her voice was soft, seductive.

"I will be back for more, promise."

He pecked her forehead and smiled, then he trotted down the stairs and joined the other men who loitered in front of the building, waiting for the bus that would drive them away.

A man called out, "to the Messerschmitt factory."

An anxious pang attacked my stomach as I watched my father board the bus, and it drove out of sight. I wondered where he would go, what he would do, and why he thought it was a good idea for us to separate. What if tanks rolled down the street, what if Gestapo decided to arrest the angry little man I was supposed to work for? So many bad things could happen. My imagination went through many scenarios, each one got more dangerous and bloodier than the previous. My stomach knotted up, a burning sour, bitter-tasting acid rose in my throat, and for a moment, I thought I'd be sick.

"Come, Ivan, let's go downstairs. The old man is there already."

I followed the others down the creaking stairs then stood patiently waiting while Mama got the address and instruction for her first day's workplace. She nodded at the man and smiled, but he didn't smile back.

"Next," the old man said.

Another person stepped forward to the counter.

"Now you be a good boy today, Ivan."

"I'm not a baby. I'm twelve years old."

"Yes, I know." She smiled.

"Be alert. That man will call you over to the counter if he has something for you to do. In the meantime, try not to get into trouble. The man said you can sit here and wait."

She handed me a book, kept her firm grip over mine for a moment. Mama looked into my eyes intensely, and it felt as if she were memorizing everything in my head.

"Here, read this in between errands. I know how much you like castles."

My mother winked at me, removed her hand, then left through the front door with Olena and Petro. The bells above the door stopper twinkled as it closed. I was alone. The walls seemed to be falling around me, I felt dizzy for a moment, abandoned.

I looked down and saw the book my mother had slipped into my hands, read the title, and smiled. '*Lichtenstein*' by Wilhelm Hauff. A faint vision of the castle back home helped me recall this Swabian romance story of a man named Albert, who was in love. He fought in a war waged in the 1500s for a magnificent castle near the Black Forest and the Danube.

I noticed a wooden chair in the corner of the room and sat my butt down. The little old man acknowledged me with a nod. I explored the old book's pages, fanning the soft, worn sheets of paper. It felt good in my hands, smelled like a well-produced tome, then I flipped back to the beginning to read. I enjoyed the book though it was challenging to translate German in my head, so the time went by quickly.

CHAPTER 38

The clock on the wall chimed noon. The old man raised his head from his work and called out to me, grumpily.

"Boy, I need you to do a task."

I jumped from the seat, laid down the book, and hurried to the counter.

The man opened the bulky register. Chimes rang as the drawer opened just like in the department stores. He took out some paper money, but it looked different than any currency I had seen before.

This banknote was brown and had a young man's face on it, a pleasant-looking fellow, and toward the bottom, there was a bird. As he reached out to hand it to me, I saw the reverse side of the note which had a picture of a man and a woman posing, standing at attention, their somber gaze toward the center showing a public courtyard of some kind with a monument. *Very stuffy currency.*

I had never seen such money. When on the farm, Herr Baumann carried koruna, a paper currency that pictured a young man on one side of the note and a woman with a flower headband on the other side. The ink was a deep blue and purple, very bright and pretty. In Lviv, they had used brown karbovanets, but the picture on the note was a little girl holding flowers in her hands, the friendliest money I had ever seen.

"Here, take this," he said.

He impatiently pushed the notes into my hand.

"Go up two blocks away from the riverside, and you'll see a tavern named Mueller's. Go in there, and the manager will have a bag for you. Tell him Krüger sent you, then pay him with this money, and return the food here, to me."

Nodding, I grasped the notes.

"There's just enough for the food, you understand?"

I nodded again. My German wasn't as good as Tato and Mama could speak, but I had learned enough from Herr Baumann to know the basics, especially when it involved food. I rolled up the bills, stuffed them into my pocket, and left. Turning in the direction away from the river, I walked fast, taking long strides, and wondered if he intended on feeding me some of the food. I hoped so, my stomach was growling.

The street was reasonably busy, the stores were open for business but they didn't have many products displayed in the windows. Some of the people smiled at me as I walked by them, and I smiled back and bowed my head. Others frowned as they whizzed by without even seeing me.

Mueller's Tavern wasn't far. It was the only freshly painted building around, red brick and white wood trim, the store window had fancy gold lettering spelling out its name. I went inside and was greeted immediately with a bag held out for me to take. I handed over the money, and the man behind the cash register smiled down at me. I nodded.

Wasting no time, I headed straight back to the old man's storefront, *or was it an inn*? I had a creepy feeling, so I looked over my shoulder. Sure enough, I was being followed by three boys, each of them a little bigger than me.

I quickened my step, and they did the same. My breaths became raspy as I jogged faster still. Soon I was running as fast as I could, a full-blown sprint. The good thing about being small was that I was also fast and could run as if the devil himself was chasing me. I must have surprised them because it took a few seconds before I heard the pounding of their shoes chasing me. I ran as if I was in the Olympics competing against Jesse Owens himself.

But they were determined and caught up to me, only steps away from the angry old man's storefront.

One of the jerks pushed me from behind, slamming his fist into the center of my back. I went flying into the air and hit the ground. I felt the concrete scrape my knees, burning, stinging. Then a hard thud met my head, the same fate as my knees, but this time I saw bright lights and stars. I smelled blood, my blood.

The only thought in my head was the condition of the package. *What would the man do if his meal ended up squished, or worse if the boys stole it away?* They probably wanted the food all along, perhaps they were starving like me. I feared the consequences if they stole it, the old man would kill me, I just knew it.

Splayed out on the sidewalk, my legs and arms were spread like a dead frog's waiting to be dissected. I heard the boys laughing at me, and angry tears burned my eyes. I closed them tight, not wanting to see their jeering faces.

Then a voice hollered out, scolding the boys.

"Damn scoundrels," the voice shouted.

Next, I heard the sound of pounding feet. I looked to my left relieved when I saw that the boys were running away. A hand touched my arm. I winced.

"Are you all right, boy?"

I twitched, then opened my eyes. It was the angry old man—he was helping me up. He brushed the dirt off my trousers. I noticed a tear and swallowed hard, worried about what my mother would say. I didn't have another good pair of pants and these had been hard to come by in the Bavarian market.

Then the old man pulled up my pant leg and examined my knee.

"Tsk-tsk. You need Mercurochrome for those cuts. Come along."

I followed the man, then looked back.

"Wait. Your food. I have to follow those boys—"

"No worries, son. I grabbed the bag."

He lifted the brown bag in the air.

"Now come along. Let's hope the sandwiches aren't all ruined. If they are, we'll have to follow the boys and smash them up."

He chuckled at his jest.

Suddenly, the angry old man seemed an entirely different person. I couldn't help smiling as I followed him inside.

He dropped the bag on the counter and led the way into his apartment in the back. The room was small but neat. The furniture appeared comfy, a chair near the heater, and a sofa against the wall. He stared at me with squinting eyes, pointed, and I sat on the wooden chair near a small table in the corner. The man opened the door of his hutch and pulled down a metal box. He placed it on the table, opened it, poking his finger about until he found the medical supplies he wanted. He dabbed me with some red stuff, I winced. My cut stung, but it was tolerable. Then he covered the scratch with a bandage, and I had to admit, it felt better.

"Thank you, Sir."

He smiled.

"Call me Herr Krüger."

"Thank you, Herr Krüger."

He nodded.

"And what should I call you, besides, boy. Hmm?"

"Please call me Ivan. My name is Ivan Rudenko."

I bowed my head. This pleased the old man because he smiled. Then he placed his finger to his lips.

"Shush. We won't tell anyone about those nasty boys chasing you, okay. It will be our secret."

I nodded.

He indicated for me to rise, and we went back to the counter. Herr Krüger opened the bag, dug out the food, and turned the wrappers to inspect them. The sandwiches had survived. He handed me a ham and swiss on rye bread. A whiff of the smoky meat, the caraway seeds, and the tangy mustard spread reached my nose. My mouth salivated. To me it was a delight, it might as well have been roasted beef Stroganov like the wealthy tsars feasted on in St. Petersburg before the revolution.

"Thank you, Herr Krüger."

I was famished and devoured the food in minutes. The old man patted my head then motioned me back to the wooden chair. I picked up the book and read it for the remaining afternoon.

Though I tried to concentrate on the story, I found myself stopping to gawk at the little old man named Herr

271

Krüger. He was an enigma, a curious person to watch. Always stern, and a bit on the grim side, as if his family tree included trolls like the ones in the Scandinavian stories. Not another smile graced his face again that afternoon. As he performed his duties, his limbs acted mechanically, his body moved with short jerks as if he had rigor in his muscles.

I caught myself staring. Thankful that he never returned my prying gaze, I opted to finish the book and turned my head down to read.

The grandfather clock that stood in the corner chimed six. People began to stream in, they came and went. Some handed paperwork to Herr Krüger, others were men returning after work. They passed me to get to their rooms where they slept. As the people paraded by, I did my best to ignore them.

Petro returned, brushing past me in a hurry, I saw him as he fled toward the stairs. I smiled and followed him. He called back to me.

"I have to use the water closet before someone else hogs it."

I laughed and went to our one-room apartment, anticipating a great story about Petro's first day of training, and the adventures of his day.

CHAPTER 39

I laid back on my ratty cot and waited for my brother. As soon as he entered the room, I bombarded him with questions.

"How did it go? Did they yell orders at you all day? Did you have to march all day? Did you shoot a gun?"

"Slow down, Ivan. I can only answer if you take a break."

He messed up my hair.

"Well?"

I sat up and leaned forward.

"First off..."

He whispered and looked over his shoulder.

"The trainer is a madman. He was the opposite of polite. No matter how well I followed his commands, he barked louder and threw more orders at me. It was like being in a race or competition all day. Stand at attention, run to the end of the field, fall in line, over and over again. Some of the other guys around me, the German boys, they seemed happy as shit to be there."

"But not you, Petro. You don't want to be a German soldier. You're not one of those Hitler Youths."

Petro raised his finger to his lips and sat next to me on the bed. Closer, he whispered.

"Yes and no. Of course, I don't want to be in the stupid German army. They are so cruel. But I do want to be a soldier and wish that I could fight with the UPA for our Ukraine, and oh what I would do to join the American army. I should have been there, in Italy, helping those Canadians"

My eyes opened wide, even I knew it wasn't a good idea to say such things around here.

"Petro, you'd better shut up, you'll get in trouble. They'll kill you—shoot you dead."

"Don't get yourself worked up. I wasn't the only one who didn't want to be there. Two other Ukrainian boys were training, too. We spoke briefly until the trainer hit one of them in the head for not speaking German."

"Ouch, that must have hurt him," I said.

"No, not too much. By that time we were all kind of numb. Plus, he's a pretty big guy. Tough, you know?"

I nodded and kept quiet, so Petro would finish his story.

"I hope to talk with him again tomorrow if we get a break. There were others like us, too. Some Polish, some Bo-hemian, some from the Carpathian Mountains, and none of them want to fight. I can tell. But they had no choice if they wanted to live. You can't refuse the German's training. The alternative is that they will kill you and your entire family."

I closed my mouth, which unconsciously had drooped open.

"Did they threaten you, Petro?"

He shook his head.

"No. That's something the big guy told me, it happened to another Ukrainian boy, the day before last. He's already gone—sent to the front."

"Oh."

My gut felt sick. Suddenly the probability of my brother being in the war became too real. Especially bad because he would be on the wrong side. The idea of our family being threatened if Petro didn't comply with the Germans scared me to death. I remembered how the soldiers had stormed into the church and stole all the gold crosses, and challises then killed all the Jews from our town, murdered by the river for no reason.

I squeezed my eyes shut and tried my hardest to repress the memory, tried to block it out before the idea morphed into a vision even worse. Too late, I envisioned my family standing by the river's edge, blindfolded, being executed with lethal bullets.

My stomach ached, and I laid down on the cot before I puked.

"Are you okay, Ivan?"

"Yes. I'm fine."

I lied. I felt woozy. Before I fainted or worse, I needed to change the subject, to get my thoughts elsewhere. I babbled the first thought in my head.

"My day was spent reading and trying to run away from bullies. Not as impressive as yours."

I smiled though I remained resting on the cot.

"Bullies? Who? I'll punch them in the jaw."

"Thanks, but it's not necessary. They won't be bothering me again."

A voice bellowed from across the room.

"Who won't be bothering you again?"

"Tato!"

My brother and I both called out.

I jumped off the bed and ran to my father, grabbed him around his waist, and hugged him tightly. His shirt was filthy and smelled of burnt oil. I didn't care. All kinds of worry left me at that moment. I felt safe with him so close—touchable.

"So, what happened? Were you a good boy?"

"Oh, it was nothing. I had to fetch sandwiches for Herr Krüger, and a couple of boys followed me back. They pushed me, but only my knees got scraped. See."

I pulled up my trousers and showed off my bruises.

"Herr Krüger came out and shooed them away. Then he gave me a sandwich."

"Very good, *dobryj chlopec*." Tato smiled.

"Is your mama back yet?"

Just then, she entered the room.

"Here I am, Taras."

He left my side to hug Mama. They talked with each other about their respective day, mumbling into each other's ears while still embracing.

"Who the hell is Herr Krüger?" Petro asked. He punched my leg to get my attention.

"It's not nice to swear, Petro." Olena's eyebrows were wrinkled-up so tight that her face looked ready to crack.

"You're not my boss, Olena. And stop making that face at me, you scare me."

My sister stomped closer and punched Petro in the arm.

"Ouch. Stop you brat."

Mama stepped between them. "There will be none of that in our family, understood?"

We all nodded.

"After your father finishes washing up, I'll lay out our supper."

"Looks like that will take a while," I said.

I jerked my head toward father with a wide grin spread across my face. Petro laughed. My mother and Olena gave little notice to my jest, they seemed to have lost their sense of humor today. I guess the sewing job was worse than it sounded. I know the thought of sitting around with a bunch of ladies sewing scared me.

Things settled down while we ate our bread and cheese dinner, and drank the broth Mama heated up. We each spoke about our day.

Petro explained how he marched all morning and then did physical stuff all afternoon in the summer heat; he was exhausted and ready for a good night's sleep.

Olena and Mama sewed with the other women in almost complete silence the entire time. "Mostly, we mended uniforms. A few women had wash duty and laundered the repaired items. I'm not sure which is the better chore," Mama said.

"You mean you had to sew the uniforms with blood-stains still on them?" My queasiness returned.

They both nodded with no additional gory details.

"What did you do today, Tato? Looks like dirty work."

Petro was quick to change the subject. He pinched Tato's sleeve between his fingers, pulling his head back as he inspected his shirt. They were both sitting on the cot.

I sat on his other side and waited for the answer. I was curious about the place where Tato worked and had no idea what a factory looked like inside. I only recalled the things that Kosko had mentioned when he had chatted with tato about the factory in Lviv.

"I shoveled all day," Tato said. "Debris was scattered everywhere since the bombings last spring. A building that size takes years to restore even with many men working. But we were a small crew, ten of us. Most of the German men are in the ranks, you know, fighting for Deutschen Vaterland. Pfft."

Tato looked down at the floor, then up at Mama. It seemed like he wanted to say something, then changed his mind. He cleared his throat.

"It was a job."

"Tell us all about it," Petro coaxed. "The factory, I mean."

"The factory was bombed last August, on the 17th by the Allies. The other men said that the summer of '43 saw many bombings land in Germany, all over. Said, the AFN Europe radio station had called it Operation Juggler."

"You get to listen to the radio?" Petro leaned forward, looking impressed.

"Yes, they listen to the American station. They probably think they can catch secret messages or something." He laughed at this. "I guess the radio news had mentioned the operation that bombed the factory. They talked about the raid and how the Allies targeted the oil refinery and the manufacturing plants."

Tato stopped and smiled. "Today they played American music on the radio. I enjoyed the music, I admit it."

"Tell us more, Tato."

I wanted to know everything, so I could visualize it in my head. I didn't know much about the Americans. I wanted to know about the music, what they joked about, what they ate.

"Well, one of the bombed factories had produced ball-bearings. Another close by made the Messerschmitt Bf 109, the backbone of the Luftwaffe's fighting force."

"Wow." I heard myself gasp. "I'm glad they bombed those targets. Now they can't make planes."

I crossed my arms over my chest and felt as if I were older. Tato reached over and ruffled my hair. Suddenly, I was a young boy again.

"It only slowed the production for so long. In a far corner of the building, I saw an area roped off with signs that said to stay away. I only caught a glimpse, but they were piecing together a few of the torn-up aircraft parts. It's still nothing close to real production. No. No other planes have been made since the bombing raid," Tato said.

"What did the fighter plane look like?" Petro asked.

"I didn't get a chance to see one of them up close, but I hope I'll get a peek at one eventually."

"If they keep getting bombed, they'll have to surrender. I hope we don't get crushed during a raid," I said.

"Maybe the Germans will give up soon."

I wondered if Tato would consider sabotaging the fighter plane to help the Allies. No, Taras Rudenko believed in peace, he didn't want to harm any side. He wouldn't kill a soul, not even a Nazi if he could avoid it. God's commandment, *Thou shalt not kill*, meant something to my father. He only wanted to keep his family safe.

"Taras—"

Mama called to get his attention. He turned around.

"Some of the women were talking about school for the children."

My attention immediately perked.

"Do you mean there's school available for our children, Leysa?"

She nodded.

"There's an abbey here that they mentioned. I wonder if they might be able to teach the children. It would be wonderful for them to be exposed to Church again, don't you think? It is, of course, the Latin Rite, but it's still the Church."

My father sighed. No one said a word. Time stretched while we each thought about the idea of school.

I liked the idea of going to school again but wasn't keen on going to an abbey. I envisioned being surrounded by a bunch of bald monks, all dressed in brown robes with rope for a belt, perhaps they would use the rope to beat us. Or worse—a bunch of old veiled nuns donned in an elaborate habit. The idea of school in an abbey sounded precarious to me.

"Let me ask around," Tato finally said, breaking the silence.

"Perhaps when I get a day off, if I get a day off, then I can explore this city. I'll find out who's in charge of the Church in this area. One man I worked with today had mentioned an Archbishop Dr. Michael Buchberger. I could send a letter to my friend, the Arch Bishop Sheptytsky over in Lviv, perhaps Andrey could put in a good word for us."

"I don't think the letter will get to him, Taras," Mama said.

Her voice, almost a whisper, as if she didn't want to say the words, but they were necessary, nevertheless.

"The Cathedral of St. Peter is the spiritual heart of the diocese in Regensburg. It's been the cornerstone of the faith for centuries. Of course, your friend, Andrey, must know of it, but no one from Galicia can help us. You know that, right?"

Mama tipped her head to meet my father's. They both leaned on each other for a moment, as if drawing strength from each other. I've seen them do this many times, but for the first time, I realized how important it was for them to decide things, together. Even war would never sever their relationship.

Petro interrupted, oblivious to the moment. "I know the one you're talking about. I saw the Cathedral today, on the way to the training field. It's beautiful, Mama. It's right in the center of the city. It's built in the Gothic style, such a beautiful Cathedral."

"Yes," Tato said, "a cathedral appeals to the heart of the worshipers, and it's where all the bishops meet, but above all, it's a place of prayer. Never forget why we have churches, children."

Mama nodded and chewed on a piece of her bread. "Wait a minute." Mama's face lit up like an angel. "Isn't that the church where the Regensburg Domspatzen Choir performs, where they sing the Liturgy?"

"Yes, Leysa, I almost forgot. They've sung there for centuries. Maybe Petro and Ivan can join them? This might be the best way to keep them safe."

My mother smiled, her blue eyes glowed with the happiness that she'd been missing for months.

"Wait one minute." Olena protested. "If it's a boys' choir, then what about me? I'm the best singer in this family. What will happen to me?" She pouted then started to cry, real tears rolled down her cheek.

"No worries, sweetheart." Mama cooed. "I'm certain there must be a girl's group as well. If not, we'll start one."

Olena nodded and wiped her eyes, accepting our mother's answer.

I wasn't sure what I thought of the idea of joining a Roman Catholic school to sing in its choir. The remaining evening sped by, and we all fell asleep without further conversation.

CHAPTER 40

Summer didn't last long. A few weeks after we arrived in Regensburg, the temperatures lowered noticeably, and an autumn nip was prematurely in the air. I wouldn't be surprised to see snowflakes fly soon.

Perhaps it was a good thing that we came to the city after all. Life in the mountains during a bitterly cold winter would have been too harsh for us without decent shelter. Last winter we had lived at the farm in Bohemia. I missed the old house, squeaky floors and all, and of course, I missed the Baumann family. I wondered what had happened to them after we left, that day we had fled and heard the shots ring out.

I thought of writing to them and inquire about how they were getting on, and then I could let them know what we were up to. No, I stopped myself mid-thought, got rid of that idea. I was chicken to know what happened to them, too afraid of what I might discover if by a miracle a letter even reached them.

Standing by the small window, I looked out toward the river. It was a dark day, overcast, and I heard the tapping of ice chips against the glass. It was sleeting. The foliage along the riverside had barely turned colors, and I had hoped to take a walk to enjoy the beauty of the trees before it was lost. Not today. I prayed the weather would warm up before all the leaves fell to the ground.

"What are you staring at?" Petro asked.

I turned my head and gazed at my brother, he looked different, harder.

"Nothing," I said.

"Don't worry, the weather will change. You'll have a sunny day soon enough, and then you can walk along the path on the river, or better yet, we can go see that castle down the river a bit. I heard they have all kinds of beautiful plants and trees there."

"That sounds wonderful, Petro. We can go together."

A smile crept across his face, and then it disappeared. "Yes. We'd better try soon before the Germans decide to send me off to God knows where."

I stopped. A layer of perspiration veiled me, my heart beating faster than the second hand of a watch. I was terrified of the truth that I already knew.

"What does that mean?" I swallowed hard.

"I'm afraid, Ivan, that's exactly what I mean. The other German boys from my training group have already been sent away to the front. They weren't ready—they still had so much to learn—but they sent them anyway. I'm afraid they'll send me and the other Ukrainian trainees to the Russian front soon. My only hope is that they remain unsure of me, wondering if I'd like to go back to the front and join the Russians as my comrades. They have no idea with us Ukrainians, if we'd like to fight with the Russians or if we hate them enough to kill them all."

Tato laughed at this remark. I hadn't seen him standing there.

"Don't worry, Petro. We will keep you safe. I've managed to talk with a couple of the local leaders and persuaded them for a favor. The Church will help us out, they will take the three of you into school soon, we're waiting for the paperwork to sign. Then you'll be excused from the training and allowed to go to the Catholic school and study to be a priest. Classes begin next week."

Olena jumped to her feet and danced in a circle, laughing. It was the first time my sister was happy for a long time.

"A priest! Tato, what have you done?"

I stopped and turned. Petro's face paled like a piece of distressed wood that I'd seen on a lake's shore, bleached by the hours of laying in the summer sun.

Tato let out a hearty laugh, so loud that it shook the room. He bent over holding his side and tried to control himself, but soon the laughter became so infectious that we all laughed along with him, except Petro.

"Seriously, I don't want to be a priest," Petro called out. "I like girls very much, Tato, and want to get married someday."

Tato covered his mouth before speaking, taking control of his mirth, then stood and leaned, one hand on the back of a chair and the other raised.

"No worries, son. They don't need to know right away that you have no intention of being a priest. First, you get into the school and go down that path for now, whatever it takes to keep you safe. Scots Monastery will take you into their fold and teach you, you'll get an education. It's the best way to keep you from being taken to the front."

Though my father had been laughing at first, his tone became harsher by the time he ended his sentence.

"Isn't that lying?" Olena said. She wasn't laughing anymore, either.

I tried to remember her last happy moment, that last day at the farm. She had held baby Herbert that morning, while

Frau Baumann heated breakfast. That seemed so long ago. I wished she would try to be happy like that again, for longer than a minute, it might make things better for her.

"Maybe, but it's a little white lie," Tato said. "While I don't suggest for any of you to tell white lies often, in this circumstance, it passes the test of decency. You see, it's a matter of life and death. Do you understand, Olena? Your brother's life depends on it, just like the time we had to hide him under the house, just like we lied about all the Jewish families that we helped sneak away."

My sister nodded, her face white as a ghost.

"You know what I think," I said aloud, feeling bold and sagely. "I think that we should all try to smile religiously. Every day. The more we smile, the better our chances of surviving this war without sadness in our hearts. Do you agree, Tato?"

He nodded at my idea, and his beaming smile lit my heart.

"So, from now on, Olena," I said, "you need to smile in earnest at least once a day. God will be watching."

She pretended to smile, I smiled back, and I meant mine.

Petro was having none of it. He scowled at Tato. Petro never liked being spoken to as if he were a child, I understood that, especially since he was older than me. I hated it, too. But my brother shouldn't be so stubborn right now. Tato was doing the best he could to keep us all alive.

CHAPTER 41

The next day when Tato came home to our small room, he burst through the door, excited. His face beamed; I had never seen him happier.

"Leysa, I have good news. Petro is accepted into the Monastery. He can begin tomorrow. God has answered our prayers."

My parents hugged for a long while, then Tato kissed my mother tenderly. They both turned their attention to Olena and me, grabbed our hands and we danced in a circle as we rejoiced together about the good fortune. We threw ourselves back and landed on the cots. We caught our breath, laughing heartily. It felt good to laugh aloud again.

"We don't have to worry about the soldiers taking Petro away to the front. He'll be safe now."

Mama looked years younger, her smile infectious.

"They said it would be weeks, but it had only taken days," Tato said. "We are blessed."

Olena added to the conversation as she always liked to do.

"I overheard one woman in the sewing circle talking about the choir. She mentioned that the Arch Bishop of Regensburg is friendly with the Führer. The Cathedral's Sparrows, that's what she called the choir. She said they sang for him."

Mama stood with her arms folded, her smile gone.

"I'm not impressed with such favor, but for our own son's sake, I'm thankful for the chance no matter who granted it, even if from the hand of an unethical bishop."

Mama began to sing. She did this whenever something troubled her, softly at first, then her song of thanks to God grew louder. Olena chimed in, and soon, the room was filled with the sounds of nightingales. My daily smile came easy at that moment.

We continued our cheerfulness for some time while anticipating my brother's return from his training. Time dragged, we kept watching the clock above the small stove.

The late afternoon turned into evening. Mama had the supper prepared, and repeatedly glanced at the door as if Petro would step through the entrance at any moment.

Our smiles long vanished, we watched the door. The songs were replaced with the quietness of anxiety. I feared the worst. My brother wasn't returning. The acceptance into school had come too late. Petro never returned to our quarters that night.

My father, too worried to eat his dinner of soup, left without a word.

I knew he was roaming the streets looking for my brother. When Tato returned a few hours later, he quietly sat awake. All night, he looked out of the window, down toward the street below, relentlessly squeezing his fist.

I tossed all night, unable to sleep. My gut was all twisted up inside. I looked toward the window and watched my father standing there, staring into the night. There was nothing to be done, that was the worst part.

An overwhelming feeling of hopelessness shook me from head to toe, and I cried silently, not wanting to bother my father with my boyish tears. He had enough troubles on his mind.

I watched the dawn's light as it slowly crept up the wall, spreading its warm golden glow across the room, chasing the drabness from the old papered walls. We woke from our half-slumber.

Mama stretched, then immediately rose and grabbed her coat. My father helped her put it on, then put on his own. They were destined for the training area, I knew without them saying a word.

Mama whispered to Olena and me.

"Stay sleeping on your cots for a bit, it's early."

She left the room, gently closing the door.

The idea of my parents walking into the enemy's territory armed only with parental anger made me nervous. I felt compelled to follow them to make sure they weren't arrested.

I grabbed my pants and pulled them up, yanked my jacket off the peg on the wall, and pulled my cap out from its pocket. I pushed my arm into the sleeve, while I hurried down the creaking stairs. The hallway was still dark, but Herr Krüger was awake. He nodded his head as I whizzed past him, I heard him calling out to me, but I couldn't stop. I had to catch up with my parents.

Spotting them, I remained in the shadows, tracking the sound of their footfall clapping against the sidewalk. The echo from their murmurs reverberated back to me, but I couldn't make sense of what they said, only mumbles and blurred noise.

When we reached the public square, I stayed at the corner of a brick building and watched my parents walk across the dark, barren space. Oblivious to anything around them, they were only concerned about finding Petro. My parents bothered the early morning birds roosting, as they trekked across the cobbled pavement.

Birds flew up and away. I heard their wings flapping, pounding hard against the brisk wind, as they took flight toward the tops of the buildings surrounding us. They settled on the rooftops, the coos whirred in the drizzle.

Remaining hidden at the end of the courtyard, I listened for any clue that my parents were successful at finding the training troop leader. But only heard them talking with each other.

"Not a soul around. What does this mean?"

Mama's words sounded hollow.

"I'm afraid to think of it, Leysa. Could they all be gone off to the war's front? Impossible. Wouldn't they tell us first?"

"I knew it was wrong here," Mama cried out. "You promised to keep him safe. Damn you, Taras."

Then my mother's contempt filled the emptiness. I heard her agony, rising like so many laments I had heard before, but this time the trigger was personal. Sorrow held me down to the spot, I couldn't move or see, only a fragmented image of my brother crossed my vision. I wished so hard that he would step out from the shadows and pound me in the shoulder like he used to do. I hated his punches but would welcome his worst rather than feel this fear and emptiness.

The smell of fresh morning bread wafted across the street. I turned and saw a vendor setting out his goods. The shelves of his stand were filled with new loaves from the bakery down the road. Everything was coming to life, doors to shops opened, people began to wander into the street. Some men were sitting on the benches reading newspapers.

Life was happening all around me, but I felt dead inside. The sound of my mother's words echoed over and over in my mind.

EDUCATION BEGINS

CHAPTER 42

Weeks went by, and we each played our part automatically without any emotional attachment. We lived like paper dolls in a box, flimsy human beings without any joy. The daily smiles were forgotten, the idea of happiness was packed away into a hidden cupboard.

Olena was sent to the Dominican Convent where they had a school for girls. She was taught by nuns dressed in long black robes with dangling rosary beads. They wore a white headpiece with attached black veils. Students were required to behave with order and discipline. There were many rules. Rules were good for Olena, they made her feel secure and at ease, preferring to being told what to do. I hoped that she'd be happy there and would enjoy being able to socialize with other girls again.

When she returned to our room one weekend, I noticed dried tear tracks down her face. Olena confided in me that none of the girls were Ukrainian. She had a hard time understanding what was said. Two nuns at the school were nasty to her, they chastised her when she'd respond to them using Ukrainian. If she said she didn't understand them using German, then they'd slap her hand with a ruler. She said it didn't hurt much, but it had embarrassed her in front of the other girls. They giggled and whispered about her when they went outside for exercise.

I told her it didn't matter what they thought or did, and that the school was temporary. She only needed to try to learn as much as possible. Olena nodded as I gave her my sage advice, but I knew in my heart that her spirits were still broken. I only hoped that having someone to talk with about it had helped her.

Underneath it all, our biggest concern was Petro. We thought of him every day, and it was a challenge to go on while our brother was missing.

Once Catholic school began, I studied hard. I attended classes with the Domspatzen, better known as the Sparrows of the Cathedral. The Etterzhausen was an excellent prep school associated with the choir. Only the smarter boys of the German Youth attended. Singing for the Saint Peter's Cathedral Choir was an intense discipline.

Every morning we had music instructions given by the Director of Music himself. We sang our lungs out for hours. When we finally were given leave to go to our other classes, I found myself feeling bruised, my neck muscles strained, my back sore, from standing at attention for hours. Most afternoons were spent on lessons and reading.

I stayed in the dormitory during the week. I was assigned a bed in the younger boy's dormitory. Mine was the closest to the window, and at first, I was happy about my good luck to have a view of the courtyard below. But soon I discovered that no one else wanted that bed. Being close to the window meant it was the coldest spot in the room. I slept with my cap and gloves on.

I could only spend time with my family when I went back to our one-room apartment on the weekends. When my parents asked how things were going, I would answer, '*the assignments were difficult, the singing lessons stringent, but I'm thankful for the opportunity and I try my best'* and of course, Tato always replied, *'your best is all anyone can ask of you.'*

At first, I considered myself lucky to be allowed into the newly formed boarding school for boys. The current leader, Theobald Schrems, planned to turn the choir and the school into one of the best gymnasiums of Germany. He invited influential people to hear the choir perform, a money-raising effort for the school. A rumor that the choir performed for Nazi leaders was accurate.

Some of the boys from the higher classes told stories about all the places they had traveled to sing. They had visited France and even South Africa. I listened to the boys when they talked during lunch in the cafeteria. I envisioned myself in such places of wonder and hoped that my father would let me travel with them when I was ready. I still needed much practice before I could perform on the big stages. *Dare I dream of being prepared by the Christmas concert?*

A few of the teachers seemed sympathetic to my situation. They knew that I was a refugee, deemed a special case, and endorsed by the Church to attend. Most teachers, however, remained silent altogether, as if I was too lowly to be acknowledged. There was no question about my place in this school, I was the lowest rung on the ladder.

The teachers used a strict program. Some instructors employed hitting boys on the back with a ruler to get a point across. The foreigners, like myself, seemed to be the favorite targets for abuse, but it was especially stressful for me during singing classes.

We had a monster for an instructor. Our voices strained to be the perfect pitch to avoid his mental abuse. He randomly doled out demeaning comments. He swished his baton and pointed the stick in our faces. If we dared make a giggle or sound, he'd roll his tubby body close to block your view from the others, gave a personal sneer, then he slapped your face. His sharp tongue constantly reminded us that the expectations were high.

"How privileged you are to be here," he said. "Influential audiences await this choir's perfect harmony. Nothing less from you miserable jackanapes."

I knew who he referred to, this choir's population was mostly German Youth, and we were expected to sing for the Führer himself. I wanted to spit at the thought of him but wasn't allowed such frankness, it would be recklessness.

The charade made me ill, so I deflected my eyes to the ceiling as I sang to the instructor's directions. My singing was decent, I knew that much, so it would keep me safer than some of the other foreign boys who had been allowed into the fold. The sparrows needed my voice, and that was the only reason I was admitted.

The first week had been the hardest. Being a curious person by nature, I asked a lot of questions but soon realized that asking questions made me a target, or worse, I was labeled as stupid. One teacher, in particular, regarded my inquiries as rebellious behavior. I received my first corporal punishment during that first week and was ordered to the Dean's office. There I had to assume the position and allow the priest to paddle my bottom. Then I did as was expected, and thanked him for the privilege of the experience. I never felt more mortified and embarrassed in my life.

After that experience, I decided a new approach was needed. I kept quiet in the classroom, my mouth glued shut, and I put off my curiosity until after school. It was difficult at first because I was accustomed to speaking out about things. I wrote all my questions down in a notebook, much like the one my brother used to carry with him. On the weekend, I opened the tablet and asked Tato the questions instead. That adjustment in self-control saved me from future paddling.

I missed our old teacher from Halych, Pan Vasyklo, with his fancy mustache and his cane that he'd pounded against the floor. He had never struck it against our hand or rump, though he'd been a strict teacher, he was disciplined. He was the prince of tolerance compared to these teachers. Perhaps it was all his years of teaching at the university in Lviv that made him immune to overreacting to stupid questions. I missed the man, and his legends told of years ago.

As the weeks passed, I noticed the choir director becoming more cross during rehearsals, until one day he turned violent. Red-faced and puffing, the Director yelled the harmony was off. He snatched a bow from a violinist seated in the front row and swatted it across another boy's face. A deep red mark streaked his cheek, but the boy didn't budge a muscle. He sat there with tears running down his face while staring straight in front of him without uttering a word or whimper. Each day more examples of the director's temper happened, and every one of us in the choir dared not make the slightest movement or sound out of order. Little soldiers, we were stiff and performed exactly as told. I dreaded going to choir.

The main coursework was taught in the native German tongue, the Masses and prayers were said aloud in Latin. Trying to comprehend what was being taught became a rigorous mental workout for me. Learning the material was tenfold the ordinary effort, but I dug into the challenge and tried my best.

There were moments when I felt discouraged. My father reminded me of how fortunate I was to be gifted with the intelligence fit enough to attend such a school. He reminded me that I was safe there and getting an education. I knew my tato was right, I had no cause to grumble. Other people were chased from their homes and had to sleep in the woods during the cold months, trying to survive.

On second thought, perhaps they were the lucky ones, I would much rather be outdoors and living in the rough. But we were in the middle of a horrible war, I was reminded of it by the explosions heard from kilometers away, but close enough that the blasts made me cringe.

I was lucky, yes, I knew. But each day thoughts of my brother and the Baumann family shadowed me. *Were they alive and breathing still, or a casualty of this God-forsaken war?* This question burned in my soul, leaving me restless. All I wanted was to dream about castles far away, to think of old kings and princes, anything other than the horrible possibilities of my loved ones' fates. Nonsensical now, childish. How could I dream of castles and of being someone great one day when I couldn't even save my brother?

CHAPTER 43

One afternoon during our recess period, I stood outside in the courtyard and watched a group of boys playing kickball. Two boys began fighting over the boundaries for the game.

"The ball was in a safety zone," the first boy, Hans said.

"There is no safety zone." The second boy's name was Fredrick. His face was bright red, matching his fiery hair.

"You're a hothead." Hans yelled out across the yard as he went to stand with the other boys and continued with more ridicules about his hair.

"Your mother is Irish, not German. You're a mongrel."

Hans ran after him and threw a punch, hitting Fredrick's shoulder.

A spark ignited, and they clobbered each other, trading punches with clenched fists so tight their hands looked like red hammers. But that didn't last long, and soon they tussled about, pulling on each other's sweaters, and the argument evolved into something more like brothers' rough play, not arch enemies at war. The fight wasn't terribly dramatic, it was more like boyish throws swapped at each other. It seemed like harmless behavior and the fight wouldn't last much longer, losing steam by the second.

Unfortunately, the headmaster showed up and blazed his way toward the boys like an arrow, breaking them apart. The headmaster dragged both boys by their collars toward the corner of the building.

I watched, hoping they wouldn't get into too much trouble. I walked over and addressed the headmaster.

"Sir, I would be happy to help. Perhaps I can arbitrate, be the man in the middle, to help resolve the issues."

He looked down at me with wrath.

"Get out of my sight, before I send you to the Front with your brethren."

I swallowed hard. All the other boys looked at me jeering, not a friendly face in the crowd. I wondered if my father found such hate when he helped with disagreements.

I stepped back, my legs awkward as if I were a newborn giraffe. I mingled back between the other boys, trying to disappear. They all stepped away from me as if I were infected with a virus. I stood alone, waiting for their focus to leave me.

The headmaster turned back to Hans and Frederick.

"You like to fight, do you, well then you two delinquents can finish it here by punching the wall."

The headmaster stood brooding down over them, his eyes sneering slits, almost as if he were cursing the boys with his thoughts, shooting darts at them and piercing their bodies.

The two boys' reluctant fists hit the solid wall.

"Ouch," Hans said.

He looked back at me as if saying, thanks anyway. The slightest glance meant a lot to me.

"Continue until I say you're finished. Punch the wall again."

Hans and Frederick pounded the wall, and the rest of us gaped at the two of them as they smashed their bones against the hardened brick. I thought I heard cracking sounds, and my own hands ached.

"Harder, harder," the headmaster said.

His eyes were wide-opened now, bloodshot and angry. I had seen eyes like that before, on the old farmer who drank too much. Some days he behaved like an angry bull. I decided to steer clear of the headmaster from that moment on.

I heard each punch as it thudded against the wall. Each strike hurt my fingers more and more as if I had pounded the blows myself. I balled up my hands tight, trying to get rid of the ache. I tried to turn away but remained glued to the spectacle.

Blood dribbled from both of the boys' fingers and down their arms, dripping, forming dark splatters on the concrete. The faint smell of rusted iron floated in the air, and I became queasy. I never did like the smell of blood. Still, I was compelled to bear witness.

The boys winced and screamed with each new blow.

"Ouch."

It seemed like a long time before the headmaster ordered them to stop.

A teacher ran to the boys on an urgent medical emergency with a cloth to wrap around their bleeding knuckles. It was Father Martin, of course.

Father Martin was the nicest of all the teachers. He understood me when I spoke my broken German, and he never ridiculed my mistakes, but instead helped me to pronounce the words correctly. He tried his best to communicate with me in my language when he recognized the confused expression across my face. His attempt sounded more like Polish than Ukrainian, but his efforts helped me immensely. For a young priest, he exuded a sense of accomplishment, his stance straight, strong, and proud. His skin was fair, and his eyes big and blue, his mannerism jovial, which made me feel welcomed.

CHAPTER 44

On a Friday afternoon, while heading home, I noticed Father Martin working outside in the garden bed. The autumn breeze was cold, it had rained earlier and left the air smelling fresh. Father Martin called out to me.

"Look at all the fall crop collected."

Proud of his efforts, Father stomped his feet and clapped the work gloves together, and let the loose soil fall.

"Did you like to garden in your hometown?" he asked.

"Yes, we all helped in the garden. We grew vegetables, and my mama loved to grow flowers. She and my sister dried them and decorated the house to make it pretty all year round. Olena, my sister, liked to wear wreaths of flowers in her hair when she danced with her friends, that is until it was forbidden."

My face burned. I had rambled on, told too much.

"It's sad that such nice things in our lives are forbidden."

Father Martin asked me many more questions about the life we had left behind and I hesitantly answered without revealing much.

"My parents live in Poland, and they've seen horrible things." Father Martin said.

"Did you see much trouble during your travels through Poland? What were the conditions like there?"

"We didn't travel through Poland. We stayed mostly in Czechoslovakia. We stayed away from towns as much as possible and traveled through the forest. I liked being in the forest. I enjoyed going fishing."

Father Martin nodded his approval.

"We noticed some travelers on the roads when we had to go through a town. Some looked as if they were dying right there on the curb. When we asked locals for work, so that we could buy bread, most turned us away and not in a nice way. I guess war brings out the worst of us."

"I'm sorry to hear this," the young priest said.

His head bowed toward the ground, he looked as if he was inwardly debating himself. I know the look—I often look at the ground and do the same thing when uncertain of what to say next. So, I broke the ice.

"In the towns, there wasn't much food in the stores anyway," I said. "The people who were unfriendly to us were most likely afraid and concerned for their safety. I don't think people from other places like Ukrainians. They blame Ukrainians for their troubles."

I kicked the dirt, with a glance, I noticed Father Martin was smiling.

"Certainly not." Then he winked.

"It's been a bad situation for us," I said. "There weren't good choices for any of us in Halych, not for the Jews, not the Polish, and definitely not for us Ukrainians. We were all scared for our lives. My father said to me one day that never in the history of our town had our different ethnic paths been more aligned."

"Your father sounds like a wise man," Father Martin said. "Tell me, Ivan, did you go to school in your hometown?"

"Well, yes."

"I thought so, you're a smart young boy."

His compliment eased me and I blathered on.

"School was banned, that is I couldn't go to Ukrainian schools. But we had a professor in our town who was expelled from the city university, so he taught us in secret."

As soon as I spoke the words, I felt my face burn, but this time in horror. I looked to the ground in shame, I had revealed our secret. Not hinted at it—I told the secret aloud. *Had this been a trick? Why did I reveal our secret?* Even miles away from home, I felt nervous for our teacher, Pan Vasyklo. The last thing I wanted was my teacher to be arrested by NKVD or Gestapo.

"No worries, Ivan. I won't tell your confidence. Besides, no one here cares about what happens in Halych. The churches in Regensburg stay out of politics, and because of that, the soldiers leave us alone. I wish whole-heartily it was the same story for the faithful Catholics in Poland. They've been traumatized by the Nazis, much like your town. The Nazis do everything in their power to prevent the Catholics from practicing their faith in Poland. Soldiers seized much Church property and sold it off to raise money. They locked up presses at the print shops to stop the spread of news. My parent's congregation was kept in the dark about what's happening at the hand of the Third Reich."

Father Martin paused a moment and looked out into the open air.

"The soldiers marched into my small hometown and confiscated the church bells. My parents said they melted them down, claimed them for the war effort."

Father Martin closed his eyes.

"The German Regime is willing to do anything to

pressure the organized Church. I empathize with what your family went through."

Father Martin's sharing made me nervous. I coughed.

"Let me help you, Father."

I bent down and finished filling the wagon with the last of the potato and cabbage crop, then began pushing it toward the dry cellar.

"Did you know that Pope Pius XII claimed neutrality in the war? The Vatican is surrounded by the enemy in Italy. Still, some Church leaders follow the progress of the German Resistance."

"What's the German Resistance?" I wondered if this Resistance was like our underground Ukrainian army—*freedom fighters*.

"The Resistance is a group of people who don't agree with the evil things that Hitler and his regime do in the name of progress and science. Some spoke out in public, of course, you can guess what happened to them."

I nodded. "They were arrested."

"That's right. Thousands were arrested for living out our Christian virtues of faith, hope, and charity. The most important, I think, is charity. To love God and others as oneself."

Father Martin whispered. "I've heard that the Vatican advised the British about the German Generals who are ready to step in as soon as Hitler is overthrown."

I covered my mouth in awe. Could it be that some German soldiers are on our side? This war kept getting more complicated to understand.

"You know, Father Martin, I think this entire war is stupid. Everything in this world comes down to two things . . . A person tries to do good, or they are evil."

"I wish it was that easy, Ivan. That black and white. But it's more complicated than that. Even our holy leader, the Pope himself, has a hard time making decisions on what to do next. Still, the Pope is a brave man and our spiritual leader. The war drags on and the brutality against innocent people increases. The Church was urged to take a stronger stance by parishioners around the world. So, in answer to the people's cries, the Pope wrote the Mystici Corporis Christi, a papal encyclical. A brave stance indeed."

"What does that mean?"

"Encyclical? Well, that's like a newsletter. The Pope called the German invasion of Poland *'the hour of darkness.'* He's against the Nazis' mistreatment of people. He wrote that all faithful parishioners should love their Church, especially the elderly and sickly members. Did you know that the Nazi scientists perform experiments with the disabled and mentally ill? Horrific. You and I, we know better. We are all equals in the eyes of our Lord."

I nodded, though my mind was filled with distorted images of freaky scientists, looming over helpless people who were strapped to gurneys, and poking large needles into their bodies. I shivered, closed my eyes, and pushed the horrific vision away. When I opened my eyes again, I noticed that Father Martin seemed troubled by his own words. He walked faster, like a man in the movies when being chased by a shadow.

"The Pope's decree was a direct response against the euthanasia programs installed by Hitler's regime," Father Martin said as an afterthought.

"So, euthanasia is experimenting?"

"No, Ivan. It is the deliberate killing of others, a way to exterminate a race of people."

"You mean like the Jews or the Poles?"

The priest nodded. We reached the cellar, opened the door, and proceeded to lift the winter crop vegetables onto the shelves.

"That's probably why they wanted to destroy all the Polish Church presses, to keep that newsletter from being printed so they couldn't warn the helpless." I kept working as I spoke.

"You're a smart young man," Father Martin said.

I blushed. No one handed out compliments lately, and it sounded foreign to my ears, yet Father Martin had given his praise twice in one afternoon. My head felt as if swimming in a sea of pride, which of course was wrong. No one should be full of themselves, especially in a time of war. The priest didn't seem to notice my discomfort, he kept on talking.

"Some priests in other parishes spoke out against Hitler, and some, well most, were arrested. All the priest-dissidents are imprisoned in Dachau, kept there in barracks dedicated for the clergy, most of whom are Polish, of course."

He grinned.

"I heard rumors there are over two thousand prisoners held there. As I said, most are Polish, but there are hundreds of German priests, too. Mostly the Jesuits, and the pastor of Berlin himself, Bernhard Lichtenberg."

I thought about his words—standing for something bigger than yourself while knowing you could be arrested. That was bravery. I think I'd be too intimidated to do that. I wondered if my father ever thought about the things he did, whether he'd weighed the risks. Our entire family could have been arrested for helping Jewish friends; it had been a risky undertaking. But we weren't caught, we were out of danger, safe in silence. *Had Tato changed his mind about the odds, now that we lived in Germany?* I suddenly yearned to go home to our room and have a conversation with my father.

"There are other resistant leaders, faithful to the Church. People like Lieutenant Colonel Klaus von Stauffenberg," the priest continued.

"He's a descendant of a noble Bohemian family and a zealous German nationalist. Yet, he's also a Roman Catholic, so he shares the same convictions of the resistance. He knew that Germany was being led to disaster by Hitler and felt his removal from power was necessary."

The priest's voice had lowered to nothing more than a whisper. He looked around. Suddenly I was aware that this conversation was probably treacherous. Father Martin bent his head closer to mine to finish the story, his voice hushed.

"Last July in Rastenburg, von Stauffenberg led a group of co-conspirators in a military coup d'état. It was a collaboration of several groups of the German resistance. They tried to overthrow the Nazi government with an assassination attempt. It failed, unfortunately. The execution ended up a blood bath. The Gestapo arrested many involved, thousands of people from all over. They've already executed over

4,000 as a warning to anyone else who might want to try to interfere with the regime."

"It's unfortunate they failed," I said.

"Yes, it's sad. Best beware, Ivan. Tell your father not to trust anyone. Spies are trying to root out other resistance members."

I nodded, afraid that my father might be scheming with others in the resistance with hopes of finding Petro. A heavy burden rested on my shoulders; I felt its weight as if I were being pounded into the ground. I missed my brother terribly. I organized the last of the cabbages in silence.

Father Martin closed the door, bolted it, and spoke. "I can't wait for them to make sauerkraut."

I couldn't help but laugh, his words sparked a recollection of making sauerkraut in the Baumann's kitchen. It seemed so long ago.

"When you're ready to make the kraut, I'm your helper. I've made it before, I'm experienced with the slicer, and everything."

"Good." The priest smiled.

Unexpectantly, other memories began to flood my mind...horrible things. *Michael*. Next thing I knew, I was rambling on, spilling my guts like an overfed fish bursting open from the knife's slit.

"I remember the day when the German soldiers broke into our Church. They took the religious pieces made of gold. Thankfully, most were still buried in the back yard. But that day we chanced to use a gold cross and chalice for the holy service. One day I'll return to our old house and dig up the remaining crosses, and return them to the Church's altar where they belong."

"That would be a nice gesture if you can someday."

"Yes, I will make it a goal. The stolen items were only things, it was much worse when they dragged the cleaning woman away from the church. Sonia was crying for help, there was nothing we could do. I felt so helpless."

I pressed my eyes shut and waited for her dark eyes to stop haunting me. "They dragged her away, along with the other Jews, down to the river. They shot them dead. Only a few managed to escape. I wonder, how far did they go? There were guards and dragnet forces everywhere. In Czechoslovakia, people were taken away to the trains, sent to prisons to be killed. To escape them once only to be caught again has to be much worse."

"How terrible to witness such crimes," the priest said. His lips muttered a prayer under his breath.

I shrugged. "I saw a woman being forced away, our parents made us stay in the house after that, we never went to the river that day. I didn't see them being shot dead, only heard it."

"I'm always saying to people I'm sorry," Father Martin said. "I'm sorry for your grief, sorry for your loss, sorry you got caught up in this war."

He slumped, his eyes closed.

I wondered if he was praying, or planning to say more to me. I stood there awkwardly, wishing I hadn't said anything. It seemed as if I upset Father Martin.

"I'm sorry, Ivan. I hope that attending this school will help your situation. When your father came to us and pleaded to allow you into school, well, at first the Bishop wasn't sure. He was afraid. Your father was honest and admitted he sympathized with the Jews, and that fact might put a target on the rest of us. Luckily enough members of the church council cared. Your father is a good man, very eloquent in his speech, and persuasive. Besides, we're lucky to have such an intelligent boy in our school who happens to also be gifted with a great voice for the sparrows."

I smiled at his words, proud of my father. I had no idea how many people Tato helped to escape at considerable risk, but my father had always said he'd keep the family safe, and I believed in my heart that he would always keep his word. But Petro was gone...now I doubted everything.

"Thank goodness the Bishop of Regensburg, stays away from politics. All these years and he never spoke openly against the regime, and because he kept such a low profile, we keep our Church open for business. And the Reverend Theobold Schrims..."

The priest made a tsk-tsk sound with his tongue.

"He traipses the choir in front of the Führer whenever he can just to stay in the Party's good graces. As it is, most of Germany is Protestant, not Catholic. But, keeping our school open is important. I guess we're lucky that the choir gets some nice donations from the Party. We all must play our part."

"I've heard that before," I said. "Isn't that like shaking paws with a rabid dog?"

The priest tussled my hair, almost like my father, as he chuckled.

"We only allow a few new students admittance each year, you're one of the lucky ones, Ivan. We need you and the others to keep the parish going, keep the faith alive, so we'll have a foundation to build the future of the Church after the war."

I felt guilty. The pit of my stomach knotted. *The next spiritual leaders of the Church?* They would be disappointed. I wasn't the one to blaze their religious future frontier.

"Is something the matter?"

"Sorry, Father, I need to get back home. I promised my father I'd help with something."

He smiled at me and bowed his head.

"Thank you, Ivan, for such a nice talk. It feels good to get things off our chest, don't you think?"

"Yes. Thank you, Father."

I turned and left, knowing that he was watching me as I walked away. Then, I heard the cart wobble away, and he was gone.

I wondered about my tato's opinion of the Pope and the Roman Catholic Church. We had always followed the Byzantine Catholic Church. *Did it matter?* No one ever explained the differences and considering our situation, it was probably a trivial matter in the Church's eyes. The fact that the Pope was against the way the Germans treated people, that was good enough for me to follow the Pope.

CHAPTER 45

It was late October, the second month of school, and strange things were going on, especially during the night in the dormitory. At first, what I saw confused me, but then I became troubled. I heard the older students talking among themselves about some kind of situation, but they stopped yapping whenever I walked by them. A big secret.

The older boys never looked at me directly. Perhaps they were envious of me because of my good singing voice. But no. I realized that anyone being jealous of me was pure folly. I knew the truth in my heart, they didn't look at me because to them I was invisible, a nothing, a non-German boy.

My fellow students were muscular with blue eyes, the majority of them were Hitler Youth. They were the total opposite of me, the privileged, the hope of Germany's future. I was a nobody. My sole purpose in being there was to serve their needs, not my own. The big question was, what were they doing in a Catholic boys' boarding school? According to Father Martin, most of the Germans were Protestant.

I had a theory. The boys were in school because the Germans were worried that the Allies would arrive soon on their home ground. The *Vaterland* was in danger. The influential Germans who remained faithful to the Führer moved their sons into any safe-haven available, protecting the future, even if it meant hiding them in a Catholic school. This presumption gave me hope.

Then it hit me like a brick. That was why new funds were spilling into the Cathedral choir coffers from the Party—so that their sons could travel the world, safely away from Germany, while performing at the concerts. And that also explained why there was so much parental fuss going on at the school.

There was a Prefect at the Domspatzen boarding school named Friedrich Zeitler. He organized and accompanied the choir on the Nazi propaganda trips to France and Spain. The choir had been doing the concerts since 1941 according to the colorful posters that hung on the bulletin board in the front of the school.

I saw him, the Prefect, one day across the lawn. We had finished a small Harvest concert for some guests of the school.

We stood at attention, watching the adults mingle on the grass, socializing. Friedrich Zeitler was with some of the guest benefactors, speaking platitudes and giving fake handshakes. Even from a distance, I detected something wrong with him, he exuded a weird feeling. He made my skin crawl.

That same night in the dorm I lay on my bed, my back toward the other boys, pretending I was asleep. I overheard one of them whispering. He had seen something bad, some kind of sexual misconduct during one of the trips to France.

My eyes were wide-opened now, and sleep was the last thing on my mind.

"My parents said that the Prefect is too close to some of the students—I mean way too close, unnatural," another boy said.

I turned around on my bed, holding my breath hoping the springs wouldn't squeak. I wanted to hear better. With the covers pulled over my head, with only a small space free, I spied. The older boy looked around, ensuring no one was listening. I lay still like a board, my blanket draped over my body, no one noticed my bed near the window. I was invisible to the group of confidants.

He whispered something about Zeitler. Squeezing my eyes shut, as if that would help, I strained to hear. Another boy spoke a little louder than the others.

"Yes, it's true. He regularly molests schoolboys, takes them to the Hauskapelle on Orleanstraße. Stay awake tonight, you'll see what I mean. Some of the other older boys wake up younger boys, and they slip out from the dormitory during the night, to do God knows what."

"You mean older boys help the Prefect?"

A third boy seemed upset, obviously the first time he had heard of this situation, like me.

I swallowed my saliva, scared from the awful images affronting my mind. I had to tell my parents, *but would they believe me?* Maybe Tato would tell me to mind my own business.

"I told my parents, and they were so angry that they confronted the Director about the incident. He persuaded my parents to keep me in school anyway, which I'm not crazy about. He promised them that things would be taken care of, but still, the man is here. The same thing is still going on," the older boy said.

"My parents are more afraid of me not attending school than of his pedophile ass."

It seemed that all their parents threatened to pull their sons out of the school but then were hesitant. *Maybe there is no safer place for the boys? Better to be exposed to a sick pedophile than to be taken prisoner when the Allied troops arrived?* I hoped that was their fears.

"Our parents need to do something," an older boy said.

"They're too worried to take us out of school, stupid. If they bring us home, the Gestapo will grab us to fight on the front. Germany's honor."

They chuckled, then I heard someone heavy walking into the room, the floorboards groaned under his weight. A large shadow cast across the wood floor. The boys rushed back to their beds—the springs squeaked as they landed onto their mattresses. I pulled my blanket down a sliver to see who it was, afraid I might be the next boy to be dragged away. I swallowed hard, my tongue felt thick and swollen. It was difficult to breathe. I prepared to kick and scream. No one would take me away without a struggle.

I looked across the room, it was Father Martin, not Zeitler. My body deflated, and I let go of my fear.

After the priest left, I laid on my bed, thinking. *Should I tell my Tato about the Prefect?* I never told my parents about the one priest who chose a student each day to whip with a leather strap. The priest said that he was a firm believer in corporal punishment even when you hadn't done anything wrong. When he finished with the whipping, he would pray for our souls. After the first month of this daily routine, the boys in school started taking bets on who would be the next in line to get the strap.

Then the one day when it was my turn, the priest mumbled something in German about me having to learn not to talk so much in class. I didn't speak too often, only when I had a question, but I guess my curiosity and thirst for knowledge was too much for him.

"Come forward, young man," the old priest had said.

His wrinkled face matched his raspy voice. He looked like shrunken rawhide, the kind that the dogs liked to chew on at the Baumann's farm. I approached the front of the room, never lowering my eyes or breaking contact with the priest's cataract-filled orbs. A duel of stares, the priest and I, and I knew that he would never win. The priest might be able to whip me, but I could hold the stare longer, I knew it.

I had won, the priest broke the trance between us. I walked to the front of the class and leaned over, exposing my butt so he could thrash me one. It was worse than the paddling in the Dean's office, I was in front and center, embarrassed.

Then I heard my brother, Petro, call out to me. I looked up and knew he wasn't there, it was only a figment of my imagination, but if he had been there, he would have said, *leave my brother alone, he has done nothing wrong.* I remained there in front of the entire class, bent over with my exposed tender parts in the open for all the other boys to witness.

Mortified, my face burned, my heart sank, but I refused to give up hope. I let my mind wander back to the stories of the old Halychyna Prince and the ancient legends my best teacher, Pan Vasyklo, had shared with us in our basement classroom.

"No one is innocent in this world," the old priest said. "Have you seen what's going on? Do you hear the bombs at night? Have you seen the hungry littering the streets? Someday you will thank me for setting you straight on the road to heaven."

He struck me; I heard the leather strings whiz through the air. The sting from the strap smarted against my skin, but I gritted my teeth and bore the pain. Each laceration was worse than the one before. I smelled the faint tinge of my blood and felt wetness on my buttock. But I refused to give this old priest the satisfaction of acknowledging my discomfort, not even after ten strikes.

When he finished hitting me, I stood straight, my stance purposeful. Looking at him, eye to eye, I pulled up my trousers. Then I turned and gazed at the other boys in the classroom. Their stares wide, their mouths agape, they were terrified. Something inside me burst, and I had to share my thoughts.

"Thank you, Father," I said.

Bowing my head to him, I feigned respect.

"I have seen many poor souls. My family and I have traveled here from Ukraine, my homeland. We saw horrors along the way. Starving families eating from the city garbage, many people who were beaten for no reason but they remained thankful to be alive. Many others grieved for their dead loved ones.

"Our train was bombed, and my best friend died. We walked for weeks until the soles of our shoes were so thin that they cracked. Every puddle soaked our socks. Along our travels, we saw towns that had been ruined by the war. We heard the cries of Jews, begging for mercy after being hunted down in the woods by packs of hungry dogs. So many people have died while you've been safe, here in this place. Yes, Father, the world is not innocent, especially not you."

I was prepared for the worst retaliation, but the priest barely acknowledged my words. He bent his head toward the floor and mumbled prayers to himself, asking for my salvation. We all watched him, surely, he was crazy. Then he lifted his head and spoke again to the class.

"Everyone, take your seats. Your regular teacher will return to the classroom in a moment."

The priest left and never used the strap on me again.

Most nights during the week after a long day of classes and voice practice, we were so tired that we fell asleep without much talking after lights out. A few giggles and jokes, and then it would be silent. That was when I said my prayers, asking God to take care of my family, and most of all, to keep my brother, Petro, safe so he could return home to us.

The room was large, lofty, with dead space above my head. *Could my prayers get caught and linger there instead of being heard?* I hoped not, I wanted my brother to return. I wanted my family to look at each other in the eye again, and share a smile. *Petro, come home.*

Home, I thought, what an odd concept. *Would Halych ever be home again?* I doubted it. The Russians had moved their wartime front and now controlled my homeland. My Tato could never go back there, he'd be arrested and sent to Siberia.

Sighing at that thought, right then, I heard a strange noise.

I raised my head and looked around. The moonlight streamed into the dormitory and cast shadows against the opposite wall. My eyes noticed one boy get out of his bed. I saw him walk out of the room alone, he tiptoed toward the hall as he slipped his robe over the striped pajamas.

I wanted to follow, it's my nature to be curious, after all. Still, something told me to stay in my bed that night. I didn't follow the boy as much as it bothered me. Instead, I lay quiet and listened to his footfall fade away as he went down the hall. Then I could tell that he climbed the stairs, his soft footfall echoing into the hallway.

Shivers raced through my body, I was afraid for that poor boy, worried for him if he was going upstairs to the Prefect's rooms. I intended to remain awake until the boy returned, but I fell asleep. When the morning light streaked through the window, it illuminated the other boys as they stretched their arms and rose from the small beds. I woke and wondered if the boy had ever returned. I didn't see him anywhere.

Later, I saw the same boy in the cafeteria during breakfast. I watched as he whispered into another, older boy's ear. The older boy responded, his brows tight, and the young boy's face turned beet red. Something was wrong, something was off with the older boy, too. I didn't know their names and was too embarrassed to ask them about the night before, so I left it. I tried all day to distract myself from thinking about what I knew to be true, but couldn't prove.

A MORALITY ISSUE

CHAPTER 47

Late afternoon there was a last-minute announcement, we all went to choir practice in the recital hall. We went over the same songs, repeating the verses over and again. It had become so monotonous for me, that I fell into my daydreaming about the Halychyna castle. Deep in the zone of fantasies instead of choir practice, I was unaware of anything else around me, until something hit me in the face.

My eyes opened wide, I saw papers covered with music scores flying in the air all around me, then they gently landed on the shiny wood floor. A music stand had collided with my face, its mark burned on my left cheek. Raising my hands, I checked my nose to make sure it wasn't broken. The smell of blood flooded my nostrils. It was only a little bit of blood. *Good*. I pulled out a handkerchief and wiped my face, cringing as the choir director continued yelling relentlessly.

"No distractions in this room."

He screamed at me, his temples bulging, his eyes popping, and hate excreting from his pores.

"You must pay full attention; it must be perfect."

That was it. I would not take this abuse any longer. I could have cowered and acted scared like the rest of the boys every time he screamed, but that wasn't my choice, *not today*. No more of the director's bullshit, no matter how lucky I was to be a member of this damned choir.

Then I realized it was Friday anyway, so I gathered my things, turned around, and walked out. I heard the man screaming at me, but I refused to acknowledge or turn around, I might have lost my resolve if I had. I hurried to the dormitory, took the things that belonged to me that I kept under my bed, and gathered my clothes from the closet cupboard. Then I left with no inclination to ever return.

I walked briskly back to our one-room apartment home. The trees were barren, all the leaves had fallen to the ground. A wind from the river whipped down the street and through the alleys. The coldness didn't bother me, I was heated with anger, and from carrying all my things. The books were heavy, but I wanted to keep them to read at night.

Usually, on Fridays, I enjoyed returning to our one-room home to see how the family was doing. This weekend, I was anxious. I'd have to talk with my father, tell him how things stood with the school and me. I didn't think he'd make me go back after I explained what had happened and what I had heard. Tato wouldn't want me there either—I hoped— I prayed.

He'll know what I should do about the young boy who seemed scared by the older boy, and he'd understand why the boy sneaked out in the middle of the night, and how he was keeping ugly secrets. Causing trouble wasn't my plan, but the boy needed help. Tato would know the correct thing to do to help the other boys.

I slowed down my pace, kicked a few rocks, and took my time. It was early yet, my family would still be at work. I rehearsed what I would say to my tato, chose the words to use that would help him understand the problems at the school. I went over the facts, the way the place made me feel, and it sounded ominous. Surely my father would feel the same.

I'd refuse to go back there if he insisted, and hoped he wouldn't push me back. I did not want to be abused again,

I'd rather stay at the house and work for Herr Krüger. He wasn't a bad man, after all.

Sometimes the roughest looking characters are the kindest. And if Tato was afraid of them grabbing me to be a soldier, well, I'd stay inside, hidden. I was not going back, no matter what...

CHAPTER 48

Later after our super, I asked Tato to come with me for a walk. Finally, I had a quiet moment alone with my father. I spoke to him plainly. He listened to my rehearsed points without interrupting me. But I could tell as he dropped his eyes to the ground, that he was distraught.

I hated bothering him with my troubles, ever since Petro went missing he and my mama hardly spoke a word. Their eyes didn't shine anymore but instead were tired and dull. No amount of joking, no amount of sweets that I sneaked out from the school cafeteria, ever cheered them up. So, as my father mulled over what I said, I was nervous about his reaction.

"Don't worry, Ivan. I will take care of the matter."

Tato's response surprised me, he sounded like his old self. We hurried back inside. He walked to the small sink against the wall in our little kitchen area and washed his face, then he combed his hair. Next, Tato put on his church clothes that had been pressed and hung on a wall hook; he looked his Sunday best. He kissed Mama on the forehead and left.

My mama read from her Bible, and Olena was writing a book report for her class. I grabbed a book and pretended to read as time passed.

I worried about what my tato was doing, was he helping the other boys or trying to get me back into the school? Maybe he thought he had to apologize for my insubordinate behavior, but surely Tato knew that something was wrong. Not one word of reprimand was uttered from his mouth toward me, for that I was thankful.

My father returned a couple of hours later.

"Ivan, you will not be attending that school any longer. For the time being, you will stay here, help the old man downstairs with his business."

I wanted to ask what happened, but the look on his face meant I shouldn't want to know. Instead of asking questions and bothering him, I gave my tato a big hug. He squeezed me back, patted my head, and I felt that everything would be right again.

Herr Krüger seemed content that I would be his helper again, and he was very good to me. Never asked to do many things, I spent much of my time reading books. Herr Krüger owned a small library in his apartment, and he let me borrow books one at a time. They were mostly written in German, I was getting better at translating the German text, and the stories fed my imagination. I went through them quickly, and after a week had completed five novels.

Each day at lunchtime, I would go up to the cafe to get our sandwiches. We would eat together, and he told me about his brother who worked for the Führer. Herr Krüger had argued with his brother and no longer wanted anything to do with him.

"I wash my hands of him." He slapped his hands and pushed as if throwing something away. "We have unresolvable issues, and I have no time for jackasses."

I zoned out for a moment and thought about what he said. It would be hard for me to never speak with my brother again. No matter what Petro might do, I could never stop talking with him. I worried about my brother, imagined that Petro was lost out there somewhere and that he might not come back to us.

Uncontrolled tears rolled down my face, I closed my eyes and prayed my hardest, more than I had ever prayed before. With each passing day, my fear grew worse. I knew my brother's odds of surviving shrunk each day.

We heard stories about bombings in other German cities, heard about the war theaters going on in other countries, and how the Germans were being flattened. Soldiers were running away from their duty, hiding.

My brother never wanted to fight for the Reich—he must have run away. Truth be told, we had no idea of what happened to Petro, none of Tato's inquiries generated any leads. It was as if Petro never existed.

"You know what they say, young Ivan, you can choose your friends but not your family," Herr Krüger said.

Then he smiled, and I forced myself to smile back.

I supposed that things are different between him and his brother. After all, his brother was Hitler's man, one of the highest Nazis. When Herr Krüger spoke of his brother, it was with distaste, and I immediately knew the truth. He looked like he wanted to spit every time he said his brother's name, and I strongly identified with that sentiment.

"My brother is a German captain of the Gestapo," Herr Krüger said. "He's responsible for organizing the raids in Poland—raids that killed thousands of Jews. He was part of Operation Barbarossa, in your homeland, and his murderous rampage began the massacre of the Lviv professors, way back in July 1941."

"That was when many of my tato's friends were imprisoned or murdered. I remember that fearful time. The lucky ones fled the University to hide."

"Yes, they can hide, but not too long with monsters like my brother. He started an even worse bloody massacre, in the Stanisławów Ghetto, the notorious Bloody Sunday massacre. It's rumored he had tens of thousands of Jews killed. My brother wears his Nazi fanaticism like a badge. He's most notorious for his brutality. He's demented and enjoys showing off his evil nature, even participates hands-on during the killing sprees. Some say that my brother has more blood on his hands than any other Nazi."

"I'm sorry."

My words seemed grossly inadequate. *How can he live with himself while knowing the horrors done by his flesh and blood?*

"Most people don't know he's my brother, thank God for small mercies, but those who do know stay the hell away from me. Oh well, we go on and try our best, right? If I can help some of you refugees, maybe the scales will balance in the end."

He shrugged his shoulders and smiled at me, but it was forced, and his eyes remained haunted.

Now I understood why our Herr Krüger hated his brother so much. I felt sorry for my friend. Living with this dreadful knowledge of the cruelty his brother was responsible for must burn Herr Krüger from the inside. *I might be the only person alive to know how decent a man he is, nothing at all like his evil brother.* I took his hand in mine, smiled at him, then I stretched across the table and hugged the man. Herr Krüger allowed it and padded my back in return.

"You're a good soul, Ivan. You are special."

CHAPTER 49

Tato's spirit broke after Petro went missing. We learned not to ask him questions when he returned from work, we left him alone. He washed up in the bathroom that we shared with three other families who lived in the building. They were also Ostarbeiter, forced workers for the German labor program. The men in our building were still cleaning the bombed factories, it was a last-ditch attempt that things could turn around for the Germans. Of course, the slower the men worked, the better.

The women had begun with mending uniforms, but now they were repairing men. The nearby hospital flooded with wounded soldiers returning from the various war fronts. Discretely, Mama questioned the soldiers with the hope that one of the injured men might have seen Petro someplace out there. Any news that he was alive would have been treasured.

The radio played on the hospital wards while she worked, and Mama heard the news reports. They were filled with German propaganda more than truth, but some facts could be discerned to the attuned ear.

Paychecks were nonexistent for weeks. Working wasn't much better than slave work. But we did have a place to sleep, and tickets were given out each day to receive food from a nearby market, though there wasn't much to choose from. Tato often came home with only bread. Mama managed leftovers from the hospital, usually unwanted cans of peas. Some days on her way home, she unearthed ingenious ways to acquire food. Mama stopped at the bakery and other places

to barter for things, returning to the room with whatever vegetables or meat she managed to scrounge. She was brilliant,
and I loved her dearly. I owed her my life.

Each day food became more scarce. We were hungry but
didn't speak about it, it only made things worse. Roads were
blocked with fallen buildings. Train tracks had been destroyed and supplies couldn't reach Regensburg. It made life
hard for everyone, but secretly I knew what this meant—The
Germans were losing, soon we would be freed from this ser-
vitude life.

We weren't starving, yet, nor being chased down in the
streets and bleeding from gunshot wounds. The patch worn
on our jacket lapels protected us from unwarranted hassles
by Germans who were afraid and lashed out at strangers.
I tried to remind myself that they lost their loved ones, too.
Many wanted no more war—only wished for this nightmare
to end—like us. But some people were dangerous, looting
and killing for scraps.

At night my parents talked in low voices. They spoke of
what they had heard about the war's status during the day
and shared secrets that only the two of them could understand. My mother was a wonder—a strong, resourceful
woman. Despite her anguish over my brother's disappearance, she worked and took care of us with her cleverness. She
became the strength on days when my father was frail.

The Christmas holiday came and passed without celebration. Still no word about Petro. We heard bombings here
and there and waited for it to be over.

February 5th, 1945

It was a bitterly cold winter day. I remember how my hands felt frozen, my fingers stiffened and were unable to bend in my hand-me-down gloves. A major assault strike happened in Regensburg. I was blocks away from our place and saw bombs land close to the river, not far from the boarding house where we stayed. The air squad aimed at the few ships that remained floating. Then they flew east and headed toward the railway depot. I ran back to our one-room home, frantic that I might never see my parents or sister again.

Thank God, they all returned in one piece and were safe. It took weeks before anyone felt at ease walking the streets again, but when we finally felt some sense of normalcy, there was another strike.

March 1945

Another bombing, this time one of the old Churches was hit. The tower bells rang out loud clangs as if in pain. They were destroyed in the strike. Like a free bird taken by a hunter's shot, the songs and pealing bells vanished, leaving a void.

The days afterward seemed to blur together into one long, tense moment. The city of Regensburg was spared many horrors compared to the destruction that other German cities experienced. We heard in the news about the atrocities that happened in Hamburg, Berlin, and the city of Dresden. Those cities were bombed mercilessly by the Allied forces.

The British used fire torpedoes that set the old cities ablaze. Some felt it had been too much, that Germany was on its knees, and lives could have been spared. I thought of my

Jewish friends and wondered why the German people had allowed that extreme cruelty to go on before their eyes—maybe they didn't know—or they were as scared as the rest of us.

Revenge isn't right, killing is never good, but I understood the anger behind the firebombs. The end was evident, Germany had failed their attempt to conquer the world. People who dared to venture into the streets talked about the war ending soon. My mind was always wondering about my brother. *Where was he?*

Even though other cities in Germany fared much worse, Regensburg was overwhelmed with fear. A haunted city plagued with stories of ghost planes that dropped real bombs on other cities.

People scrounged for food, then hid in fear of revenge from others who were hungry. Those brave enough to wander into the street spoke of the ongoing threats. The future was precarious in the city. Crude conditions existed and there was no access to the necessities needed to maintain good health. The train tracks were useless, all bombed. Travel on the Danube was impossible, all ships sunk. Any boats seen by a plane above became an instant target, so the smaller fishing boats remained moored.

People's souls were broken. I could see it all in their eyes as they passed by on the streets, their diminished mannerisms as if waiting to be whipped. The people were in limbo, aching for the official end.

Herr Krüger said to me one day, "what did they expect? We dropped bombs on the most prosperous cities, marched in and took over countries, and we didn't expect them to fight back? It was an insane plan from the start."

He sounded like my father.

LIBERATION

CHAPTER 50

Early spring 1945

I looked out of the window and noticed people rushing to the street.

"Herr Krüger, something is going on," I said.

I jumped from the chair and looked through the door's glass panel. There was activity everywhere, people abuzz, walking the streets. This hadn't happened for months. I watched as they poured into the street from the storefronts. A group of women strolled together arm in arm, all heading for the stone bridge, as if in a parade.

I went out and stood on the steps alongside Herr Krüger. He looked as puzzled as I felt. The air was cool, a refreshing breeze from the river drifted over me. The sun was warm as it kissed my bare arm after I rolled up my sleeves. A group ran in front of us toward the riverfront, shedding their work aprons along the way and waving them up in the air.

In the distance, I heard motors humming and getting louder. Moving vehicles were close.

Jumping off the stoop, I joined the others flocking to the streets. I heard the faint cry of Herr Krüger...

"Wait, Ivan..."

I wasn't about to wait—I needed to see what was happening. I sprinted ahead of them all, reaching the old stone bridge first.

On the road across the river, I spied war-time vehicles forming a line. Loud engines rumbled, as they clunked onto the old stone bridge and drove across. I felt the vibration under my feet, sending ripples through my entire body. They rolled across the expanse like giant turtles from the Galapagos Islands.

Thankfully, this bridge was too significant to be bombed. It was a timeless pearl from the Middle Ages that had already survived many wars. The other modern bridges were destroyed into twisted metal pieces that collapsed into the water. No one had the heart to bomb this ancient bridge which had aided many a brigade of armies as they crossed the Danube. A sight so beautiful—this age-old bridge—it never had a load as important as this spectacle.

Two war trucks and four Jeeps, American Jeeps, driven by American soldiers, drove across the timeless arches. The people lining the sides of the streets waved to the Americans and tried to touch the warm motorcars as they passed ever so slow and steady.

I waved to them, too. Excitement filled my entire being. I felt lighter than air as I jumped up and down, and flapped my arms.

Smiling with grins ear to ear, the American soldiers waved back at us. I had never seen such happy soldiers. They were real people, authentic American Joe's, and such friendly faces. I waved until my arm hurt, and watched as they crossed. Then it hit me, the war must be over, at least here in this part of Germany, because the Americans were here, in Regensburg.

Crazy with glee, my head was swimming. Without thinking, I jumped from the rock railing where I had been teetering onto the hard pavement and fell. I sprang back up on my feet and ran toward our one-room home, eager to tell anyone about what I had seen. It was an answered prayer— a miracle.

I cried out freely in the street, "we are free!" and celebrated the glorious moment with any passers-by who offered a return smile.

Some of the German residents were hiding inside of the buildings, I noticed some peeking through their curtains as I ran past. They were scared, understandably so, but there was also a look of relief in their eyes. Not a soul wanted the war anymore, the casualties had been too much for anyone to tolerate.

I reached the rooming house, everyone there spoke of the news of the German fall. Men stood in the lobby and carried thin newspapers looking for phantom details. People spoke of how they deserted their workplaces and joined the crowd in the streets to greet the liberators.

Spanning the room, I soaked in the ebb of elation brewing, it carried me to a hopeful place. *Now my brother will return.* Among the smiling faces, I spotted Herr Krüger. The old man stood alone by the counter brooding, holding a letter tight in his grip.

Something was wrong. I knew he would welcome this happy news, *so why so distressed*? I bolted and reached him as he crumpled the letter and tossed it into the dustbin. Herr Krüger slumped, his blue eyes filled with tears. He was crying, tears dripping down his face, streaking his wrinkled skin, leaving a faint white trace.

He looked up at me.

"My brother is dead."

His voice sounded grave and far away.

"I'm so-r-r-ry. Did he die because of the war?"

"He died by his own hand. But yes, it was because of this horrid war. The Third Reich turned him into a monster." He sighed. "My brother was a monster. The thought of it makes me so sick and ashamed. I hate knowing that my flesh and blood was so cruel—You see, my brother couldn't live with himself after the things he did—at least I hope that was it. It's that or else he was a coward, afraid of what the English will do to him once they arrest him. He didn't give them a chance to show mercy. Besides, he didn't deserve it. No. Even he must have known he didn't deserve mercy. Still, he was my brother...and somehow, he managed to touch my heart. I wonder what that says about me?"

"It says you're a good person, Herr Krüger."

Reaching out, I hugged the old man.

"The evil reign has ended," he said. "It's over, thank God. Germany officially surrendered. "

The old man patted my back. I let go, deliriously happy, but at the same time sad.

"Did you hear, boy? The war is over. Everywhere, it's ended."

I gazed into the old man's eyes and felt pity for him. I knew the near future would bring him pain with the bad memories people harbored. Much had to be accounted for, no matter how remorseful. Paying the price for being on the wrong side of the war was a daunting thought.

Many people hated any German. *Would the Americans sympathize with my family? We were living in Germany, too.* I wondered if we should go back to Halych. *Old Halych, you*

seem so far away. I felt a tinge of homesickness, and the euphoria from the soldiers' parade faded. Too much information
and feelings to sort out.

A vision of my brother smiling about the news crossed
my thoughts, and I wondered where Petro was when he
heard the war was over, what had happened to him. *Did he
also end up a casualty of the war? No, I would know if he died—he
still felt real to me*—my mind refused to accept that he could
be dead.

CHAPTER 51

The commotion continued for days then slowly things settled down, somewhat settled anyhow. News spread that the Allied countries occupied Germany, Austria, and Italy. Millions of refugees had been torn from their homelands and now categorized as displaced peoples. The United Nations Relief and Rehabilitation Administration sectioned off areas of Germany. The Americans were assigned to set up a military government in the DP camp region that included Regensburg.

I was older and wiser than my years, and curiosity propelled me. I listened to any conversation that seemed of interest, especially anything about the USA. The initial troops that arrived drove through the city and then continued onward. We all waited in suspense for another group of Americans to arrive who would lead our area. No one knew what to expect.

One afternoon I spied an American man walking into the city, smiling and waving to everyone as he passed. I ran to him and began asking a barrage of questions. Though Tato had warned me not to bother any newcomers, my curiosity couldn't be contained any longer. I knew in my heart that my father would thank me later.

"Sir, what's happening here?" I saluted him. "Will more troops arrive and stay here for a while? Do you understand German?"

"Well, hello there."

The man answered in English. He bent his tall frame and tousled my hair as Tato did. His big hand was surprisingly gentle. Like the other soldiers, he smiled at me, his eyes were a soft brown, his skin pale-white like mine, but he wore freckles across the bridge of his nose.

"Ja," he said in German, "Ich spreche nicht gut deutsch…I'm not that good at speaking German, so try to follow my words. Versuche meine Bedeutung zu verstehen."

I laughed aloud.

"I don't speak German well myself," I said in broken English.

"What nationality are you," he asked.

"I am Ukrainian," I answered proudly, and stood stretched as tall and straight as I could manage. "I traveled here from Halych."

"Wow, that's a long way. I've traveled a bit to get here, too. Soon, there will be more of us coming. We'll be setting up a field hospital nearby—it's a place to treat the people with injuries. We'll be bringing people from the POW camps that we liberated, and wounded soldiers, of course."

"Do you need help? I can fetch things for you and be your assistant."

The man laughed aloud.

"Sure, kid. You can help us clean them up. What's your name?"

"I'm Ivan. Where will you and the other soldiers be staying?"

"That's another big job. You see, we'll be cleaning the existing prisons and camps to use for the freed prisoners and refugees. We'll also be building shelters for the wounded soldiers. We'll have lots of supplies coming this way."

I looked up and noticed he was chewing gum. He must have noticed me staring because he held out the pack and nodded for me to take a stick. I grabbed one and unwrapped the gum then started to chew, surprised at the fruity juiciness.

"Dyakuyu," I said. "I mean, thank you."

"You're welcome." The man responded in English. "Kid, do you have a place to stay?"

The sun shined from behind his helmet and glowed around his head as if he was some kind of holy saint. I drew in a deep breath, happy that he acknowledged me and he was concerned about my predicament.

"Yes, Sir. My father was lucky to find a room for us to sleep in, over there."

I pointed to the building. It was old and looked worse now from when I first laid eyes on it. Riddled with pitted holes gouged from shrapnel from the bombs that had flown onto the outside layer of cement.

"There's a good man there, a German, Herr Krüger. He helped us, and a few other families, too."

I hoped that if we kept saying Herr Krüger was good, they wouldn't mistreat him for being German and the brother of such a rotten guy.

"Good. Good. Hey, do you think your father could help us out?"

I nodded. "Yes, certainly. I'll go get him right now."

I ran and called aloud as I raced to our room.

"Tato, Tato. Hurry. An American is asking for your help."

My father grabbed my arms and bent his head to listen, but now I was almost eye to eye with him, I had grown taller this year. I told him about the soldier, then he followed me down the stairs. Tato held his hand out to the soldier as we got close.

"Hello, my name is Mr. Rudenko, but please call me Taras," Tato said. "It's so nice to meet you. Thank you for liberating the people in this city. Many are not German as you probably know. We have escaped to here from places even worse."

The man nodded and returned Tato's handshake.

"My name is Hank, I'm an American soldier with the medical unit, and I'm scouting out the town, getting ready to bring our field hospital here. Do you know the area? Could you help me make sense of the place?"

"Hank, I'm your man. Follow me, I'll show you what you need to see. There's a nearby hospital, which you'll want to commandeer."

I stood and watched as my father and Hank disappeared down the street. Tato yelled back at me over his shoulder, "tell your Mama I'm working with the American, and you stay with her, keep her and your sister safe."

My plans were dashed. I was supposed to be Hank's assistant. I headed back to watch over the family, knowing in my heart that Tato was the right man for the job. My father was almost in charge again. And he was right, the situation was dangerous. Some people were banding together, stealing food, and anything else they could get their hands on. There were rumors of some people being killed. Reminding myself of such misery, I stayed with my mama and sister to protect them.

As the weeks went by the Americans became more organized. The liberators needed volunteers, so Mama, Tato, Olena, and I helped them. We packed survival kits consisting of a blanket, toothbrush, and soap, to be distributed as people wandered into the camp area. We helped to prepare food — mostly soup, and served the long lines. My father had already joined a committee to help organize us Ukrainians and now they were busier than ever as more Ukrainian people flocked into Regensburg. The military government was calling us Soviets or Poles, but we were neither and refused to be labeled as such.

As many more refugees arrived, they were assigned a house to live in or a cot in the barracks for displaced people. We cleaned the old prison camps with disinfectants, a disgusting job. Then filled them with new cots and blankets supplied by the United States.

Injured people were directed to go to Hank and his crew. They used the German hospital in the next town, which proved to be a much more efficient place for their surgery needs. A mere week after the first soldiers crossed the bridge, the hospital was buzzing with doctors and nurses from the Fifteenth Division of the US Army.

I enjoyed bringing lunch to the Americans from the food tent. I chatted with my new friend, Hank, as we ate. He told me stories of his hometown in Kansas. My imagination grew with ideas of how wonderful it will be to live in America, I might be someone important someday after all.

Hank explained how they marched into various towns in France and through Germany to liberate people. His favorite tale was about entering the German hospital here, near Regensburg. He tore down the Nazi flags that littered the entryway and halls. He found the biggest USA flag available and hung it smack in the middle of the front wall for everyone to see when they entered. The German patients there didn't dare complain because the American medics treated them as well. *Imagine that...Americans are generous.* I didn't know then that the months would turn into years.

The United States military ran the DP camps for refugees and displaced people in the area. They were in charge of the temporary military government. They set up housing, brought in food and medical supplies, and recorded the people who kept streaming in. Many wandered in from the outlying areas and had been homeless for a long time.

When people entered the gates, they were immediately dusted to keep bug infestation down within the camp. Women, men, children lined up with arms raised and were puffed with a dust cloud of disinfectant and bug killer that blasted away the fleas and ticks. It was a strange thing to watch.

Then the people were ushered to the next section where we handed them a bowl of soup and a piece of bread. Many had been hungry for a long time, so we instructed them to sip the food slowly, so they wouldn't get ill. I helped by serving soup, and eventually, the lines became smaller...but that was only the beginning.

CHAPTER 52

The spring and summer months of 1945 flew by, and my curiosity grew with each new development. A group of Ukrainian refugees had already formed a committee before the United States arrived, and of course, my father was involved. The Americans were great to work with and took pride in trying to be the best DP camp in Germany.

Ukrainians were classified in their records according to their citizenship. This meant Ukrainian Displaced Peoples were listed incorrectly. Our community members were listed as Soviet, Polish, Romanian, or Czechoslovakian citizens or worse as non-Poles or doubtful Poles, or even undetermined nationalist. The military government refused to classify Ukrainians as a unique national group. *Was it because our statehood had been taken away after WWI, and they didn't recognize our borders before the war?* It made no sense, and my father would often return at night, frustrated.

My father came home one night in a good mood. He told us how another Ukrainian man tried to explain the situation of Ukrainians to a soldier. He said, *'if there's a horse stable, and a cat wanders into the stable then gives birth, are the newborn kittens or horses?'* Tato said that a few of the Americans laughed, so perhaps some progress was made on our behalf. Our community leaders remained persistent.

September 2nd, 1945

I officially walked to Ukrainian school again, but this time, I walked alone. My brother was still missing. I felt lonely inside, wishing Petro was with us again, wondering if he'd ever find us.

The school was set up by the Ukrainian Relief District Committee. Rooms located at Neupfar Platz, in the old Dresden Bank smack in the center of Regensburg served as classrooms. It was only a few rooms and very crowded so they broke students into morning and afternoon sessions to accommodate us all. We numbered over one hundred students that first day, all eager to learn.

Student applicants had streamed into Regensburg during the summer. They answered the questions given by the committee, hoping to pass the exam and become students. I watched as wide-eyed kids marched up the steps to the interview. The people were thirsting for education and normalcy in their lives.

My tato had told me that many lived in Ganghofer Siedlung, a refuge location. Other students lived farther away and would be housed in dormitories. I reminded my father about what happened in the dorm where I had gone to school with the Sparrows, but he assured me that things would be appropriately monitored. And I knew they would because I believed in my tato now more than ever. He was right to leave the forest and come here to Regensburg. The Allied countries came to our rescue.

Our principal of the Ukrainian Gymnasium in Regensburg was Mykola Velychko. He once ran a school in Ukraine but was here with us, thank God. On our first day of class, he gave a speech and inspired us all to do our best work. We represented our families, our culture, and our future as Ukrainians.

Classes met every day, and I enjoyed learning again. It was much easier studying using the Ukrainian language. We didn't have fancy classrooms and there were only twelve teachers. But they were dedicated to us students, answered all our questions, and they never resorted to hitting us.

Speaking Ukrainian with the other children gave me joy I hadn't expected. You never know what you miss until it's gone then found again. But we were no longer children, we were survivors—young adults who knew our ancestors were counting on us to carry the torch. There were great expectations on our backs.

After school, I took some time off and hung out with my new friends, a couple of boys my age. Dmytro was a tall lanky dark-haired teenager, who enjoyed history like me. Andriy was a plump adolescent, who liked to joke a lot, and he also enjoyed mathematics like me. We bonded quite well, the three of us played chess whenever a teacher lent us his board and played capture the flag when we were outside.

Most importantly, we enjoyed listening to music on the radio—we spent hours tapping our feet and daydreaming to the new tunes sung in American English, with all the funny slang words they used. The songs were upbeat and happy.

It was Friday after classes, the three of us decided to head over to the recreation area to talk with the American soldiers hanging out. Nearby there were trucks and tanks lined up in a row, that always impressed us. I spotted Hank, waved, and called out to get his attention.

"Hello there, Ivan. Who are your friends?"

"Hank, this is Andriy and Dmytro. Guys, this is Hank. He was the first American soldier I ever spoke with."

My friends shook hands with Hank.

"We've heard of you and all your doctor friends," Dmytro said. "Someday I want to be a doctor. I enjoy helping people."

"I wish you the best. Study hard," Hank said.

"So, did you go to school?" Andriy asked.

"Yes, and I studied hard."

Hank chuckled. He told us a few stories about his high school sweetheart; she was named Darleen. He spoke of his college friends, embellishing the tales of pranks they played on each other. The entire time Hank's eyes mirrored happiness, and longing at the same time...the same kind of light that glows in my father's eyes when he remembers his younger years.

"I like your stories, you're funny," Andriy said.

"Hank, can I climb into one of those tanks?" I said. "Every time I walk by them, I wonder what they look like inside. How they're designed and put together."

"Ivan, do you imagine yourself a soldier?" Hank said.

"No, not at all. I only wonder how it's all put together inside—does the dashboard look like an automobile's? Or like a train's controls?"

"Our friend Ivan dreams a lot, Hank," Dmytro said.

"That's okay. Dreaming is a good thing. All right then, Ivan, the young man with a million questions. Come along and I'll let you climb into one."

I felt my heart beating fast and the rush of excitement propelled me to run toward the monster machine. I looked up. It was huge. Gray and brown with weird wiggly designs painted on its sides. I stood beside it in wonder. Hank climbed up first and I followed, felt the metal under my hands and smelled oil and diesel fuel. Hank opened the hatch. I heard a loud creak then stepped down into the hole, and slipped into the worn leather seat inside. All around me were buttons, levers, and things I was dying to push. I wanted to pull them all.

"Don't touch anything," Hank called down, his voice echoed in the hull of the tank.

"I won't." Still, I wished I knew enough to turn it on and run around the town with it. The idea of it got my adrenaline going and I wanted to move but I couldn't. The inside was cramped and smelled of perspiration, but knowing the entire size of the machine made me feel almost invincible. After I explored for a time, I climbed back out. My friends gawked at me as if I had done something dangerous.

"Hank, how old does someone have to be to enter the army? How long do they train to use this tank? Is it designed by an engineer or a mechanic?"

"Hold on there, Ivan. My, you're a giant question mark today."

Hank laughed and we all joined in. We had lots of questions for Hank that day, and he obliged us with his honest answers. He enjoyed himself as much as we did, his smile never-ending. Hank told us more stories about his home, back in the USA.

"My favorite holiday is the 4th of July—Independence Day," Hank said. "There's always a parade in the morning down Main Street. The marching band plays, later we go over to the lake and listen to music on the radio, great music."

Hank closed his eyes.

"And there's lots of food. Cold fried chicken—nice and spicy, potato salad, an apple pie that melts in your mouth, and chocolate brownies, mmm…"

He opened his eyes and sat upright.

"Then, in the evening, the town shoots off fireworks over the park's lake. Beautiful colors fill the sky and reflect on the water, rippling away, and you can smell and see the smoke fumes left behind. They bang so loud that it's really easy to pull a girl up close and wrap your arms around her."

Hank kept smiling but he wasn't with us right then. I liked his 4th of July holiday—Independence Day. It sounded wonderful and I wanted to be an American, too.

"It's getting late. I have to go back," Dmytro said.

"Well thank you, boys, for stopping by." Hank waved as my two friends capered away back toward their quarters.

"Ivan, thank you. I enjoy spending time with you. You gave me a gift today."

My face must have revealed my confusion. I never gave Hank anything but a headache with my endless questions, but he explained without me having to ask.

"You ask a lot of questions but more important is that you're a good listener. Letting me remember my home, listening while I talked about the things I love—well, it helped me from being homesick. Reliving my memories brings me back home. For that I am grateful."

"Glad to help you. I know what daydreaming is like. I do it too, all the time. Whenever I get stressed, or I'm afraid or don't understand the things around me. I go to my fantasy world and dream of Old Halych and the lazy river near my hometown. I miss my old teacher and his stories. He encouraged me to keep dreaming, and to never stop."

Hank smiled, then wrapped an arm around my shoulder. "He's right. Never give up on your dreams, Ivan. You can be whoever you choose as long as you never give up hope."

I smiled and shook Hank's hand. While walking home, I thought about Hank and how he seemed a lot like my tato.

CHAPTER 53

My father often returned to our little room with strange, sad stories. One night his tale was frightening, and it made me wonder why some found the path to forgiveness, and others did not. I was glad we stayed in our one-room apartment instead of the camp after my father told these stories.

"Whenever people are crowded together, there's bound to be unintended situations. We get on each other's nerves," my tato said. "But worse, you never know how people will react to each other. The refugee camps are crowded to the max with all sorts of people. So to ease the tensions, the military government tried to separate the people into groups, you know, sorted by nationality. We already grouped as Ukrainians, even before they started the policy. But then later, some people pretended to be Ukrainian instead of German or Russian, because they're afraid of being beaten by the other people in the camps, the Poles and Czechs and more. No one trusts the Germans or Russians."

"And who can blame them," Mama said.

"Yes, we all understand that, but the violence is not needed." Tato swung his head, side to side. "Some men banded together and ransacked the supplies. They stole the reserves for themselves. Now there's less for the rest of us, but still, we're lucky there's enough food for everyone. The Americans are doing a great job of supplying food and blankets. There's plenty to go around compared to a few months ago."

My mama nodded and continued her knitting.

"The military guards will keep a close eye on the sections of the camp where they caught the thieves," Mama said.

"Yes. They will try. Some of the people in the camp are spies," Tato said. "They were caught but never revealed much about who they worked for. The authorities are troubled by this and don't know how to handle the situation."

"That's horrible. It's hard to feel safe when things like that are happening," Mama said.

"On a few occasions, the homeless Germans in the camp were surrounded and beaten by the others, and in one incident, a man was killed. I suppose that's why others tried to pretend they were a different nationality. There's a lot of fear and hatred in people's hearts. I hope we can change the tide, and help everyone to forget the horrors of the war, at least a little, so we can get on with the business of life."

My father closed his eyes, I knew he was praying for our Petro. He and Mama have been walking around with sullen faces for months. I wanted to take away their worry, to let them know my brother was fine, but I couldn't because I didn't know my brother's fate either. It's hard to go on when part of us was missing, but we must. I willed myself not to lose faith.

"Tato, do you remember once you said, *'fear of death takes away the joy of the living,'* I think you need to remind yourself of that."

I swallowed hard, hoping I hadn't offended my father.

He reached over and hugged me.

"Yes, of course," Tato said. "We will find our Petro. In the meantime, it stands to reason that we Ukrainians need to organize ourselves. We know who we are and can identify who's lying. And if we stay together, we can be much more productive and protect our interests. We don't want revenge, what we want is a school for the children, art and poems for us all to enjoy, and peace—always peace and freedom. The Americans are good and allow us to organize. And why not? It makes their work a little easier."

Tato laughed. Music to my ears, I missed his light-hearted way. It was a welcomed sight to see him smile again.

In our area of the camp, things were thriving—many had poured in during the summer months from the countryside to test for school. Entrance exams had been given before students could take part; it was very organized.

The Ukrainian Central Committee immediately set up a post office. We had our stamp and tried to get letters to loved ones, to reconnect families, all with the cooperation of the military overseers. This was important. A stamp with our own recognizable identity—a woman with flowers in her hair, dressed in embroidered skirts and carrying a basket— a man dressed like a Kozak holding a staff in his hands, managing the river, these images reminded us of our beloved Ukraine, which was always in our hearts. It encouraged us to go on.

The adult Ukrainians who had participated and promoted the arts before the war set up small plays and music venues. Churches sprang up—Ukrainian Orthodox Catholic and Byzantine Catholic. Genuine Masses were said with real priests. A choir was established with the director, Yosafat Pachovsky. These community activities collectively helped people to stay positive and forward-thinking. It was better than dwelling on our losses.

The Ukrainians also organized their scouting group, Plast. The Scouts program was intended to add normalcy for the younger people and helped retrieve respect for life, and dignity for all. We were a group of Ukrainian patriots reaching for the best in life, and trying our best to honor our heritage.

'*Never take things for granted,*' my father often said. More valid words had never been spoken, we all learned that lesson from the war. One day you have, then the next it's gone, like an elusive fog floating between the hills of life.

School went well, despite some obstacles like the cramped classrooms. We valued the honor of attending school. We were Ukrainian again, living and breathing our esteemed culture...

We finished the first semester successfully with optimism until the unthinkable happened.

CHAPTER 54

December 1945

People were beginning to feel comfortable being Ukrainian again. Our DP community was planning holiday events to celebrate the Christmas season. I was thirteen, taller and pimpled-faced, but my love for the holiday hadn't changed. I was hopeful that this year, my family might honor the holiday as we should.

I missed our old home and the many holiday customs we had abandoned, like the Christmas Eve meal preparation and the caroling house to house in the cold night. I fondly remembered the Christmas spent with the Baumann family. That had been special to me, to share and learn about their customs. It had been a joy to be with them, and I worried about what had become of their little family, and baby Herbert.

One day in December, days before the holiday, Olena and I were reading a short story. She had found a magazine discarded at the hospital where she worked and brought it home so we could translate the American story together.

Tato stormed into our crowded one-room apartment, his expression burned of dark fury. Upon seeing him scowling in the doorway, Olena dropped the magazine, the pages splayed open on the floor.

My stomach knotted and I had to sit down. Adrenaline zipped through my veins as if I were in danger. I presumed there was news about Petro. *Did they find him? Was he sick, or worse?* Something bad had happened.

"What's wrong?" Mama said.

"A group of men representing the Soviets came to the military headquarters and spoke with the camp leaders. They demanded that all people declaring themselves to be Ukrainians had to be immediately handed over to their custody. They claimed that we were in fact, Russian. Even those of us from Galicia and western Ukraine. They said that those areas are currently under Russian rule."

My father understood the situation better than most. He knew that if anyone was handed over to this Russian convoy, they would immediately be sent to Siberia, or worse, killed.

He told the events without care that Olena and I were in the room, he didn't try to conceal anything from us any longer. I supposed that after Petro's disappearance, he thought we ought to understand what's going on and be prepared for the worst. Or perhaps he had become jaded, too much water under the bridge to tolerate anything else after pushing for our freedom for such a long time. My father was worn out.

"You should have heard them, Leysa. They spoke as if they owned us. As if we were some people not worthy of living and breathing like them, mere cattle."

He pounded his hand down on the old table. The few dishes we had placed there rattled, and for a moment I thought some might break. I worried we would have to share one plate again, and the thought of that made me sad because we had come so far to actually each have a plate of our own. For some reason, that seemed important.

"I was with the other Central Committee members discussing the extra activities for our community, you know, the things we talked about. We were planning the final details for the Christmas pageant when they intruded. The Soviet men marched into the headquarters and petitioned for the Ukrainian refugees to be handed over. Like we didn't have a word to say about the matter. They mouthed on about an agreement with Poland or something, some kind of exchange program, sending people back to their home country. Agreed to by the Big Three Allied countries. A resettlement operation called *Vistula* or some sort."

My father flayed his arm in the air.

"The Lieutenant in charge picked up the papers and read the request, but before he could respond with something stupid, we rushed into the room. We raced in there shouting objections. I told the man on duty how we feared for our lives, and that we could not be handed over to a Russian death squad. We demanded that he have the military government review the situation before they responded to the Soviets' outrageous request."

Tato mumbled under his breath and pounded the table again.

"Those pompous Russians stood there huffing and puffing about their rights as if they owned us. I wanted to punch them all."

He held up his arm, prepared to strike.

"Taras, please," Mama's voice quaked.

Tato dropped his arm and hung his head for a few seconds.

"Taras, sit."

Mama pulled out a chair.

"Thankfully, the man in charge granted a review of the situation before any actions were taken. I don't think the

Americans are about to jump to the Soviets' demands, anyway. But now, we have to ensure that other people's politics don't dictate our future—so that we can have a future of our choosing. Leysa, there are so many international rules. I never dreamt that our government would have been kicked out of the Versailles Treaty after the First World War, but we were. If the Americans have their hands tied by the other nation's rules—well, let's pray that it won't come to that."

My tato pulled off his cap, and rested his head into his hands, hiding his face. For a moment, I thought he might be crying, but I was wrong. He lifted his head, his expression enraged.

"I know why they are doing this, Leysa. They're afraid that we will tell the truth and then the entire world will know that the Soviet government is a monster."

Tato raised his arm in the air, his voice almost shouting.

"The Russians want to silence us still, to keep us under their NKVD thumb, or worse to kill us all."

A loud banging stopped my tato mid-thought. Someone in the next room yelled, "keep it down."

Tato took a deep breath.

"This time their genocide won't be silent. We will not go anywhere to lay down and die, not without kicking and screaming, and the Americans will listen. We have their ear now. I pray that the Americans will listen to reason."

"What else can be done, Taras?"

Mama looked old; lines surfaced her face. She had found a way to hide the furrows in the past few weeks, they had smoothed over, but now I could see the deep creases of worry.

"We have ideas. We are writing letters, sending them to the people who have the power to help us—even the president's wife."

My mama laughed at that, and soon, my tato's frustrations ebbed as well. His anger melted when he gazed at Mama's face. Their eyes met and they spoke a silent language between them, a secret communication. A smile slipped through as Tato took a deep breath.

"We will make this work, we haven't traveled this far to give up," Tato said.

My mama kissed the top of his head and began rubbing his shoulders.

"You will figure this out, you and the committee. I have faith in you all."

I was relieved that the anger melted, and they remained hopeful.

Five months later, May 1945

Tense months dragged, but the committee wasted no time. They petitioned the military government. The Americans were good people, but they also were beholden to some universal agreements. Some Ukrainians who had been living in Poland were forcibly sent back to Russia by train to honor an exchange program agreement between the two countries. Immediately the people sent back to Russia were killed upon their arrival.

This knowledge helped our case, proved the threat. But it felt awful to think that some people were still being forced onto trains to their deathbeds.

School continued as if nothing was wrong, we worked hard at our studies. I knew that we had bigger troubles. If we were handed over to the Soviets—I couldn't bear thinking of the consequences. Re-living the hell on earth, watching them imprison my father again—and this time my mother as well—the thought was too staggering to contemplate.

Each night when I went upstairs to our quarters, I saw the desperate expression on my tato's face and his tired eyes. Even my mama's back rubs didn't help his stance. I was only thirteen, but I felt as if I was much older. *How much more anguish could people be exposed to before they burst from exhaustion.*

GOD'S
INTERCESSION

CHAPTER 55

May 31st, 1946

I stepped outside to a warm spring morning, dewdrops kissed the flowers in the pots lining the street. A boat horn blew. The river sounded more rapid than usual, spring thaw and rains had filled its edges to the brim. The smell of fresh fish drifted in the intermittent breeze. My excitement grew — I made plans in my head to grab a fishing pole and try my luck at catching dinner for tonight, after the celebration at school. *Who had a pole I could borrow? Herr Krüger?* I would figure that out later, I was in a hurry to get to class. The last day of the school year had finally arrived.

Our school was lucky to have twelve professional teachers from various parts of Ukraine who volunteered to teach. The enrollment kept swelling with more students arriving from the countryside every day. The Ukrainian community planned a celebration for the few graduates, later in the afternoon, with a gala after marking the first school year's official close.

I was sitting at a desk, waiting to be excused. The morning air was stuffy in the crowded classroom, adding to my misery. We all wanted to leave and prepare for the party, except me...I wanted to find a pole and catch that fish I had been daydreaming about for hours. The taste of freshly caught fish might ease the anxiety I've been experiencing lately.

I'd been in Regensburg too long. I craved the outdoors — to smell the forest once again, feel the dirt under my boots, and hear the wildlife's spring ritual mating calls — that seemed like the right place to be right now. With my brother still missing, my family couldn't appreciate the end of the war—there was still so much unfinished business. My parents' biggest fear was that Petro might be dead, though I didn't believe it for a moment.

The bell rang. As we gathered our things to leave the classroom, our principal stepped to the front of the room, slapped a ruler on the desk, and asked for our attention.

Pan Velychko was sweating, rubbing his collar. Something was wrong.

"I'm afraid I have some bad news to announce." His voice wavered, he cleared his throat. "Listen, please. We have to cancel today's event."

The room filled with cohesive mumbles of disbelief.

"Sorry, sorry. Please listen, people." He slapped the ruler again to gain control of the room. "We cannot hold our commemoration celebration as hoped. Children, go directly home with your parents and stay safe. If your parents couldn't make it here today, go back to the dorm with your friends without delay. And stay together."

There were parents in the classroom, who had traveled for miles to be there on the last day and to take part in the graduation gala.

"Pan Velychko, what's the meaning of this?" a man said.

"Don't the children deserve the recognition?" a woman added.

"What good reason could there be to deny them this?" another woman blurted. "We have been through so much. Shouldn't they be allowed some joy in their life?"

Our principal stood frozen; hands clasped behind his back. His sweat now glistened as the sunlight beamed through the window and traced his face.

"Please, let me explain. You will all find out soon enough. We have no choice. I'm sorry to announce that we canceled the commemorations. We received some unfortunate news. A few of our students have been abducted by the Soviets."

People gasped, like one giant breath of disbelief, then panic ensued. The adults all spoke at the same time.

"Please, calm down," Pan Velychko called out. "Go to your homes and stay safe. Our committee is working on a solution. We are working on it now, as we speak. Please don't be frightened. Have faith the kidnapped children will be returned."

Nothing the principal said comforted them, and the classroom was emptied. I was the last to exit, nodding to Pan Velychko on my way out.

I ran to our quarters, looking in all directions and praying the Soviet soldiers wouldn't grab me on my way there. I thought about how sad my parents were since Petro went missing, and if I were snatched, they would be devastated.

"Tato, Tato." I cried aloud as I entered the room.

Only my mother and Olena were there. Mama stood and reached out her arms. She took my hand in hers.

"Your tato is talking with the other men. They are planning something to get our children back. We learned about what happened after you left. I wasn't able to stop you. I've been so worried."

Mama hugged me so tight that I couldn't breathe.

"I'm fine, Mama." I let go and sat on my cot.

My sister had resorted to her sassiest tone. "Ivan, didn't you worry when you saw that Mama and I weren't at school?"

"No, I didn't, Olena. I was with my friends. We were making plans for vacation. We all want to go camping together."

"Unless your tato and the others can fix this, no one will be going to camp this summer."

My face burned. How could Mama say such a thing? I knew the abduction was terrible but were we to stop living our lives again, right when we got them back.

"I don't care, I'm going camping, and that's final." I stood and stomped my foot then ran from the room, rushed past Herr Krüger, and out the door, then seated myself on the stoop and pouted. I knew I was acting like a child and shouldn't have lost my temper, but I had been dreaming of going away to camp...it had kept me going every day. I needed to connect with nature again, to be away from all this turmoil and worry in Regensburg.

My father returned a few minutes later, stared at me for a moment, then grabbed me by the shoulders.

"What's wrong, Ivan? Did you hear the news? Don't worry, I'll keep us safe. We will make this right. I promise."

Looking up at my tato, I squinted when the sun hit my eyes. Tears stung them, but I refused to cry. I was angry, not sad, and I was no longer a baby brother. I was a teenager. My older brother was twenty already, he had been missing for so long. I missed him.

So many missing pieces. We can't allow the Russians to control us again, it must never happen. My father and the committee would fix this, I had faith in them. All I needed was to go to Scout camp before I burst. I longed to be in the forest again, smell the fresh air, and to feel free. Room to breathe and dream once more. I was smothering with all the realism around us.

My tato pulled me up by my hands, then squeezed me so tight that I was reminded of bears hugging. For a second, all I wanted was to stay there in that moment with my father, feeling loved and safe from all the evil surrounding us.

He sighed, then said, "*dobryj chlopec.*" After a few moments, he released me, pushed me into the building, and we went upstairs together.

Word of the kidnapping spread throughout the area, fast. Some families panicked and fled—hiding away—afraid of the worst. Many still harbored traumatizing memories of what the Russians did—like Holodomor. I often thought of that poor woman who washed clothes with my mama that one day, how the woman still struggled with her loss every day of her life. How horrific it must have been for her to watch her children and parents die before her eyes, and not a quick death, but laborious starvation until her loved ones were nothing more than skin and bones. To find her husband hanging from a rafter, unable to live with the nightmare, overcome with grief.

I shook inside, my chest collapsing of air, as I still heard the woman's haunted wails echoing in my mind.

I didn't blame anyone who tried to hide, I would most likely do the same with those kinds of terrible memories.

The Soviets made our lives hell. They forbad our schools and churches and shot political prisoners. When they retreated from Galicia, they implemented their scorched-earth policy—blowing up buildings to leave them as waste for the Germans. They destroyed crops and burned food storage, even flooded mines. We had heard all the horror stories from other Ukrainians who were in the camp.

Our community was desperate to stay out of harm's way and petitioned for months to the military government. Ukrainians were not Soviets, we weren't Czechs or Poles, either. Now more than ever, we needed to stay together, united as a people. No one could erase our culture, our uniqueness.

Despite all the fear this news of the kidnapping generated, most of us Ukrainians remained in Regensburg. We organized a plan as fast as bees around a hive. The need was urgent—our friends must be returned to us.

The Ukrainian community masterminded a plan within hours. There was no time to debate options. It was a simple plan, yet moving—One Voice.

Men, women, and children—we all gathered in the street with a sense of urgency. Side by side we walked through the city with our priests from the various Ukrainian churches leading the way.

We marched singing hymns in our Ukrainian language, songs of thankfulness for God's blessings, songs of our Ukraine, and what home meant to us.

We carried hastily painted home-made banners and waved flags—as many blue and yellow flags we could find stowed away in our belongings. Some were sewn in short notice with any cloth we could find. The children gathered the items in a flurry and the women sewed, some men, too.

We walked deliberately into the center of the city, carrying our flags and signs, and only stopped when we reached the front of the headquarters of the temporary government.

I stood in the middle of the crowd behind dozens of others; we packed the Platz. I was wedged between two older women who were dressed in black as if attending a funeral. They carried a banner between them that said, *"free the Ukrainian students."* I felt like a prop in the middle to emphasize their message.

Appeals were spoken aloud by some of the men up front, perhaps they were the priests saying another prayer, I couldn't make out who the speakers were or hear their petitions. But whatever they said, it was short and to the point.

Then suddenly, a solemn silence unfolded like velvet, as if some kind of magic was sprinkled over us. No one spoke a word, stiller than a library, as serene as a church while waiting for the confessional. The void of sound persisted. Quietness filled my ears. I swallowed hard, hearing only my heartbeat.

Eerie as it was, I recognized that this was a momentous event. This was the power of people—but something bigger than us all—we were prayerful together for a common goal named freedom.

Then together, we knelt on the hard, dirty, wet, cobbled street. We were a flock of people kneeling before other people who held our destiny in their hands. *Birds in a hand, would we be captured or freed?* We hoped for justice. By demanding the kidnapped children back, we were also insisting that they see us for who we were—Ukrainians, not Russians.

In our humility, we kneeled and prayed for God's intercession—for his will to be done—just like it said in the prayer *Our Father*.

No loud cries of praise for glory, nor calls for justice were uttered, only mumbles. Like the hum of bees or the sound of a breeze swaying through the branches of willow, a great force of nature was released.

I knelt with the others, not giving a care that the pavement was hard on my knees. Side by side, we prayed, and the power of our communal prayer revealed itself, a supreme strength like I had never known before or since.

A peacefulness flooded my spirit, and for a moment I knew in my heart that things would work out. An imaginary road unfolded before me, throwing away the barbed-wire and bricks that scattered the way and clearing a path for me.

I was capable of forgiveness and soon forgot all the iniquities of the war. My soul moved on to a brighter future—my destiny lay before me to be fulfilled. These devoted people, my fellow Ukrainians, no matter which region they had originated from, we all had something special and in common—our dream of freedom.

I knew those watching us as we joined together would feel the power, too. We would have the children returned.

Time was lost, I don't recall how long we knelt on the hard road, but whatever we said in our collective prayer, it worked. Like an electric current, our compelling display of unity in peaceful protest for the return of our beloved children moved the military government in charge.

They granted our wishes. Russia, the Soviets, had no control over our future any longer. We received sanctuary. Our young fellow students were returned the following morning...

But there were a couple of surprises we hadn't foreseen.

CHAPTER 56

Most of the protestors returned to their places to sleep. Only a few remained in the city to hammer out the details of the agreement with the military government. My tato decided to stay at the headquarters with other committee members to assure the students were returned in good health with no strings attached.

"Take your mama and Olena back to the room. I will see you all soon, I promise," Tato said.

I looked over my shoulder, as I watched my father walk away to join the other leaders. I knew how lucky I was to have a great man for a father.

We walked home without speaking to each other, Olena, Mama, and me. It was a warm evening, humid after the short spring rain earlier in the day, and barely a star visible in the overcast sky. We ate dinner, canned peas and a small piece of meat called chipped beef. Not the fresh fish I had dreamed of eating, but I realized how lucky we were to have food.

We prayed again, this time in private, or as private as we could be in a one-room apartment.

Three hours passed, and I was tempted to walk back to the city's center to find my father. I tested various scenarios in my head as a cover story, so I could slip out without Mama asking questions, and then, the door burst open.

"Blessed be God! You'll never believe our good fortune," Tato called out.

He was giddy, more than I had ever seen Tato before, and he looked as if he was about to dance some kind of jig.

I jumped off the cot and saw him. Behind Tato, stood my brother. Petro was alive and present.

A quickening rushed through my body. *Was my chest caving into my heart?* It was impossible, but there he stood. So overcome with joy, I could not speak.

Part of me, deep inside, was afraid this was another dream, a mirage, not Petro standing there in front of us. *Tato had brought him — Petro must be real this time.* I closed my eyes and blinked a few times.

Petro held out his arms, and Mama pulled him close. She cried with happiness, muttering to herself prayers of thanks, then Mama repeatedly kissed his forehead while tears streamed down her face.

Olena sat on the bed, she too had tears running down her face. Tato plopped himself down next to her, wrapped his arm around her.

"Isn't it wonderful. Our prayers have been answered," he said.

Olena bobbed her head, she was speechless, too.

I was the only one frozen, afraid that this was another dream, afraid that I'd wake up to find it wasn't true. After worrying about my brother for so long, wondering if I'd see him again, I even imagined him — talking to me like a ghost, and now he stood in front of us as if nothing had ever happened. I felt drool drip from my mouth, so I snapped it shut and wiped my mouth with my sleeve.

I stared at him, *had he changed? Was this the same brother?* No, not the same, he was twenty now, a man. Something else seemed different about him, a far-away look in his eyes. He was my brother in physical form with his lanky arms and legs, same face, and brawny forehead. But his blue eyes...they looked haunted now. Tainted, his spark was gone.

Hundreds of thoughts ran through my head, memories of our younger days mingled with my fears of losing him to the war. I remembered the sound of his laughter when he joked. The way he sat so straight in class, such seriousness, always carrying his notebook. All the times I imagined him speaking to me when he was missing, the ache I felt when I looked into our father's eyes, wondering if he was dead.

I searched my brother's face, looked deep into his eyes again, wishing to see them sparkling once more.

Petro broke away from Mama's grasp, marched over to me, and grabbed me by the arms.

I flinched.

"You've grown so much, Ivan."

I felt his hands—firm—real.

He pulled me into his arms and hugged me.

I collapsed into his chest. I smelled his sweat, felt warmth penetrating through his shirt, felt, and heard his heartbeat—steady beats, his breathing—moving, alive. My big brother had returned, it was Petro.

I wept with joy. I didn't deserve such happiness but would greedily take all the luck that passed my way. Whatever had happened to Petro didn't matter now, we were together again. My brother was alive.

Petro went to our sister next, and the tearful blubbering seemed unending. After a few minutes, we gained our composure. His presence was becoming real to us. It was quiet only for a few minutes. Then we barraged Petro with a million questions. This time it was our father doing most of the interrogation.

"Come, sit. Tell us everything. Where have you been, Petro?"

"That last day when I was here in Regensburg the commander received orders. We were directed to move, so the training group marched out of the city without a chance to tell anyone. We were supposed to go to another city to join more soldiers. Linz perhaps, I'm not sure where or what was going on, but we traveled for days."

Petro wiped his hands on his pants.

"Then one night I heard a commotion going on in the camp. The officers were arguing about going to another country, I think. I'm still uncertain of what they said. But the Germans seemed very upset by the correspondence they received. They were quarreling among themselves, that's when the two other Ukrainians, you know the boys I befriended in training. I told you about them, right?"

We all nodded.

"Well, they thought we should use the opportunity. So, we made a rash decision and used the diversion to slip away. We crawled away from the camp, while they were still arguing. I thought we were quiet enough to go undetected. After a few hundred meters or more, there was a field. We got up and ran. Then I heard shots behind me."

Petro had begun to pant between his sentences.

"The soldiers knew we escaped. I never ran so fast in my life. They shot at us, in the back. I was so frightened, I thought I was a dead man."

Mama handed Petro a cup. He stopped a moment and took a sip of water. The memory had shaken him up, he was almost out of breath.

"It's all right, Petro. Take your time. You're safe now," Tato said.

Petro nodded and took another moment to clear his head. The room was quiet as we waited to hear more.

"Well, I ran into an old farmyard. I looked back and saw one of my friends fall. I think he was shot dead. I have no idea about the other fellow, there was no sign of him at all. I ran into the barn and hid under some hay. Soldiers came in and looked around, I heard them call at each other, but then they left. I think they thought I wasn't worth their time. As I said, they were supposed to go somewhere. They were all heated up about some plan."

Petro drew in a deep breath and blew out. His face looked pale, and I wondered how long it had been since his last meal.

"I stayed put for the rest of the night and slept in the hay-loft even though it stunk like hell. The next morning an old farmer came out to the barn. He called out to me that it was safe, I could come out, for all I knew it could have been a trap but I chose to believe in him. I was tired of being buried in hay."

I laughed aloud at that remark, and Petro shot me a smirk. Yes, underneath his anger and fear, this was my brother. That one gesture, his cockeyed smile, laughing at me, it made me feel confident that he'd be all right. I blew out a sigh of relief.

"The farmer was kind, he gave me normal clothes, fed me, and then sent me on my way. Told me never to return."

"Thank the Lord. Bless that man," Mama said.

"So, after that, what happened? You've been gone a long time."

Tato seemed concerned, even though Petro was here, safe and sound.

"Then, I met up with an American troop from the USA. One of the soldiers said I could tag along and help them, you know do some camping chores, which I did for a bit until they received orders to rush to some other town. I think they were supposed to help free some people in one of those concentration camps. They said I couldn't come with them because I was a kid plus not trained or authorized for that kind of work. Geez, some of the American soldiers were practically the same age as me. Strong fellows, though, ready to fight for freedom."

Mama nodded.

"So, they impressed you."

"Yes, they did."

"What happened next," I prodded. "And what does *geez* mean?"

Petro laughed and punched my shoulder.

"That's something the Americans say. Kind of like when we say *oiy* or *bozhe*. Anyway, after they left. I wandered on my own trying to get back to Regensburg, I almost made it, too. Until I was caught off guard by a small band of Soviet soldiers. They took me captive. I gave them my name and told them I was from Galicia—that was a big mistake.

"They said I must be a soldier from the Galicia Division of the Waffen SS. I tried to tell them that they were wrong and that I was running away from the Nazis. That I wanted nothing to do with any of those extremists who were siding with the Germans. They wouldn't believe me. They insisted that I was fighting for that Stepan fellow that you talked about, Tato. They thought I was a radical like him. They forced me to go with them, seized on the spot."

My mother's face was as white as a ghost.

"I thought Stepan was arrested?"

My tato nodded.

"Did they mistreat you, Petro, hurt you in any way?"

Mama kneaded her hands, prayer beads twisted around her fingers. A shimmer of light reflected off of her crystal rosary and it made me wonder if that was a sign, *would everything be all right?*

"They pushed me around and stuff, but I'm okay. Bruises heal. They brought me to a place and held me in a sort of jail, I have no idea where I was, it was dark and smelled foul. And then, some other kids were put in the same cell as me. I heard them talking in Ukrainian and realized they were from Regensburg. I couldn't believe my ears. I told them who I was, and at first, they didn't believe me. They probably thought it was a Russian trick or something. Then I mentioned things about you. They soon realized you had to be my family—I knew too much for you not to be."

Petro smiled, then swallowed another sip of water.

"They helped me leave when they were being released. It happened so fast... things were confusing. Some guards had just swapped duty right then while the others were being released. They whispered for me to pretend my name was Ivan Rudenko—and it worked—they let me leave with the group of students. For once, I tricked a Russian. God, thank you! And you too, Ivan. I used your name, after all."

Listening to my brother's story, I knew my family was blessed. It was all just a matter of coincidence, timing, being in the right place. My family never let fear rule over our ethics, well, at least we tried. I thanked God for my Tato and his lessons. I thanked God for every blessed moment, the good and bad.

Even though I was thirteen now, I knelt beside my cot and said extra prayers of thanks that night, like I did when I was a boy.

The second surprise came to our community with welcoming arms. Our school was given a proper building—a real school. We now had nearly 200 students attending our gymnasium. More teachers came forward, twenty so far, as more students enrolled. Many practiced taking their final exams to graduate. Our little Ukrainian community was thriving despite the circumstances that brought us here.

Together, we performed plays, sang in choirs, practiced our arts, set up a postal service, practiced faith in our churches, debated our politics, planned scouting activities, and celebrated our culture. It seemed as if the flood gates were opened to the parched fields, and the life-giving water spilled into the plains of drought. Wildflowers and life-giving wheat bloomed so that we could reap and nurture our souls.

CHAPTER 57

Summer 1946

Time waited for no one. I learned much since we left Halych, even more since the war ended. Walking alone at times, I tried to make sense of all that had happened. Life wasn't a dream, and I knew now that war for any generation was nothing to fantasize about.

I will turn fourteen on my next birthday, days away. If the war hadn't ended when it did, I would have been next in line to get pushed into some country's army.

War was an ugly business and must have been just as horrible ages ago for the Goths and the Kievan Rus' people who followed Yaroslav the Wise, the Grand Prince of Kyiv as they fought for Christianity. Religious freedom was worth fighting for, and people's rights to have their beliefs were paramount. *But at what cost?*

Ukrainians and the Kozak code have always believed in an individual's freedom. But, nothing in life was free, I knew that now. But fighting for freedom didn't have to have such a heavy cost, didn't have to use weapons that caused detrimental ruin.

People's tenacity was the most essential tool...even if it took years, our faith, hope, and charity were by far the most powerful of all weapons. I recalled what my father said years ago to Mama, *"what good is living without a soul."* We all must do our best without crossing lines that turned us into the monsters we are against. That was what caused war...the monsters people created in themselves.

"Ivan, did you hear?"

Olena crashed into me and hugged me so hard I thought that she was going crazy.

"What's going on?"

It was nice seeing my sister so happy.

"They're going to have Plast camp this summer, and we're going."

She jumped up and down, clapping her hands as if she was some little child.

"Are you kidding?"

She shook her head without missing a beat. "It will be so much fun. The C.R.U.E. put together our registration and arranged it all. They said that we would benefit from having some cultural activities to help round our education," Olena said.

"You know what this means, right? You'll be camping with the scout troop, probably sleeping in tents and on the ground again if there aren't any barracks."

Olena turned her head up.

"I know, but I'll see my friends again. They said Ukrainians from the other DP camps will be there. We can look for our old friends from Halych," Olena said.

"I'm happy for you, Olena. And for me, too. It's going to be great fun."

Summer Camp couldn't have started soon enough. I longed to be outdoors, away from the beat-up city. We met up with some old friends from Halych at *Oselia*. That fat boy,

Yyri, was there, though not chubby any longer; he looked tall and strong now. I still didn't like him, he seemed to look down on me as if I was that younger boy who told lies. He never understood me.

Most of the others from Halych only remembered my sister. Olena lit up when she saw her girlfriends from our old school. I watched them from afar, totally confused by their constant chattering and jumping up and down.

Then I spotted one girl who was off to the side by herself, quiet. She was lovely, with soft-looking blonde hair braided and pinned to her head. Her eyes glimmered, like those movie stars on the magazine covers. Her face glowed, her cheeks so pink and smooth looking. I wanted to touch her face to find out for myself what she felt like.

*Later I'll ask my sister about that girl, her name, her friends, her age...*as I contemplated my plan, I noticed that the girl had her eye on me. She walked toward me, her body seemed to float as she drew closer, and my heart skipped beats.

I broke out in a sweat, my hands felt clammy. I sniffed to check if my underarms smelled, and tried to remember if I had combed my hair.

She stood to my side and smiled up at me.

I was in heaven.

"Hello, my name is Kateryna."

Her voice sounded as soft and pure as her hair looked. She gazed up and blinked.

"Well, who are you?"

I felt my face burn up.

"Oh, please forgive me. I'm Ivan. Ivan Rudenko. Do you go to school here?"

"Here at Plast camp?"

She giggled.

"No. My family recently arrived in Germany. We want to emigrate to America."

I smiled at that.

"My family wants to go to the United States, too."

She sighed.

"We are sponsored to go to Canada. Alberta, Canada."

I wasn't sure where that was, or how far away it would be from wherever we ended up going, but we would both be Americans.

Awkwardly, I asked her if she'd like to walk with me. There was a nice path in the woods and we strolled. I pointed out the different kinds of trees and told her stories about my family's travels.

She shared her own experiences and explained how her family arrived from Vienna. We talked about all the beauty we found in the woods, and how both of us were nature lovers. We had so much in common, and from that moment on, talking with Kateryna became easier.

Each day afterward, I looked forward to spending time with her during our free-time. We explored the area, hiking as we sang, and read poetry together under the trees. We shared possibilities, our dreams, and what we would do once in America. We repeated our daily stroll for the next three weeks while at camp, a routine I welcomed.

I found myself daydreaming of Kateryna all morning while working on my badges with the other scouts, anticipating our time together during the afternoon. No matter how much we shared, I wanted to know more about her and craved to hold her in my arms and kiss her. One afternoon I found my nerve.

We walked along the nearby river. There was a nice flat area near a natural pool, and I laid down a small blanket I had taken with me for her to sit on. It was shaded and cool, the water rippled, the small fish swam in circles in the deeper waters between the rocks, and we laughed as we watched them. Then we sat quietly for a moment and listened to the water gently splashing, peaceful, and content on the outside, enjoying the warmth of the day.

But inside my head, I was cursing myself with rebukes for not being honest with her about my true feelings. I was a coward. Finally, I took a deep breath and a chance.

I leaned closer, turned her face to heed mine, and I looked into her eyes, fixated on their bright blue color. Then I closed my eyes as I kissed her, softly touching her plump lips. We shared the first kiss.

Happiness filled me, I was floating as light as air, and a new strange feeling came over me. I tingled inside and out and wanted our kiss to never end. Her breath was warm, her skin so soft, as I lovingly touched her cheek and neck. My head told me one thing, my heart another.

She responded to me, as natural as could be, and soon passion took control. She wrapped her fingers in my brown hair, tugged, and then gently circled them against my skin seductively when we kissed again.

We ventured another touch, cuddling, embracing each other as we closed the space between our bodies. Then, I lowered my head to rest on her chest, heard her life beating, and smelled her sweet perfume of violets.

I discovered a deeper appreciation for her with each slow stroke nestled against her milky skin, as my fingers gently wandered her body, and as she sighed back to me in excitement. She leaned over and kissed me on the top of my head, and encouraged me to continue to touch her, as she massaged my back. The remaining afternoon went by too fast and felt surreal. I was in love with Kateryna.

I knew eventually, we would each have to leave and go our own way. I'd never see her again. After summer camp, she and her family would travel to Canada to relocate. I wanted to beg her to stay with me, to come to Regensburg to school, but I knew how silly an idea that would be. I had no way to take care of her, and we were too young to marry, but I loved her so.

Young love had touched my heart. It felt so good and at the same time, it hurt.

Ukrainian scouts gathered from all the other DP camps in Germany. We were all from different areas of Ukraine. Some of our families planned to travel to Canada, like Kateryna, others to Australia, South America, wherever possible once their paperwork was completed. Our futures looked different, yet our experience of the three weeks together created long-lasting memories.

The scoutmasters encouraged us to be creative. At night we entertained each other and sang songs around a large campfire. We performed skits and the fun of it helped us to escape from our reality for a while. I imagined that I was an

American movie star when I acted with my group. We performed a mock scene from Romeo and Juliet, making fun of the poetic lines, but when it was time to serenade the heroine, I stared and smiled at Kateryna.

We all worked together and built extra cabins for future Plast campers. We were encouraged to express our ideas with each other in a civil manner. We finished projects together and this made a significant impact on us all. I had never felt this good around others, and for the first time in my life, I felt a need to nurture my ties with outsiders, people other than my family.

We forged bonds that summer. At first, it seemed like we were sharing simple friendships and scout activities. But by the time we had to say good-bye, we realized that we shared more than Plast camp…more than three weeks.

We shared the experience of surviving World War II as Ukrainians.

Those memories proved to be the cement in our future — we had no clue how important, or tightly bound, those bonds became. Our destinies were intertwined, and we didn't even know it.

Eventually, we would pick up the torch that our parents handed us, and blaze a way for future Ukrainians who dreamed of freedom.

I was heartbroken when we returned to Regensburg from Plast camp. I thought of Kateryna all the time. I drove my family mad with my brooding, and short temper. Tato reprimanded me, and I promised him that I would try to be more agreeable. But he didn't understand how much I had lost the day I said good-bye to Kateryna.

Classes resumed in the Regensburg gymnasium. After school, I still helped at the hospital when I could. I had more activities to keep me busy than ever before in my life. Choir practice was three times a week. I went to a weekly Plast meeting, and attended Ukrainian dance lessons twice a week.

Our lives were filled and continually challenged intellectually. In school, I did my usual studies, but in the evening, I studied with Petro. Together, we learned the English language and read from books loaned to us by soldiers.

Our teachers and parents expected us to do our best and were never afraid to pile on the pressure. The stakes were high, always more to do, to learn, and I often became overwhelmed.

Some days, I felt as if I would choke from all the tension. My nerves were overwrought from the rushing reality of everything that was permeating my brain. It was those moments when I sought out my father. Tato always knew what to say to put things back into perspective, that part never changed.

CHAPTER 58

Spring 1947

School finished for the term and I wanted to goof off, I was depressed and missed Kateryna, but Tato expected me to do my work. As always, my father was right. We were the future hope for generations to come, but we could only become a beacon if we took things step by step, building a strong foundation.

"Someday we will be citizens in a new country, so we need to be able to offer something to the country, to show we are worthy of the honor," Tato said. "But Ivan, you can only be good for others if you take care of yourself first. Don't waste your time worrying, or pinning away for a girl that lives far away. Instead, use your time wisely. Enjoy the doing, then the result will be sweeter."

I took my father's advice. Though I cherished the time I had spent with Kateryna, I continued with my dreams. I knew that was what she would want me to do. Every night I prayed she was happy.

Summer 1947

In August the 6th World Scout Jamboree was held in Moisson France. They called it the *Jamboree of Peace*, and twenty-five thousand scouts from seventy different countries attended. Unfortunately, the Ukrainian Scouts weren't acknowledged by the organization. We never received invitations, so we stayed close to Regensburg and camped on our own.

Three older boys from the Lion Troop of our Plast company, Wolodymyr, Vladymyr, and Bohdan, decided they would crash the jamboree. They made their way to Paris on their own without invitation, passports, or any type of travel itinerary.

When I heard about this shortly after they left, I was jealous. How I wanted to go, to see others from different parts of the world. Even the Girl Scouts were attending the jamboree, perhaps Kateryna would be there from Canada. I knew it was a long shot, but I wished I had known before they left, I would have begged them to take me along even though we weren't close friends.

When the three teenagers returned, the rest of us scouts happened to be sitting around a campfire. They joined us and told the wild stories about their trip to France, and about the people who helped them cross the border along the way. The boys were surprised when a small group of twenty Ukrainian scouts from the Munich DP camp were announced. They leaped to the stage and performed skits and danced dressed in Ukrainian Hutsul costumes for the other scouts. Bohdan said that it had given him chills. At the end of the day, the scouts sang together by the campfire. It sounded like a great time.

Flags flew in the breeze on the main stage, one from every home country of the attending scouts. But of course, not the Ukrainian flag. When the jamboree ended, all the scouts from the various nations, spilled into the main field. They rolled a balloon twelve meters wide and painted like a globe, on top of their heads. Then the boys showed us their patches and hats they brought back. Their stories went on all night.

I listened in awe to their wondrous adventures. I decided that night that somehow, I would go to the next jamboree. We were lucky, to be given this chance to be a Plast Scout again. I vowed that whenever my family left this place, I would somehow keep the Ukrainian Scouts going. Perhaps if we arrived as Ukrainian Scouts from another nation, then we could raise our flag with all the others. I dreamed of that day...

Ukrainians were being sponsored all over the world and that would ensure our culture never died. We were going to places where freedom was allowed, and we would have the right to practice the traditions and customs that we hold dear.

I swore to myself that after we relocated to the United States, I would work hard and save my money so that I could go to one of the world-wide jamborees. Then I could reconnect with my new friends and meet more. Perhaps one day I might see Kateryna there. I spent a lot of time fantasizing about Kateryna that summer, musing about the previous summer, and dreaming of meeting her again someday.

Late 1947

Our excitement grew with each passing day. Finally, in the fall, we had a Scout meeting house to use for activities. We shared the hall with other DP Scouts who were Polish, Belarusians, Latvians, Lithuanians, Estonians, Slovenians, and Yugoslavs.

One of our leaders, Bohdan, painted murals on the walls, depicting scouting themes. It was a wonderful place to hang out with my friends between our duties and I met new friends.

No matter our nationality, we all shared the same anxieties associated with the war fatigue. And we all grew excited about the rapid changes happening—the promise of better days to come. It was a fantastic time to be a teenager.

Many prominent visitors arrived at our DP camp. The Plast troop was always present to welcome and entertain the guests. High ranking officials from Canada were impressed with our organizations when they visited. We had many scientists and cultural artists, and soon more sponsorship invitations arrived from that country.

As the invitations arrived, more people left the DP camp, most headed to the United States. My family waited for our turn to be hosted. We were part of the last remaining people in our DP community. Like a bad joke, my family had been there even before there was a camp. My father had started a small group of Ukrainian activists even before the Americans appeared on the scene. I wondered if our turn would ever arrive...our hope and dream of freedom still hung in the air.

CHAPTER 59

1948

Regensburg was mostly comprised of Germans, now. Many Ukrainian and Jewish refugees, as well as others seeking asylum from various countries like Poland, Latvia, Lithuania, and Czechoslovakia, had already left the DP camp. Ukrainian Americans who were already US citizens helped those of us still waiting. The sponsors promised housing and jobs until we were ready to support ourselves, that was the requirement.

There was a visit from the prominent Archbishop Ivan Buchko, who conveyed our status to the Pope himself. Shortly after, the people in our Regensburg camp connected with sponsors led by churches, women's groups, and the like. Paperwork was completed in record time.

Those of us dreamers who remained anticipated future travels to America. We had a *"Week of Ukrainian Culture"* and were visited by high ranking Generals and American politicians. They must have been impressed because of a keen interest in our fate seemed to top their list.

My family and others waited a bit longer. I began to wonder if my tato enjoyed helping others so much, he purposefully stayed behind. He worked diligently to help, cleaned up messes, both the physical and the diplomatic kind.

Each morning I woke, went to school, read, and helped wherever I could. After school, I volunteered at the hospital, even though Hank had returned home already. They still needed extra hands. I often got the worst jobs, like bedpans, but I did it while holding my nose. It wasn't as bad as sneaking people into sewers, and it had to get done. Better it be me than my mama or someone like her.

My family had been living near the Displaced People Camp in Regensburg, in a one-room apartment, for four and a half years. We attended classes with the other Ukrainian refugees. When our friends graduated from the gymnasium, we celebrated with them.

Friends we had met through Plast, who lived in different camps run by the other Allied countries, were also given a path to citizenship. Many traveling to Australia, South America, and Canada.

All our dreams were coming true. Some of our friends wrote and let us know that they made it safely to their new country, and wished us the best. Each letter ended with promises to stay in touch... a tether to keep Ukrainians rooted together somehow, despite the distance.

One afternoon I received a letter from Kateryna.

When I realized it was from her, my stomach flipped and I almost swallowed my tongue. I hurriedly opened the envelope, and quickly gazed at her dainty handwriting. She drew a flower in the corner, so sweet.

She wrote that her family was very happy and doing well. She was attending school, studying Horticultural Science, at Olds College. She remembered the summer we shared fondly and thought of me often. She closed with promises of writing again soon. Her words hung in the air, and I drifted into daydreaming about her.

Each day I waited for the mail, only to be disappointed. After waiting months without any more letters, I figured she had moved on to some new love.

I was brokenhearted. I stopped going to the post office and spent more hours down by the river staring across the water as I fished, wishing I was back in the woods.

Autumn 1948

The big day finally arrived. Tato received notification that our family had a sponsor, but first, we had to report to the clinic for a health check.

The very next day Mama, Olena, and I entered the health office and sat in chairs that were lined up against the wall. While we waited my mama coughed. A couple of women who were also seated in the waiting room turned and stared at her, then turned sideways on their chair to avoid breathing the same air.

I felt affronted, why would they look at her like that?

A nurse stepped forward, out of nowhere, and led my mother into the examination room first. Only minutes passed. Mama came back out.

"Come on then, put on your coats."

Her voice sounded gruff, not like Mama at all. She marched out without waiting for us. We followed her back to our one-room home, without a word spoken, and climbed the stairs.

I entered the room, noticing how small the place looked, even a snail couldn't fit in the corner. My tato was sitting on the bed reading a paper. He looked up when we arrived, his expression puzzled.

"We were taken off the list."

Mama broke down and sobbed. Tato leaped to his feet and hugged her. She pushed him away. I couldn't believe my eyes.

"I'm so sorry, Taras. They said we can't go because I have this cough. Stay away from me or else you'll be sick, too. You and the children should go on without me."

We all looked at each other.

Was my mother mad? I swallowed hard.

"Absolutely not," Tato said.

"We can all wait with you, nurse you to good health. Then we will go to America together."

Once again, his voice made me feel safe, and I knew everything would be fine. But again, more bad news...just days later.

On November 25th, Scoutmaster Mykhailo Ivanenko died. He was only sixty-eight, but he had been sick for a while. Four priests said his funeral Mass, and after all the prayers were said, a group of us from Plast laid green wreaths on his grave.

He was loved by all at the camp, not only Plast, but also the other Ukrainian Youth Association called SUM, the Veterans from the underground, the local chorus groups, and all the camp residents who remained. He had united us from the beginning, working well with other people like my father on the committee to set up our little community.

My father took the news hard, and he vowed to help organize a monument in his honor.

A NEW FUTURE

A NEW REPORT

CHAPTER 60

January 1949

My family received word that it was our turn again. This time, we all passed our health tests without even a sneeze, then were asked all kinds of questions about our past activities back home. We passed the questionnaire and met the requirements set by the Displaced Persons Act of 1948. We prepared to travel to the United States and were assigned a seat on a train, then passage on an American troopship.

I can't recall how long it took us to travel to the port. I was more interested in the book I was reading. *Kingsblood Royal* by Sinclair Lewis. One of the servicemen in the hospital had given it to me as a departing gift. I never thought that such a book existed.

I became enthralled in it as the main character, Neil Kingsblood, discovered his black ancestry and was kicked out of the white neighborhood where he lived. Even though his skin was white, every part of his life changed because of his black ancestry. The story gave me great pause. *Would the people in the United States treat me and my family unfairly because we were different? I* hoped not, but as I read the book, I prepared myself for the worst.

When I was a small child everything affected me, any small change and it bothered me. But after this war, I was immune to the changing scenery. So much had happened, and I thought that I could survive anything. *But could I survive rejection in our new home country? I* knew how I felt after Kateryna stopped writing to me. I felt inside-out. *How would*

I feel if Americans treated us badly to our faces? I sat in the train's booth and read the book until we arrived at the port.

We boarded with a throng of others, onto the largest ship I had ever seen. That's when my attention left the book behind.

My curiosity shifted focus, I was a child again asking questions. My mind opened and I became a sponge, scampering around the ship as much as allowed, snooping in the various sections, and inspecting the equipment. Whenever I could, asking the crewmen questions.

The immensity of the ship inspired me, and I found myself dreaming of being an engineer. I had passed my graduation exams, which the school had given to a small group of us, last minute before leaving. I was ready for college, as soon as I turn eighteen.

At night I laid in my hammock in the men's dormitory and imagined drawing up prints of ships, then bridges, and anything else huge. I envisioned the angles, how things would fit together, often keeping myself awake all night with these new fantasies.

I dreamed up buildings, tall, wide, impressive designs. I played a game with myself, envisioning the position of every connecting corridor, each plumbing stack, and broom closet. It was a challenge for me to create a frugal design in my head.

I had read about Frank Lloyd Wright, a great American architect. His early designs influenced the Arts and Crafts style. Later he designed with more open plans for both houses and buildings he designed. He blended structures into its surroundings using what he called, '*organic architecture*', like his famous *Fallingwater* house in Pennsylvania. His Prairie house style and later his Usonian style, both shared the idea that family life revolved around the hearth. I liked that idea.

The man had a troubled home life, his many marriages were a bit scandalous, and his own home which he named Taliesin was burned twice. He rebuilt it despite it all and taught students in his home. His family motto was '*the truth against the world*' and I wondered what was his truth. I wanted to be intellectually like him, but there was much to learn. I reasoned it was best to start with my surroundings.

I was permitted to visit with the Captain, and I questioned him about the ship, about the way the ports work, about the new country we were about to embark on. The Captain was generous with his time and answers. I imagined grandeur from his high praise of the Port of Authority. He told me about the New York International Airport, too. How President Truman came to the dedication opening. How they had a groundbreaking ceremony last September for the site of the United Nations' world headquarters.

The Captain praised New York and all the big stuff that happened there. Musicals and plays like *"Kiss Me Kate"* starred on Broadway. He told me all about baseball, and how Babe Ruth, an American hero, had recently died. But Joe DiMaggio would keep seats filled for the New York Yankees baseball team...

There was so much I needed to learn about my new home. I read like a fiend, trying hard to catch up. I questioned as many crewmen as possible, to find out what I could. I wanted to be a good citizen.

The weeks onboard also proved an excellent time to people-watch. We were a group of strangers chasing the same dream, freedom. Many people had forgotten how to smile since the war. Perhaps they had a bad experience in their DP camp, or more likely they had lost a loved one, or worst of all, they were a survivor from the concentration camps.

Nightmares hounded many people. Sleeping in a group atmosphere was often hard on the nerves. Some men cried aloud in their sleep, which was worse than dealing with the rhythmic snorers.

My family's journey hadn't been easy, but we were luckier than most, we survived together without permanent damage. We saw and heard horrid things, but we were still alive, still hopeful, and never lost our dreams.

Other passengers on the ship slept in private cabins, they were regular folks, who had chosen to visit Europe as their vacation spot. *To inspect the damage done?* I pondered that one afternoon. *Had they come to see the war-torn cities—to gloat?—To count their blessings?*—Or to observe and then write about the scenes, so that they could explain to the rest of the world that we needed to prevent this atrocity from ever happening again.

The Allied forces won, yes, but at such a cost. I'm thankful for one thing the war had taught me—that freedom remained the ultimate dream.

I enjoyed spending time on the deck though it was cold, and most often I was assaulted by a horrid smell drifting up from the ship's exhaust pipes. So, I turned around and faced the ocean, looked out at the expansive grey sea, and guessed how many meters away we were from our destination. After weeks at sea, the ship finally entered the harbor of New York City.

The ship's horn blew and I rushed up to the front of the deck, anxious to see the cityscape. It was a bitterly cold morning, the wind bit through me even with my hat and gloves on, my face and hands burned.

As the city became visible, I tried to make sense of it. I wanted to see the buildings and all the wonders I had heard so much about, but I could barely see a few feet in front of me. A storm had rolled in and hit, as the ship docked. My luck had run out.

Standing on deck for what felt like hours, I strained to see, but the snow washed the sky in a wall of white, all the buildings that I had glimpsed now disappeared. I trudged back to the cabin, disappointed.

We were instructed that all passengers had to remain below deck because of the storm. We ended up confined in our cramped quarters for days. It was hard to remain smiling.

My nerves were shot. Tempers were short with so many people living and breathing in tight accommodations. Everyone around me spoke with sharp tongues and I found it best to stay to myself.

Then the flu spread among the lower decks and our floor was quarantined. The ship remained docked at the shore for an extra week without permission to dispatch. The ship rocked with the blizzard, the hammocks swung, and after a bit I became dizzy. This continued for days. We were trapped in a metal prison made of steel and bolts, and couldn't leave to be processed.

I closed my eyes and pretended I was someplace else. I remembered my hometown, my Halych, and the castle by the river. I thought about the spring flowers, my mother's tortes, and the way the tobacco smelled when my father smoked outside on the stoop. I pictured all the old men, sitting in the park, gossiping about this and that...

I forced myself to hold on, closed my eyes, and tried to remember the plans I dreamed about all these years. I couldn't let them shatter like the ice on the upper decks now after we've come so far.

I waited, what else could I do. The agony of anticipation doused my spirits instead of lifting them. I began to question if we would ever find the freedom that we dreamed of for so long.

CHAPTER 61

The storm finally passed after two days, and soon afterward the quarantine was lifted. We were allowed to move about the ship. Everyone crowded the corridors to get out of the lower deck. I slipped past the others and ventured up to the highest deck for some fresh air. I drew in a deep breath and exhaled slow.

My lungs felt alive again, the air crisp and refreshing. I peered over the ship's railing and watched the waves hit against the hull. The water surrounding the boat looked dirty, not at all as I had envisioned. I had expected a blue ocean and the sound of seagulls, not the poop of them on the deck.

My fantasy crumbled. I had visualized that there would be grand receptions, marching bands, fireworks... all the fairytale stuff that Hank had spoken of. All the images of how I thought things would be... were wrong. *Of course,* I shook my head. This was a major world city in a free country with an international port, ships, and boats coming and going in all directions.

I wondered what else would be different from how I had imagined it. I looked out, across the water, at the cityscape. I wanted to estimate the measurements of the tall buildings, but I hadn't a clue how far away they were, I had no idea of the height. But they were the largest I had ever seen. Tall gray spires stood like blocks of geometric pieces, like a child's game. The buildings were rather drab compared to the colorful marble and slate roofs that covered European churches and landmarks. Sadly, most of those were gone now, perhaps even the old wooden castle in Halych. Poor

Halychan Castle, now the Russians would take it all. They claimed to own all Ukraine, my homeland was doomed.

Staring out at the vastness of the city for hours, I imagined the details on the tall skyscrapers that weren't visible from afar. There must be pillars and art deco embellishments on the modern buildings. Hours passed and my excitement grew for the first time in months...this was it. We were in America. Everything was new here, a new beginning. Any day now, our paperwork would be processed, and we would be on our way to our sponsor family.

The sunlight dissipated, with the evening sky another brightness grew. In the distance, the city lights glimmered like tiny stars sparkling in the sky. They were beautiful.

I wasn't able to see the glitzy signs of Broadway as Hank had described to me, instead I stared at a blanket of twinkling lights, proof of life in a cold city. The sensation excited me and I felt optimistic. So many things were possible here, I knew it in my bones.

I gazed toward the Statue of Liberty, her outstretched, beaming arm was a wonder. I remembered the other grand and fantastical stories that the soldiers told me. *Were some of them true?* Tato came to the railing and stood beside me.

"There you are, Ivan. You've been out here for hours — you must be freezing. It's a beautiful statue, no?"

"It's not like I thought, Tato. I thought freedom would be something different. More colorful or glitzy, I guess." I sighed. "I dream too much."

"No, Ivan, you can never dream too much. You need to understand what it means to be free. It's not a statute, a city, or a movie screen story... Freedom is a way of life."

My father blew on his hands, then rubbed them fast while thinking of the right words to say to me. His eyes narrowed thoughtfully, that little something he did before dolling out his sage advice. I took a deep breath myself and smelled the salt air.

"If you have a positive attitude, Ivan, and the endurance to live each day to its fullest, then freedom paves a path for you to realize the dreams that you sow. Freedom allows you to work for whatever you want—not take whatever you want. Freedom lets you choose your fate, without the government or anyone else telling you what you can and can't become. Freedom allows you to choose to be you. It's not free— it's freedom. A kingdom you create."

My father's words touched my heart, and a new light began to glow inside of me. Yes, a positive attitude, like the smile we forced each other to express when things were dire while first in Regensburg. If I dreamt and worked hard enough, I could be that engineer someday. Then I would be special—extraordinary—and do amazing things to help others in the world.

"Tato, I want to go to a university, up in Rochester, and learn Engineering."

My father reached up and rubbed my hat, as if he moved it to tousle my hair, pretending that I was still a boy.

"That's a great dream, Ivan—I will help you realize it."

I took a deep breath, thanked God for our blessings, and vowed to work hard to keep our culture alive. I was an Ukrainian American, and proud to be so.

Together we walked away from the edge, and the following day, my family was processed and allowed to enter the

United States. Our host family had bus tickets waiting for us, and then we embarked on our long bus ride to Rochester, New York.

There my father worked as a laborer, hefting sacks of grain over his back as he unpacked trucks. He gladly did this heavy manual work because it meant providing for us, his family, and our new life. Years later, after he made connections with Ukrainian friends of influence, he became an employee in a credit union.

My brother, Petro, worked hard for a construction company owned by a fellow Ukrainian-American. On his free nights, he sang beautifully in a choir, and they performed on the weekends at Churches and various Ukrainian events. He also wrote articles for the local Ukrainian newsletter, that habit of his, of jotting down notes, paid off.

Olena and Mama sewed in a large factor that produced men's suites. They both sang in the church choir and belonged to the Ukrainian Women's League of America.

I was the lucky one. My family must have thought I was special, after all. My father enrolled me in college for engineering. The first semester was filled with English classes and mathematics, and I studied like never before.

I joined Plast, too. I continued in the scouts for years and became a counselor for the younger troops. I looked forward to the summer weeks spent camping in the woods, in the nearby North Collins.

No matter how old I grew, I never forgot what my father had said about making my freedom. Freedom's a place made with work and dedication, not only dreams. Freedom is a mindset we create, where our dreams are nurtured by our deeds.

During the early years in the United States, we sat together in the evenings and went over civil studies, and prepared for our citizenship tests.

A few years later, I was proud to call myself an American citizen, though I never forgot my Ukraine.

EPILOGUE

Now that I'm an older man, I remember my family's journey with amazement. I have no idea how we managed to travel such a long way on foot, in a war-torn countryside. To see so much death, and yet still succeeded to keep our faith in humanity. My parents were the strong ones, they kept us protected from much of the exposure to scary scenes.

I often remember my boyhood friend Michael, and others who perished during the war and pray for them daily.

After I joined Plast in Rochester and saved enough money, I attended a scout jamboree, but I never met up with Kateryna again. I heard through the Ukrainian pipeline that she became a scientist for the Canadian government, was married and had children. I was happy for her. I moved on myself, married, and had two blond children of my own.

Despite my happiness, dark images from my boyhood still pop up in my daydreams, never completely leaving me. I endured the tragedies that were flung at us, but I can still see the dark eyes of Sonia in my dreams. Many of us managed to become successful, productive people despite the haunting memories. But then again, maybe our success was because of our personal histories, and that our adversities gave us our strength of character.

My father had been imprisoned and mistreated by occupying governments because he dared to speak out for people's rights and a free Ukraine. I can't imagine being that strong, but I try to be like him each day. He's passed away now, but all those who knew him well will always cherish his passion for freedom.

In America our new neighbors knew nothing of his bravery, never gave him his due, but those of us in our Ukrainian community, we remembered. His strength and conviction will always be revered for generations. We owe our freedom to him and those like him who led us away from tyranny. Someday history might acknowledge his sacrifice, and the many others like him, who courageously toiled to make the world a better place.

May all the Ukrainians who perished during the war, either by soldiering or by murder, rest in peace. Today, Ukraine stands proud as an independent free democratic country. Forever live the dream of freedom.

The End

AFTERWORD

Hope for the Truth

Approximately six million Jews, or about two-thirds of Europe's total Jewish population before World War II, died by 1945 via pogroms, mass shootings, and gas chambers. We refer to the horrendous event as the Holocaust, or *Shoah*. The majority of the atrocities took place in occupied Poland's death camps known: Auschwitz, Belzec, Chelmno, Majdanek, Sobibor, and Treblinka. Other ethnic groups also suffered a great loss, though not with such outrageous, shameful means.

Five million Poles had horrific fates at the hands of the Nazi regime. They were arrested, beaten, killed, or often died in prison. Many were Catholics or Jews, or sympathizers.

Those who referred to themselves as Ukrainian experienced a total death count during World War II much higher than any other ethnic-national group—over eleven million people. The actual count could be higher. *(Note, some Ukrainians were also Jewish, most were Byzantine or Orthodox Catholic.)* To date, there is no full account of all the lives lost. Scholars who wrote about the war and tried to record the events factually for future reflection have been denied access to the Soviet archives, blocked to all the secrets. Some truths may never be uncovered.

The Nazis occupied Ukraine for three years after overtaking the Polish occupying government in Western Ukraine, the area known as Galicia. Later, Russia regained its occupation of all sections of Ukraine.

We know that there were four and a half million Ukrainian soldiers killed in World War II. Some aligned with the Russian troops, others aligned with the German troops, as in the case of the 14th Waffen Grenadier Division of the SS (1st Galician) in 1943. The fighting was often like our American Civil War, brother against brother. The SS Waffen solely fought the Bolsheviks.

This tactic by the Germans, to create foreign SS units to fight Communism, also happened with French units, Dutch, Latvian, Estonian, Croatian and Belarusian units and more. Most Ukrainian soldiers were drafted to fight in this regiment with the perception that it would lead toward Ukraine's independence.

Many Ukrainians were forcibly recruited as soldiers; the Germans needed bodies at the Eastern Russian Front. Ukrainian men often feared that if they did not join the ranks, then their families would be arrested, or they would be killed, though the odds of surviving the front was ominous.

The majority of Ukrainian war victims did not fight in the war at all. Approximately eight million civilian Ukrainians (that we know of) died or disappeared during the war years, the highest loss of any country during this world war, though only Ukrainians considered Ukraine as a country instead of an occupied territory. Even the Allied forces and liberators didn't recognize the Ukrainian borders and referred to them as territories of the takers.

Many people were forcibly 'recruited' as workers, known as an *Ostarbeiter*. Some were lucky and earned a meager wage, others were abused, many women raped and mistreated. Some women became pregnant, some babies aborted and used in Nazi experiments. There are horror stories that war survivors prefer to forget, to survive.

The American Displaced People's camp of Regensburg closed in 1950. Those who remained in the gymnasium went to another city to finish school. Some refugees remained in Germany to restart their lives, but most displaced Ukrainians were blessed to have sponsors in various countries.

Like many nationalities who immigrated, Ukrainians created neighborhoods in their new home cities, assembled churches, and civic clubs, formed Ukrainian schools, and taught their children the language and culture. It seemed an important thing to do after Ukraine was occupied by the Soviet Union after World War II.

Many people tried to connect with their families in the old country, but as the years passed, it became harder with the division caused by the Iron Curtain. Money sent to those who remained was never received, packages were intercepted and stolen by the corrupt authorities. Ukrainians who remained under the U.S.S.R. occupation lived meager, oppressed lives. Treated as second class citizens, they were forbidden to participate in their own culture. Arrested if they did so, they were imprisoned, sent to Siberia, usually accompanied by additional allegations of spying.

Churches in Ukraine other than the accepted Russian Orthodox were confiscated, closed, or destroyed. People were steered and schooled only in the Russian language. The country of U.S.S.R. tried hard to convince the world that they were the originators of the great Rus' culture and not Ukrainians. Russian leaders purposefully corrupted history to meet their version of the truth and prohibited any authors, theologians, and scientists from swaying others away from their propaganda and the false version with the truth.

Those brave enough to promote the facts were most often arrested. People like historian Yuri Dmitriev, who spent over thirty years investigating crimes done by the Soviet regime, uncovering graves and pushing to identify the murderers. He and his colleagues from the Memorial Society uncovered the mass graves of victims of the Great Terror of 1937-1938 who originated from over 85 countries and were found at Sandarmokh Clearing in Karelia. Immediately after the discovery and before going public, Dmitriev was arrested with phony charges. Dmitriev was released only to be re-arrested for the same dismissed fake charges. Attempts to cover up Dmitriev's discoveries and re-write history is ongoing, unfortunately. This is only one example by the Russian government to cover up truths and hide the facts from worldwide knowledge.

The final chapters of many victims' stories remain hidden and unaccounted for because of political barriers to the truth. The death count of Ukrainians taken by Russia after World War II remains a mystery.

Many people throughout the world still deny or are ignorant of the truth about the Holodomor, caused by the Soviets. Some don't recognize the millions of deaths, the genocide of Ukrainians, much like those who deny the Armenian death walks. Documentation and information are being leaked out slowly, ever since the fall of the Iron Curtain. To date, Russia still holds many secrets, refusing to hand over important artifacts and documents, refusing to share truths with the world.

After Ukraine declared independence, people could meet with family and friends again, and talk about historical events. Thankfully, world-wide support kept the Ukrainian culture alive despite the attempts to erase them. Backing from Ukrainian groups in Canada, Australia, Venezuela, the United States, and other countries, nurtured the new generations. They were taught in their new home countries, where there was freedom to live the Ukrainian traditions. Private Ukrainian Schools promoted the language and encouraged the culture to thrive.

The language, literary works, dance, songs, embroidery, Easter egg or Pysanky decorating, cuisine, and more are still taught. Ukrainians around the world never forgot who they were, and this gave native Ukrainians hope while suffering under the Soviet rule.

In August 1991, those who kept the dream of a free Ukraine burning showed up with nearly 90% of citizens voting. The Act of Independence passed. Elections immediately took place.

Later, on August 28th, 1991 more than 200,000 from the Lviv Oblast declared their willingness to serve as the Ukrainian National Guard. The dream had finally come true with an eruption of new life and hope and they were willing to protect it

Proudly, fellow Ukrainian Americans and other Ukrainians around the world celebrated as the country of Ukraine claimed their independence. By December 1991 most countries acknowledged Ukraine as an independent nation.

With travel back and forth now allowed, reuniting family and friends who immigrated with those who had survived, and their extended offspring, mushroomed. Many Ukrainians from other countries aided the newly formed Ukraine to stand on its feet by offering financial support and investing in new businesses.

Ukraine still fights to keep its freedom, as they deal with rooting out corruption. In 2004-2005 the Orange Revolution occurred, peaceful protests by citizens who demanded a re-vote after the fraudulent election results. The contested elections were annulled and a revote was ordered by Ukraine's Supreme Court on December 26th, 2004. The world watched the new elections in suspense, waiting to see if Ukraine's democracy would stand the test, and were relieved once the second election was declared successful, with the new inauguration in January 2005. The Orange Revolution ended.

There is an ongoing struggle against deep-rooted corruption by Russian sympathizers still rooted deep in the underworld. Each new election gives more promise to the people that someday the evil will be expunged. The world observes and supports the Ukrainian efforts to remain a democracy and end corruption.

Today Ukrainians fight to keep their freedom intact as outside forces threaten to tear pieces away. More recent events have severed the country. In March 2014 Ukraine was in high alert after Russian troops aggressively overtook parts of Ukraine and claimed it again for themselves.

There is a hidden Russian agenda, their real reasons revolve around oil reserves and other natural resources, and money. Pretenses of their support for the people with old Russian ties who had emigrated to some of these areas (after

taking over land post Holodomor and after the forced deportation of Crimean Tatars on May 18th 1944 when 8,000 people
died) was a mere smokescreen for the true goals.

Ukraine has endured more hardships than most countries, more oppressor occupations, and yet they refuse to let
go of their unique identity. Historically, the world has repeatedly disregarded them as sovereign, refusing to accept them
into the fold with other European countries. Yet the Ukrainian culture has contributed much to the world with their art,
music, and literary works.

Today Ukraine offers abundant talent with new artists,
musicians, and other contributors, as well as keeping alive
the old traditional songs and dance that have endured despite
their previous banishment. Ukrainians protect their heritage
and keep alive the deep-rooted belief in freedom and democracy.

Let's help keep the freedom in Ukraine alive, by accepting the country into the fold with other nations, and by
appreciating them for the exceptional people they are—
lovers of liberty and freedom, seekers of peace, and God-lov-
ing believers in life.

Ukrainians will forever hold freedom, dear.

WORD INDEX:

Mnohialita - a popular saying in Ukrainian that translates to something similar to "many years of a happy, healthy life"

Pan and **Herr** are equivalent to Mr. in Ukrainian and German respectively

Pani and **Frau** are equivalent to Mrs. in Ukrainian and German respectively

Tato is equivalent to dad, daddy or father in Ukrainian

Dido is grandfather in Ukrainian

Holodomor – the famine-genocide caused by the Russian government against Ukrainians

khustka is a colorful printed scarf worn by Ukrainian women most often on the heads

Plast is the name for the Ukrainian Boy Scouts organization

Oselya - summer camp for the scouts

kompot - cooked seasoned fruit, most often drunk warm

druzhyna - dear wife or similar to the expression my better half

tryzub - a symbol used to represent Ukraine and their traditional beliefs, often seen alongside the country flag, can represent the Holy Trinity when a cross is added to the inside of the design, also referred to as a trident

kapusta and **sauerkraut** are similar recipes of shredded cabbage

babka, **kolach**, and **stollen** are types of bread
varenyky and **pierogi** are recipes of stuffed dumplings in Ukraine and Poland respectively, the most
common filling is potato or cabbage
syta – a warm drink brewed and made from honey
often served during holidays
Kozak is a Ukrainian freedom fighter
Oblast – a region or area, similar to a county
NKVD is the Russian secret police
OUN Organization of Ukrainian Nationalists which
later split into a dozen factions each with varying
platforms but all sought a free autonomous nation
of Ukraine
OUN-B is the OUN faction run by Stepan Bandera
who later aligned with the German SS troops to
fight against Bolsheviks.
OUN-M is the OUN faction run by Andriy Melnyk
who never conspired with Germans but fought
against them, as well as against the Russians,
Czechs, and Turks.
UPA – stands for the Ukrainian Insurgent Army
then changed to the Ukrainian People's Revolutionary Army who fought against Russia, Germans, and
other bordering countries who tried to occupy
Ukrainian lands.
Heiligenacht – the night before Christmas in German
Gestapo- German secret police

Einsatzgruppe – German death squad

Lviv-Holovnyi Railway Station - Holovnyi means "main"

Gymnasium – is the term used in Germany for school

Ostarbeiter - Nazi term for foreign slave workers, who were gathered from occupied areas to perform forced labor in Germany. According to Pavel Polian, (a Russian geographer and historian, Doctor of Geographical Sciences with the Institute of Geography of the Russian Academy of Science), over 50% of Ostarbeiters were formerly Soviet subjects originating from the territory of modern-day Ukraine.

CRUE (Central Representation of the Ukrainian Emigration)

pysanky - Ukrainian Easter eggs created using dyes, bee's wax, and stenciling tools.

FROM THE PUBLISHER

Thank you for reading DREAMER by Elisabeth Zguta, we hope you enjoyed the story.

Please leave an honest book review, short or long, at the storefront or reader group where you recommend books online. Your opinion matters. Reviews help a book become visible to the world, and guides other readers to find this story. Thank you for your support.

If you want to know more about this book or the author, visit our website and follow for future posts.
EZIndiePublishing.com or ElisabethZguta.com